The new novel by the author of *The Man in the Gray Flannel Suit* and *Ice Brothers* is a unique adventure, the story of a man deep in love, and in trouble, over his head in an intrigue of huge dimension, whose seaman's sense of peril beneath the surface of all things guides him between vicious "partners" and that as yet untested part of himself—his errant yet magnificent courage.

FIRST-RATE ADVENTURES FOR MEN

SOLDIER FOR HIRE #1: ZULU BLOOD (777, $2.50)
by Robert Skimin
Killing is what J.C. Stonewall is paid for. And he'll do any job—for the right price. But when he gets caught in the middle of a bloody revolution in Zimbabwe, his instinct for survival is put to the ultimate test!

SOLDIER FOR HIRE #2: TROJAN IN IRAN (793, $2.50)
by Robert Skimin
Stonewall loathes Communists and terrorists, so he is particularly eager for his next assignment—in Iran! He joins forces with the anti-Ayatollah Kurds, and will stop at nothing to blow apart the Iranian government!

THE SURVIVALIST #1: TOTAL WAR (768, $2.25)
by Jerry Ahern
The first in the shocking series that follows the unrelenting search for ex-CIA covert operations officer John Thomas Rourke to locate his missing family—after the button is pressed, the missiles launched and the multimegaton bombs unleashed . . .

THE SURVIVALIST #2:
THE NIGHTMARE BEGINS (810, $2.50)
by Jerry Ahern
After WW III, the United States is just a memory. But ex-CIA covert operations office Rourke hasn't forgotten his family. While hiding from the Soviet occupation forces, he adheres to his search!

THE SURVIVALIST #3: THE QUEST (851, $2.50)
by Jerry Ahern
Not even a deadly game of intrigue within the Soviet High Command, the formation of the American "resistance" and a highly placed traitor in the new U.S. government can deter Rourke from continuing his desperate search for his family.

Available wherever paperbacks are sold, or order direct from the Publisher. Send cover price plus 50¢ per copy for mailing and handling to Zebra Books, 475 Park Avenue South, New York, N.Y. 10016. DO NOT SEND CASH!

THE GREATEST CRIME

SLOAN WILSON

ZEBRA BOOKS
KENSINGTON PUBLISHING CORP.

ZEBRA BOOKS

are published by

KENSINGTON PUBLISHING CORP.
475 Park Avenue South
New York, N.Y. 10016

Printed in the United States of America

Acknowledgments

Mr. Hugh A. O'Haire Jr., a writer for *The New York Times,* was kind beyond the call of duty. He allowed me to study the voluminous files on drug smuggling which he personally has built up over the years to give background for some of his own magazine and newspaper articles. His enthusiasm for my attempts to write a novel on this subject also gives me cause for gratitude.

Captain Ralph M. West, U.S.C.G. (Retired), who has commanded many Coast Guard cutters, also gave me both information and encouragement.

Mr. Daniel Starer, a professional researcher, showed unusual ingenuity in checking figures in a twilight world where statistics are not advertised.

Betty S. Wilson, my wife, started urging me to write this novel way back in 1964, when I feared that I could never gather enough information about drug smuggling and the people engaged in it. She also served as a full editorial assistant, the only typist who can read my handwritten corrections and as a researcher who knows the difference between dull and interesting facts and figures.

To Betty, who taught me that both god and the devil usually speak to us through people who look quite ordinary.

S.W.

AUTHOR'S NOTE

This novel is strictly fiction, but it is based on the blunt fact that drug smuggling is a multibillion-dollar industry nowadays. The files of *The New York Times* and Coast Guard and police records show that drug smuggling is as real, and as melodramatic, as any other kind of war.

In addition to consulting official records, I have based this novel on many stories I heard during seven years of living aboard a yacht which was based in Miami and which often cruised the waters from Long Island Sound south to the Bahamas. As World War II Coast Guard officer, I also was given much information by men who are still active in that embattled service. The Coast Guard could put a stop to activities of the sort described in this book, but it would need many more well-equipped ships, and many more men—in short, much more money from Congress. Professional drug runners nowadays form a much bigger army and navy than the old rum runners ever did and they deal in vastly greater sums of money. Thousands of amateurs hear of all the "easy money" being made and try to get into the "action." The result is seldom reported because no one involved wants to talk about it. This book, of course, is fiction. If it were factual, I'd be afraid to write it.

*I've seen the devil of violence and the
devil of greed and the devil of hot desire . . .*
Joseph Conrad, Heart of Darkness

1

Just about the last kind of madness I ever thought I would get mixed up in is the drug-smuggling trade. Because I was a professional yacht captain or boat bum of sorts, I of course was aware that many people used all kinds of drugs and some of my friends brought a few pounds of marijuana home from voyages to Mexico. During the many years that I was based in Miami, I read that in point of fact, the illegal importation of drugs was becoming a bigger business than the tourist industry there. I saw a lot of young fellows driving expensive sports cars or ripping up the harbor with big speedboats who were said by waterfront gossips to be cleaning up "millions of bucks" in drug runs, "stashing the loot" in Swiss banks and preparing to retire before the age of twenty-five. The newspapers were often full of stories of shootings, knifings and disappearances which were said to be the result of underworld drug wars. All this clearly had nothing to do with me, Andy Anderson, a responsible skipper, navigator on ocean races and yacht delivery-man, the son and grandson of square-head sailors, square men who prided themselves on making square deals. I was an aging would-be Errol Flynn—not the alcoholic actor, whom I knew slightly during his last sad years, but the fantasy of a hero, nothing like the sort of villain who got involved in drug running. When I thought seriously of the drug trade, I wondered if I could make a few dollars in rewards by turning in some of the sly characters who hinted that I could make big money on the side without any risk at all simply by giving them a job and a berth on one of the large yachts I was delivering and looking the other way when they went about their business. It might be possible to work with the feds and trace a few of these small-timers to their underworld connections, but the role of informer did not much appeal to me and I suspected that it could turn out to be highly dangerous.

Many of the young fellows who sailed aboard the ocean-racing yachts with me smoked pot as freely as any other kind of cigarette, and a few of the rich people, the owners of fancy motor yachts and their friends, made a production of carrying little gold spoons and snuffboxes.

As an old athlete I never smoked anything, and I didn't see why I should work hard to acquire a new bad habit. I'd had enough trouble handling booze over the years without getting messed up with even worse drugs.

Although drugs were all around me in Florida, the Caribbean, various parts of the Mediterranean, South America, Australia and other parts of the world where my work occasionally took me, they somehow never seemed quite real to me. They were the stuff of melodrama and crime which one read about in the newspapers, the sickness of the slums and sometimes the business of real killers whom sane, sensible men knew how to avoid. No one I knew well ever got involved with them deeply until young Seymour Clayton grew up.

They called young Seymour "Tad" when he was a small boy to differentiate him from the other Seymours in his family, and though he went through a stage of objecting to the nickname as "too cute," it stuck. The Clayton family and mine had been oddly intertwined for three generations; my grandfather's first job in America had been skippering a yacht owned by Tad's great-grandfather, and my family had worked for the Claytons on and off ever since, sometimes on yachts and sometimes in the many enterprises they owned ashore. Tad seemed to me to be a normal enough rich kid until he left Harvard at the end of his freshman year and became what we used to call a hippie, although the hippie movement was then well past its height. I too had left Harvard after one year, but I had become what some might call a boat bum, a guy who was always available to crew on the ocean-racing yachts and who made a living of sorts for many years without disturbing his status as an amateur by selling sails, marine insurance, and sea

15

stories to the boating magazines. Perhaps I was my generation's version of a hippie—I had certainly said to hell with the conventional route, which led from classrooms to respectable office jobs, commuting to the suburbs and all the rest of it. Maybe for that reason Tad liked me, despite the fact that we wore our hair at different lengths. He hung around me a lot during a few years when he would have nothing to do with his father, and I sometimes took him as a deckhand on delivery jobs. For a while I was the only link between Tad and his father. That was a curious position, because they both trusted me and I wanted to be loyal to both, but they were furious at each other. That's a strange thing about the Clayton family. For generations they have been great at many things—making big money, winning yacht races and getting famous in several ways—but they are lousy at raising their own kids and for that reason the whole clan seems to be petering out. Of course I'm no one to criticize . . . I have fathered no children of my own at all.

At first Tad and I got on together pretty well. Perhaps I was sentimental enough to think that he was giving me a chance for a sort of secondhand fatherhood and perhaps I was opportunistic enough in some corner of my mind to hope that the great rich Clayton family would eventually find ways to reward me if I helped to steer their son and heir through his years of confusion. I have always been ridiculously optimistic, and I was sure that sooner or later Tad would "turn out all right." My rosy predictions soured a little when I noticed that he was going out with some rather peculiar-looking boys more often than with girls and when he started to give me lectures about the true health and joy of bisexual life, but I was trying not to be any more "square" than I had to be and I had always considered tolerance of all kinds a virtue I should try to acquire. I had long liked to consider myself a sort of seagoing closet intellectual—a quarter of a Harvard graduate, a world traveler, in sum a true sophisticate. So who was I to *reject* a young man, as the saying went, for discovering tendencies in himself which, thank God, were foreign to me? Anyway, I figured that he'd outgrow this queer business—that's how sophisticated I was. Whenever Seymour, Tad's father, asked me how his son was doing, I left his odd friendships out of the report.

Tad's use of drugs bothered me less than his homosexuality at first. Almost everyone his age who wore long hair and funny clothes was making a great mystique of pot and pills, and the drug culture was by then so widely accepted—at least among those who had the money and the interest—that it was even considered chic. I became alarmed only when I found that he was selling the stuff and importing some of it on yachts which I commanded when I took him along as a deckhand.

I might never have found out that he was carrying drugs aboard my ships if he had not been so proud of it and so glad of a chance to act superior to me. The day after we finished taking a big sports fisherman from Acapulco to Palm Beach he came up to the little apartment I kept in Miami as a home between jobs.

"You sure live crummy," he said, glancing around the small, sparsely furnished rooms.

"I'm hardly ever here."

"You're such a sucker," he said.

"In what way?"

Before answering he opened the leather bag that hung from his shoulder and took out one of those limp-ended cigarettes. It flared up when he lit it. He blew out the flame, inhaled deeply and let the smoke stream from his nostrils.

"Andy, how much money have you got in the bank?"

"None of your damn business."

"How old are you?"

"Old enough to be your father and damn glad I'm not."

"I bet you don't even have a pension figured out. What are you going to do when you get too old to play sailor?"

This was a question I had never liked to think about, and I didn't much appreciate it coming from a rich kid like Tad. I did not have an answer so I replied with another question: "What makes you so damn worried about me all of a sudden?"

"I feel guilty."

"What have you done now?"

"I made a pretty good haul on this last trip. I think I ought to give you a share."

He reached into his bag, took out a roll of bills about three inches thick, detached a rubber band and counted out ten of them on my kitchen table. I had never seen bills like that. Each one was for five hundred dollars. But I wasn't so much surprised as angry. For some reason I had trusted him. He knew as well as I did that a yacht can be impounded if the feds discover drugs aboard her, and though the fines involved usually are not much, a delivery skipper like me can quickly lose his reputation and any chance for more jobs. My rather precarious living was being risked by a rotten rich kid who preferred the dangers of smuggling drugs to the humiliation of calling home and asking for money.

"I could be blackballed—"

"Save your virtue by yelling all you want, but stash it away somewhere. Someday you'll need it."

I needed it already for all kinds of reasons, but I guess I needed my self-respect or at least a grand gesture more. I picked the money up and threw it in his face, real Errol Flynn style.

"Take this and get out of here before I turn you in," I said.

With curious dignity he picked the bills up and put them in his bag. "I'm not going to get mad at you," he said. "You're just doing your thing like you've been programmed to do. But don't you ever get tired of it?"

"Look, Tad, I'm sure this business looks very glamorous to you now, but it's bound to get dirty. I feel sorry for you," I said, "if you can't see that this could ruin your life, *and* that you might be dragging other people down with you."

"I guess we feel sorry for each other. That's one kind of friendship, isn't it?"

"No, I really feel sorry for you," I said hotly. "You're going to keep on with this drug stuff. Sooner or later you'll get caught. You'll start making bigger and bigger deals and sooner or later the feds or the tax people will catch onto you."

"I've studied the odds on that a lot more than you have. People like you enjoy thinking that people like me always get caught. You'd go crazy if you ever realized that *most* people in this trade never get caught, wouldn't you?"

"If the feds don't get you, some of the people you'll have to deal with will. You're just on the edges of it now. Wait until you get into the real drug wars."

"There are winners and losers in every war. Hell, there

19

are risks, Andy—I know that. But plenty of people retire from this trade rich and clean as a whistle. You just don't hear about them."

I suspected that he was right and that made me madder than ever. It's not a fair world—some people work a lifetime and get nothing while a few others probably do cheat their way into quick wealth and get away with it. My problem was that I just was not built that way. My conscience would drive me crazy, or perhaps that was just a way to say I was too scared to take that kind of chance. No, there was more to it than that.

"For God's sake," I said, "what could be more ugly than the drug trade? Are you going to start hanging around schools trying to get kids addicted, or do you just bring the stuff in for people who do that?"

"I've been dealing in grass and cocaine. Grass doesn't hurt anybody as much as booze or tobacco. Even Freud said that cocaine is good stuff, and the people who can afford to buy it are smart enough to make their own decisions—"

"Even *if* all that were true, you're dealing with the underworld, the same sports who twist the arms of people who can't pay the loan sharks and scare little idiot girls into being whores. Damn, I'd like to kill those people, not help to make them rich—"

"Sir Galahad rides again. You live in a whole damn world of organized thievery from Moscow and Washington right down through Madison Avenue to the people you call 'sir' when you trot their yachts around the ocean for them, but you're going to starve to death in virtuous dignity."

"I'm not going to starve to death, for God's sake. What kind of imaginary world do you live in? I'm really worried about you, Tad. You've got yourself off on a kick that's never led anybody to anything good. For God's sake, you'll probably be inheriting millions of dollars before long and your old man would be glad to give you anything you need now, just so he wouldn't have to worry about you. Why do you have to sweat it like this?"

Tad smiled, a curiously boyish grin for a man who apparently considered himself a clever criminal. "The old man? I don't need him. And if you really knew him as well as I do, you'd know why I think the drug trade is a damn sight cleaner than he is."

With that Tad got up and left, slinging his leather bag over his shoulder like a soldier's kit, and slamming the door after him with something like righteous indignation. He left me feeling stunned. I had spent a lot of time around Seymour ever since we were kids, and I had seen Tad grow up into the twenty-three-year-old young man he was that winter. But suddenly I had discovered that I knew nothing about this father and son.

I did some thinking that night after Tad left my apartment. The immediate question, of course, was whether I should tell his father that the boy seemed to me to be headed for serious trouble. If I was the father of a boy like that, I'd like someone to tell me about it, but what, after all, could the father do? Tad wouldn't even talk to his father on the telephone. What unimaginable sins had Seymour committed to make his son hate him so?

I couldn't even guess. Seymour was a mild-appearing man fifty-seven years old, a year younger than I. He had an older son and an older daughter, Cyrus and Judy, who seemed to have turned out more or less all right, as far as I knew. In view of his many successes, he must have been

21

a forceful businessman and I knew him to be a fierce competitor when he raced his big yawl, but he didn't really seem capable of the role of family tyrant or perpetrator of mysterious deeds which would make his son think that the drug trade was cleaner than his father's family or business dealings. Obviously I was getting involved in psychological currents here which were far too murky for me to even try to fathom. There was nothing I could do but simply accept the situation and make up my mind whether it was worse to rat on Tad or be irresponsible enough not to report him to his father. That was too tough a question for me to answer quickly. I did nothing for several days, perhaps because I knew that Seymour would eventually call me, as he did every month or so to check up on his son. Somehow I might feel less guilty for ratting on Tad if I didn't initiate the call myself. My delicate moral sensitivities were complicated by the fact that I did want to stay in Seymour's good graces. In the back of my mind I guess I always thought of him as the only rich old friend I had to whom I could always go in time of trouble. If I ever really did end up broke and too old to play sailor anymore, Seymour could probably be counted on to find some sort of job for me, or to direct some modest windfall my way. This was an attitude I hated but, after all, my family had worked for the Claytons for three generations, off and on, and they had always been our anchor to windward.

Seymour's call came on the following Sunday afternoon. All the members of the Clayton family have a distinctive way of speaking, very precise, a tenor tone with echoes of both Harvard and Wall Street, if Wall Street has a regional accent. The Clayton voice can sound snobbish, but perhaps because of his long business training, Seymour always pumped a lot of hearty friendliness into his.

"Hello, Andy," he said. "I was hoping to find you in. How was the run down from Acapulco?"

"Fast," I said. "The boat is owned by an oil company so I didn't try to save on fuel."

There was a slight pause before he said with a try at sounding casual, "How did Tad make out? Did he pull his weight?"

I took a deep breath. "Seymour, I'm worried about the boy," I said.

"Something new?"

"This is going to come as a shock to you, I'm afraid, but he really seems to be heading into trouble."

"What kind?"

"Drugs."

"That's nothing new," he said with a sigh. "Are you afraid he'll overdose?"

"He's selling the stuff. He brought some back from Acapulco."

"I wish I could say I was surprised. I knew he must be getting money somehow. He hasn't asked me for any in a long time, and I didn't figure he was working."

"I don't know what you can do, but that's a tough world he's getting into."

"I better come down there. I don't know if he'll talk to me, but I guess the least I can do is try. Why don't you meet me at the Bath Club around four tomorrow afternoon and bring him if you can. If you can't, I'd like to see you anyway."

*　　　*　　　*

The hotel in Coconut Grove where Tad rented a room by the month said he had checked out the day before. That evening I toured the bars where he usually hung out, leaving notes, and I dropped in at the Jockey Club, but I could find no trace of him, which I told Seymour when I met him at the Bath Club the following afternoon.

"It's about what I expected," he said. "Let's sit down and have a drink."

We sank into overstuffed chairs on a terrace near the swimming pool. Seymour looked as tired as he sounded. His hair appeared to have grown more white in the year or two since I had seen him and he had put on too much weight. His face had a worn look. He did not resemble any stereotype of a big-time stockbroker or family tyrant who might cause his son to hate him; he could more easily have played the part of a kindly if weary physician or professor. His body looked soft, but there was a lot of strength in his tired face. A waiter took his order for a vodka martini and mine for a ginger ale.

"Still off the sauce?" he said to me with a smile.

"Still."

"You're smart. You look well, Andy. You look ten years younger than I do at least."

"No worries . . ."

"I used to think you were crazy. No real job, no career. But you seem to be ending up well."

"I'm ending up broke and without a family. That's the bad part."

"Family—Lord God!"

When the waiter brought the drinks Seymour took a big swallow of his martini and ordered another immediately.

24

"There's no point in wringing my hands about Tad," he said softly, as soon as the waiter had gone. "He's my son and despite everything I still love him in my way, but I don't think a sentimental approach would help right now. How heavily is he involved in the drug business?"

"He's just beginning, I think. But he seems to have ambitions, and that's what worries me."

"I suppose the first question is whether I should turn him in to the cops before he gets into worse trouble."

"That occurred to me, but I don't know that it would really turn him around. And I doubt it'll do much for your relationship."

Seymour shot me a look that said he didn't appreciate my comments, however true they might be, but then his expression softened. "I still think it would be the wisest move, but I can't do it. Anyway, I have no proof, and I couldn't ask you to do it. I suppose I could hire detectives . . . Damn. There must be a better way to handle this."

"I hope so."

We watched a pretty girl in a yellow bikini dive into the swimming pool, climb out and run to the dressing rooms. No one else was nearby.

"Tad ought to know that I'm not made of money anymore," Seymour said. "My brokerage business is going to hell—these are crazy times."

It occurred to me that Tad wouldn't care much about this, or might even be glad, but I said nothing.

"I'm pulling in my horns," Seymour said. "I'm going to sell out, consolidate and retire. I'm getting old, I'm not well and I don't know what the hell I've been working so

25

hard for anyway."

"Maybe you'll get a chance to do some sailing."

"I don't even feel up to that and the boat is costing me so much to keep up these days that I'll probably have to get rid of her. Things are tough, Andy. You may not believe it, but when I discharge all my business obligations and family responsibilities, I may not have a hell of a lot left."

That meant that he would be down to his last few million, I figured, but he probably did feel poor. Apparently he had suffered a business defeat and the damage to his ego undoubtedly hurt more than any deprivation.

"I'm sorry," I said.

"I'd like you to tell Tad this. It's time he came home and helped the whole family face some kind of reality. I've got to be setting up trust funds, making up a new will and all the rest of it. I'm worried—I've got ulcers and my heart isn't too good. Time is what I may not have. So if he wants to set matters straight with me, he better see me soon."

"I'll tell him that."

"Otherwise, I'm going to have to cut him out. There won't be enough money left to just spread it around for old-time's sake. I'm going to leave money only to those who need it and those who can use it well."

I had a certain horrible hope that I would be numbered among those chosen few, but of course I wasn't even kin or an employee.

"I'm not sure that Tad is going to care much about wills," I said. "I sense that part of his whole trouble is an independence kick."

"Probably, but he ought to know the truth." He paused before he added, "Tad's a homosexual, isn't he?"

"Bisexual, he calls it," I answered, momentarily surprised that he knew. I'd never seen any of the overt mannerisms of a homosexual in Tad, and somehow I doubted that he'd told his father.

"I never thought that could happen to anyone in my family, but they say you have to accept it. A lot is written about it nowadays. They call it an alternative life-style . . ."

I nodded and couldn't help wondering—perhaps somewhat naively—how a man who showed this much concern could be quite as bad as his son seemed to think he was.

"I'm damned if I know what his mother and I did wrong. I still don't know whether we were too strict or too easy on him."

"I don't think anybody knows much about how it all gets started . . ."

"He's an intelligent boy. They told me at his school that he has nearly a genius I.Q."

"I wouldn't doubt it."

"And he has a strong will—no one can doubt that. With a high intelligence and a strong will, he may come out all right. I haven't given up on him yet."

The waiter brought his second martini and he ordered a third. After that he did not talk much more. He just sat staring at the still water in the swimming pool.

I got busy with the spring trade of bringing yachts from Miami to New York, and though I tried to look

27

up Tad between trips I didn't see him for about two months. Finally he picked up one of the messages which I had left at the Jockey Club and called me at my apartment.

"Can I come to see you?" he said.

"Make it as fast as you can. I'm supposed to fly to Venezuela for a delivery job."

"Can I come?" he asked with a laugh.

"Poison, kid, you're poison. But I have a message for you from your father, so come on up."

When he came bounding up the stairs to my place a half-hour later, I was startled by his appearance. His dark brown hair, which had hung below his shoulders, had been stylishly cut to ear-length. The blue jeans and dirty T-shirt which he usually wore had been replaced by a natty gray suit. He was even wearing a necktie, a conservative maroon with his initials embroidered on it.

"What the hell happened to you?" I asked.

"I'm a businessman. I have to look the part."

"Some business, if it's what you were talking about."

"They don't like longhairs in South America," he said. "I just came back from Colombia and Peru."

"You better not get yourself thrown into jail down there."

"I was just doing research, pure research." He grinned. "But I did do enough business to buy myself a new car. Want to see it?"

It was a new Mercedes roadster, jet-black with red leather upholstery. The wages of sin.

"Get in and see how comfortable it is," he said. "I'll take you for a spin."

"I'll get in, but before we go anywhere I've got to have

a serious talk with you."

"You told my father I'm into drugs and he's mad clear through. I figured that."

"He's sick, Tad—ulcers and heart. And he said his business is going bad. He's going to sell it and retire."

"Too bad."

"He's going to be setting up trust funds and drawing up a new will. He wants you to get in touch with him. If you don't, he's going to cut you out."

"I don't want any part of his money. I can make my own. Before I'm through I'll be able to buy or sell him."

"If you don't get yourself jailed or shot. Anyway, he's still your old man, Tad. Why don't you be big about it and give him a call?"

"No." Then, after a pause, "You think I'm a real bastard, don't you?"

"You got it."

"You don't know enough about all this to judge. I know what would happen if I called him. I'd just be back into the whole nightmare."

"It wouldn't hurt you to call."

"Now *there* you're wrong—I at least am an expert on what hurts me. Now, do you want to go for a ride or not?"

"I'm afraid not."

"Andy, I know what I'm doing. I'm not stupid!"

"Your father told me that."

"Dad said that?" He sounded startled.

"He said that you have almost a genius intelligence and a very strong will, so you may turn out all right. He said he hasn't given up on you yet."

"Old Dad with his stiff upper lip. He gave up on me

years ago. Anyway, it doesn't matter. I have a message for him. Tell him if he needs money, come to see me. In just about a year or so, I'll be able to get him all he wants."

With that as an exit line, Tad roared away in his shining roadster. His mysterious hints about his father, I decided, were bull. Young bull versus old bull.

2

For about a year after that I did not see much of Tad,
but I was aware that he was making rapid progress in his
"career," if that's what one could call it. Utilizing his
family's connections, he joined all the best clubs, and
photographs of him, often with beautiful young women,
began to appear on the social pages of newspapers. He had
never seemed to be such a proper young aristocrat before
and I was astonished until I remembered reading

somewhere that the people who run the drug racket try to acquire as many highly respectable minions as possible. A few of the big-time drug smugglers even headed charity drives in Florida and became chairmen of PTA committees, anything for a reputation which might place them above suspicion. Apparently Tad's role was that of a Miami prince. He must have had publicity men pushing him. Most people can go to even the fanciest parties without getting their pictures in the papers so often. It seemed unlikely that Tad's own small-time beginning efforts as a drug smuggler could have earned him such eminence so quickly. Probably this bright young beginner from the right side of the tracks had caught the eye of someone with some rank in the mysterious world of drugs and Tad had been promoted from the equivalent of apprentice seaman to maybe lieutenant junior-grade. At the moment it must seem like a rich, easy life for him. Maybe he was right in believing that a smart man could pile up a fortune without ever being caught, but my experience with navies of all kinds was that eventually they have to fight a war. I wondered what Tad's duties actually were with his new comrades-in-arms.

In the first part of that winter three men were gunned down in a motel near Miami and there was a series of other murders and many disappearances which the newspapers declared to be drug-related. I wondered if Tad felt himself to be beneath, above or in the middle of such battles. I wanted to talk to him—to tell the truth, my moral indignation at his career was laced with considerable curiosity. I was, therefore, pleased when he finally telephoned me at my apartment and asked if he could see me.

"Come on up," I said, and couldn't resist adding a barb. "Are you beginning to feel the heat?"

"Very funny. I work in an air-conditioned office and I have an air-conditioned apartment. No heat where I am."

He looked even more respectable than he had the last time I had seen him. His hair was now cut as short as though he worked in a bank and he was wearing a crisp seersucker suit with some sort of narrow striped club tie. He had put on enough weight to rid himself of that hungry, gaunt look which had distinguished him during his hippie days. Mr. Establishment.

Gone also was the tense, alternately exuberant and angry manner. He seemed calm, businesslike and even a little subdued as he walked into my apartment. He didn't smoke anything at all. He even refused a beer.

"I'm on your drink, ginger ale," he said.

"Is this true moral reform or the precautions of a man on sentry duty?"

"When are you going to take me seriously, Andy?"

"When are you going to take yourself seriously? How goes your game of cops and robbers?"

"There have been a few shoot-'em-ups lately, as I guess you've read. Nothing too close to me, but a little unsettling. I knew one of the guys."

"The killer or the killed?"

"Please don't make jokes, Andy. I have something serious I want to talk to you about."

He sat down at my kitchen table and folded his hands in front of him, as though at a board meeting.

"You've seen the light," I said. "You're going to quit while you've still got a whole hide. Thank God!"

"I asked you not to make jokes." He sounded hurt.

"That was no joke—I had real hope there for a minute."

"Andy, how much can I trust you?"

"Not much."

"I know, you tell my old man everything I say. But I don't think you'd tell anyone else."

"That's your risk. I hate secrets, especially when they involve breaking the law."

"Virtuous Andy! I suppose you never take a captain's ten percent when you bring a yacht into a shipyard, and if you should be tempted, you'd report it on your income tax."

"Men don't get themselves shot for that."

"So we're both law-breakers, right? I can't stand this righteous act you put on."

"Have your friends gotten you into the pimping business yet? I understand that's one of their more profitable sidelines."

"I want to talk seriously!"

"There's nothing very jokey about pimping. Have your friends taught you yet how to pick up little runaway girls at bus stations and break them in as whores?"

"Come off it, Andy! Drug running is no worse than rum running was. From what I hear, your father and my grandfather were kind of partners in that line there for a while."

"I'm not sure that drugs and booze are really just the same, but I suppose you've got a point."

"Try to stay off the moral kick for a while. I'm going to concede you a point. The in-fighting in the drug trade is dangerous."

"You're a slow learner, but you do finally manage to put things together. I guess that's what a near-genius I.Q. can do for you."

"I've learned a lot about my business. Research—that's what I've really been doing more than anything else."

"Are you going to write a book about it?"

"I don't think that would make me too popular with a few of my friends, but I could." There was a pause before he added, "Andy, what do you hear from my father?"

"Nothing lately."

"The *Wall Street Journal* says his business is in real trouble. There's even talk of it going into receivership."

"He has lots of businesses, doesn't he?"

"They're all related. *Forbes* had an article on it. They entitled it 'A House of Cards?'—with a question mark."

"Tad, I don't know one damn thing about big business, but I'd be very damn surprised if Seymour really went broke. I think he knows how to take care of himself."

"Oh, I'm sure he won't be asking for food stamps, but he's hurting. That's one of the facts I'm trying to put together."

"Call him. That call is long overdue."

"Maybe. Can I talk to you?"

"I won't charge you for listening. I'm no damn psychiatrist."

"At its lower levels the drug business is very dangerous and doesn't pay much over the long run."

"Then it's like any other military outfit."

"Now just listen for a change—no more jokes. The drug business pays pretty well at the middle levels but is

35

even more dangerous there."

"I'm listening. A lot of lieutenants always get killed."

"But there's a lot of really big money to be made at the top of the business, more than any general ever gets, and life at the top can be almost a hundred percent safe if a man knows what he's doing."

"But first you have to get there, even if that's true, and I bet the climb isn't safe."

"Not everybody has to climb. Some just fly."

"Flying always has its risks."

"Let's forget the figure of speech. Let me give you one more fact I've learned. It's much safer to make just one big haul than a lot of little ones."

"It's even safer to make none at all."

"And that way you may not be safe from poverty. What I'm *saying* is that a man has a good chance to get away with any *one* . . . well, crime. People get caught because they establish a pattern and the law of averages catches up with them."

"Tad, do you think that's a brilliant original observation?"

"Not everyone realizes it," he insisted. "Not everyone realizes that if a man decided to commit just one big so-called crime in his whole life and never repeated it, the odds would be very high that he'd get away with it. And if it brought him enough money, he could retire without ever being tempted to do it again."

"What's this leading up to? Do you want me to help you to commit the perfect crime? Excuse me, so-called crime?"

"Right now, at least, I'm not going to ask you to do anything. You're an old friend of the family and I like you, Andy. I'm just trying to educate you—"

"From the mouths of babes . . ."

". . . comes the truth, sometimes. Now let me tell you a little about the drug business. There's very little danger in transporting the stuff if you use your head at all. The trouble comes in loading it and unloading it, in buying it and selling it. That's what I've been doing most of my research on."

"I'll take your word for it."

"There's very little danger of any kind from the Coast Guard or feds. The danger comes from informers, hijackers and people who may think you're trying to muscle into their territory."

"The whole damn thing is dangerous!"

"Not necessarily. One—just one—really big run could be planned like a real military operation by people who had the brains, the knowledge and the resources. It would have at least a ninety percent chance of succeeding."

"Just what would you call a really big run?"

Tad smiled. "What do you care? I thought you weren't really interested in this sort of thing."

"I'm not." Or was I . . . ?

"I'm talking about bringing in about ten tons of stuff. Any big yacht or vessel of any kind could handle that."

"You're talking about marijuana?"

"Only if we were going to go small-time."

"Never mind the 'we.' And what's big-time?"

"Cocaine. That ought to appeal to your fine moral instincts. It's too expensive for schoolchildren or poor people. Only the very worthwhile can afford cocaine— people who have every opportunity to know what

37

they're doing."

"How much money would be involved in a haul like that?"

He suppressed a smile. "The last time I checked, cocaine was bringing somewhere around twenty-five thousand dollars a pound to a wholesaler in New York. Figure it out for yourself. That means it would bring fifty million dollars a ton, five hundred million for ten tons. Of course, it would be difficult to buy the stuff in such quantity, but for some people it might be possible."

"How much would it cost to buy?"

"That depends on where and how you . . . sorry, just a figure of speech . . . buy it. Almost all the coca is grown in Peru and Bolivia. If you can buy it directly from the little labs in the hills or the big pharmaceutical plants in Colombia that process the coca leaves, you can get it for less than a tenth of what you can sell it for in New York, but it would probably be better to let someone else transport it to a loading port. That might double the price but there'd still be a healthy margin of profit."

"Why don't all the big-time crooks do it?"

"Quite a few *do* do it, although not on the scale I'm talking about. A lot of capital would have to be involved and an operation like that would have to be carried out by some really high-caliber people."

"It would never work. A million things could go wrong."

"Given time, I could show you that the risks are very small compared to the possible profits. Even if we got caught, the chances of going to jail are slim and the fines would be surprisingly small. Getting caught and even being hijacked are dangers that can almost be planned out

38

of the whole operation. There's a bigger problem."

"What?" He's said "we" and I hadn't said a damn thing.

"Raising the money to buy the stuff and for operating expenses. Then we would have to figure out what to do with the profit, maybe a couple hundred million dollars. How would we ask to be paid: in cash, gold or some other commodity? How would we launder all that money, find a way to pay ourselves that would look legitimate? Anybody who spends a lot eventually has to explain to the government where the money came from. I can figure out theories of how it might be done, but it would take someone with a bank or some kind of big business to make the thing actually work."

He paused to gauge my reaction before going on. "You see what I'm getting at. I know only one person who could raise the capital and figure out how to funnel all that money into legitimate channels."

"Your . . ."

"Of course. My father."

"He'd think you were crazy."

"He'd maybe say it's too grandiose. I shouldn't start with the big figures. What if we scaled it all down to a modest profit of, say, thirty million dollars? That sound sensible? How about ten million or even five—?"

"There's *nothing* sensible about the whole damn thing. Your father is a legitimate businessman, Tad. After all these years, he's not going to go crooked."

"His father was a legitimate businessman, but he financed your father in the rum-running business and they both cleaned up. I bet they figured a thing or two about laundering money back then."

"I don't think any sensible man would think for a moment of actually trying it."

"Come with me and talk to him. If he knows you're interested in it, even as just a game"—he eyed me carefully—"he'll think about it more. He never takes anything I say seriously."

"No, you're on your own with this one."

"I bet if you were really interested dad would come in with us. He has a lot of respect for you."

"I'm good at boats. Period."

"Damn it, you'd come in quick enough if you knew dad was behind me. I'd say this is a chicken-and-the-egg thing—"

"Tad, you're young and you're a dreamer. Your old man is hard-boiled, and I only have small dreams—no big deals like yours. Look, if this whole scheme of yours doesn't get off the ground, are you still going to stay in the drug business?"

"I've already quit," Tad said. "I wanted to quit before I got a record—my skirts are still clean. Only people with a clean record should try to set up a deal like this. One crime—isn't that what I started to tell you about? One big crime and no more. What I've really been trying to do is to plan the greatest crime of the century."

"Marvelous, such modesty. But you've already built up to this one with a lot of small drug deals. You've established the pattern you were talking about."

"But I never got caught. Most of the time I was just doing research. Nobody's mad at me. The boys think I just got so scared by all the shooting that I didn't have the stomach for it. That was a good out for me."

"What are you going to do now?"

"I'm going to see my father."

40

"That's the best news I've had yet."

"It'll probably take him some time to make up his mind if he's interested at all, and the various arrangements could take months. We won't need you until it's all set up. Then we'll want you to run the ship for us—"

"Forget it. I may not be so damn moral as I pretend, but I'm a for-real coward. I'd never get a wink of sleep if I got into a deal like that."

"You'll do it if dad asks you. I know you, Andy. If dad was in on it, you'd know the whole thing was safe. He'd protect you. Even if we got caught, you could pretend that you were just a poor dumb delivery captain who didn't even know what the cargo was. At worst, you'd probably get off with six months on probation."

"At worst, I'd get killed by hijackers."

"Hijackers have to know where to find you. They can be avoided. Think of the bright side, Andy. If we do this, you'd make more than a million bucks for yourself. Maybe much, much more. I try hard to talk small because I really don't want to sound grandiose, but figure it out yourself. If coke is worth fifty million dollars a ton in New York, ten tons would be worth five hundred million. How about a hundred tons? A slightly bigger ship . . ."

"You'd never be able to buy that much of the stuff."

"Maybe. If not, we could fill up our holds with grass. Good marijuana can bring a million dollars a ton in New York. Now don't tell me marijuana is a clear and present danger. Its use is pervasive and nobody has proved it's bad for you, and in some cases it's been *proved* therapeutic."

"Running an operation that big would be like fighting a private war—"

"I'm only talking about a hundred tons, or even ten.

41

One small ship. The trouble with you, Andy, is that you've been programmed to believe that easy money is not only immoral but impossible. But there really is such a thing. And it's no sin to realize it."

"I'm going to try to forget that."

"I bet you can't," Tad said, and laughed too easily.

3

I did not really take Tad's grandiose scheme seriously, not then, but he was right about one thing—I couldn't forget it. It was just a pipe dream, of course, the kind of idea a crazy, mixed-up rich kid would play with for a while before going on to something like transcendental meditation, Scientology or a candle-making shop, anything to keep his little mind busy until it was time to go home, accept a lifetime allowance and be a good boy again.

"Easy money—there really is such a thing." Sure, for Tad there was such a thing waiting for him if he didn't keep on pissing off his daddy. But for me, not bloody likely.

Even so, I couldn't help but wonder what I'd do with a million dollars. I was human, after all. Decent, I like to think, but no saint. Tad had said there would be an opportunity to make much more than that, but in my dreams a single million was plenty. What would I do with it?

Settle down and get married. At the age of fifty-eight, I had, face it, what almost amounted to a lust for the very kind of life I had fought so hard to avoid in my youth. After almost forty years of roaming the world on yachts of all kinds, I was just as bored by the sea as other men are by their offices. And at sea or in foreign ports I was lonely, so lonely that I was thinking of getting a damn dog to talk to. But I'd tried that once and had felt terrible when the poor little devil was swept overboard in a North Atlantic gale. Dogs can't hang onto anything and don't belong on boats.

Marriage and a square life for this old squarehead— that's what I really began to dream about when Tad tried to tempt me with all his talk about easy money. I wanted, I confess, a wife and a house in the country and enough money for my old age and a shore job if I had to have any job at all—those things interested me much more than dreams of expensive cars, fast women or fast yachts.

The idea of running drugs in order to turn respectable was ludicrous, of course. Weren't there other ways to give up the boat-bum life and turn respectable?

With my peculiar skills I could make much more money at sea than I could ashore. Three thousands bucks a month plus expenses was my basic wage when delivering yachts and the best I could do ashore was some precarious commission deal. I'd tried selling yachts, real estate, insurance and "investment securities"; as a salesman of anything I was admirably *honest*, lots of people said, but nobody ever bought anything from me.

Hell, I was right back to Tad's fantasy again. But for someone like me it would be better to take a job as an attendant in a parking lot than to run drugs, and if I really wanted "easy money," I should marry one of the fat blue-haired widows who occasionally expected me to deliver more than their yachts.

But I didn't want to marry a fat blue-haired widow. I wanted to marry Pattie, a woman I had loved for years. We were made for each other, except that she had three kids and almost no money, and I had to keep sailing the seas in order to keep up my alimony payments, among other things. I had learned not to be too bitter about the alimony I owed—the mistakes of one's youth have to be paid for and my former wife wasn't able to make much of a living for herself—but they did make my fantasy of marrying Pattie and supporting her three children pretty farfetched.

A quick million, though, made in one big run, would be an answer . . .

"Pattie, we've got no more problems," I imagined myself saying. "We'll buy a house big enough for all of us and I'm never going to have to go to sea again!"

45

"Where did all the money come from?"

Now *there* would be a problem. Pattie was closer to being a candidate for canonization than any person I'd ever met, even if she was a surprisingly sexy saint, and she would be properly horrified if she learned that I was getting involved in drug running.

If she knew I was going to go into it, she'd be furious, all right, but what if she found out about it only after I'd brought it off successfully? Would even a saint object to the arrival of so much money if all the risks and dangers and such were in the past?

That would be quite a test of anyone's morality. Pattie laughed every time I called her the only sexy saint in history, but she did tell me once that she tried her best to be "a practicing Christian," and she meant every word of it.

I had known Pattie for eight years. I had met her at an AA meeting in a church basement. Like me, she was an alcoholic who had not had a drink in almost a decade, but we both still had to work hard to stay sober. Pattie laughed a lot, as many drunks who have managed to kick the booze do, but she took the basic Christianity which is the essence of AA more seriously than anyone I knew. She kept taking moral inventory of herself, she really knocked herself out to help others, whether they were drunk or sober, and she often visited her former husband in a state mental hospital because she was convinced that she had helped to put him there before she got off the booze. From what I could gather, her former husband had been too drunk himself to be hurt much by anyone during their entire disastrous marriage, but Pattie still felt that part of the responsibility was hers and she kept

46

going up there to hold his hand, even though he rarely recognized her.

Just by looking at her and hearing her talk, no one could guess that she had ever had problems like that. She was thirty-six years old when I met her, fifteen years younger than I, and she was still making a living of sorts singing old-fashioned torch songs in piano bars over on the Beach. During the days between engagements she did typing at home for students at Miami University and took care of her two daughters and son.

"I'm a third-rate singer and a fourth-rate typist," she said to me, "but we get by."

In point of fact, her typing was accurate, if slow, and her voice was sweet and full of emotion. She might have made it big as a singer if she had got the proper training and experience when she was young, instead of her disastrous marriage. But the reason I loved her was a quality the students with papers to be typed and the drunks in the piano bars rarely noticed—a unique combination of serenity and warmth that was enough to give religion a good name even with me.

She had said she'd marry me even if I was in port only about one week out of every six and despite my financial problems. But her son, who was eight years old when I met her, hated me on sight and so much tension was generated every time we all got together that she was afraid that marriage might send us both back to our cups. Especially my cups, because Tommy's inexplicable rage at me and my inability to do anything about it upset me very much. For eight years we had been saying that we all had to give each other time. She also said that she wanted to pay off all her debts before she got married; she still owed the lawyers for her divorce and who knows how many doctors.

Money. We needed money more than time, and Tad's fantasy drug run—the greatest crime of the century, as he called it—kept running crazily through my mind as a sort of solution. But if I actually went into such a deal, it seemed unlikely that I could keep it a secret from Pattie forever; I always had a curiously intense urge to tell her the truth about myself. And for a woman who based her precarious sobriety on the serenity of religion, drug running might offer dangers worse than the law or hijackers. So, the *hell* with the whole idea . . .

The strange thing—the truth—is that Tad's fantasy had a strong effect on me from the moment I heard about it; it had a dynamic all its own, even if, as I was then almost certain, it could never become a reality. It got me thinking about the importance of money in my life. It also got me to examining the part my squarehead kind of honesty had played in making me whatever I was.

I was working as a yacht deliveryman essentially because I liked to pretend that I was too honest to be a good yacht broker, which was the only kind of reasonably good job I knew how to get ashore. But if I continued to avoid the easy lies which almost all salesmen have to employ, I would have to give up the future I wanted with Pattie.

Ridiculous. What I should do was forget all that false pride and look for a job as a yacht broker. It was conceivable that I could make a reasonably good income doing that, and if I had to tell a few lies to sell bad yachts to nautically ignorant people, that at least would turn my own small-scale fantasy into a reality.

So that was the first of many strange results of Tad's scheme—it made me examine my life and led me to try my best to defy Tad's prediction that I could not forget his offer. Instead of brooding more about it, I called Mark Johnson, who ran the Lauderdale office of some big-time New York yacht brokers and designers. I had sailed with Mark on many ocean races, and he had told me to give him a call "if I ever got sick of having no money in my wet pants."

"Andy," he said with great good cheer. "Are you looking for a delivery job?"

"Not this time, Mark. I'm sick of having no money in my wet pants."

He laughed. "I figured you'd wise up sooner or later. Come up and have lunch with me. I'm sure we'll be able to figure something out."

In some ways the job he offered looked good. I was to get a small guaranteed salary. He'd give me access to his listings of used boats, steer customers to me and we'd split the commissions. I would also try to sell the lines of new stock boats he handled.

"Have you got a place to live here?"

"I can commute from my apartment in Miami."

"That would be a waste of time. We have all kinds of yachts tied up here, waiting to be sold. Most of the owners would be glad to have a free caretaker. Pick one and move aboard."

"What if I have company?"

"We're not prudes around here. Have you got a steady roommate these days?"

"I'm not sure," I said.

49

*   *   *

That afternoon I told Pattie I had a surprise for her and I wanted to tell her about it in style at a good restaurant. I don't think she guessed that I had got a shore job; I had been talking about getting one ever since she knew me and never had. Probably she thought I was going to tell her that I was going to take a two-week vacation. We'd been talking about that too.

For this great occasion I chose a good Cuban restaurant on the top floor of a hotel which offered a dramatic view of the Miami harbor. It was good to sit near a window, looking at the ships heading out through Government Cut to the open sea and know I would never have to go out there again if I didn't want to. No more long, lonely sea voyages, with nothing and no one to come home to.

Pattie was looking great that night. She was wearing a green silk dress which flattered her pretty figure. In the candlelight and the fading twilight she could have passed for a twenty-five-year-old, at least in my eyes.

We ordered red snapper with that green sauce the Cubans do so well, and on a whim I had the waiter serve ginger ale in champagne glasses.

"Now what's your surprise?" she said. "I'm going to bust if you don't tell me."

"You're not talking to a sailor," I said. "You're talking to a Lauderdale yacht broker. I've swallowed the anchor. I got a shore job."

"Oh, Andy . . . are you sure you really want that?"

"I'm sure."

"Why? What made you finally do it?"

There was something about Pattie's face that really

made it almost impossible for me to lie to her, even by omission. I ached to tell her all about Tad's crazy scheme and the way it had made me look for an alternative, but in the very back of my mind I suppose I felt that my fascination with the scheme was even crazier, and I was afraid it might show. And maybe not *just* for the money . . . maybe I was looking in part at least for a new way to beat the establishment, for all my fine and true thoughts of a little house in the country . . .

"I just got to thinking that my life has been too rootless," I said, reflecting that this at least was true enough, but the evasion still didn't make me feel good.

"Where are you going to live?"

"Mark, my boss, says I can live on any one of maybe a hundred yachts they've got moored in Lauderdale, waiting to be sold."

"That sounds like fun."

"Would you like to come with me, Pattie, you and the kids?"

She reached out for my hand, but suddenly she looked scared.

"Will you do it?" I asked. "We can go down tomorrow and pick a boat. Do you want a houseboat, a big cruiser or a schooner? Now how many men can give you a choice like that?"

"Andy, not many, but we have to think about this."

"Haven't we thought about it for years and years?"

"Changing a dream into reality is never easy. If it was just me, I'd get up and go right now, but we have to figure the effect on the kids—and what the kids might be like for you. Being around them every day is a lot different from one week in six."

51

"The girls would love it, I'm sure, and maybe if I saw more of Tommy . . ."

"Maybe. Maybe we should begin by just visiting you a few days at a time."

This made me angry. I was almost never angry at her, but I hadn't taken a shore job to live alone most of the time.

"Pattie, I think we've been putting off decisions too long," I said. "It's not as though we were kids. To tell the truth, I think I've gone about this whole thing all wrong."

"How?"

"I don't know what I'm waiting for," I said, taking a very deep breath. "Pattie, as you know, I've been in love with you for years. I've never loved anyone else. I have a fairly good job now and can come home every night like any other sensible man. So I have a proposal to make. Will you marry me?"

She began to cry, which was not exactly the reaction I had expected. She covered her face with her napkin for a few seconds, turning toward the window. There was an awkward silence.

"Yes," she said finally. "Of course I want to say yes, but I'm scared to death."

"Why?"

"The kids would have to change schools."

"That's no reason. The Lauderdale schools are better anyway."

"It's Tommy. You and he . . ."

"I know, he hates me, but I think that's getting better. To tell the truth, I don't much blame him. Who wants his mother to go running around with a crazy sailor? At least now I'll be here all the time."

"I'm still worried about him. With the kind of childhood he's had—"

"Easy does it. One day at a time."

"I'm afraid you and he would get to fighting. I don't know how even you and I would get on, day in and day out. Maybe one week in six was just about right for people like us . . ."

"I never liked the other five much. Pattie, I've taken the leap from ship to shore. Now, forgive the flowery language, take one more leap with me."

"All our AA friends . . . we'll miss them if we move."

"There'll be plenty of meetings in Lauderdale. I'm told that practically half the population up there are members of AA."

She looked at me for a long moment, then spoke in a calmer, if tentative voice. "Andy, you're right about one thing, of course. It's crazy that we're not married. In the long run it's probably just what the kids need— respectability, a father coming home every night, the feeling they're just like everybody else. Why in hell am I so scared?"

"Well, I'd be pretty scared if I thought I was going to marry me. It's been a long time since I liked to look in a mirror."

She smiled. "You'd be unbearable if you did. One of the AA women—and I'm not saying who—said she thought you should be in the movies."

"I actually had two chances of sorts," I said, relieved at the change in her mood. "Did I ever tell you about that?"

"No."

53

"I helped Errol Flynn take his schooner to Jamaica once when the poor old boy was on his last legs, and I spent a drunken weekend in Frisco once with Sterling Hayden—both old sailors who had made it big in the movies. They both said they could help me to get small parts. And they both advised me not to try it because the business isn't healthy. After one look at them, I believed it. So my great acting career is still out to sea."

"You could still make it. You could be out chasing the young chicks like all the other roosters your age."

"I'm hung up on a chick who can understand me. So far I've found only one."

"And I'm giving you a hard time instead of being grateful. Of course I'll marry you, Andy, and I hope you really know what you're getting in for. Tommy can be more trouble than you realize. And you don't know it yet, but when I get depressed, I can be a real bitch. The girls are fine—they adore you and maybe they'll make up for the rest of the package."

"I always wanted a family, Pattie. The worst part of the life I've lived was the prospect of ending up alone."

"Well, you've got one now, God help you . . . Do you really feel like eating right now?"

"No."

"Let's go to your place and cry together." She grinned and squeezed my hand as she guessed the sudden unsaintly thought in my mind. "And then, if it's not too late, let's drive to Lauderdale and look at some of those boats. I want to see where we're going to live. Come along, love."

At a little after ten o'clock that night we arrived at Pier 34 in Lauderdale, a big marina where Mark Johnson kept many of the yachts waiting to be sold by his—or now "our"—brokerage house. Floodlights bathed it in a yellow glow. Perhaps a hundred yachts, power and sail, varying from about twenty-five to a hundred feet in length, were moored at the finger piers. Parties were in progress aboard many. Music from dozens of tape decks and radios mingled into a carnival cacophony. An unusually high percentage of the population of Lauderdale seemed to be made up of girls in bikinis, and they were out in full force, strolling with men in dungarees, ice clinking in their cocktail glasses.

"I don't know if I'd really like living here," Pattie said. "It looks like a bad place for a couple of reformed drunks trying to raise kids."

I had imagined that life could be kind of fun aboard a big yacht at a Lauderdale marina—for a while, at least. Maybe I had been reading too many John D. MacDonald detective stories about Travis McGee. Pattie was right, of course; a perpetual party was a poor place to take a mixed-up teenage boy and two little girls, never mind a man and a woman who had trouble enough staying off the sauce in ordinary situations.

"If we can find a boat we want to live aboard, maybe I can wangle a quieter place to moor her," I said.

We examined several yachts which Mark had said to be available. I was glad when Pattie passed up the Travis McGee-type houseboats. Even though we weren't going to go anywhere on whatever temporary home we picked, I was still old-sailor enough to want to live aboard a good-looking vessel of some kind, something with a little grace and flair in addition to comfort. A schooner which Mark had told me about was so old that she looked depressingly ready for the ship-breakers or Davy Jones' locker, but a big North Sea ketch which was named the *Far Away* attracted us.

"Now there's a boat with a little romance," Pattie said.

"You have a good eye. She could go anywhere—she's one of the few that really can."

"Can we look at her cabins?"

"She'll be locked up, but Mark said the dockmaster can give us keys to almost anything here."

It took the dockmaster a while to find the keys to the *Far Away* on his pegboard, but he finally located them. The vessel had four nice big double cabins, and a comfortable main saloon. She also had a husky diesel engine. I figured she was about a fifty-tonner, and I was somewhat ashamed to find myself noting that this wouldn't be a bad vessel for smuggling. The Coast Guard would probably suspect sailing vessels less than fast powerboats. If we were going to be carrying a cargo worth millions of dollars and wanted to stay outside the twelve-mile limit or even the two-hundred-mile limit . . . But why in the hell was I going on like this? Tad's scheme was just a crazy fantasy that his father would laugh at and that I wanted no part of in any case. Right? Right. Maybe.

Fantasy—I guess I'd always craved a romantic role of some sort to dream about acting out. Some "romantic role"—I'd be the bad guy this time. And very likely the fall guy. An illegal cargo worth ten or more million dollars—the owners of such a cargo could never call in the law, no matter what happened. A prize like that would attract every kind of thief on the South American, Central American and Caribbean waterfronts, never mind our domestic brands.

Madness, but Tad had been right when he said I could never forget his damn scheme. Sure, it had made me reassess my life. And because of that I now had a life with Pattie. But the fantasy had taken hold of me in a way I was beginning to find scary . . . seductive . . .

"This is really cozy," Pattie said. "With all this room, the kids could each have a cabin. Maybe I could fix up that place up in the bow as a kind of office and keep on with my typing business."

"If I can turn myself into a good salesman, you won't need that for long," I said. "This can, like they say, be a new life for us, Pattie. We may never be millionaires, but on this boat we can sure live as if we were."

It was after midnight by the time I took Pattie home and returned to my apartment, which looked shoddy indeed after the teak-paneled interior of the *Far Away*. I was tired, but for some reason I had trouble getting to sleep and tossed all night. Both half-awake and asleep, I had strange dreams of fighting sea battles.

"We are the descendants of the Vikings," the ghost of my grandfather seemed to be telling me, as the old man himself had often said when I was a boy. "We ran all over Europe for centuries. Our long boats got clear up the Danube to Moscow. We were the ones who really discovered America."

Had the Vikings been troubled by moral scruples when they stormed ashore, butchered the men with their long bronze swords, grabbed the women for their pleasure or for enslavement, and burned the houses? What would the old Viking captains say if they knew their great-great-great-grandson was afraid to run a cargo of some white

57

powder a few thousand miles for profits greater than any they could ever imagine?

Dreams, fantasies and memories of violence filled my mind. Machine-gun fire. I'd heard enough of it in World War II. Our little PT boats didn't sink any Jap battleships or big carriers, the way people hoped they would during the first part of the war, but some of them worked out pretty well as fast gunboats along the New Guinea coast and in the Philippines.

I was good at it—damn it, I was a good PT-boat skipper, if nothing else. I had named my boat the *Angry Angel*. I did not get her cut in half by a Jap destroyer, I didn't get sunk and involved in heroic rescues of my own crew, so I never got elected President, but I did kill quite a few Japs.

It was not a heroic business, just efficient. New Guinea was like a checkerboard in those days, with the Japs holding the red squares while we were moving into the blacks. At night they would try to build up their forces at the pressure points by moving their troops up and down the coast in big self-propelled barges. We didn't have much radar in those days, so our planes couldn't get them in the darkness, and they kept so close inshore, almost under the overhanging branches of the jungle, that our cruisers and deep-drafted tin cans couldn't get near them. So we sent in our PT boats, the *Angry Angel*, the *Happy Hooligan*, the *Sexy Sally*, and all the other raffishly named craft in our squadron.

Some of our boys thought it would be a turkey shoot, but the Japs had heavy machine guns mounted on those barges, and sometimes mortars. The biggest of those Japanese steel scows carried a couple hundred men, all of whom were armed with rifles and grenades which couldn't hurt a tin can much, but our PT boats were nothing but plywood over gas tanks. Quite a few of our PT boats turned out to be the turkey in those shootouts.

Not me, not ours, the good old *Angry Angel*, PT 111. Numero Uno, some of our Chicano boys used to call her, the Big One, the Triple One. We were proud of her, all seventy feet of her plywood hull. They crowded her decks with 50-caliber machine guns, and with twenty millimeters when they turned her into a gunboat, and she was so heavy that her speed, our greatest protection, fell from her theoretical forty knots to not much more than twenty. But we were still a hell of a lot faster than those troop barges.

I guess I sort of invented my own way of fighting. I'd leave our base before the moon came up and keep well offshore until we came to Jap territory. It was largely a matter of timing. When we headed toward the jungle, I'd throttle the boat way down, so there would be no big white wings of spray to be seen in the starlight, no pounding hull to be heard, and no roaring engines, just that low chortling sound those big Packards used to make when they were barely turning over. We'd go so close to that black jungle that we could hear the night birds and smell the swamps. I'd try to get right into the shadow of the mountains before the moon came up. There I'd cut the engines to produce total quiet. If there wasn't much current, we let her drift, and if we started being pushed onto the beach we'd drop a small hook on a light line which we could cut fast. I had my men trained to be as silent as any submarine crew. We listened, for hours we listened, waiting for the distant rumble of the diesel engines on those troop barges, the clatter of rifles on steel

59

decks, and the constant jabbering of those Japanese soldiers, the sharply barked orders and sometimes the laughter—they never did learn to be quiet. With our engines dead and our crew mute, giving orders in whispers or with hand signals we had worked out, we always heard them long before they heard us, and in the shadows of those mountains nobody could see far, especially when the moon went under clouds.

I got quite good at estimating distance and direction with my ears. When I figured I had a pretty good fix on where the Jap barge was, we'd run one engine dead slow, cut our anchor line if we had used one, and almost silently, with just that small, happy chortling sound, we'd move into position. I never liked to use star shells; they blinded us as well as them, and we usually dealt at such close quarters that we would be revealing ourselves as well as our target. In those days I had damn good night vision and we had a kid from Oklahoma who could see in the dark so well that we called him Radar. Radar and I would stand together at the helm and pretty soon we'd sense, rather than see, that those sounds ahead, the voices, the clicking of metal against metal and the rumble of the diesel engines, were turning into big blobs which were even darker than the surrounding night. We got pretty good at estimating ranges under those conditions. It took nerve, but I always liked to get as close as possible, closer than a thousand yards with just one of our engines ticking over, sounding as if it were chortling with a kind of secret delight. Our men waited at the guns silently; they even knew how to cock those fifties and twenties without a click. I never even had to raise my voice when I said, "Open fire," started all our engines and jammed the throttles down.

We came in close with our guns hammering and our engines roaring, fast and sudden. There was plenty of light to see by then. They carried a lot of ammo on those barges and often drums of gasoline—there were more fireworks than on the Fourth of July.

I never circled those burning barges the way some of our guys did. Before the Japs had a chance to shoot back much, I went across their bow, dropped a depth charge set shallow and turned away into the night, getting out of there as fast as I could. One 300-pound depth charge often lifted a hundred-foot barge right into the air, breaking it in half. After that we didn't have much to worry about except small-arms fire, which sometimes continued from officers on rafts.

There was no quarter given or asked at that stage of that war. If we sank a barge close enough to shore to permit the troops to get to the beach and fight again, we ran in and dropped another depth charge. Nasty stuff, but those Japs were giving our boys fits in the jungles, filling our cemeteries at Milne Bay. Our job was to kill them without getting killed and we did it well. Remember, the Japs had asked for it at Pearl Harbor, and we didn't weep when we gave it back to them on those dark nights on the Guinea coast. We were scared—of course we were scared when we rode those plywood boats on top of 2,000 gallons of gasoline. When the Japs blew up, it meant we wouldn't, not that night at least.

We were professionals, scared, bumbling kids who had become professionals, and we were proud of it. Now on this sleepless night thirty-five years later, I thought of that and recovered some of that remembered pride. If I

61

ever was crazy enough to try to make a big killing in the illegal trade, I'd know how to arm my ship and how to fight her. If a bunch of hoodlums tried to hijack us, they'd learn what it was like to run into a professional, a hit man with some real experience.

Tough talk, maybe just an old dry drunk mumbling to himself at three o'clock in the morning. When you came right down to it, how would a civilian arm a privately owned vessel in what was supposed to be a time of peace?

It was all right to dream of somehow using my connections with the Naval Reserve to steal machine guns, depth charges and hand grenades, but how on earth would I even begin? Weapons were not left just lying about naval bases, ready for any old reserve officer to carry off. It would be easy, and ludicrous, to get caught stealing guns even before Tad's scheme got off the ground.

It was undoubtedly possible, of course, to buy weapons of almost any sort illegally, but how would I go about it? I had a vision of myself going into some waterfront bar and saying to every shady-looking character I met, "Hey, Bud, do you know where I can pick up a few machine guns?"

Somebody would surely set the law on me. Perhaps Tad had made connections while he was doing his "research" on the drug trade which would enable him to buy machine guns from the underworld, but such purchases would tip off the whole network of organized crime that he was off on some adventure of his own and would almost certainly cause him to be closely watched.

No, it would not be wise for me to try to steal guns, and even less wise to start dealing with the underworld at the start. Then how to arm a ship? The National Guard kept supplies of fairly heavy weapons in armories in small towns and cities all over the United States. If I could meet someone active in the Guard and get him involved in our giant scheme, maybe he could find a way to steal machine guns without much risk.

Crazy. Every time you took another man into your confidence, the risk of betrayal would increase. I'd have to find a way to buy weapons for our ship legitimately. Abroad? Foreign officials were generally even more touchy about guns than American authorities. Anyone who tried to buy machine guns anywhere in the world would be subject to immediate arrest.

It should be *possible* to make a small ship into a pretty tough customer without military weapons. Semi-automatic rifles, shotguns and even submachine guns were available at many sporting stores, and a gunsmith could easily change a semi-automatic weapon into an automatic one by altering the firing pin. I was hardly a gunsmith, but I could read manuals and the specifications for all those weapons were available in libraries . . . Of course even light automatic weapons would not be enough protection, but grenades could be fashioned out of dynamite. When my grandfather, in a fit of rebellion against the sea, had bought a small farm in the Adirondacks, he had bought dynamite to blast tree stumps, and I was sure I could find a way to get the stuff legally. To use dynamite effectively as a weapon, I would have to make sure how many seconds it took to burn each inch of fuse. I'd have to conduct experiments to see how long a fuse I should use to explode a stick of dynamite or a package of it at the end of a twenty-foot throw, or as long as I could heave it. Dynamite could blow up too close to one's own ship, or the fuse could sputter long enough to allow a cool enemy to throw it back at you—timing in this, as in all fighting, would be all-important. And surprise. Dynamite could be a potent weapon simply because one could appear to surrender to a boatful of hijackers, motion them close, and then drop a package of closely fused dynamite on their deck. The resulting explosion would, if it occurred, resemble the explosion of the Japanese troop barges . . .

What kind of crazy man was I to lie in my room the night I had proposed marriage to a woman, a near saint, with my mind full of such fantasies of mayhem? Since I was much too sane, and too cowardly, to take Tad's great scheme seriously as a game, never mind an actual project to undertake, why in hell did my mind keep dwelling on it? I knew, but I wasn't ready to face it yet . . .

I thought I was nuts. The temptation to get drunk after so many years of sobriety became almost overpowering. I telephoned an old AA friend, a lawyer, waking him out of a sound sleep.

"Sorry, but I'm in trouble," I said.

"Tell me about it," he said groggily. "Say, Andy, can you wait till I get a cup of coffee? Call me back in five minutes."

"Sure."

"Now promise you won't have a drink inside of five minutes."

"Promise."

The minutes crawled by slowly, but he called me back in about three.

"Now what's bugging you, Andy?" he said.

I wanted to tell him about Tad's whole insane scheme and the way I could not get it out of my mind, but . . . well, if there was even a one-percent chance that we ever were actually going to try it, I'd be crazy to start talking about it, even to my most trusted AA brothers. And I was crazier still to be thinking this way.

"I proposed to Pattie tonight and I guess the whole idea of marriage has got me scared," I finally explained to myself.

There was of course some truth in that too, and this semi-confession kind of semi-calmed me. Twenty minutes later, after thanking my friend, I lay down and finally slept.

There were no sweet dreams.

4

At about eight o'clock the next morning the telephone woke me up. It was Pattie.

"I haven't been able to sleep," she said. "Last night I called practically everybody in AA that I know."

"I made a long call myself."

"God, maybe we shouldn't be putting each other under this strain."

"Pattie, if you don't want to get married—"

"I *do*. But it's all so complicated . . ."

"How?"

"Sally is going through a very religious stage. She's thirteen, Andy. At that age many girls become almost fanatics."

"Will it help if we get married in a church?"

"We're Catholics, Andy, or I was and Sally very much is. She just assumed we were going to have a Catholic wedding when I told her we were going to get married. She was so happy about it that I couldn't—"

"What will your church have to say about your divorce?"

"They're fairly reasonable about that these days. It probably can be worked out, but it will take time."

"I don't want to hurry you."

"You're not. I want this as much as you do." She broke off for a moment before saying, "There's just one thing, though. If we're going to be married in the Catholic Church, you're going to have to turn Catholic. *That's* what I meant when I said it was complicated, and it's a lot to ask. It seems crazy but I don't know what else to do."

"I don't have any religion except the 'higher power' we talk about at AA, but if it will make Sally happy . . ."

"It apparently will. I can't figure out the morality in this. I know you're never going to believe in any dogma, never accept any church authority. In effect you're going to have to lie if you turn Catholic, but can a lie told to make a child like Sally happy be such a terrible sin?"

"I don't know. Will it make you happy if I take the vows or whatever I have to do?"

"Yes. I'm still a Catholic and I do want to make Sally happy. She'd be so shocked if I weren't married in church. I couldn't do that to her."

"That would be no way for me to start trying to be a father to her."

"You'll have to take instructions and I'm afraid it will take time, maybe months, but of course we can keep on seeing each other."

"We'll do it any way you want."

"I don't think we should live together full-time, though, until we're married. Isn't this crazy? I think it would be somehow worse for the kids if we lived together before we got married than if I just kept on being your part-time mistress."

"You were never that."

"Lover then. Whatever. Look, if you go to Lauderdale and live on that boat, I'll be there every minute I can without hurting the kids. We can have a lot of mornings together if you don't have to be out working."

"We'll figure it out."

"One day at a time. I think maybe we're really going to make it, Andy."

When we ended that conversation I felt pretty confused. I loved Pattie. No doubt about that, but I had spent most of the night remembering the war with pleasure and trying to figure out how to blow up hijackers. Even now I couldn't stop my mind from trying to answer all the hundreds of questions posed by Tad's crazy scheme, but I had just agreed to join the Catholic Church because that seemed the best way to make some people I loved happy. What kind of a man was I, anyway? I was glad nobody was around to answer that.

The immediate solution to my problems, I figured, was to forget my fantasies about the big score, so to speak, and to work to establish myself as a yacht broker and make some honest, respectable money. That, after all, was a legitimate business which had proved surprisingly lucrative for some people and I presumably had all the right qualifications. Not many people knew more than I did about yachts.

How should yacht brokers dress? Not like boat bums—no dungarees, no khaki shirt. Yacht brokers were like bankers in that they dealt with large sums of money and had to look responsible above all else. I put on my one good suit, selected one of my three proper shirts and one of my five ties. Pretty soon I'd have to buy a conservative wardrobe, but I better make a few sales first.

My first potential customers that day were a plump young physician from Akron, Ohio, his plump young wife and their three plump children, the oldest about ten. They had had "lots of experience sailing on the Great Lakes, where conditions are even worse than the ocean," the doctor told me, and now they wanted to buy "a good auxiliary for exploring the Bahamas."

Fine, except he had only $30,000 to spend, "not a cent more." That limitation restricted him to very old boats, most of which were full of rot, to very small, cheaply built new boats or maybe a sound thirty-footer about ten or fifteen years old if I could find one. Going through the files in Mark's office, I discovered the specification sheets for a fine Seawind ketch that was moored just a few miles away. She was a trim little vessel, a good buy, but the doctor's wife took one look at her small cabin and said, "I could never live here, I need a *much* bigger galley, a shower and at least three separate cabins."

For thirty grand that was impossible, of course, but I guessed that good salesmen never should be blunt.

"You might find the room you want in a powerboat," I

said, "one of the older ones."

"We don't want power," the doctor said indignantly.

"But couldn't we just look at one?" his wife asked.

I decided that the thing to do was to show her the most luxurious interior her money could buy and to hell with the kind of hull which surrounded it. This turned out to be an ancient jerry-built cruiser, plywood and plate glass, but with plenty of room in her bulbous hull, and she had new rugs and curtains.

"This is *lovely*," the wife said. "We could all be quite comfortable here. I wouldn't mind moving aboard and starting for the Bahamas right away."

"Is she really seaworthy?" the doctor asked.

Well, there it lay—was I an honest man or wasn't I? A sale would mean $3,000, half for me and half for my boss, and I loved the idea of making a deal the first time out. Still, I had a quick mental image of that couple with their three plump children out in the Gulf Stream in that shoebox. The beginnings of a norther were whispering in Fort Lauderdale that day and the Christmas decorations which had recently been strung from lamp post to lamp post in the marina were already beginning to swing in the rising wind.

"Is she really seaworthy? Well, sir, with all your experience on the Great Lakes, I guess you're as good a judge of that as I."

"She's got a good high bow," the doctor said, sounding very professional. His profession, not mine. "Is the cockpit self-bailing?"

"She's got scuppers," I said factually, pointing out two small holes in the linoleum that covered the plywood deck.

"How's the engine?" he asked.

"We'll start it and see."

The engine, which was basically a Chevrolet motor, ran, which seemed to impress him.

"How much horsepower has she got?" he asked.

"Oh, she's got lots of horsepower—about a hundred and fifty, I'd say."

"A very powerful vessel."

"You could say that."

"Of course I'll want to have her surveyed to make sure she's sound."

"Of course. I can give you a list of recommended surveyors."

Mark had a list, all right, a dozen names of fellows whom we in the business called "poets." They'd inspect any vessel with a fine show of thoroughness and write reports with phrases like "a fine example of yachts of her type," "a well-tested design by a well-known builder" and "truly luxurious accommodations for the price." Those "poets" could wax lyrical about even a sunken barge without ever writing anything which could actually be proved to be false.

"We'll take her subject to survey," the doctor said. "We only have two weeks and we want to get started."

I figured that the least I could do was to ask him not to sail until he got a good weather report if he planned to cross the Gulf Stream, but I'd better wait until he signed a contract. The survey and the details of the sale would take at least twenty-four hours, and by that time the norther would probably be howling loud enough to give him the message.

Mark took me out to lunch that day to celebrate the fact that I had made a sale on my very first try. He had two martinis and it took guts for me to stick to my

72

ginger ale.

"Do you suppose that guy will actually put his kids aboard that floating greenhouse and try to cross the Stream tomorrow?" I asked.

"If he does, he'll probably make it. And when he comes back we'll sell him a bigger boat, something a little more comfortable at sea."

"What if he sinks?"

"You can't worry about that in this business. It's his funeral. We just sold him what *he* wanted."

My ginger ale didn't taste very good, and neither did the steak I ordered. Compared to this, the illegal trade didn't seem so bad.

That evening I saw the doctor and his family busily gluing letters on the transom of their newly bought yacht. They were naming her the *Blood Vessel*. It seemed to me that anyone who gave a boat a name like that deserved to sink, but that observation did not make me feel much better. The doctor's plump children looked happy. It was calm there in the marina and the Christmas lights were flashing merrily.

The next day the doctor sailed, despite the norther, but the man who filled their gas tanks told me he had more sense than I had thought. With the weather as it was, he had decided to try the Keys rather than the Bahamas on this vacation, and he had headed down the inland route, not out the inlet. Which made me feel much better, but did my conscience have a right to feel relieved?

It was ridiculous to worry about that. Besides, I had a new customer to try to satisfy, the representative of a big corporation this time, who wanted to buy a fishing cruiser aboard which to entertain customers. This was a prime prospect, for he was talking about spending maybe two hundred thousand dollars, but unfortunately for me, he knew his business and planned to shop around a long time.

Mark told me that if I made one sale out of ten tries, I would be doing well, but I got discouraged after three days of showing boats to people who didn't know what they wanted, couldn't afford what they wanted, or were too smart to buy without looking at practically every hull afloat. My spirits weren't exactly lifted when Pattie telephoned to say that Tommy had come down with bronchitis and seemed terribly depressed (probably by his mother's impending nuptials, I guessed) and she didn't think that she should leave him for a few days. It was lonely there in Fort Lauderdale with the crazy tropical Christmas lights blinking on the boats that milled around the harbor and with Christmas parties going full blast in every cockpit and bar. I made a lot of AA meetings in unfamiliar church basements, but I didn't know anybody in the Lauderdale fellowships and it would take time to find any real friends.

I had enough sense not to drink, but I was feeling sorry for myself as I sat in a restaurant with a view commanding the inlet, watching the fishing cruisers roll in from the sea, and one big motor sailer, the *Laughing Gull*, head out, probably for the Bahamas. I had delivered her to the Virgin Islands once. She was a good vessel, the proud property of a fine old yachtsman. I didn't know whether I was glad or sorry that I had swallowed the anchor. The roaming life had often been bleak and lonely; although I kept telling myself that things would soon change, I couldn't help feeling impatient, depressed. There was just a glow of twilight left on the

74

eastern horizon, and I could see the norther pushing up the waves against the Gulf Stream out there. The *Laughing Gull* started to roll as she escaped the arms of the breakwater and her skipper headed her into the wind to hoist her steadying sails. Before dark tomorrow she'd probably be moored in Nassau . . .

Before going back to the *Far Away* with the intention of turning in early that night, I toured the wharves to see if any old friends were in port. Moored between two trim sloops I saw an astonishing hulk, the wreck of an apparently big, brand-new houseboat. Her metal and fiberglass were still gleaming, but her big windows had almost all been smashed, the stanchions round her foredeck had been twisted, and the glass deck itself had a jagged crack about twenty feet long, like a fissure in ice. Her little mast tilted at a crazy angle and the forward end of her deckhouse had been bent into concave curves. On her afterdeck a short muscular man in swimming trunks and a gray sweatshirt sat in a canvas chair with his feet up on a battered rail, a six-pack of beer by his side. He had a round head with short-cropped black hair and a vaguely Oriental face. There was, I was sure, only one man on earth who looked like that.

He was called the Eskimo, and he was one of the best professional sailors in the world when he was sober, and better than most when drunk. Back in the days when we both served on the foredeck of John Nicholas Brown's famous big black yawl, *Bolero*, I'd seen him climb the hundred-and-twenty-foot mast hand over hand on a halyard as though it took no effort at all. There was no better man when it came to wrestling in a four-thousand-square-foot spinnaker in a gale. Whether he actually was part Eskimo, as he claimed, I never was sure, but when

75

we took the northern route together in the 1952 transatlantic race, he said he could *smell* icebergs in the fog ahead. And apparently he could, because when we followed his directions, we always skirted them. He was one of the best yacht captains in the world until the booze really got to him and he became even wilder than most of us boat bums. Perhaps because he was so short, only about five-foot-seven, and many people did not realize that he was sort of a sawed-off giant, he got into a lot of fist fights. With vast understatement, Esky told me once that he was "not good at taking criticism." This meant that owners who objected to his drinking habits quite often were hurled overboard—Esky rarely actually hit anyone except cops, whom he thought could take it. But the owners often called the cops after they had been rescued, usually by Esky himself, and after three or four cops had splashed into the harbor, Esky often found himself in jail. Eventually some hotshot owner of a racing yacht usually bailed him out and hired him, because Esky's reputation as a winning helmsman was even greater than his notoriety as a wild man. Now, however, I suspected that he'd reached the end of his road. Why else would a top racing skipper be aboard this wreck of a houseboat?

"Esky!" I yelled. "What the hell is a nice girl like you doing in a place like this?"

He jumped up, bounded to the wharf and clapped me on the back hard enough to make me brace myself.

"Andy, you old bastard! You're just the man I need—"

"What's happened to you?"

"Man, I got a story to tell. If you can write it up and sell it, will you give me half the loot?"

I had sometimes been called the Shakespeare of the

boat-bum set because I had often picked up a few bucks by writing up the ocean races for the boating press, or sea stories for men's magazines. When I was fresh out of my one year at Harvard, I had had ideas of becoming another Joseph Conrad or at least a Somerset Maugham, but I never got beyond *Yachting Magazine* or *Argosy*. These literary triumphs were enough to impress my fellow sailors, however, and they often came to me with tales to be written up. Mostly they were too wild to be publishable. Especially Esky's tales . . .

"What's happened to you now?" I said.

He took me into the battered deckhouse of the houseboat, where splintered furniture lay in a pile, got me a cup of coffee when I refused the beer, and told me this story.

Until about six months ago, he'd been captain of a fine old schooner, the *Iron Yankee*, which was based in New York. He liked the job and was on his good behavior, no drinking except beer. The only trouble was the owner's wife, who was in the process of getting a divorce from her husband. "She wasn't a bad-looking old crock," Esky said, and she spent a lot of time aboard while her husband was on business trips.

"That old lady and I got along pretty well together," Esky said, "and pretty soon the husband smelled a rat. He paid the mate to take pictures of us. In the end it didn't make much difference, because she had all kinds of pictures of him dating from way back, but he fired me and kicked her off the boat. She didn't seem to care much, but she felt bad about me getting fired and maybe she wanted to keep me, so she decided to buy her own damn yacht and make me skipper."

Instead of asking Esky's advice about the purchase of a yacht, she had bought this houseboat on the recommendation of a friend. The friend (who probably got a commission from the dealer) and the salesman had told her that the houseboat was seaworthy; they had described it as "a real seagoing houseboat" and the salesman had been foolish enough to use those words in the bill of sale, as the manufacturer had in his advertisement.

This had outraged Esky's nautical morality and he wanted to show the salesman up. "If this is really a seagoing houseboat, I suppose I can take her to sea," he said to the man, when he took delivery of the craft at the 79th Street Pier in New York. It was late November and fall gales were sweeping the harbor.

"Of course," the salesman said uneasily.

"Well, my owner has given me orders to take this bucket south. Seeing she's seaworthy, I'm going to take her outside around Cape Hatteras."

"Now, in November?" the startled salesman asked.

"Well, is she seaworthy or isn't she?"

"I said she's seaworthy and she is, for her type."

"You didn't put nothing about types in that bill of sale. Not in your ads, either. I believe what I read, so I'm going to take this thing to sea. I'll survive because that's my business. When we see what happens to your seagoing houseboat, you'll hear from us."

I imagine that there was a look in Esky's eyes which made the salesman disinclined to argue. Anyway, Esky took that houseboat out on the open Atlantic in the teeth of a fall gale. She had powerful twin engines and he bounced her right into the seas while being careful to stay on the flying bridge, where he wouldn't get hit by flying glass.

As he had expected, the superstructure was smashed long before he got to Cape Hatteras, but the hull held out long enough for him to crawl in the inlet at Cape May, New Jersey. After emergency repairs to the bottom, he had continued down the inland water route to Fort Lauderdale, where he had been ordered to go.

"I got your seagoing houseboat here," he had said to his owner over the telephone. "Come down and take a look at her."

The lady who owned the boat was indignant, not so much at Esky, whose friendship she wanted to keep, as at the people who had sold her the boat. Legal proceedings wre instituted and Esky had been ordered to leave the wreck "as is" until the matter was resolved. Which was why this great racing skipper was living on a hulk that looked like a demolished crystal palace.

"It all ought to be written up for the boating magazines," he said. "People ought to know."

"Esky, the boating magazines try to sell boats, not warn people off them."

"They at least ought to print a picture of this thing." The bellow of his laugh suddenly rang out. "Andy, you should have been with me. Man, it was like standing under Niagara Falls when I headed this thing full-bore into that sea. I had parts flying off her like confetti. It was a glorious sight, I guarantee you."

"What are you going to do next?" I asked.

"I don't know. Man, I'm sure getting sick of the yachting life. They say that punk kids are making a fortune by running dope in from Colombia. Sometimes I'm tempted to try that."

I stared at him, not so much startled that he would

consider getting involved in illegal running as that the subject should come up at all. Maybe it was the adventure of it that was so appealing, the idea of being pitted against dangerous odds at sea, the game of working out a detailed strategy that would insure untold profits for two old sailors like Esky and me. But all I said was what I'd been telling myself for some time now.

"You'd be crazy, Esky."

"I don't know. In the last few years they've been bringing that stuff in mostly by plane, but I hear that the government has set up some new radar systems, and now they say they're going back to boats. They're looking for skippers—a guy I know and trust pretty well told me that."

"In the long run you'd get nothing but trouble, big trouble, Esky. You're smart enough to know that." Who was I really talking to?

"I ain't so sure. More than fly-by-nighters are mixed up in this. They got an organization, you know, real big-time with protection at the top. Those boys take care of their own—"

"In more ways than one sometimes. You've read about all the shootings—"

"They shoot people who try to muscle in, but I'd just be an employee. They need real sailormen to carry valuable cargos like that. Those punk kids have been piling their boats up on reefs all up and down the coast. The Mafia navy screws up a lot."

"How much would they pay a skipper?" I asked, trying to sound casual.

"Sometimes a hundred grand a run, can you believe that?"

"That's a lot, but if you ever were crazy enough to

want to risk your ass, you could probably do better on your own."

"I've thought of that," he said, "but there's a lot of business to it and you need protection—not just from the feds, but from hijackers. I doubt if the Mafia or whatever they're calling it these days flies a house flag, but people know which boats are theirs and bloody well leave them alone. That's what I've heard, anyway. Maybe it's all scuttlebutt."

"It would be plenty hard to find out. It's almost impossible to get facts . . ."

"You sound interested . . ."

"Hell, I have no intention of . . . but I guess a man can't help but be interested when they're making millions of dollars every day. It's *interesting* . . ."

"It sure is. Maybe we could make enough in a few runs to retire for life and buy your own damn yachts. How I'd love to show up on the starting line of a transatlantic race with my own new cutter, one built to my own design. I been drawing up a boat like that for years. I never thought I'd get a chance to get her built."

"Don't jump too fast. I don't want to be reading about you in the wrong part of the newspapers."

"I'm just *thinking* about it, trying to build up what information I can. Hell, it really ain't no different from the rum-running days, from what I hear, except it's a lot bigger, and I guess that plenty of men got rich then, plenty of folks whose children are real respectable gentry today."

Since my father had done his share of rum running I couldn't think of any good answer to that. There was a moment of silence, during which I heard the mullet jumping close alongside the broken windows of the battered houseboat.

When I finally left, I walked slowly back to the *Far Away*, the cabins of which were damp and musty. I flicked on an electric heater. A small motor cruiser went by with Christmas lights blazing and people singing in her cockpit. Her wake caused the old North Sea ketch to roll a little, straining at her docklines as though she were dreaming of the sea.

Suddenly I felt exhausted, and that night, at least, I enjoyed the sleep of the innocent.

The next day Pattie called me with the news that she had found a priest in Fort Lauderdale who would give me instruction. He turned out to be a nice round-faced Irishman, full of boyish enthusiasm for his religion and most of life. He gave me a whole armful of pamphlets and books to read. After carrying those back to the *Far Away*, I went to work at Mark's office. That day I sold a fast fishing cruiser to a soft-spoken, dark-haired fat man who looked to me as though he might be planning to use it for running, but he turned out to be a well-known Florida politician. How did a man on government pay make enough to buy a big fishing cruiser? Maybe *he* was on the take from the drug boys; rumor had it that they had a lot of the authorities in their pocket. Hell, I had no reason whatsoever to suspect my customer, except that he had once, according to Mark, been a district attorney. I apparently had reached the point where I saw dark intrigues in every corner.

5

For about six months I lived in an odd kind of limbo, planning to get married, studying religion, trying to sell yachts—which proved harder when the stock market dipped—and finally forgetting my insanity about Tad's preposterous idea. I didn't hear anything from Tad, and since his father had stopped calling me I figured that they had somehow mended their fences and were in touch with each other. In any event, I was too absorbed with Pattie and my soon-to-be new family to give the Claytons much thought.

Pattie and I finally got married. In a Catholic church as she and her daughters wanted, and my whole new family moved aboard the *Far Away*.

This was the first time I had ever had a family. Both Pattie and I realized that we were not exactly the stereotype of the American dream, but ex-alkies trying hard to stay reformed, a sixteen-year-old boy who was still just about as mixed up as his early childhood had been, a fourteen-year-old girl who with touching sincerity hoped to be a bride of Christ, and a ten-year-old, Susie, who I guess was the most normal of all of us, perhaps because her mother had straightened herself out and her father had been taken away before she was badly hurt.

Part of my damn foolishness had always been a tendency to think that life was going to turn out to be either heaven or hell—that was true of a lot of my friends in AA and we all tried to kid each other out of it. I had had rosy dreams of family life, pictures of my new daughters bringing me my slippers and my newspaper, I suppose, and of myself teaching Tommy how to navigate or splice manila, interesting him in the sea enough to get him over his hostility toward me. Of course it didn't turn out to be like that, but the tensions of this newly created family were eased as much as possible by Pattie, who so much wanted to make it all work and who was so grateful to me for trying to help build something for all of us that she seemed to forget that I was getting as much good stuff as I was giving, though also taking my share of hassles.

Our main problem was Tommy, who had so many problems that I kept telling myself that no one in his right mind could stay angry at him for long. He was physically small, like his real father, and I sensed that that was one of the problems he had with me; I was about six inches taller than he was, and almost a hundred pounds heavier, and I must have seemed a threat. Sometimes I tried to see myself through his eyes. I liked to think of myself as a fairly gentle person, and in point of fact I hadn't hit anyone since I was sixteen years old—not a bad record for a man who had hung out in bars for more than twenty years. But obviously there was also a lot of violence in my nature. I was always doubling up my fists and sticking them in my pockets when I was crossed, bunching up my shoulders and glaring at people who annoyed me in a way which was a kind of aggression in itself. No wonder I sparked an answering hostility in him.

He was a cocky kid who had survived a tough world. His mother told me that his father had often hit him in drunken rages, and the boy had rarely cried, had never been willing to testify against his father to the cops. No wonder she loved him and couldn't stop herself from crying when she tried to tell me what he'd been through, but the boy was sometimes hard for me to love. Sympathy, of course, was easy. My own background, which hadn't been nearly as rough as his, had been hard enough to deal with and could easily have steered me into major trouble at his age. But my sympathy didn't make me any less worried, or him any less difficult. He regarded himself as tough, all five-foot-seven, all one hundred and twenty pounds of him.

"Don't worry about me, Jack," he actually said to me once. "You better worry about yourself."

He was wiry, muscular and fought a lot with kids his own age. He had been hanging out with a fairly rough bunch in Miami, a few of whom were old enough to drive motorcycles and jalopies. They drove up to see him when he moved to Lauderdale and introduced him to some of the locals they knew. By the time Pattie and I were married, I had arranged to have the *Far Away* moved to a wharf at a boatyard on the New River which was much quieter than the marinas. Part of the deal was that I was to act as a sort of night watchman at the yard, and I worried when Tommy's friends began to use the place as an after-hours teenage hangout. At any hour they would arrive in their crowded old cars or on motorcycles. Most of them were too young to drink legally, but the boatyard soon became so littered with beer cans and pint bottles that the owner objected, and he claimed the kids were smoking pot.

"You're bringing me more trouble than you're supposed to prevent," he said. "You're a good guy, Andy, but if you can't control those kids, I'll have to ask you to leave."

"I guess you've got to be firm with Tommy," Pattie said, when I talked to her about it. "He's always needed a father. Just try to remember that he's got no clear idea about what a father is."

Feeling rather self-conscious, I asked the boy to come into the after cabin of the *Far Away* for a serious talk. He looked both hang-dog and defiant.

"I know, you don't like having my friends around," he said before I could start.

"I don't like being asked to leave this place. It's the only quiet mooring I can find and your mother doesn't like the marinas."

"We're not the only ones who leave beer cans and bottles around. Half the workmen are alkies. Why do they always blame every bottle they find on us?"

"Let's just keep the place cleaned up anyway. It's a free mooring. We can't beat that."

"I'm not going to pick up *their* crap. You know I don't drink at all. I'm not an alky like—"

"Finish it."

"Like you, damn it. No wonder you hate to see people drinking so much. My friends can handle it, even if you can't."

"I've been handling it pretty well for quite a few years."

"Well, my friends don't have to keep calling up people all the time and going to meetings, like you and mom. I think you got her into it. She was fine before she met you—"

"Let's not get into that right now," I said, trying to keep the anger out of my voice. "We have a practical problem. I'm going to take a walk through the yard every morning. If I find a lot of beer cans and bottles around, you'll have to tell your friends to keep out."

"They'll come anyway. Are you big enough to throw them all out?"

"I'm big enough to call the cops and I'll do it. Don't mess with me, Tommy. I'm trying to help."

"I know, mom says I need a father . . . *I* say it isn't you."

He turned and ran ashore. Pattie saw him go.

"I'm sorry," she said.

"It'll take time," I said, trying to sound more hopeful than I felt.

The hassle with the beer cans and bottles continued until I got into the habit of going out with a big plastic sack and picking them up myself, feeling noble, and resentful, all at the same time. Giant confrontations should be avoided until our new family had some chance to get established, I thought. Easy does it. One day at a time.

Fights with Tommy were not easy to prevent, though. He bought a stereo with money he said he had earned himself—though how, he never explained—and played it so loudly in his stateroom aboard the big ketch that life was almost intolerable for the rest of us. He also smoked pot in his stateroom and the smell of that worried his mother. In AA Pattie had learned that marijuana and booze usually go together with the younger generation and she was terrified by the whole pattern. Her first husband had smoked a lot of pot, and to her the whole nightmare was starting again.

I started by talking to Tommy gently, but in the end I'm afraid I said, "I know you don't want me to try to act like a father, but damn it, I'm the master of this vessel, if nothing else. If you can't keep your music down to the point where the rest of us can stand it, I'm going to throw your machine overboard. And the next time I smell pot being smoked aboard here, I'm going to roust out your cabin and throw any of that stuff I find overboard. Don't mess with me aboard this vessel, Tommy."

Big deal, I thought. My surrogate-father bit with Tad had ended with me fantasizing about a drug run, and here I was going on an anti-pot crusade, for God's sake . . .

"Yes, Captain," he said. "Aye aye, sir! Is that the way you want me to talk?"

"It's better than a lot of the shit you've been giving me."

"How do I ship out of this outfit? It's not the Navy, is it? I'm not in for four years. I didn't volunteer."

I started to worry . . . hope? . . . he'd run away. Pattie lived in dread of it.

"What do you want, Tommy?" I said. "Your mother and I want to help you make sense out of your life. What do we do?"

"They have boarding schools, don't they? I met a guy the other day who went to one and he said it wasn't bad. 'Better than parents,' he said. I can't stand you and you can't stand me. I can't make a living for myself yet, and I'd like to get myself an education, so how about a boarding school?"

"You know, that's probably a sensible idea," I said, with a certain amount of surprise. "We'll look into it. Meanwhile, please let's try to get on together. You may not think that we can make much of a family here, but we're doing better than if we all tried to fly off on our own somewhere."

"I know," he said. "I *know*," and I'm darned if he didn't start to cry. I tried to put my arm around him and at first he didn't resist, but then he twisted away and ran ashore again, the way he ended almost all our confrontations. Still, it was a breakthrough of sorts. Maybe now he wouldn't even want to go away to school.

I was wrong. Somehow he got all the literature on

89

Alfred Academy, where his friend went. I'd never heard of the place, but it was accredited and was in Jacksonville, relatively near, close enough for us to visit him fairly often. It also had a summer school. It was designed for kids who had money but no real homes, I guessed. Tad might have gone to such a school, from the way he talked about his father.

"I hate the idea but I also hate the tension here," Pattie said. "And I hate his friends, all that pot-smoking, boozing lot. I'm afraid they're into shoplifting—I heard a couple of them boasting about 'boosting beer' and selling it. I'd do anything to get Tommy a new start."

"It's one possible solution," I said.

"How much would it cost?"

I had noted that the answer in the catalog Tommy had given me was seven grand, plus another $1,500 for the summer school, but I didn't want to scare Pattie. "I don't know, but it's nothing we couldn't handle."

"I may get a job singing at the Rose Room again if business picks up for them."

That was a forlorn hope. Business was bad all over the Beach that year, and young strippers were more in demand than middle-aged *chanteuses*. I had a feeling that along with Esky, we were all going out of date, like wooden yachts. Still, I'd made six grand on my sale of the fishing cruiser to the former district attorney. The stock market showed signs of recovering and people said that boat sales would soon pick up . . . "We can handle it," I said to Pattie. "Get him enrolled, help him to get started soon as possible. At least it's something positive."

"I'm *grateful*," she said, tears coming to her eyes.

90

"So am I," I said. "You know, Pattie, since we've been married, we've had lots of problems, God knows, but I'm not lonely anymore, and I don't wake up in the middle of the night with the feeling that my life is empty, and for sure I don't have to pick up dowdy old broads in bars every time I need to get laid. Hey, it's a great life." And mostly I meant it.

Except for one thing—I began to worry more about money than I ever had before. My expenses, even without eight-and-a-half grand a year for the boarding school, were much bigger than I had figured; I had never really been aware of the effects of inflation until I started to try to fill all the needs of a family of five. While I had been in the yacht-delivery business, I had been on an expense account most of the time, and it had never occurred to me that the simple process of staying alive was so damned expensive. The small salary Mark guaranteed me hardly covered our grocery bills. Our rent was free, but there were clothes, doctors, dentists, ten thousand "incidentals" and a big life-insurance policy I'd thought it wise to buy when becoming the head of a family. Pattie's work with the typing agency continued when she moved to Lauderdale, but most of her earnings went for buying a newer car, which we needed when her old Volkswagen bug finally gave up the ghost. Our livelihood really depended on any commissions I could make selling yachts, and that was a strange, unpredictable business; sometimes I'd make three sales in quick succession and then go for months without a serious nibble. Except for the fishing cruiser, most of the boats I sold were small. My savings account, which had

91

never been fat, lost weight almost every month, and although I thought I'd do better as a yacht broker when I gained experience and became better known as a salesman than as a skipper, it was often pretty hard for me not to get panicky.

Of course that feeling of panic, of building terror, is one thing that had led me to drink in the past. I had only two answers to it—the AA meetings, which I attended almost every day during this period, and my love for Pattie. My breakthrough with Tommy was minor, of course, but it was progress nonetheless, and I was enjoying spending time with Sally and Susie. They were rapidly becoming very much their own people, with their own enthusiasms and ways of tangling with the business of growing up, but they shared enough of themselves with me so that I finally began to feel as if I really was their father. That was a luxury that I never thought I'd have—but the drawback, of course, was that my feeling for my new family also added to my worries about money. And I admit I began again to fantasize about Tad's scheme. Just as an intellectual exercise, I kept telling myself, a safety valve of sorts. By then I assumed that Tad had either given up the idea or might even be executing it, having found someone else to skipper his ship. So I felt relatively safe indulging in my fantasies, trying to figure out what kind of vessel would be least likely to draw the attention of hijackers and Coast Guardsmen and at the same time offer optimum speed and ingeniously concealed storage space for the cargo. I had gimmicks in mind that outdid James Bond. And because there was no possibility of them ever becoming reality, I didn't have to feel the least bit guilty about them. Or so I told myself whenever in fact I began to feel guilty. It was all just a useful distraction from my worries, a way to stay on the straight and narrow . . .

Newspapers and magazines suddenly seemed to me to be unusually full of stories about smuggling. It was fact, not fantasy, that at least one and perhaps several huge underworld organizations existed and were bringing about three billion dollars' worth of illegal narcotics of all kinds into the country every month. Thousands of smaller gangs and countless individuals were fighting for their share of the trade. Not only had drugs become bigger than the tourist business in Miami, they were said to be the biggest industry in the whole nation of Colombia, and marijuana was reported to be the biggest cash crop in the Hawaiian Islands. Maybe Tad was wrong to think only in terms of cocaine—that stuff was easier to transport because each ounce was so astonishingly valuable, but marijuana might be easier to buy and to sell because it was both produced and used by so many more people. In California, even back in the days when I had sailed there, masses of people believed that they had a God-given right to smoke pot and a moral obligation to fight the government's "tyrannical" outlawing of the stuff. There and, increasingly, in Florida, the situation was much as it had been in the days when the government had tried to prohibit booze: a hell of a lot of people were rooting for the smugglers, and thought the law was wearing the black hat.

As my "intellectual curiosity" about the drug trade grew, I found myself going to the local library and leafing through a lot of books, back magazines and old newspapers to learn more about it.

Among other things, it was apparently true that the smugglers were turning more and more from airplanes to ships. As Esky had said, the government's radar system was working too well and airports were too rigidly controlled to suit the pilots. Out-of-the-way landing strips which the smugglers had built for themselves were too easily detectable in aerial photographs, and parachute drops went astray too often and were too frequently observed by fishermen and bird-watchers, even in the depths of the Everglades. Besides, ships could carry far bigger cargos. Sometimes a mother ship would lie in international waters and let fast ocean-racing speedboats of the "Cigarette" type take the cargo in, but transporting cargo from one vessel to another in the open sea was never easy. Nevertheless, the old rum runners had operated succesfully with mother ships and speedboats for many years.

Elaborate procedures like that might not be necessary. The whole east coast of the United States was honeycombed with small harbors, inhabited and uninhabited, where the right ship sailed by the right people could unload without much more than a one-percent chance of getting caught. The big-time smugglers were apparently realizing that. Now that Miami was becoming so famous as a center, the smugglers were landing their goods in Georgia, in the Carolinas, in Long Island Sound, and in New England, where the huge fleets of summer yachts reduced the chances of being chosen for inspection.

Sometimes I tried to imagine what the men who controlled the trade were actually like. Were they all movie Mafia types, dark men with white ties on purple shirts who talked in hoarse, whispery voices à la Brando's Godfather? Or were they very sophisticated businessmen who held legitimate executive jobs or high political offices as fronts? Maybe I'd already met a few of them, maybe I'd delivered some of their yachts, but I had such a reputation as an honest skipper that no one ever approached me except small-timers who didn't know any better. Or crazy kids like Tad, who no doubt thought that my skill as a skipper and navigator and my World War II fighting experience were a perfect combination for his scheme.

My curiosity about the runners was fanned by my conversations with my old friend, the Eskimo. Often I strolled over to his battered houseboat and sat in his wrecked deckhouse with him while he drank beer and told me about the visits he was getting from a man who said he might be able to get him "another kind of delivery job."

"What kind of a man is he?" I asked.

"Oh, just a young fellow. He could be any kind of salesman, nicely dressed."

"Did he get into any details with you?"

"A hundred grand a job—he told me that, but he didn't say how long the voyage would be. He did say that some of their skippers pick their own boats, charter them themselves or even buy them. He said money can be borrowed for that purpose."

"How serious do you think he is?"

"How serious are you, Andy? You want to go in with me?"

"Hell, I'm just playing with the idea—"

"Well, I tell you, I was a lot more than playing with the idea until last night."

"What happened?"

"A young guy I've sailed with a couple of times came to see me. He owes me a big one because I got him back when he fell overboard one night in conditions that didn't make it easy . . . Anyway, this young guy came to see me last night. He didn't look too good. He said he was hooked on drugs and he sure looked as though he was into something bad. Anyway, he said he'd heard through the grapevine that I was 'available,' as he put it, and he told me not to do it."

"Why? Was he afraid you'd get hooked too?"

"No, he said the people who are really running the business these days are a new breed. A lot of them started in Vietnam. They've seen a lot of killing, he said. They know what they want, how to get it, and they don't let nothing stand in their way. He said those guys will kill you very easy and they wouldn't worry about it afterward. He also said he was afraid they'd hire me because they know I can take a ship anywhere in the world, but they'd find out, if they don't know already, that I've been known to take a drink or two, and that just before the end of the voyage, as soon as they could see the harbor, they'd give me the deep six. That way they wouldn't have to be afraid of my ever talking and they wouldn't even have to pay me nothing. They'd see no reason *not* to do it."

"No wonder they're running into a shortage of skippers."

"Hell, they're setting up a regular nautical training school for their own kind, according to my friend. They even use satellite navigation systems, everything our own Navy has. Radar, loran, gyro compasses—all the best stuff is routine on their ships."

"I bet they still don't have many really good old navy skippers."

"They don't need much more than some old tanker men. Most of these voyages turn out to be routine. No fancy tactics to avoid the Coasties. The poor old Coast Guard is so busy putting out buoys, running ice patrols, stopping illegal immigrants, and rescuing damn fools that they've got practically nothing left for patrols."

"So the smugglers have almost a free hand."

"It seems their only real problem is each other. The trade hasn't really been organized yet. It's too big for any one outfit, even the damn Mafia. They got about twelve different organizations fighting it out, trying to establish territories and hijacking each other."

"So you're not going to be 'available' to them? You're giving up on the idea?"

"You're fucking *A*—that's no crowd for the old Eskimo. I may have been wild in my time, cracked a few heads, but I ain't never killed anybody. I don't want to get to be like them and I sure as hell don't want to be deep-sixed by them, which is probably what would happen. No thanks."

"What are you going to do?"

"There's a big new twelve-meter season shaping up and someone's going to want me on a foredeck. Not much money in it, but a lot of fun, and nobody's going to knife me in the back. I've put out a few calls, and I imagine I'll be getting a job before long."

Only a few days later Esky stopped by my ship to tell

me that he was on his way to California. He was a smarter man than I'd figured, I told myself, maybe a lot smarter than I. He at least had the good sense to give up even the fantasy.

Well, it was a good game to play when I woke up in the middle of the night and lay there worrying about how I was going to pay my bills.

A game? How about an obsession?

6

I had long since concluded that Seymour was not in the least interested in his son's plan when I got a note from him which had been forwarded from my Miami address. He could not have tried to telephone me, because I'd arranged for the telephone company to give my new number to anyone who called the old one. Letters were more Seymour's style; he had telephoned me only during that period when he was so worried about his son.

Nowadays he must be feeling more relaxed.

The letter was typed by a secretary on that expensive Bluff House stationery which had not changed since the days of my early youth.

Dear Andy,

It's been quite some time since we've got together and I've been wondering how you're getting along. I saw an announcement in *Yachting* that you've gone into the brokerage business with Mark Johnson. He's a good man and that's a good outfit. I wish you luck.

As I think I indicated to you last time we met, I'm thinking seriously of selling the *Patrician*—I hate to do it, but my health is such that I don't do much sailing these days. I'd be willing to give you an exclusive on her because I'm sentimental enough to want her to go to someone who will take care of her, and I know you appreciate the old boat. I have some ideas on all this and also about replacing her with something more manageable—I'll always want some kind of boat. We should get together for a chat. I have lots of important things to discuss. Is there any chance you could fly up and spend a weekend here at Bluff House? I'll be available for the next few weeks, but then I'll have a fairly heavy schedule of business travel, so make it as soon as you can. Tad sends his best.

As ever,

Seymour

I read this letter twice, then three times, more

intrigued with each reading. It might mean that Seymour simply had not taken his son's prattle seriously enough to make even an oblique mention of it, but of course he wouldn't be likely to discuss such a thing in a letter, no matter what he thought about it. It was possible that he simply wanted me to sell his yacht and buy another one, but he had "lots of important things to discuss." Maybe the business about selling his boat was just a good cover story—my God, how quickly I was beginning to think in all that melodramatic language . . . But the more I thought about it, the more that letter seemed to me to mean that Seymour might well be in on the deal and that the whole project was really going to turn from fantasy into reality.

My heart beat fast as I read the letter for the fourth time. I was sure of it. If Seymour just wanted me to help sell his boat, he'd simply write me a brief note to say that—and ordinarily he'd do that kind of business with Sparkman and Stephens, the top outfit. He wasn't the kind to go out of his way to do me such a big favor, and never before had he asked me to spend a weekend at his house. He wanted something from me—there was no doubt about that, and it was not likely to be my services as a beginning yacht broker or just the pleasure of my company. Besides, he had made it clear that Tad was with him. This promise to give me an exclusive on a possible sale of *Patrician IV*, which should bring a couple of hundred thousand dollars at least, would persuade Mark to pay my expenses for a trip to Long Island, I thought, already working out the details of implementing Seymour's cover story. For a rich man, Seymour had always been remarkably close-fisted with employees, and clever about getting other people to pick up checks . . .

I decided to take Pattie with me on this trip to Long Island. I certainly had no intention of telling her anything . . . I hadn't *entirely* acknowledged to myself what the purpose of the trip might be—after all, I was going to see an old friend, and so forth . . . I was going to negotiate the sale of a yacht owned by an old friend. I needed, in a way, a cover story for myself. Pattie calmed me down, and if I was going to have a deal with Seymour and Tad, I'd better keep my cool, as they say. Beyond that, Pattie had been under a lot of strain with her warring son, who had just gone off to boarding school, and she needed a change. She could get a friend in to look after the girls, and the trip would do her good. And beyond that, I think I wanted to appear at Bluff House as a full equal, a weekend guest with his wife, not an employee who'd come when called. I needed to establish right away that I was going to be a full partner in . . . well, in any enterprise we developed.

She was pleased with the invitation. I called Seymour, and though he sounded surprised to learn that I'd been married, he of course said he'd be happy to have me bring Pattie.

He asked if Mark would pay my expenses, and for some reason, I said I would take care of them myself. Full partners, I reminded myself. And let the devil take the hindmost. Which he might well do . . .

"Tell me more about the Claytons," Pattie said, as we settled into our seats aboard the plane. "I sense they're pretty important to you, but you never talk

102

about them much."

"Ancient history . . ."

"But they say the past is prelude?"

So I tried to tell her about the past, both that of my family and Seymour's. It was just as strange, and maybe "melodramatic," as the present and the future might turn out to be, except that one rarely accuses the past of being melodramatic; you can't challenge the reality of what actually happened.

My grandfather, old Lars Anderson, who was called "The Captain" by most people throughout his long life, got command of a good Swedish brig out of his home town, Stockholm, in about 1875, when he was only twenty-three years old. He didn't mean to immigrate to the United States, but soon after bringing his ship into New York for the first time, he got drunk ashore and was hit on the head or drugged, he claimed. Two days later he came to, and found himself lying in an alley without any money and without all his papers. His clothes were disheveled, his face was bruised, and he looked so terrible that when he staggered out on a street to look for help, a policeman put him in jail—or so his story went. He could not speak English and none of the authorities could speak Swedish. Although he was a victim, not a criminal, he said, he was booked on vagrancy charges and spent two weeks in a crowded basement cell. By the time he got out, his ship had sailed for Stockholm—his first mate, he claimed, had been only too glad for a chance to take command.

Lars worked as a stevedore on the docks until he earned enough money to make himself appear respectable and arranged to get copies of his master's papers.

When all was in order, he toured the shipping companies of all nations, looking for a job, but his mate had apparently spread the word that he had jumped ship and was a drunk—which he may have been for some time, I guessed, but he always denied that. According to him, he had been sandbagged on his first spree. No one believed him and the only job he could get was as a yacht skipper, a big demotion for a master mariner. Old Commodore Clayton hired him to command the first *Patrician* because he said he liked his looks . . . My progenitor was a huge man who looked the way Vikings or square-head sailors were supposed to look.

Lars took the job as a stopgap measure, but it lasted almost fifty years, until he retired at the age of seventy. There was no talk about amateur standing in the yachting circles of those days; skippers were strictly professionals, high-ranking servants approximately on the level of butlers, even when they became famous for winning races, as Lars did.

My father, Peter Anderson, was brought up on the fringes of the Long Island yachting world his father worked in. As a young man he served aboard the yachts, but he wanted to be much more than a flunky. He was bright, good-looking and affable enough to become something of a protégé of the old commodore, and with a little help from the Clayton family he worked his way through Harvard. After that he went to work for the Claytons, not as a yacht captain but as a junior executive in an importing business, which was one of that family's many enterprises. After serving in the Navy during World War I, he was made a junior partner in the importing business, which dealt partly in

104

Scotch whiskey.

According to my father, he got along so well with the commodore that he incurred the jealousy of the old man's son, Seymour, the one who became the father of the Seymour I was about to visit now. All the bad things that happened to my father, and they were plenty, he blamed on this rivalry—if such it could be called, because the Clayton clan was not about to allow the son of a subordinate to shoulder aside their own kin.

Or so dad told the tale. I believed it when I was young, but less and less as I grew older. I think that my father's real enemy was alcohol—the stuff he drank, not the stuff he sold—as it was for so many members of my family. He had a brief, brilliant career in the importing business. When it appeared that Prohibition had come to stay, he used his knowledge of importing Scotch whiskey to establish a Canadian company—with or without the help of the Claytons, although he always claimed he was doing nothing but following orders all along.

Much of the whiskey which my father brought into Canada legitimately found its illegal way across the Great Lakes to Detroit and other midwestern ports. Someone with a lot of nautical knowledge assembled quite a fleet of old sub-chasers and fast speedboats of new design which could outrun anything the Coast Guard had. My father got rich, though he claimed that he had no direct connection with the bootleggers. He kept on claiming that even in 1927, when he was arrested and accused by the newspapers, at last, of being "the admiral of the Clayton rum-running fleet."

The lawyers got him off with a small fine, but he had been disgraced. As part of the Clayton's effort to disavow any connection with him, they wouldn't even talk to him.

"They'd made a thousand dollars for every one I got on that whole operation, and I was no more a bootlegger than they were," he told me over and over again as I was growing up. "But they made me the fall guy. With all that bad publicity, somebody had to fall, and they picked me."

At the time he was dropped by the Claytons he felt not much more than a sort of moral outrage . . . he'd cleaned up enough to retire in style. He began playing the stock market and for a year his dreams of becoming a millionaire to rival the Claytons themselves seemed to him almost to materialize, until the crash of 1929 put an end to him. He went bankrupt, took to the bottle in earnest and finished his days as a wavering drunk.

Much of the time he was in hospitals and rest homes while I was growing up, and I hated to visit him because he looked so terrible and did nothing but spew out his hatred for the Clayton family, which he still held responsible for all his "bad luck." According to him, their brokerage house had even given him the advice that had caused him to invest his savings in worthless stock.

His denunciations of the Claytons confused me because my mother was grateful for the small pension they eventually arranged to give him, and my grandfather, the old captain, loved them. After his retirement he was often asked to sail aboard their yachts and was treated as a sort of family retainer. When I reached the age of twelve, my grandfather took me with him on a visit to Bluff House.

To me, at that age, the Claytons seemed to be a royal family that, appropriately enough, lived in a palace and traveled aboard a royal yacht. The old commodore, who was almost eighty then, was the aging emperor. His son, Seymour Senior, was the working king, a man about the same age as my father, but a vigorous, kindly person, a strange contrast to the unshaven, gaunt-faced figure for whom I had to try to play the part of a son. Seymour Junior was a year younger and much smaller than I was in every physical dimension, but he had the confidence and, it seemed to me, the condescension of a prince. I hated these people, and admired them at the same time. Every minute I was with them I was ill at ease, but I tried hard to make them like me. After all, our living came from them, my mother had explained to me, and although I hated to admit it to myself, they represented just about everything I wanted to be.

As I grew up, the Claytons sort of semi-adopted me. They kept telling me how much they loved my grandfather, never mentioned my father, and soon asked me to crew aboard their yachts, not as a professional, but as a friend. "Amateur" yacht racing was in. They encouraged me to call the younger members of their family and their friends by their first names, and Seymour Junior's older sister, Julia, gave me the nickname Dandy Andy, which some of the older members of the clan picked up with what seemed to me to be a mixture of amusement, admiration and maybe some condescension.

I was a big, strapping, straw-haired kid, better than most at almost any team sport, but not good enough at tennis or golf to be embarrassing. Somewhat to the surprise of everyone, I turned out to be a good student at the high school in City Island, where we shared my grandfather's house, and Seymour Senior helped me to get a scholarship at Exeter Academy, which I hated but which was clearly the first rung of my climb to the Olympian heights.

Seymour was at Exeter with me. He was two years behind me because he was younger and because his ill health in early childhood had prompted his family to take him out of school for a winter of traveling in warmer climes. On the surface, at least, we were close friends. He often invited me to his home for weekends, and if there was an ironic ring in his voice when he called me Dandy Andy, I could set it down to the fact that he also had a rather wryly humorous attitude toward life in general. He was only a fair student because he never worked hard and he was too frail for excellence in any athletics, but his congratulations were genuine when I was asked to play on the varsity football team and made the honor roll. "After all, somebody has to uphold the family honor," he said. "Better victory by proxy than none at all."

The idea of a rivalry between Seymour and me never occurred to me in those days; he was too obviously fortunate in almost all aspects of his life, too complacent and self-assured. Whereas I might scramble for pennies all my life, he had millions of dollars the day he was born, and all the social graces that went with them. So how could he possibly be worried?

Still, I sensed that we never really were friends. There was a glass wall between us. The fact was, of course, that neither one of us could forget that he was rich and I was poor. In those days that made more difference than it

108

might now.

When I was seventeen years old, my father killed himself, either on purpose or by accident, by driving his ancient Packard, the last remnant of his salad days, at sixty miles an hour into a large elm tree on City Island, only a few blocks from our home. I had no logical reason for more than token mourning, but when I went through his room to pack up his papers and his few tattered garments, I had the most profound sense of sorrow, not only for him, but for some reason for myself. My mother too had more reason for relief than grief. She had been taking care of him as an invalid for years, had been arguing with him, screaming at him—but now the house was so silent, she said, that she couldn't stand it. Only my grandfather was calm, and he was so old by that time that he rarely moved from his chair in the corner and seemed more like a ghost than a man.

My mother went crazy. Or, as the doctors said, she went into a profound depression and needed to go to a quiet place for a good long rest. As a seventeen-year-old, already more than six feet tall, maybe I should have been able to handle all this, but I panicked. Among other things, I did not see where I was going to get the money for the enormously expensive quiet place which the physician recommended, or for a housekeeper to care for my grandfather. In this moment of need, no member of the Clayton family came near me, but I got a letter from a lawyer saying that my father's pension would continue for the rest of my mother's life, that my grandfather's small pension would be increased to take care of his increased living expenses, and that the Clayton family would be "glad to take care of the medical bills of both these people during this emergency." The lawyer added a postscript: "We assume that with their pensions your mother and grandfather can take care of your immediate needs with the help of your scholarships. If not, we will be willing to discuss the situation."

My gratitude was mixed with resentment that no member of the family came to my father's funeral, and none even wrote me a letter of condolence or recognized in any way that I had suffered a loss and might be going through a bad time. Even when I finally got back to Exeter, Seymour's expression of sympathy was perfunctory.

"Sorry to hear about the sorrow in your family, Andy," he said to me blandly. "It must have been tough on you . . . Could you help me with my Latin? I flunked the last test, and the dean is talking about giving me the old heave-ho."

An alcoholic can't blame his drinking on anything or anyone but his own alcoholism. Other people, especially with the warnings of their ancestors, could have sailed through such a time of stress without taking to the bottle, but I got drunk for the first time on the night following my father's funeral and I had a bottle of his Scotch with me when I returned to Exeter. After rather contemptuously helping Seymour with his Latin, I went to my room and started sipping, a process which didn't hurt me, in my own opinion at least, for about ten years.

The stress, the booze and the precocious growth of my body and mind, if not my emotions, soon worked changes in me. At the age of seventeen I felt myself to be a man alone in the world, not a little boy with fond parents taking care of him, like Seymour and most of my other schoolmates. I made friends with college students considerably older than I that I met when they came back to Exeter for football games. In those days I'd become something of a football star, despite the fact that games of all sorts had begun to bore me and I never totally put my heart into them.

One of my college friends came from a family that owned a cottage at Southampton on Long Island. They invited me there for spring and summer weekends. Southampton was flossy enough in those days, but not as imposing as the North Shore, and I didn't feel myself to be essentially the son and grandson of Clayton hired hands. When I mixed with crowds of young people on the Southampton beaches or helped friends take small boats out of Shinnecock Inlet for a day of fishing, I felt inferior to no man. On hot August days or moonlit nights, when the beaches were so crowded that it was almost impossible to find enough space to spread a blanket, I learned that cold beer can dissolve shyness and that a young man could strike up conversations with attractive strangers who cared not a damn about his pedigree.

A man on his own in the world is entitled to his share of drinking, I thought, and I soon learned that to be on one's own does not necessarily mean that one has to suffer the torments of extreme loneliness forever. There was such a thing in the world as girls, I discovered, and a few were just as lonely and mixed up as I was, as much in need of more than hand-holding at the movies.

The sexual revolution of that era did not give me the freedom from guilt and fear which the next generation claimed to enjoy. I was not aware that I was in the

111

vanguard of a revolution. I just thought I was bad, a wild man out of control, but I comforted myself with the thought that the whole world was going crazy. This was 1937, after all, the year that Hitler repudiated "the guilt clause" of the Versailles Treaty and the Japanese sank the *Panay* in the Yangtze River. War was in the air. Schoolboys and college kids even got up an organization called Veterans of Future Wars, which demanded pensions and bonuses before we got killed, not after. I was an early member. At about this time I also became aware of Errol Flynn, and almost consciously took his movie image as a model. After all, I was as big as he, and some of the more nearsighted girls said I was as handsome. Like him, I was a sailor, so why couldn't I live the dashing life he led on the screen?

In the summer of 1938, Seymour Senior asked me to crew on the *Patrician IV*, his brand-new Sparkman and Stephens yawl. I went because the boat was so beautiful and I knew that many parties surrounded her. He and his son both raised an eyebrow at my escapades ashore, but I got the idea that he expected no more from a square-head sailor, the descendant of a long line of them. And no one could question that I was damn good on the foredeck when it came time for wrestling in a big genny in a gale.

That summer I heard that I had been accepted by Harvard and was to be given a scholarship. Young Seymour himself had given up hopes for Harvard and was aiming only at Williams. My head swelled up bigger than my shoulders, and Seymour Junior's sister, Julia, remarked to me, "Andy, you're not so dandy anymore— you should calm down a little."

"The world's on fire," I said poetically, and with a

112

straight face. "Don't ask me to play dead before I have to."

The Claytons got so tired of my carousing ashore and my thinly veiled arrogance that they might well have got rid of me despite my usefulness aboard their yawl, but I contrived to make something of a hero of myself in true Errol Flynn style. In September of 1938, just before I was to report at Harvard, the first hurricane in recent history hit New England and Long Island Sound. When we got the first warnings of it, the Clayton family and I, together with a mixed bag of their friends, were aboard the *Patrician IV* about seventy-five miles to seaward of Montauk Point. We were coming home from a cruise to Nova Scotia and Seymour Senior said the barometer must be broken because it was falling so fast.

We soon found out that the barometer wasn't broken, but we damn near were. The wind piped up to Force Ten, maybe more than a hundred miles an hour, and the seas looked like the Adirondack Mountains. None of us had seen a storm like that. We lay to under a storm trysail and spitfire jib for a while, and when the yawl started to dive through the seas, we turned and ran for it, trailing three anchors on long warps to slow us down. Seymour Senior was in command, and I will say for him that he knew his business and remained calm, but he was never a strong man physically and seasickness weakened him. The vessel was rolling and pitching like a bucking horse, no matter what we did with her, and Seymour Senior quite literally lost his grip. He was hanging onto a mizzen shroud when the yawl gave a snap roll, and he fell into the cockpit, breaking several ribs and knocking himself dizzy.

"You better take over, Andy," he said to me, as I carried him below. "I don't think anyone else can do it."

This was not really fair to Seymour Junior. He, like his father, had been remarkably calm throughout the storm and he was not visibly seasick. Although he was a skilled helmsman he had never bothered to learn much about navigation, but plenty of yachtsmen depended on friends or professionals for that while acting as skippers. Perhaps the reason his father turned the yawl over to me was that Seymour Junior didn't look or act like a sailor, nor a man of action of any kind. Small, frail, soft-voiced, he just did not inspire much confidence.

The women and the rest of the ship's company were so seasick and scared that they rarely stirred from their bunks. Seymour Junior and I took turns at the helm.

"We're going to be all right if this thing doesn't last too long," I said.

"How far off the beach do you think we are?"

"Maybe fifty miles."

"How fast do you think we're going?"

"Too damn fast. Two knots, maybe three or even more. God knows what the current is doing, but these seas are sure pushing us."

"Then maybe we only have about ten hours before we hit the beaches. Could we put out more drogues?"

"They don't seem to help much," I said. "I think we ought to lie ahull."

"She'd roll her sticks out. She might roll clean over."

"But she'd come back, and sideways she'd drift slower."

"I'm against it. This wind will die or change before long."

"We can't take a chance. Let's get those warps in."

"I don't have the strength," he said, "and anyway—"

"Take the helm. I'll get the warps in. Your old man put me in charge and we're going to lie ahull."

Lie ahull, sideways to the seas, we did. And it was a nightmare, with the vessel rolling onto her beam ends, first on one side, then the other.

"I don't think the rigging can stand it," Seymour Junior said.

"It's better than beaching her in a hurricane surf."

Shortly after dark the starboard main shrouds parted and the mainmast went over the side. It was still attached to the ship by the lee rigging and smashed against our hull with every roll. This was a job for axes and we had three aboard, but only one of the guests was strong enough to try to help, even in this emergency, and Seymour Junior was ineffective as he tried to hack away at the steel shrouds with one hand and hang onto a rail with the other.

I felt guilty because Seymour had warned me that we might roll our sticks out. Somehow guilt made me angry and anger gave me strength. This was a situation made for me and my Errol Flynn act. I might not be a man with the most refined social graces, but I was good with an ax. I attacked the remaining steel rigging with all the fury that I imagined my Viking ancestors had shown to their enemies, and it was not long before the last remaining strands snapped, and the heavy spar, with its lethal splintered butt, bobbed safely clear astern.

The one guest who had tried to help congratulated me before scurrying below, but Seymour just went and sat glumly clinging to the wheel.

"Goddamn thing never would have happened if you had just let her run," he said finally. "You should have listened to me."

I did not try to answer. The wind continued to blow, hour after hour. By the next night, when it finally died enough to let us get under way with the engine, we could clearly see the flash of Montauk light. If we had let the ship continue to run, we would have beached her and been pounded to death. Not one of us would have survived.

Seymour Junior stared at the flashing light for a full minute before he said, "You were right. I was wrong. I'll tell dad—you deserve credit."

Credit I got, almost literally. Seymour Senior offered to pay my way through Harvard if my scholarships ran out and signed me on as navigator for the following summer, when he was planning to enter the Halifax race.

"I won't be able to pay you without hurting your amateur status," he said, "but I'm going to buy a lot of new sails. Make a connection with a sailmaker and I'll order them from you. That's what a lot of the boys do."

"I'll try."

"And take a navigation course at Harvard. You're a natural-born navigator, but you'll need to know the newest celestial stuff."

A naval science course at Harvard taught me theoretical navigation. That and a course in creative writing were the only ones I enjoyed. The idea of turning into Joseph Conrad as well as Errol Flynn began to take possession of me. Girls and boats were a hell of a lot more interesting than history and, after all, I needed them for *material*.

The next summer, that of 1939, was my undoing as a respectable student. All kinds of things happened. I helped the Claytons to win almost every race they entered, which was not hard, because the *Patrician IV* was a further development of *Dorade* and *Stormy Weather*, and with such ancestry, she was an almost unbeatable boat. I had sort of an affair with Seymour Junior's oldest sister, Julia, the one who had called me Dandy Andy first. It was hardly true love; it bore too much of the ambivalence that characterized all my dealings with the Claytons. Julia and I got along well enough, by my standards at the time, and the idea of marrying into the Clayton family seemed somehow natural, as if it were merely formal recognition of a family tie that already existed, at least for me. But at the same time I was strongly repelled by the thought of marrying money and becoming one of Seymour Senior's whipping boys. (He was always hard on his sons and in-laws.) My confusion was both decreased and increased when Julia told me that she loved me but *obviously* couldn't ever marry me—for a Clayton no explanation was necessary. I told her that she'd regret her snobbery when I became famous.

"How are you going to get famous?" she asked, buttoning her shirt over her rather meager breasts.

"You'll *see*," I said. "You'll see."

I proceeded to help the Claytons win the Halifax race in pea-soup fog, a feat which spread my reputation as a wizard of navigation. At that point, Hitler invaded France. My mother was given shock treatments and did not recognize me when I visited her in her "quiet place."

117

The owner of the *Flying Yankee*, a fine new cutter that we had beaten in the Halifax race, asked me to take his boat south for the Miami-Nassau race. I could be skipper when he wasn't aboard, which was most of the time, and he'd buy not only his sails, but his insurance through me. I also met a reckless college girl who said she'd marry me and go as cook. The owner said that arrangement was all right by him. Compared to that, how could Harvard compete for the affections of a square-head sailor?

7

After I reached this point in my story, there was not much I had to tell Pattie. She had heard me recount the tales of my international sprees at plenty of AA meetings. She knew that I had always kept in touch with the Claytons and had helped them win a transatlantic race. She also knew that young Tad, Seymour Junior's son, had recently been in touch with me a lot, though I had been careful to tell her nothing of his plan.

That still hurt. Keeping such a large secret from Pattie, to whom I had long confided everything, didn't sit easy with me. Nor did my lie to her that we now were visiting the Claytons because they were listing their yawl for sale with me for old time's sake. She kept asking me why I was so nervous. Sooner or later, of course, she would have to find out if we actually put the thing into action, but I hoped to keep it from her until I could show her a million dollars in the bank. And if Seymour found a way to launder our profits it was possible that Pattie never would have to find out. I could announce that Seymour had made me a partner in a great stock deal. Or the whole thing could never happen at all—I was, I realized, basing a great many assumptions on Seymour's rather bland letter. In any case, I'd try to be a professional smuggler if I was to be any kind at all, just as I was a professional sailor, and I doubted that professional smugglers told their wives much. The old Eskimo had said it pretty well . . . a man who couldn't keep his mouth shut had no business even thinking about this business . . .

My mind was so preoccupied with these thoughts that I hardly was aware when the plane touched the landing field at LaGuardia.

"Here we are," Pattie said. "You've made the Claytons sound so fascinating I can hardly wait to meet them." Fascinating? Maybe. But she didn't know the half of it, I thought ruefully. And neither did I, as I later discovered.

At the airport I resisted the absurd impulse to rent a Cadillac or a Mercedes to impress the Claytons and instead rented a Ford compact. The Long Island

Expressway had not changed much since I had last driven it, almost twenty years ago. I felt a curious sense of homecoming as we turned off the expressway and reached the town of Setauket, where I used to get off the train when I visited the Claytons. In the old days I could usually guess my standing with the family by the way I was met. If I'd recently helped them win a big race, Seymour Senior or Seymour Junior would meet me. Otherwise it was a chauffeur and if I'd disgraced myself lately, no one showed and I had to take a taxi.

Maybe that's why I had rented a car this time. I didn't want any of those little tests, despite the fact that I was pretty sure that Seymour or Tad would be eager to meet me now.

From Setauket we drove to Old Field, where the Claytons had for generations owned about a hundred acres. Their land surrounded a small private harbor which yachts reached by following a torturous channel through the Narrows and up Conscience Bay.

Conscience Bay! It had always seemed ironic to me that the Claytons had built their imposing mansion, which was certainly a prize they had won in some pretty rough commercial games, with a fine view of Conscience Bay. Sometimes Julie and I had anchored a small sailboat behind an islet there to make love, and with the rather sardonic humor of so many members of her family, she had suggested that we write lyrics for what could become our song—"We Went Astray in Conscience Bay."

Poor Julia. She spent most of her time in Palm Beach now, a fat, blue-haired widow whose only passion seemed to be for winning bridge tournaments. I was lucky that there had been "obvious reasons" why she couldn't marry me.

"This sure is lovely country," Pattie said. "It looks more like Connecticut than Long Island."

"Every place where rich people build houses ends up looking like Connecticut."

She laughed, and I took a good long glance at her before I turned through the open iron gate which marked the entrance to the Claytons' driveway. What a fine-looking woman, with a figure that would be good for any age, and a warm, understanding face—the advantages of youth and age combined. The Clayton women, both those who were born to the name and those who married it, tended to fade or bloat up fast. It was odd to think that a couple of penniless middle-aged alkies like Pattie and me had been allowed by some forgiving higher power to hang onto our looks and vitality so long. Odd, but a kind of evening of the score. I was thankful for it . . .

The Claytons had sold some of their land to developers since my last visit. Comparatively cheap little houses—although each of them probably cost far more than I ever could afford—were drawn up in rows in front of the gardens of the great estate, like the tents of a hostile army. But who was I to mourn the death of spacious lawns and orchards? The Claytons were still making do with about thirty acres surrounding their private yacht harbor.

The lawns that were left had been cut recently and there was that sweet smell of new-cut grass in the air, a fragrance I had long associated with that place, and which brought back all sorts of memories—chasing fireflies under these elms with Seymour, playing tag and hide-and-seek with their friends, the sense that I could

122

never fit in with these people.

The formal gardens which two old Italians had tended for decades had been seeded with grass. Only the hedges and several rather forlorn-looking nude marble men and women stood to mark the paths which had divided beds of snapdragons, hollyhocks, roses and the whole catalog of other summer blossoms. A small marble cupid who had once burbled water into the pool which surrounded him now appeared to be kissing air, and leaves filled his moat. The grounds of Bluff House had fallen upon evil times, but the outbuildings of the old mansion were as trimly painted as they had been in my youth. The swimming pool looked newly cleaned and filled, a ritual of spring. The tennis courts had exchanged their clay for some new green plastic composition, the nets were new and the surrounding chicken-wire fence had recently been replaced.

Bluff House itself had not changed at all. "The two-faced Tara on the Sound," Seymour had once called it. It was a sort of copy of an antebellum Southern mansion, with tall white pillars facing the driveway, and even taller, fatter, more ornately topped ones facing the big terrace overlooking Conscience Bay.

"Wow," Pattie said as the house first came into view, "I suppose they say it ain't much, but it's home."

"That sounds like something Seymour might have said. He told me that they call it Bluff House because his grandfather won it in a poker game, but the big sand bluffs in front of it are quite a landmark. You can see them from all over the bay."

We parked at the side of the gravel driveway and, carrying our suitcases, approached the imposing front

123

door. It was opened before we touched it by Seymour—a good sign, I thought.

"Andy," he said, "I'm delighted to see you. And I'm so glad you brought your bride. I was sure that you'd marry a good-looking woman and I'm not disappointed."

He took the small suitcase she had been carrying and even offered to take my big one. We crossed a wide foyer and turned into a long hall with bedrooms opening off it, like staterooms aboard an ocean liner. He put us in his best guest room . . . one old J. P. Morgan himself had once occupied, I'd been informed. About thirty feet square, it boasted a huge four-poster bed with a crocheted canopy, enough other furniture to start a classy antique store, a bathroom which was downright Roman in its splendor and a big bay window with a view of the private harbor, in the center of which the *Patrician IV* lay at her moorings in an undiminished glory of shining varnish and brass.

"I've never been *anywhere* so beautiful," Pattie said.

"It's been a long while since such a beautiful woman has stayed here," Seymour said with a smile. "It's about time."

He was not much to look at, even in his beige linen suit, Brooks Brothers pink shirt and Racquet Club tie, but he sure had learned to sweet-talk a woman better than he had when he was young. Although he had gained a little more weight since I had seen him and was quite pear-shaped, he had acquired a tan, and that look of weary resignation which had distinguished him during our last meeting had been replaced with something like boyish enthusiasm. Of course now he apparently was on good terms with his son and maybe his business

124

difficulties had been resolved. A man who was secretly excited by plans for an adventure might also lose his look of weary boredom, but why on earth would a man who had so much going for him take such a risk?

Suddenly I felt sure that Seymour was going to tell me he had talked his son into acting sensibly and I was ashamed of my own disappointment.

"After you get settled, come into the living room for a drink," Seymour said. "Virginia hasn't been feeling so well lately, but she'll join us in a few minutes."

We sat around a coffee table made from the polished rudder of the *Patrician II*. I remembered his wife, Virginia, as a rather aloof, pretty but not very exciting girl, the kind who had been brought up in one big mansion, married into another shortly after graduating from Smith, and who read a lot to find out what the great world was really like. Now I was shocked as she entered the room; she looked as though she had found what the world was like in all its worst aspects. She had one of the saddest faces I've ever seen—thin, drawn and older than anyone not yet sixty should look. Virginia had a vacant stare and that abstracted manner which I've seen with people who are on heavy tranquilizers. She shook my hand and smiled like a good little girl without giving a sign of remembering me, told Pattie that she was happy to welcome her to Bluff House and sat down on the edge of an overstuffed chair. She seemed to be staring out the window at the yawl, but I guessed that I could have drawn the shade without her noticing. Folding her thin white hands in her lap, she sat without saying a word. It occurred to me that Tad had rarely spoken of her, and I was beginning to understand why.

"Virginia hasn't been a bit well lately, but she's getting better now," Seymour said.

Virginia gave the ghost of a smile.

"Tad will be here in the morning," Seymour continued. "He's anxious to see you, but he's been taking some courses at the university over in Stony Brook. He's got a room there and he's studying for his final examinations."

So Tad had gone back to college! I couldn't imagine how Seymour had talked him into being a good boy again. Perhaps Seymour was lying, making up the story for his wife's sake, or maybe Tad had invented a college career to explain his absences. More likely I was kidding myself and Tad had just straightened out. I certainly must be a despicable character to regard that as such bad news.

A black man in a white coat took our orders for ginger ale, Virginia's for tea and Seymour's for a vodka martini. Seymour smiled at me in a way which made me wonder if he read the look of disappointment on my face and fully understood the reason for it.

"We have a lot of business to talk about, Andy," he said. "I have some ideas about selling the yawl and about a replacement. I'm afraid I've reached an age when I should have a powerboat."

"I can understand that. I still love sail, but it's a lot of work."

"After dinner, we'll go into the library for a talk if the ladies will excuse us. I thought that tomorrow we could all run the yawl over to City Island if you feel like it. I don't want to be bothered by people coming to see her here."

His talk about the boat sounded so sincere that I began to doubt my sanity in imagining that he wanted to talk about Tad's scheme, but would he really have asked me to fly 1,500 miles to discuss the fairly routine business of selling a yacht I already knew well? As for finding him a powerboat, I could probably do better in Fort Lauderdale than I could here; there were more good yachts concentrated in Florida than anywhere else I knew. No, he must have some important reason for wanting to see me, giving me the big hello and his best guest room. Nostalgia and old-time friendship had never exactly been Seymour's style; he would never treat me so well if he didn't want something from me now, or in the future.

Unless I was going paranoid about the Claytons, as my father had been, unless Seymour was mellowing with age, unless he was truly grateful for my efforts to help Tad through a bad time and wanted to do me a favor by throwing me a yacht sale . . .

I didn't know where I stood, and suddenly the suspense was too much as I sat sipping ginger ale and staring out the window at the beautiful shape of that well-remembered yawl. I wanted to say, "Look, Seymour, let's go into the library and talk business *now*."

Somehow I could not do that. I'd look ridiculous if all he had on his mind was selling a boat, and if he had more to talk about I shouldn't appear too eager. After all, my share in the proceeds of any enterprise we might undertake had not even been discussed with Tad. My position in a large-scale operation had to be established— I still wanted to be a full partner. If anything was afoot, there was bargaining to be done, and so far no member of my family had ever come out ahead in a business

127

transaction with the Claytons. I'd have to watch my step every inch of the way.

The tension of such thoughts, together with my uncertainty about whether I had simply been nuts to imagine that Seymour might undertake Tad's grandiose scheme, made me so nervous that for the first time in a long while I really longed for a drink. My eye followed Seymour's martini glass as he raised it to his lips. Well, let him drink. The more he drank the better, if we were going to begin some bargaining sessions.

The risk of being driven back to the booze by the tension and secrecy was a real danger for me. Why was I, then, apparently willing to undertake it?

Money, of course. But also deep concern about Pattie and the kids and relief from all those damn bills piling up every month, with age coming on fast and not a cent of savings or a pension. Which kind of tension did I prefer? At least this run would offer some action. "Adventure" was a word I'd always loved, even if it had long sounded phony.

Someday I'd find an adventure to make me rich . . . that hope had continued on all through my worst years . . . I'd gone through a period of hoping to strike it rich as a skin-diver and had once joined an expedition looking for sunken Spanish galleons. We actually found a few artifacts and a little gold, but not enough to pay expenses. Still, I'd risked my life diving deep, and for what? For money, sure, but also for some sense of vindication, for proof that my whole boat-bum life wasn't wasted, that it could manage something big.

Baloney . . . well, some baloney . . . Ever since I'd witnessed the palace life of the Clayton family I'd wanted

128

to taste it myself, and royalty in America meant money. At the age of fifty-nine, I still needed to prove I was as good as anyone else—and beyond that, I still, God help me, had a kid's love of excitement. Maybe my craziness was as simple as that—I was bored with selling silly yachts to silly people and wanted to go to sea again with a mission more profitable and exciting than delivering some rich man's big toy to some other part of the world where he wanted to play with it. No, that wasn't all of it . . . but, face it, it was a part . . .

Seymour had another cocktail, and he sipped it slowly. The butler passed canapés, hot pastry with cheese inside. I wasn't hungry. Seymour kept smiling at me and I wondered whether he was enjoying this game of cat and mouse. Or was he in the slightest bit aware of my feelings? After all, he probably *was* just going to talk to me about changing yachts.

Finally we went into the big oval dining room with the crystal chandelier which had so impressed me when I was young. It had not been cleaned in some time and the sparkle was gone from it, but it was still enough to make Pattie marvel, and Seymour told the story of how his grandfather had bought it in Paris and personally packed every piece of it for the long voyage home.

I don't remember what we ate. Virginia touched almost nothing, I recall; and I was rather grateful that I was not the only person who had lost his appetite. Seymour chewed happily while complaining that he should be on a diet, and Pattie kept saying how good everything was, but I have no memory of what was on our plates. The white-coated butler seemed to take a very long time to clear the table and bring dessert. That, whatever it was, took a very long time for the others to eat, and afterward there was coffee, served in gold-edged demitasses. I felt as though maybe six hours had passed before Seymour said, "Well, ladies, would you excuse Andy and me for a few minutes? We have some business to discuss."

Virginia did not appear to hear him.

"We may need quite a few minutes," Seymour said as he stood up. "Don't wait for us. I have some new books I want to show off to Andy after we have our little business chat."

He wouldn't need many minutes to talk about selling his boat, and he had never showed off a book to me in his life. My hopes rose, alone with a sickish feeling of both guilt and anticipatory nervousness as I followed him to his high-ceilinged, paneled library.

8

Seymour sat in a leather armchair on one side of the brick hearth and motioned me to a chair facing him. A newspaper had been folded into the shape of a fan under three white birch logs in the fireplace. I wondered when it had last been lit, whether the shelves of leather-bound books in this room had ever been read, whether anybody had ever really loved anybody in this house—whether anything here could really make sense. I had a curious feeling of disorientation, as though I was not quite sure where I was, either in time or space.

"Well, Andy," Seymour said, after lighting a cigarette in a long black holder. "I guess we really do have a lot to talk about."

"Selling the *Patrician* shouldn't really be so complicated."

"No. As you may have surmised, I have more on my mind than that."

I only nodded.

"Tad told me he talked to you . . ."

"Often."

"What do you think of his plan?"

"It's interesting."

"Yes . . . though I must admit that I was more than a little startled when Tad batted it up to me, even outraged—it's not the sort of thing that would usually engage my attention."

"Nor mine . . ."

"I realized, of course, that Tad was determined to do something of the kind, with or without me," Seymour continued. "He is my son, after all. My first instinct was to play for time . . ."

Which explained the long delay. I said nothing.

"I told Tad quite truthfully," he went on, "that I knew almost nothing about the world he talked about and that I never invest time or money in anything without thorough research—complete research. He'd picked up a lot of street knowledge, but I wanted more than that."

"It's not, I'd think, an easy field to research. Too much secrecy involved."

"Of course, but we've been putting as much together as we could. Just from reading back newspaper and magazines files, we've been able to draw a rough sketch of the situation. My first reaction was amazement at the sheer enormity of the trade. The *Times* recently ran an editorial on it. Apparently fifteen *billion* dollars' worth of cocaine alone is brought into this country every year. The breakdown on figures for marijuana and all the other stuff is not yet clear to me, but the *Times* said that the total worth of all narcotics smuggled into this country every year is close to fifty billion dollars now and it's growing fast. This situation isn't even comparable to the old bootlegging days in terms of money. We're talking about a major national industry, one of our biggest."

"Even bigger than I thought, if your figures are right," I said. I had read the same editorial in the course of researching my fantasy, but I wanted to see how far Seymour's interest had taken him.

"All the figures are startling. According to our research, something like thirty million people in this country buy cocaine, marijuana or both more or less regularly."

"My guess would be that more than that smoke grass."

"Perhaps. Excuse me for droning statistics, but I'm trying to get all this into some sort of perspective. The federal government has estimated that the trade in the Southern states alone brings in something like five billion dollars in tax-free cash every year. The government calls it 'dangerous money.' It's unaccounted for and can be used for bribing officials or illegal contributions to political campaigns."

"I hadn't thought of that." Though of course I had

133

read about it.

"The government spends more than a billion dollars a year to stop smuggling, but it's about ninety-percent unsuccessful. Some say they catch only about two percent of what's brought in. They don't have the forces to cope with such a huge business and, beyond that, maybe a lot of people in high places don't want to see a golden river stopped."

"Tad said that the smugglers fear only each other."

"So it seems. Here are a few more interesting facts we picked up. Five million dollars will buy a hundred tons of marijuana in Colombia. That would sell wholesale for at least fifty million here. Did you ever hear of such a mark-up? I don't have comparable figures on cocaine yet, but I understand that that is even more profitable. It's not surprising that qualified pilots get fifty thousand dollars for flying in about twenty-five thousand *pounds*. The captains of ships which can deal in tons, not pounds, of course stand to make much more."

"So I hear."

"With this much money involved, you'd think that running would be conducted by serious, sane men, but a lot of crazy, flamboyant characters are in it. The *Times* called them 'cocaine cowboys' in its editorial. Some are Colombians, some are Americans of various sorts. They haven't been very good at remaining invisible. Some of them bought a huge estate down in Florida, had it fenced and patrolled by lions, real lions. They posted signs that said 'Trespassers will be eaten.'"

"Not exactly calculated to avoid publicity."

"No. They operate more quietly here on Long Island, and now that the pressure is put on them in Florida, they're bringing more and more of the stuff in here. In the past few years, I understand that a hundred million dollars' worth was landed in Long Island ports."

I sensed that he was trying to assess my interest when he paused and glanced at me before stubbing out his cigarette. Assess away, I thought. Out of perverseness and just plain wariness, which I had never really felt with Seymour before, I wanted him to have to convince me. Besides, I still needed to be convinced.

"The method of operation is much like the old bootlegging days here. The ships that bring the stuff from Colombia lie just beyond the twelve-mile limit off the South Shore of Long Island. Fast speedboats use the little inlets there to bring the cargo in. They get lost in the crowd of summer yachts. Some say that only about one percent are apprehended. All kinds of people are involved—all ethnic groups, all ages. Respectable businessmen who are being run under by taxes and inflation are getting into this, too."

Like we know who, I thought. The irony of it seemed lost on Seymour, though. He was clearly a man in trouble.

"People are getting killed, too," I said.

"I understand that." He looked at me closely. "And just because the trade is enormous and profitable for a few doesn't, of course, mean it would make sense for us. I'm also not entirely insensitive to the moral issues involved . . ."

"No, of course not," I quickly answered, noting the slight edge of defensiveness in his tone.

"Tad points out that the intelligent use of certain drugs can be therapeutic, and we do all use some of them

135

in one form or another. There are strong arguments against that line of thought, of course, but perhaps it's a philosophic question that everyone has to answer for himself. Freud himself apparently used cocaine and recommended it to his patients and fiancée. John Hancock, the signer of the Declaration of Independence, is said to have smuggled booze and other goods into this country before the Revolution."

How we do go on in the service of our conscience, I thought . . . ."I'm not sure that Freud would have been so enthusiastic about cocaine if he knew as much about it as doctors do now," I remarked, "and I'm even less sure that John Hancock's smuggling stuff past the British is exactly comparable."

"I guess I agree with you there," Seymour put in quickly. "I suppose that my *basic* belief is in freedom, including the freedom to use drugs if an individual so chooses."

"I'm not so sure about that." Except, of course, it was true of booze, surely a drug . . .

"I am. My conscience, such as it is, is troubled more by the question of whether it's ever right to break the laws, instead of trying to change them. And to profit in the process. I also concede I can't really think of smugglers as freedom fighters."

"Then how have you justified getting involved in it?"

"I've *tried* to be truthful with myself about this. The fact is that if I thought I could make a hundred million dollars or more in the trade without any appreciable risk, I'd probably do it. How many people would really say no?"

"Not many."

"So I've pretty much laid aside the moral considerations and have turned to practical ones. Do you share my feelings so far?"

"Yes and no." But I was sitting there, listening . . . apparently for practical purposes it was more "yes" than "no."

"The question is, of course, how much risk would be involved? There's no such thing as investing money with no risk at all, including so-called legitimate enterprises. The risk is always greatest when one is entering a new, unfamiliar field, when you try to play ball in somebody else's back yard."

"And this back yard is in a pretty tough neighborhood," I reminded him.

"So I gather." He lit another cigarette and leaned back in his chair. "I must confess that even the word 'kill' seems so far removed from my own little corner of the world that I can't quite take it seriously. That annoys Tad. In the course of his research, he found this in a newspaper and gave it to me."

From his polished pigskin wallet Seymour took out a clipping and unfolded it. For some reason his wallets always looked brand-new.

"This is a UPI dispatch out of Washington, dated August 4, 1978," he said, holding the paper up to the light. "I won't bother you with all the details, but it seems an informer, when describing the cocaine business, said, 'When we make the buy we don't pay money—instead we kill the couriers who bring the merchandise.' Which of course raises the question: Why would anybody in his right mind get into such a business?"

137

It seemed he was looking for an answer from me . . . "Well, anybody who stayed in the business long would be asking for it, but it might be possible to make one big run and get away with it—"

"Yes, I suppose it would take time for the people who are already in the business to figure out what one was doing, and by that time we'd be home free—transportation shouldn't present much of a problem, especially if you're helping us. The danger is in the buying and selling. We're doing more research on that. Which is why Tad is enrolled in the college; it gives him the use of a research library—"

"So you really are going into this seriously—"

"We're *investigating* the situation seriously. We're planning an operation, simply as a matter of theory, Andy. The decision of whether to go ahead with it should wait until we get all the information. Just as in any other high-risk business venture."

Could it be, I suddenly wondered, that Seymour was simply playing for time, concocting all this to keep his son out of trouble as long as possible, letting him go ahead with research and initial planning so he could discover for himself how crazy the scheme might be? "How much longer do you think you'll need to collect information?" I asked.

"Not too long. We've already made a lot of progress. I think I now understand how we could sell the product without much risk."

"How?" I asked, mentally retracting the fatherly concern I had attributed to his motives only moments before.

There was a slight pause before he said, "Andy, I'd like

to put you in charge of transportation. I think we should run this like a military operation—if we get into it, that is. No one should ask to know more than he needs to know to do his job."

There it was—no matter how he phrased it, he was not making me a partner. Like old times. "I'm afraid I have some questions about that," I said, trying to keep my voice calm. For the first time in a long while, I thought about my father—his ghost almost appeared at my side. Maybe he'd been right when he said that the Claytons had just used him, made him their fall guy.

"What?" Seymour asked, his tone touched with ice, as though a square-head sailor had no right to ask questions.

"In the first place, are you really planning to put me in charge of transportation and nothing else?"

"What else do you have in mind?"

"Shall we call it guard duty? I may sound like an alarmist, but this is a literally cutthroat business. Aren't you going to have to have a fighting man in this operation? You don't have much experience in such things . . . I'm not trying to play the combat hero. I know you, Seymour, and you've got just as much guts as anybody else. I'm talking about military preparations. If we're going into a business as dangerous as this, we've got to be able to take care of ourselves, and I think I know how to do that."

"Right. Okay, you'll be in charge of transportation and defense. This is beginning to sound like a government operation—"

"I hope more efficient than most. Now how do you think you can sell the stuff without huge risk?"

"Does that really have much to do with transportation

and defense?"

"Seymour, let's get down to it. If I come into this at all, I'm a full partner. I want to know *everything* about the deal before I decide."

Seymour smiled. "You're blunt, Andy, and I appreciate that. We have to be honest with each other. But have you considered the fact that Tad and I may not want a full partner?"

"Then you got the wrong boy—"

"Don't be too hasty, Andy—"

"Don't *you* be too hasty. What are you going to do? Are you going to interview a lot of yacht captains, explain your plans to several, see how many bite, and make a choice? Is that your idea of maintaining secrecy?"

"No . . ."

"Seymour, I'm it. You can't get anybody better. And to put it crudely, unless you're going to get as tough as those boys who kill anybody who knows too much, you might begin to worry about what you've already told me."

Seymour mustered up his businessman's smile. "There's no point in getting hot under the collar, Andy. After all, we're old friends. Of course we want to do business together. We can work out some form of limited partnership—"

"Unlimited."

"If I'm going to put up capital and you provide only services, we can't really have an unlimited patnership—"

"Just how much capital are you willing to put up?"

"I think I can raise whatever we need. The amount will depend on the scope of operation. Tad talks about ten tons that would be worth maybe five hundred million dollars wholesale in New York. I doubt whether we could buy that much all at once anywhere without sending the price way up when we buy and down when we sell. Our preliminary research indicates that the coca leaves are grown mainly in Peru and Bolivia. The leaves are processed in small laboratories in the hills of Peru and in bigger outfits in Colombia. Apparently only about thirty-five thousand tons of coca leaves are produced a year. More than half are consumed in leaf form by the locals— they chew the stuff. About five hundred tons of the leaves are sold legally for cola drinks and medicine. That gives less than seventeen thousand tons of the leaves for the market, worldwide. It takes about a hundred and forty pounds of coca leaves to make one pound of cocaine. As far as we can figure out, that means that there are only about a hundred and twenty tons a year available for export. I've read that the world demand is somewhere between a hundred and a hundred and seventy tons annually. Ten tons would of course be a very large share for newcomers to buy all at once."

"How much do you think we could handle?"

"We have to do much more research before we can decide that. Of course we could get a ship that could carry fifty tons or more as easily as ten. I'm not committed totally to cocaine yet—our cargo could be a mixed bag. Marijuana would be much easier to buy. It's grown all over the world in such huge quantities that one big buy could escape much attention. Good grass has a U.S. beach value of close to a million dollars a ton. Not so bad . . ."

"The grass is bulkier and harder to transport, but it

could be done. You still haven't told me how you can sell the stuff without much risk."

"I don't know who we'd sell it to yet—it would have to be one of the very large syndicates—but I have figured out a mechanism for transferring the money. We won't have to get involved in carrying suitcases of thousand-dollar bills or trucks of gold bars. My mechanism will also take care of turning our income into accountable profits for us."

"How?"

"In theory my mechanism isn't a complicated process. Suppose I have or can acquire land, mineral rights, oil-drilling rights or stock in privately held companies that have no easily assessed value. Say that I personally believe that these properties are worth a hundred million dollars, that I'd be glad to sell them for that. If someone agreed to pay me four hundred million dollars for those companies in a perfectly legal sale conducted through normal business channels, I could agree to deliver three hundred million dollars' worth of narcotics to him. 'The greatest crime of the century,' Tad likes to call it, and maybe the sheer size will be a hazard. I haven't thought all this out."

"The danger point, as I understand it, is the delivery. Will you get paid one way or another before we give them our cargo, or would we have to give it to them before your sale of stocks or whatever was consummated?"

"We'd have to work out as simultaneous an exchange as possible. Some risk of a double-cross would be involved for both sides, of course. Even in enterprises like this there has to be a moment of trust—"

"We'd be trusting some pretty odd people."

"The big syndicates might trust us first. They'd have the power to take care of us if we tried to cheat them . . ."

The very words we were using didn't sound quite real to me—"double-cross," "take care of us." Would they soon begin to sound normal?

"Your business is defense and transportation, mine is finance. We'll make a good team. Tad is in charge of intelligence."

"How would we divide the profits?"

"We could each acquire stock, one way or another, in a company that held the properties we were going to sell legally. When the deal was consummated and the cash was in the company account, we could cash our stock in. Of course, we would have to pay capital-gains taxes. We would be smart to stay on the right side of the government on that."

"How would the stock be divided among us?"

"There may be more than three of us. We'll probably have to take some more people in to raise enough capital and get the manpower we'll need. With so much profit possible—"

"The fewer involved, the less the risk. We might do it all by ourselves, just us three."

"We'll certainly keep the group to a minimum."

"You still haven't told me how the stock will be divided."

"I believe we'd have to think in terms of rewarding the three of us and any other major working partners equally for our services. Anyone who invested capital in the enterprise would have to be rewarded separately according to the amount he provided. The profits would of course have to be great to make up for the risk. We

143

shouldn't be too close-fisted. There should be plenty to go around. If all this works out on a large scale, the three of us should make more than ten million dollars apiece, just for our services, maybe much more. Would you have any complaints about that?"

"Hardly," I said, shaking my head. "The damn thing still doesn't seem real."

"It didn't to me for a long time, but the research is sinking in. Billions of dollars are being made out there every year, Andy, by people who are hardly as smart as we are, no tougher in any real sense, and with fewer resources than we can manage. There's just one big question. Where do we buy the stuff? From whom? And how?"

"How are you going to answer those questions?"

"Tad is going to take a run down to Colombia. He'll be a rich college student writing a thesis on the economics of drugs and he'll have the papers to prove it. He says he also has some connections at the street level down there. He's going as soon as his term ends, in a couple of weeks."

"How long will it take him?"

"We don't know. I worry about him a little, Andy. He's smart, but he's heading into tough territory with some tough questions."

"I think he can handle it."

"I do too, but maybe he shouldn't go down there alone. I'm still afraid that he's not too stable. Can you go with him?"

"What would a student be doing with a friend like me?"

"Wouldn't a man like me send a man like you to

144

accompany a boy like that on such a trip?"

"How about my travel and living expenses?"

"I'll advance you whatever you need and subtract it from our profits, when and if."

"Thank you," I said, and immediately was aware that my father had probably thanked Seymour's father at the start of their questionable enterprise.

"Well, that's enough of business for one evening," Seymour said, his smile warming. "Tomorrow we can talk about selling the *Patrician*. Meanwhile, let's try to relax."

Relaxing isn't easy with a deal like this in the wind, I thought. Or with the confusion of crosscurrents and undercurrents that had run through our conversation. But beyond my new fears was a growing excitement. This alone acted on me as a kind of drug, a stimulant stronger than any I'd ever known.

I found Pattie reading in the big canopied bed. She had on a blue nightgown, and her pink shoulders seemed to glow with health.

"Come look at the sky," I said.

She put her book down. "The sky?"

"It's a beautiful night."

I went to the window. From this side of the house we could see the harbor with the reflections of the moon and stars surrounding the silhouetted hull of the graceful yawl, but I found an even better view when Pattie came toward me. Her full breasts swayed slightly under her thin nightgown and they were even more beautiful than the moon and stars. Fountains of life . . .

Familiar but undiscovered—that's what her beauty seemed to be. I kissed her.

"I thought you wanted me to look at the sky," she said with a smile.

"You look at the sky, I'll look at you."

All the sexual organs were lovely, nonaggressive, made to give pleasure and life, to express love, not hate. How come people of my generation had been brought up to fear those parts of our bodies so much, to think that they were disgusting? I knelt and buried my head between Pattie's breasts. She stroked my head, understanding my feeling without the need for words.

We had what for me was an incredible session of love-making and I seemed strong enough to make it last forever. I was not even aware when it ended, because dreams of Pattie replaced her flesh.

9

I slept until ten the next morning, which was most unusual for me.

Dressing quickly, I hurried in search of her. I found her having breakfast with Seymour, Virginia and Tad on the terrace overlooking Conscience Bay. Tad looked like a prince of the realm here on his home turf. He was wearing highly polished brown loafers, sharply pressed gray flannel trousers, a white turtle-neck shirt of some soft, thick material and a blue blazer with a red monogram on the left breast pocket. His hair was still cut short, and he had taken to slicking it down like an old-fashioned dude. His face was so deeply tanned that his big even teeth seemed very white when he smiled.

"*Buenos días, Capitan!*" he said, snapped to attention and gave me a salute. I was pretty sure that he didn't mean it to be condescending, but his military burlesque reminded me of the days when a few salutes had been meant.

Pattie was lying back in a deck chair. "Good morning, darling," she said cheerily. "I'm glad you had such a good sleep."

"We've got a fair wind for City Island," Seymour said. "I figure we should start in about an hour. Pattie has been good enough to say she'll stay here and keep Virginia company. Then she'll be able to drive the car over and pick us up tonight."

That would give Tad, Seymour and me a chance to work out more details of our plan. The whole crazy fantasy seemed to me to be turning into reality with dizzying speed. The residue of guilt was still with me, and the fears, including going to work for the Claytons. That had been disaster for my father . . . It was a grand June morning with brilliant sunlight and singing birds in blossoming fruit trees all around us, but for some reason the very beauty of our surroundings seemed almost sinister to me. I guess I just wasn't made for great mansions; when I first visited here as a child, I felt scared and out of place. The people here were not my friends any more than they had been my father's friends. Even my

148

grandfather had been used by them; they had made a proud master mariner into a retainer, and the fact that he had accepted that role seemed worst of all. Suddenly I felt very bad and my face showed it.

"What's the matter?" Pattie asked.

"Just a headache," I said. "You go ahead with your breakfast. I'll go back to the room and take an aspirin."

In my room I sat with head bowed on the edge of the canopied bed. I'd had a grand night, all right, but I had also committed myself to the smuggling business—the whole thing was actually going to come off. Soon I was going off on a cockamamie voyage to South America with Tad, a princely bisexual drug freak. And his own father was encouraging him in this madness. What a combination.

Probably, I told myself, I could still get out of it. Not too late for me to say I was simply scared, and Seymour would probably trust me enough to be sure I wouldn't turn on him. I could go back to Lauderdale and try to sell yachts. Probably Seymour would be too angry at me to entrust me with the sale of the *Patrician*. Still, one way or another Pattie and I would somehow manage to pay the bills. Somehow . . . ?

It would be one damned uphill battle all the way, and I was getting older. My body suddenly seemed to be full of aches—perhaps my exertions of the previous night had been too much for it. Soon I'd be sixty, and old men don't necessarily make the best yacht brokers any more than they make the best lovers. They're not asked to go on the big ocean races where contacts with the new hotshots are made. Life as a yacht salesman would be dull, coasting downhill, and damn it, both Pattie and I deserved more

149

than that after all the hell we'd been through over the years.

One big run could change all that. One great run. Ten million dollars at least would be my share, Seymour said, and if nothing else he was a clever businessman who wouldn't undertake any hare-brained scheme . . . Ten million dollars . . . I couldn't even imagine owning such a sum . . .

We'd have a big house, a good boat, the best colleges and trust funds for Pattie's kids. We'd travel all over the world. The best of medical care whenever anybody in the family needed it. No more damned killing worries . . .

What kind of coward would turn down a chance for all that?

Pattie came into the guest room looking concerned. "Are you all right?"

"I'm fine. The headache is going away." Actually, for the first time my head was starting to throb.

"What's this about Seymour offering you some kind of a temporary job?"

"Tad's going down to South America and he wants me to go with him. It's a sort of hand-holding deal, but he has some odds and ends of business down there that he wants me to do—"

"Would Mark give you a leave of absence?"

"Probably."

"Well, it should be a good change for you, and I can't see how it could hurt to stay in the good graces of a family like this. I know you've had trouble with them, but still, in your business, contacts with people like Seymour . . ."

"I guess," I said, managing a smile. She was so easy to lie to, so easy to conceal things from. She trusted me and she even wanted to trust Seymour and Tad. She couldn't even imagine what we were keeping from her.

"I'll miss you." I was just beginning to realize how true that was. No Pattie to guess my moods and give me a dose of hope, as she was now. She was, I realized, the only person in my life who had that ability, and the realization was brought home even more by the seeming lovelessness among the Claytons, a family I had once wanted to belong to.

Pattie sat down on the bed next to me. "You'll be back soon. You know, I can't help feeling rich as hell in this room. And *confident*. I bet that no one who ever slept in this room worried about money."

"You'd lose. J. P. Morgan especially worried about money."

"I mean about paying bills. I'm sure everything is going to turn out to be just great for us."

"Keep your fingers crossed," I said. "Pray a lot. Knock on wood. Rosy predictions always scare me."

"Damn it, you deserve a streak of good luck. If anybody does, you do. It's high time you got what you deserve."

I kissed her while wondering if God always gives people what in some inscrutable way they deserve. What do smugglers deserve and what do they get, even if they succeed for a while? It seemed that I would soon find out.

Seymour's oldest son, Cyrus, joined us while we were having breakfast on the terrace. I had never known him well and I would not have recognized him. He was a plump, bald, diffident man who couldn't have been older than about twenty-eight, but who looked forty at least.

151

This was the son who, Seymour kept saying, "had turned out all right." He was accompanied by his wife, Helen, a thin, nervous woman, quite pretty, but she never sat still and rarely stopped talking.

"Good morning," Helen said and, interrupting the introductions which Tad attempted, added, "Is it true you're going to take the boat to City Island today?"

"That's the plan," Seymour said. He looked irritated.

"Why didn't you tell us?" Helen said. "Cy saw Weaver putting food aboard. We never would have known you were going if Weaver hadn't told him."

"I didn't know you were so interested," Seymour said. "The last few times I've asked you—"

"This is different. If you're going to sell the boat, this could be our last sail. It really should be treated as a sentimental occasion. That's what you said, didn't you, Cy?"

"Something like that," Cy replied with a slight stutter. "I just thought that Judy—"

"Judy would be furious if she found you had taken the *Patrician* on her last sail without her," Helen said. "You know how she loves the boat. And I must admit that Cy and I feel pretty much the same way."

"I'm sorry," Seymour said, his air of irritation giving way to his practiced urbanity. "I'm afraid I've been so busy lately that I just thought of this as a practical matter, but I guess it will be our last chance to get together for a sail . . ."

"Of course," Helen said. "You want to go, don't you, mother?"

"What dear?" Virginia asked, trying to bring her blank eyes into focus on her daughter-in-law.

"This is going to be our last sail on the *Patrician*," Helen said, raising her voice as though Virginia were deaf. Perhaps she was, but no one else shouted at her.

"Oh?"

"You want to go, don't you?" Helen said, lowering her voice a little.

"Oh no, dear. I have things to do here . . ."

Her things to do almost undoubtedly were to sit and stare, I thought; the poor lady was obviously on some sort of medication which left her barely awake. She reminded me of my mother during the long depression she suffered after my father's death. I had blamed my mother's illness on the loss of her husband and on the near poverty she had to endure throughout her old age, but being Seymour's wife and the mother of Tad and Cyrus might not exactly be considered the happiest of fates. Anyway, I had seen depression enough in my own life to know that it's a disease that can strike without apparent reason. I felt sorry for Virginia. Whatever her trials or interior chemistry, her face was a pitiable mask of resignation.

"Helen, why don't you and Cy stay here and keep mother company?" Tad said. "There's no reason to make this into a sentimental occasion. The boat probably won't be sold for months, and we can get together for a last sail any time we want."

"But she could be sold any time, couldn't she? And Cy and I are going up to Maine. Judy won't be here. You know she has all kinds of plans for the summer. This really will be our last chance for a sail."

"Judy will be hurt if you just take the boat away without telling her," Cy said.

"Well, we don't want to hurt Judy," Seymour said. "Give her a call. If we don't start pretty soon, we won't get in before dark."

Tad gave a shrug of exasperation. "I'll call her," he said, "but I can't understand why everybody is getting so sentimental all of a sudden. Usually I can't get anyone to go with me when I take the damn boat out."

Apparently both of Seymour's older offspring permanently occupied the guest cottages on the old estate, because Judy appeared soon after Tad called her. She was somewhere in her mid-twenties and looked a lot as my Julia had at the time we had had "our thing together," as she had called it. Just as I had been crazy enough to take Errol Flynn as a sort of model for myself in my youth, Julia had tried to play Katharine Hepburn. Judy was not old enough to have been much affected by the screen image of the young Katharine Hepburn, but perhaps she was a copy of a copy; she still seemed to be trying, without a great deal of success, to combine the aristocratic but still earthy charms of the great actress.

"Hello," she said to me. "So you're the one that dear auntie called Dandy Andy."

Had Julia exchanged heart-to-heart reminiscences with her niece, true but upper-class confessions? I was still naive enough to be embarrassed by that thought.

"I can remember times," I said ruefully, "when she said that Dandy Andy didn't seem so dandy anymore."

Judy's laugh was more shrill than her model's would have been. "Daddy, have you got some champagne aboard?" she asked, turning to Seymour. "We ought to do this last voyage in style."

At his father's direction, Tad brought two magnums of

champagne from the house. As we all started to walk down toward the boat, I got sore that Pattie had been asked to stay behind to keep Virginia company and to come get us that evening in the car.

"Pattie, if you want to go, I can arrange it," I said to her.

"I don't, really. To be honest, this bunch is beginning to give me bad vibes, and I love champagne too much to let myself be around it. You be careful."

"Don't worry about me. This may be a sentimental occasion for them, but for me it's strictly business."

I did not look forward to a day without Pattie on a trip that obviously would soon develop into a drinking party, but I was soon glad for the opportunity to watch Seymour and Tad in action together with the rest of their family. After all, it seemed they were going to be my partners in some serious business, and the more I understood them, the better. Seymour usually gave the appearance of a perfect gentleman, strong but kindly and well-mannered. In his youth he had been rather cowed by his father, the old commodore, whenever he went aboard a boat, but now all this had changed. As soon as Seymour stepped aboard the *Patrician IV*, he almost became the old commodore and started giving orders to his family in every direction.

"Tad, check the oil in the bilges," he said. "Girls, you can start taking off the sailcovers. Andy, you can start singling up the lines."

"What do you want me to do?" Cy asked with a slight stutter.

"Just don't get in the way," Seymour said, and I didn't

think I had ever seen an example of worse petty cruelty.

Cy went below without another word. Soon Tad came up.

"The bilges and oil are all in order," he said. "I do wish you'd pick someone else for those messy jobs. The engine room needs cleaning. I've got smudges on my pants."

When Tad was with me, there was never a hint of the limp-wristed homosexual in his voice or manner but, to my astonishment, there was a sardonic, perhaps defiant hint of the swish in his style as he obeyed his father's orders.

Seymour glared. "Tough," he said. "I told you to clean out the engine room weeks ago. See if you can help Andy with the lines if you're not afraid of getting your hands dirty."

There was no reason why Seymour had to make a big deal of sailing one of the best ocean-racing yawls that was ever built forty miles up the sound on a bright June day. He was an experienced and skillful yachtsman, even if he never had bothered to learn much about navigation, and his whole family had been brought up on the water, but he managed to create a gratuitous atmosphere of tension as he cast off the mooring lines and began threading his way out of the little harbor and through the familiar channel which led down Conscience Bay to the sound.

"Tad, you take bow lookout," he shouted. "There are a lot of floating logs around here. Andy, I think we'll use the drifter. Ladies, see if you can help Andy to roust it out and hank it on. Tell Cy to put some water on for coffee."

I had long ago given up trying to understand or even look for the roots of homosexuality, but it struck me as odd that Seymour treated his sons with such contempt

156

that they acted almost like women might when faced with a chauvinistic man, while he apparently encouraged his daughter and daughter-in-law to act like men. Tad remained sitting languidly on bow lookout while Cy served the coffee. The women worked the sails. Nobody seemed very happy, despite the spectacular grace of the great yawl as she made a good eight knots on a broad reach up the shining sound in the June sunshine.

There was no need for a bow lookout when we were completely surrounded by open water and I sensed that Seymour had put Tad into a sort of isolation up there on the prow as a form of punishment, or maybe just because he didn't like to be near him at the moment. Tad soon came strolling aft, and though his father did not order him back, he was gruff when he said, "You can take the helm now if you can manage not to jibe her. The course is two seven eight."

Tad was a perfectly good helmsman, as I had found when he had gone as deckhand with me on delivery jobs, but he was obviously nervous as he climbed onto the wheelbox of the big yawl and he grew more so as his father stood there and watched him.

"Meet her—don't let her yaw like that," Seymour said. "My God, look at your wake—it looks like a sea snake."

Tad spun the big wheel, first one way, then another, and I suspected that he was over-steering on purpose, just to bug his father.

"Oh dear, dad, I just can't seem to get the hang of it," he said, with that new hint of swish. "You better take over. This just isn't the sort of thing I'm very good at."

"Andy, for God's sake, will you take over?" Seymour

said. "I've got to go below and show Cy how to ice that champagne."

I felt sorry for both Seymour and his sons, but the fact that he and Tad were so difficult with each other had to be taken into account when I planned the long voyage to South America and back. Since the profits would diminish and the risks increase as our crew on that trip was expanded, I'd been considering the possibility of taking no one else; three good sailors could handle a seventy- or eighty-foot motor vessel, and if we were prepared right we might be able to face the danger of hijackers with some confidence. Tad's usual cheerful efficiency as a deckhand simply disappeared when he was in the presence of his father, however, and Seymour, I realized, would always be shouting orders, not really doing any work himself. He would certainly tell me that I was captain of a smuggling ship, let me do the navigating and defer to me in any real emergency, just as his father had in that hurricane long ago, but most of the time Seymour would be acting like a yacht owner with a professional skipper. He would be in charge of everything but the dirty work.

An image of my old friend the Eskimo flashed into my mind. He was too smart to work with the new breed of hoodlums and realized that his reputation as a loud-mouthed boozer virtually insured that he'd end up dead through any association with that bunch. But he would probably volunteer to go to sea with me readily enough. Esky had always been smart in his own way, smart enough to live the life he wanted, and if he realized he had a chance to make a million dollars, the old dog might learn all sorts of new tricks. My confidence in my ability to run a successful operation rose the moment I thought of taking Esky with me and it plummeted when I thought of trying it with no one but this strangely warring father and son. As soon as things firmed up enough for me to get a time schedule in mind, I'd give Esky a call. He said he'd gone to California to work on the Twelves and I knew people out there who could put me in touch with him.

While I was thinking all this, Cy came up with a magnum of champagne in a mop bucket filled with ice cubes. Tad found a large supply of plastic wine glasses in the galley. Because they had no ginger ale aboard, I drank soda water, which tasted flat. Following Tad's example, they all made a grand gesture of throwing their glasses overboard after the climactic toast to the great yawl. Those which landed rightside up floated and bobbed astern in the wake. It was a strange new world, I thought, in which a bickering family of rich people felt no real joy or even much nostalgic regret on a sentimental occasion like this, in which they used unbreakable champagne glasses that survived the toast to the passing of an era. Everything I thought of as strong was apparently weak, and much that I thought of as fragile showed an odd ability to survive. I didn't know whether this was a good omen or a bad one and I tried to tell myself that I didn't believe in omens anyway. A good ship and a good crew were what could survive, and I was determined to put them together. Seymour could handle the finances on this operation and Tad could handle the intelligence, but the voyage would be my business, and I'd do it right, no matter what the Claytons had to say about it.

After we had moored the yawl at Minneford's yard in City Island late that afternoon, Seymour said, "Cy, take the girls up to the restaurant and order a lobster dinner

for us all. Call home and tell Andy's wife that we're here.
Andy and Tad and I will clean up here and join you in a
few minutes."

As soon as the others had left, Seymour mixed a
martini for himself in the galley.

"I'll have the yard do the cleaning up," he said.
"We've got to firm up our plans."

"I want to start for South America next week, as soon
as school's out," Tad said. "Are you going to come with
me, Andy?"

"I guess."

"Can you start so soon?" Seymour asked.

"If we're going to do this thing, let's do it."

"Right. Get your friend Mark to take care of selling
this boat while you're gone. If I give you personally an
exclusive on it, you'll still get your share of the
commission. Send the money to me and I'll use it to buy
you some shares in our holding company. You should be
able to prove that you bought the shares legitimately."

"How about my living expenses?"

"Will two thousand a month do it?"

"How about three? I have three stepchildren."

"Okay, three it is. Now, while you're down there, you
might see if you can buy a suitable vessel for us on the
spot. It would save half a round trip."

"I might pick something up in the Virgins. I'll stop
there on the way home. You sure you want to buy, not
charter?"

"We may have to make alterations or we could suffer
damages which could raise eyebrows when we returned
her to her owners. It might even be cheaper to buy. In
this inflation, we might sell her a year later with a profit if

160

you get a good deal."

"Do I have a free hand in choosing a vessel?"

"It's your business more than ours. Consult with me before you commit yourself, but I'll trust your judgment."

"I have some ideas on that," Tad said.

"You better leave it to Andy, son."

"He knows ships but I know the trade. There are different theories on what kind of ship is best."

"Like what?" I asked.

"In one way your ideal runner is very fast, like an ocean-racing cigarette boat—but of course that *looks* like a runner. Some think that something that doesn't look the part is best, like an old gaff-rigged schooner, even if she is slow."

"I thought for a while of using the *Patrician*," Seymour said, "but she couldn't carry much tonnage. She'd be great for coming into Long Island because everyone knows her and no one would suspect her, but the further south we took her, the more attention she'd attract. Everyone would want to know what I was doing down in South America with her. A famous yacht like this we *don't* want."

"I don't want sail anyway," I said. "I want something fast enough to outrun most hijackers and patrol boats. The voyage is bound to be dangerous; the shorter we make it, the better."

"How about one of your World War II PT boats?" Seymour suggested. "There must still be a few of them around. We could put in new engines."

"I've thought about that," I said, taking a sip of flat soda water. "But the truth is that those boats were never

161

built to outlast the war. Their hulls have loosened up long before now, and even if we found one, it would be nothing but rotten plywood. And those boats could never carry anything like ten or more tons."

"You sound like you already know what you want," Tad said.

"Maybe a sea-going motor yacht, faster than a trawler, about twenty knots or so would be enough. She should be rich enough to fly the New York Yacht Club pennant plausibly, but not so fancy that she'll attract a lot of attention. A good stock boat would be right, but we need something damn near a hundred feet long if she's going to carry any real tonnage fast. She could cost a million or more."

"I agree," Seymour said. He could try to bargain me down on my living expenses, but he was no piker.

"With fuel costing so much, there are quite a few big vessels like that for sale," I said. "I'll go through our files in my office and see what's available in the Virgins."

"Then everything's set," Tad said. "We go to Colombia next week, figure out how to buy the stuff and get a boat. Maybe we can do the whole job this summer, before the hurricane seasons starts."

"We don't begin until we're really ready," I said. "There might even be some advantage in the hurricane season. It could scare off the competition and I read weather reports pretty well."

"I agree with Andy," Seymour said. "Now there's just one big point I want to make. So far, I'm committed to no more than research. I'm not going to make the decision to *do* this thing until we have every bit of information we can get on every aspect—"

"Information on how to buy stuff big goes out of date fast," Tad said. "If I find where I can make a good deal, you're going to have to move."

"Don't let anybody panic you into buying before we're ready. If we have the money, we can always find a way to buy. I want to plan this thing the way Eisenhower planned D-Day."

"Eisenhower had his supplies all ready and waiting to go," Tad said.

"But I doubt you could store the stuff safely down there," I said. "We should be able to move it the minute we buy it."

"That makes sense," Seymour said, looking at me speculatively, maybe even a little surprised. Planning was supposed to be his specialty. "While you're gone, I'll wrap up the details on a deal to sell the stuff," he continued. "Next we'll buy the boat. And last of all, we'll buy the cargo."

"You haven't mentioned crew," I said.

"You think the three of us can't handle it alone?" Tad asked.

"In case of emergencies, we'll need one more man. I have one in mind."

"I don't suppose I need ask whether we can trust him," Seymour said.

"You needn't ask."

"Who?" Tad said.

"No names until I find for sure I can get him."

"Okay," Seymour said. "But get him for wages, not shares. About twenty grand and expenses should do it."

"This man should get a hundred grand."

"Why?" Seymour asked.

"He's that good. I wouldn't ask him to go for less."

"Well, we want the best, but no commitments until I give the final go-ahead. Just line everything up so you can move fast."

I wondered again if Seymour would back out at the last moment, if he was just playing this complicated game to somehow make Tad see the error of his ways and straighten out. But then I remembered that Seymour had promised to pay me three grand a month and my expenses for a trip to South America. Whatever his concern about Tad, the Seymour I knew would never put out that kind of money unless he expected to get it back.

While we were talking Seymour had two martinis, and then two more at the restaurant where we had dinner. He also had wine and brandy. He showed few effects other than spilling his glass of water and a certain exaggeration of his dignity, a general slowing down. But if he drank so much now, how would he react to the stress of a long run? Seymour was an alky of sorts—it takes one to know one. After even two martinis, he'd be no good in an emergency. I was damn glad I'd decided to ask Esky to come with us. Esky drank too, but very little at sea, and the two of us could damn near sail a square-rigger alone.

The Clayton family bickered so much that I found it hard to enjoy the lobster dinner they bought for me. Were all patricians so nasty to each other? Seymour even criticized Tad's table manners, which were better than his own after all those martinis.

When Pattie arrived, she looked so warm, so *cheerful*, so undominating and undominated, that I hugged her the moment she came into the restaurant.

"Let's go," Seymour said.

"Wait a minute," I said. "Pattie, have you had dinner?"

"I can get something when we get back."

"The hell you can. You'll have a lobster before we leave."

"Of course," Seymour said. "I'm sorry to have been so thoughtless—I was a little tired."

He ordered two more brandies while Pattie ate, and so did the rest of his clan. Only Tad abstained. He had told me that he'd sworn off booze for the duration of this operation. I felt a curious sense of triumph; for the third time I had spoken up and had forced my will on Seymour. There would be many occasions, far more important ones, when that would be necessary, I figured. These small victories were a good start.

That's what I figured.

10

I felt tired that night and went to bed early, but I couldn't sleep. Because we did not like to be in a strange room that was totally dark, we had left a light on in the bathroom with the door slightly ajar. As I lay staring up, the crocheted canopy of the four-poster began to seem like a net poised over me. Like I was trapped.

Maybe I was suffering nothing but guilt. Forget it!

Start planning.

The thing to do was to try to follow the produce in my mind from point of origin to point of sale. The point of origin was Colombia or Peru. Peru was out of the question, I suddenly realized, because it was on the Pacific side of South America. If we picked a cargo up there, we would have to bring it through the Panama Canal, where there could be all sorts of inspections and observation by pilots. That left Colombia, which was widely known now as a drug capital of the world and a beehive of intrigue, as our only point of origin. I had heard that there was one good thing about Colombia: since drugs had become the country's chief national product, some officials there, at least, could be counted on to cooperate with people who wanted to export their goods. If the right palms were greased, it probably would not be hard to get a cargo out of that country.

Greasing palms . . . the very phrase sounded like something from the movies and made me feel out of reality . . . How the hell would one actually go about greasing a palm? There were always at least a few honest officials in even the most corrupt countries, and it would be my luck to run into them. Probably Tad would be more effective in this department. I'd better stick to transportation and defense.

The cheapest and perhaps the safest way to buy would be at the laboratory. This probably would be inland, or at least far enough from the waterfront to demand trucks. Tad had talked of hoping to import ten or more tons of Beverly Hills' favorite party commodity and Seymour had said that if we couldn't find that, we could supplement our cargo with grass. We'd probably end up with thirty tons, maybe even more, of narcotics of one kind or another.

For the first time I tried to visualize the sheer bulk of it. Several large trucks would presumably be needed to carry it. If we paid some trucking outfit to move the stuff from the laboratory to the wharves, where we could load it, word would soon be out along the whole waterfront. Perhaps we could buy or rent trucks which we could drive ourselves, but in a country like Colombia, how could we load a ship with such a cargo in secrecy? Fast small boats or planes could easily track us after we left the harbor and hijackers could jump us anywhere.

Safe in my bed now, I began to sweat. This was a battle I was preparing to enter, and with the proper strategy battles could be won. A deal probably could be made which would require the manufacturer to deliver the cargo to us at the waterfront. There it could be loaded aboard some sort of local freight boat which we could buy or charter and which would head out to sea, where we could transfer the cargo to our vessel without fear of hidden witnesses. If we made a really smart deal, we'd tell the manufacturer to bring the stuff to us several miles offshore and pay him only when we took possession. The crew of the boat that brought the stuff to us would get a good look at us and our ship, but they would not know what course we were going to take home. We could insist that they carry no radio and inspect them to make sure that they could not transmit immediate information about us. We might even disable their engine. By the time they got back to shore, we could be well out to sea . . .

So far, so good. I imagined the delivery boat and our vessel lying to in the open sea a few hundred yards from each other. If we got a calm day, we could put over big fenders and lash the ships alongside each other, but we couldn't count on that . . . even a slight ground swell could smash us. No, the delivery boat should unload her cargo into big rubber life rafts. The cargo could be packaged in waterproof bales of manageable size and left right in the cargo nets. Then we could just haul the raft alongside and pick it up.

How? A fast yacht would have no cargo booms and no hatches, no holds. Some kind of temporary mast, maybe an aluminum tripod, would have to be devised if we were going to load thirty tons. The cargo could be carried below, a bale at a time, and stowed in the main saloon and staterooms. But with thirty tons of cargo and full fuel tanks for a voyage of some 3,000 miles, a light motor yacht would look like a deep-laden tanker and would lose much of her speed. Besides, fast engines were always more liable to breakdown.

Maybe we should forget the idea of using a yacht for this business and switch to a trawler. Of course, many smugglers used trawlers, but they were usually scruffy old shrimp boats which attracted immediate suspicion. We should buy one of the powerful brand-new steel or fiberglass trawlers such as those the big corporations used, the bigger and fancier the better. It should be something so impressive that no one could easily imagine her to be in an illegal trade. She might cost more than a million dollars, but that would not really matter. Seymour would find that banks are more willing to finance good commercial ships than large yachts, and a modern trawler would be much easier to sell when we were through with her than a big yacht.

A big trawler of the latest design might make up to twelve knots when pushed, not much, but she could maintain her speed in the teeth of a gale. She would have the holds and booms to handle sixty tons of cargo or more, and that would permit us really to plan for a big profit. If ten tons could bring five hundred million dollars, sixty would be worth three thousand million, three billion dollars! The mind reeled. Of course we could never buy that much, but even if we had to settle for a tenth . . . this could indeed be the greatest crime of the century. No exaggeration.

Did I really want to become famous by making such a record? In what history book would our triumph be celebrated if we were successful?

It was all madness, of course, but it was no lie that I was hooked on it, and the decision to ask Seymour for a big new trawler sounded marvelously sensible. Those were, after all, sensible ships, much less likely to break down than fast yachts. I could think of several companies in New Orleans and St. Augustine which could quickly provide one, complete with all the latest electronic gear. Maybe Seymour could line up such a purchase while I was in South America. The idea of giving an errand to him rather pleased me—I would of course ask him to consult me before making any final decision.

After breakfast the next morning, Seymour asked me into his library and gave me a check for $3,000 to cover my first month's living expenses. I took that opportunity to tell him my thinking about buying a big new trawler instead of a fast yacht.

"I'm glad you're still flexible on this, Andy. We have to think every detail through without preconceptions. I like your idea of a modern trawler; I've been a little worried about the idea of a big yacht. A lot of people are aware that my 'financial empire,' as some of the papers have been calling it, is in trouble, and some eyebrows would be raised if I went out and bought some sort of huge luxury yacht. A commercial vessel would be a lot easier to explain. I have my finger in a lot of little companies, some of which might be expected to diversify enough to get interested in commercial fishing. A trawler would be much easier to finance, too. I'll get right on it. If I find the proper vessel I'll give you a call. We might buy her right away. If you run into delays down there in Colombia we could find a crew that would take her out fishing. After all, you won't want her holds to be smelling too sweet."

His readiness to buy a trawler both reassured me and unnerved me. Seymour was dead serious about this, all right. The fantasy had taken a direct turn into reality.

Money in my pocket usually makes me feel confident, but the check I'd just taken from Seymour was different; from the moment I cashed it, I began feeling more and more nervous. The details of planning my immediate trip to Colombia with Tad seemed absurdly complex. I had to get my passport renewed. I'd have to get inoculations and vaccinations, traveler's checks. I'd have to ask Mark for a leave of absence and see if Pattie and the kids could continue to live aboard the ketch at the boat yard in my absence. Right now we should return to Lauderdale. I felt as though everything had to be done immediately. I paced the floor like a man with great decisions on his mind.

"Take it easy," Pattie said. "One day at a time . . ."

"So much has to be done—"

"What kind of business do you have to rush down to Colombia for?" Her tone was mild, but I thought she maybe sounded suspicious.

"I told you. Tad's doing research for some kind of a college paper on the economics of drugs. All I know is I'm going to be paid to nursemaid him."

"You said there are some other odds and ends of business Seymour wanted you to do down there."

"He wants me to look for a new boat for him," I said, improvising. "They've got some pretty good native-built boats down there in Colombia, may be good buys with great hulls. They use South American hardwoods as good as teak but cheaper."

This seemed to satisfy her, but more and more I hated lying to her.

"You seem awfully tense," she said to me a few minutes later.

We flew back to Miami, where Tad said he'd meet me five days later with tickets for our trip to Colombia. Sally and Susie were glad to see us, and when Pattie telephoned Tommy at his summer school, the boy said he'd take a bus to Lauderdale and spend the weekend with us. Could he bring a friend? Pattie said he could.

Tommy greeted me with more warmth than usual, but he and his friend played rock and roll music so damned loudly in his stateroom, and the smell of marijuana soon became strong. The idea of giving my stepson hell for smoking that stuff while I was planning to import it— and, worse, by the ton—seemed almost a logical part of this whole crazy world I was stumbling into. I balled up my fists, stuck them in my pockets, and went ashore to get my vaccination.

I felt lousy, I couldn't see my AA friends. I would be an outlander, as I would be tonight even in my old home. A man who could not tell the truth about himself was always an outlander anywhere.

Well, no point in beating upon myself. Better to let my mind dwell on the challenge of the future . . . If we got a big trawler, where would we unload our cargo in the States? When we had been planning to use a fast yacht, I'd always assumed that we would use Seymour's private harbor at Old Field, but except at high tide a big new trawler would draw too much water for Conscience Bay and a big fish boat would look rather odd at Seymour's yacht dock. Besides, I didn't much like the idea of leaving the cargo totally under Seymour's control after it had been unloaded. It would be better to choose a more neutral territory.

Where? In a lifetime of sailing the east coast I had made mental notes of many secluded coves, some of which had wharves—maybe I'd been a smuggler at heart for a long time. A closet smuggler, yet. Florida was too hot for smugglers these days, but Georgia, the Carolinas, Virginia, Chesapeake Bay, New Jersey, Long Island Sound and New England—the whole coast was honeycombed with small harbors occasionally used by fishermen and rarely checked by the thinly stretched forces of the Coast Guard. Ideally we would rent a secluded summer cottage on the water, and I immediately thought of just such a spot in Maine—Red Rock Cove, it was called, a tiny harbor surrounded by forest on all sides except for one summer estate with a pier. I'd picked up a fine big Alden schooner there for delivery to Boston only about a year ago. The owner had died, and the estate, like the schooner, had been put up for sale or rent. Maybe it was still available, it had looked like a white elephant. I should call Seymour and ask him to find out.

It somehow comforted me that I knew the precise kind of ship we would use and exactly where we could land our cargo. Maine would offer lots of hazards—fog in summer, gales in the fall and blizzards in the winter—but bad weather would not bother a modern trawler with all the latest navigational instruments. It might, in fact, be wise to approach the coast in very bad weather, when we would be invisible and when the Coast Guard would be busy with rescue missions. The coast around Red Rock Cove was so deserted that we might get in and out without being observed by anyone, especially in foul weather.

A trawler could unload fifty or sixty tons in jig time. We could store the stuff in that big Victorian mansion with the weathered shingles and let the purchaser worry about trucking it away.

A new thought hit me then: the danger of our cargo being hijacked *after* we landed it? With conceivably as much as a billion dollars at stake, anything could happen. That meant we would have to stand guard until we were paid, that a strategy for defense would have to be invented. While Seymour conducted business, Esky, Tad and I would have to be hidden nearby with the shotguns, rifles, submachine guns and sticks of dynamite I'd planned to arm the trawler with. And if they jumped Seymour . . . well, we would be faced with becoming killers as well as smugglers.

The confidence I'd begun to generate suddenly dissipated. Why didn't I just stop? The relief would be enormous, but then I had a truly evil thought: why not go ahead, make my millions and *then* confess in the protected sanctuary of an AA meeting. Many crimes had been confessed in such meetings. I could repent without giving *all* the money back—I could give great donations to help starving children and the church. With all my tens of millions of dollars, I could be a modern Robin Hood. Who was I really stealing from, anyway? Rich customers who wouldn't feel cheated when they bought our stuff. I'd be an entrepreneur in the old tradition . . .

It didn't wash, of course. I was incurably caught up in a dream of adventure and wealth. I was seriously tempted to drink, but I knew I could not let myself touch the stuff; the servants of the devil, I thought dramatically, like those of God, must remain sober if they are to be effective. In the old days I used to telephone a fellow AA member when I felt myself in trouble. Now I called Seymour. His calm voice almost gave sanity to the damned scheme . . .

"That sounds good," he said, when I told him about Red Rock Cove. "I'll have a real-estate agent up there look into it for us right away. And I've already called two

176

of those shipbuilders you told me about. They're sending me the spec sheets on several new trawlers. I'll mail them to you at the Bogotá Hilton. I've already made reservations for you and Tad."

All sounded so respectable, so simple, just like any other routine business trip.

11

Pattie drove me to the Maimi airport an hour early,
as she always had when I flew off for routine delivery
jobs. We did not like to get jittery if we ran into heavy
traffic and we enjoyed relaxing in a restaurant near the
gate where I was to depart. In the past these had
sometimes been festive occasions, when we knew I
wouldn't be gone long and would bring good pay back,

but this time I was very nervous and Pattie of course sensed that.

"What's the matter?"

"Nothing. I just don't like leaving you."

"Can't you give me any idea how long you'll be gone?"

"I've never had a nursemaid's job before."

"Is Seymour afraid he'll be kidnapped or something?"

"That may be in the back of his mind, but I think he's more scared he'll get himself in jail. Who knows?"

Tad met us at the gate five minutes before the flight was scheduled, as he'd arranged to do. He was faultlessly dressed, the perfect gentleman student, in a fawn-colored gabardine suit and highly polished loafers, and he carried a thin, expensive-looking leather briefcase. Even horn-rimmed glasses.

"Good to see you, Andy," he said, slapping me on the back, and kissed Pattie on the cheek. The diffidence and limp-wristed manner he'd shown to his father on the old yawl were hardly imaginable in this young man.

When I gave Pattie a farewell kiss and hug, Tad appeared to watch somewhat quizzically.

"Come on, we better go," he said, and led the way to the first-class compartment. He had our tickets.

"Why first-class?" I said.

"We're VIP's this trip . . . I like your wife."

"So do I."

"Married love. You make it look almost real."

I thought of his parents—mostly of his mother—and was sorry that he'd grown up with such a skewed example of marriage. But then so had I. So had most of us, I reminded myself.

"You're too young to understand," I said.

He laughed, took off his glasses and put them in his breast pocket. His eyes appeared very large in his narrow face, light brown, almost faunlike, I thought. He smiled at the stewardess, a pretty dark-haired girl in an orange uniform, and the smile she gave him back made me a little envious. It had been a long time since I'd been able to get a smile like that from a pretty stranger.

The first-class compartment was full. A lot of rich people flew to Bogotá, I knew, but this was not the ordinary first-class crowd. Only a sprinkling of fat executives sat waiting for their drinks. The other passengers included young men and women in blue jeans and T-shirts, a thin black man in a bright pea-green suit, stylishly dressed women of all ages and four small children whose distraught mother kept telling everyone that she was a pilot's wife.

When I had taken long flights in the past, I usually slept, read or sat staring at the cloud formations. This was not Tad's style. As soon as we were in the air, he was out of his seat, chatting with the hostess, laughing with a young man who had "Ask Me" printed on his T-shirt and helping a young woman who wore a wide-brimmed red hat to put her coat on the shelf overhead. Within half an hour he appeared to know everyone in the compartment. He acted like the host of a very merry party.

A very strange party. Here we were, hurtling at six hundred miles an hour through the sky toward a terrifying mix of promise and danger, for Tad and me. And from the look of some of the other passengers, I guessed that they were not heading toward a humdrum life of security, respectability and pensions either. A few of the passengers, led by Tad, broke into song. It was a curiously old-fashioned ditty for him and oddly incongruous for that crowd. "I've been working on the railroad, all the live-long day . . ."

It reminded me of the days aboard my old PT boat, the *Angry Angel*, when the men, led by a gunner's mate who played the harmonica, had often sung that song. World War II on the New Guinea coast . . . There had been times then when I had suffered a dizzying sense of unreality. There we were roaring along on a plywood speedboat loaded with high-octane gas and TNT, out to kill some Japs or be killed, characters from an adventure story or a comic strip. But it was reality then all the same, just as reality for me now was speeding through the thin air at thirty thousand feet, on my way to smuggling, and whatever that would be prelude to.

One day at a time—easy does it—don't project. A few of the old AA slogans still seemed to help, even though I had disqualified myself from the fundamentals of the search for sanity. No point in brooding about that now. In for a penny, in for a pound. What would Colombia turn out to be like?

"We have fair winds and will arrive in Bogotá a little ahead of schedule," the stewardess said in Spanish, then repeated the message in heavily accented English before going on to say, in both languages, that the weather in Bogotá was clear and the temperature was fifty-eight degrees.

I had imagined Bogotá to be a tropical city, hot and humid like the other banana republics I had visited. But the fact that it was so much colder there than I had thought did not really surprise me; this was a trip on which the unexpected should be taken for granted. With an aplomb which rather pleased me, I put my head back to rest and soon slept.

I did not awake until the pilot asked us to return to our seats for landing. Tad was in the aisle, sitting on the arm of the seat occupied by the woman with the wide-brimmed red hat, and the stewardess was trying to get him to obey orders. I looked out the window. We appeared to be descending over a moonscape—a high plateau rimmed by tall, jagged mountains, silhouetted in black against the sky. There was a thin thread of a river winding around an enormous city, its first lights aglow in the gathering dusk. Neither the Pacific nor the Caribbean, which I knew Colombia bridged, were in sight. We were eight thousand feet up in the Andes over Colombia's capital city of Bogotá.

"Is that river navigable?" I asked Tad, as he sank into the seat beside me.

As though to answer, the pilot announced, "If you look down to your right, you can see the famous waterfalls of the Rio Bogotá at Tequandama. They are four hundred and seventy-five feet high . . ."

I glanced out the window, saw a plume of spray between two mountains, very rugged country. But I shifted my gaze back to the city lights of Bogotá, the country's financial center, remembering that Tad had enumerated its four major export industries as coffee, emeralds, and pharmaceuticals of both the legal and illegal varieties . . .

"Please put the back of your seats up and fasten your safety belts tightly," the pilot announced. "There is some turbulence near ground level."

183

No question about that.

The plane landed with a heavy thud, but after a frightening swerve we straightened out and sped smoothly along the runway. Soon we found ourselves in a huge international airport, not much different from those in Miami, New York, London.

"How big is Bogotá?" I asked Tad.

"About two and a half million. Mostly *mestizo,* part European and part Indian. They ain't very big, but don't get 'em riled at you."

Most of the people who swarmed around us as we waited for customs clearance were black-haired, copper-hued and looked slightly Oriental to me, not especially sinister for "the world's biggest narcotics marketplace."

When the customs inspector came to us, his inspection of our luggage was cursory, at best, but of course nobody brought stuff *into* Colombia. What they brought was money to buy, and as Tad said, "the government ain't about to stop that."

The taxi that picked us up was a Chevrolet so old that I wondered if it would survive the trip to our hotel.

"The Hilton," Tad said, and added in both English and Spanish, "Slow—no hurry."

The speedometer on the battered dashboard soon pointed to ninety, and though that was probably in kilometers, not miles per hour, the car still rattled and shook alarmingly. God knows how fast the man would have driven without Tad's words.

The Hilton of course turned out to be like any Hilton anywhere. "A home away from home," a placard in the lobby said, but nobody I knew ever had a home like that,

184

unless some people grew up in New York's Grand Central Station. Seymour had reserved two bedrooms and a living room for us. All had doors opening on the hall, and that pleased me because we were provided with various routes of escape and with the means to screen anyone who knocked on one of the three doors. Such fantasies might be ridiculous, of course, but we had come to this place to buy a huge amount of narcotics, and some fairly undesirable elements might get the idea that we were carrying a lot of money or might be food for considerable ransom. Nothing unrealistic about such suppositions. I wasn't armed; trying to carry a gun through customs in South America or on any airline these days in any part of the world is asking for trouble. But Seymour had said he'd see to it that I got a gun once I was down here. I wasn't sorry to leave him the job of supplying the tools of my new trade; one can buy pistols anywhere in the world if one knows how and I never knew how.

Our suite was ornately furnished—Grand Rapids Spanish, VIP-executive style. There was a huge bar with a kitchenette.

"Your father is certainly setting us up in style," I commented, after Tad had tipped the bellboy with a ten-peso note. "Do you think maybe we're playing it too rich?"

He sprawled in an overstuffed chair. "Do you want to know more than you have to know?"

"I'm a full partner in all this. I hashed that out with your father."

He looked at me for a moment, surprised and then apologetic. "Old dad doesn't tell me much," he finally said. "All right, on this trip you're sort of a front, Andy.

185

One of my roles is the rich college kid down here to do research on a paper about the economics of legitimate drugs. A family like mine wouldn't send me down here alone. I'm trying to get away from the hippie-student image—big-shot businessmen and government officials wouldn't give me any information at all if they thought I was that. They hate hippies here. A lot of savvy people, the kind I worked with in Miami, will of course figure that this rich-kid bit is a front for me. I have some contacts that I made on the street when I was here before. I'm just going to look up old friends and mix socially with as many people on all levels as I can. A lot of guys will figure that I came down here to buy, maybe buy big. I hope I won't have to say anything. I plan just to listen. People should come to me and try to make deals."

"Sounds okay—"

"I hope I can get a quick picture of this scene and get some contacts lined up firm enough to get into details. If I don't figure it out damn soon, old dad is going to come on down himself, which I sure as hell don't want."

Tad called room service and ordered up a bottle of Scotch.

"I thought you were going to try to stay off stuff of all kinds for the duration," I said.

"Don't begrudge me a drink. No insult intended, but I'm no alky. I can tie one on tonight to relax my nerves without looking for the bottle in the morning . . . Don't take me wrong, Andy. I admire you for staying off the stuff so many years. But get off my case. I really can take a drink or let it alone."

Maybe, but under the stress we were heading into, he'd probably let himself drink a lot and that was going to make my job as bodyguard or whatever the hell I was that much harder. It meant that I would be around booze a lot more than usual, and that I'd have to resist it without any help from AA or my wife. When a waiter arrived with his Scotch, he opened the bottle and I got a whiff.

I went to my bedroom when Tad poured his Scotch in a glass and shut the door. I walked over to the window to take a look at the city. The Hilton Hotel was in a new skyscraper, and I was standing some twenty floors up. Almost directly beneath me stood a cathedral which looked as old as the surrounding mountains, an old Spanish church with twin steeples and an orange roof which had been often patched, the tiles overlapping in different shades. That cathedral had not been built for a man to look down on. How strange to stand thinking about drinking and smuggling while staring down on a steeple. . . .

12

The next day we were told that a package was waiting for us at the main desk. It turned out to be the gun Seymour had promised and it gave me a touch more confidence. I was . . . pardon the immodest expression . . . still a natural-born fighting man, but I liked to have more on my side than the instinct I knew I had. Tad agreed to do as much of his socializing as possible in his own hotel suite so that I could keep an eye on him. He was to play the role of a party boy with almost unlimited resources while he waited for the dealers to come to him. On the few occasions when I put in an appearance, I played the part of an amiable drunk, but most of the time I just sat in my bedroom, close enough to the thin door to hear what was going on.

What went on, as far as I could make out, was a lot of earnest conversation in Spanish and English, laughter and occasionally singing—it was like eavesdropping on any Miami cocktail party. I felt ridiculous as I sat there in semi-darkness, my gun at my side. Where did paranoia start and reality end?

When I read the local papers, one of which was in English, it was hard to answer the question. There were a lot of kidnappings and killings in Bogotá. Some of them seemed to be politically inspired—"conservatives" and "liberals" obviously were hard at it in Colombia, as they were in so many other parts of the world—but there was also a lot of talk about drug wars and drug-related murders. A home away from home—Bogotá was a lot like Miami.

The reason for all this violence in the trade seemed pretty obvious. Most sellers demanded immediate payment in huge amounts of cash, and there was always that moment when one side could grab the cash without delivering, or the other side could grab the product without paying for it. A moment of trust is necessary, even among thieves, or no business could be conducted at all, Seymour had said. He'd devised a clever scheme to avoid dealing in large quantities of cash when we sold our cargo, but how did he intend to buy the stuff without the danger of carrying a lot of money around? Did he intend to arrive with trunks full of thousand-dollar bills?

Unanswered questions about how we were going to get any stuff we bought aboard our ship and how we were going to guard it in the process kept me awake at night. When I mentioned it to Tad he just shrugged and said, "There are ways that these problems can be handled. Other people are handling them every day. It's just a matter of research and meeting the right people. . . ."

At first he seemed remarkably confident for a young man involved in such a complex deal. He spent a lot of time on the telephone locating old friends, and troops of them arrived for the parties he gave every evening. They were sleek young people, for the most part, the same sort I'd often seen in good Miami restaurants and nightclubs, the women gussied up, the men in straight business suits.

Tad was obviously a social creature, never mind the work. He also was capable of a kind of easy sexuality I both envied and somehow scorned. A very beautiful young woman stayed over with him the second night we were there. Before taking her into his room, after all the other guests had left, he came in to assure me that he wasn't being kidnapped.

"I don't want you running in with a gun to interrupt us," he said with a smile.

The next morning they invited me to have breakfast with them, which she prepared in the kitchenette at our suite. She had admirable breasts which were clearly outlined under the thin material of the silk pajamas she had borrowed from Tad, and I spent a lot of time staring at my plate. She and Tad seemed almost loving with each other, touching a lot and exchanging compliments, but she soon left and I never saw her again. Tad never mentioned her. I wondered, in my old-fashioned head, how such an apparently intense affair could be so short.

"You want me to find you a girl?" Tad asked.

"No thanks."

"You being faithful to your wife?"

"It isn't hard."

"Why?"

"You're too young to understand. Or I'm too old . . ."

"You been married twice, haven't you?"

"Yeah."

"And you still got your first wife on alimony?"

"Old debts—"

"And now you're supporting your new wife and three of her kids?"

"I'm what they call a family man."

"Goddamn, you're supporting two broads and three kids, and you can't even get laid. Is it really that good when you get home?"

"Like I said, you're too young to understand."

"Damn, I hope I *never* get old enough to understand that."

It's possible that Tad enjoyed shocking me, or imagining that he did. At any rate, he staged a very wild party two nights later that had, he assured me, "nothing to do with business." I could believe that. These were no stylishly dressed Colombians. They were students, American, French and German, whom he had met at some bar where they all hung out and who all wore blue jeans, sloppy sweatshirts and sweaters. They drank pink wine from bottles that they brought with them, smoked grass and lay around the floor on blankets and pillows, listening to rock-and-roll groups called Yes and The Styx, which they discussed with great seriousness. They put most of the lights out, but it was obvious that some of the couples were making love in a casual, almost indolent way, and without any desire for privacy, which was available in Tad's bedroom. Before long the couples began to merge into small groups and these gradually came together in the center of the big room, a tangle of nude bodies, some of them, I admit, quite beautiful in the dim light. Much good-natured laughter, a few small shrieks of excitement, but all in all I guess it was a curiously subdued orgy, almost well-bred.

An hour or so after I retreated to my room, Tad came to my door wearing only a towel around his waist.

"Come on out," he said, sounding a little drunk. "We're having a ball."

"I'm going to bed."

"You're missing a hell of a good time."

Probably so, I thought as I lay down to try to sleep. Maybe I'd missed good times all my life because I'd never even been able to conceive of such impersonal, almost emotionless sex, although I wondered if it was fair to call it emotionless. The sounds of a good deal of heavy breathing were now replacing the laughter. Somehow it all scared me the way booze did. If I got involved with it, I might not be able to stop. The people I knew who went in for this sort of thing a lot seemed even more screwed up than I was most of the time, and neither Tad nor his new friends seemed to be much of an exception. Salvation through copulation, any kind any time—that was another kind of religion, or addiction, I couldn't believe

193

in. Like I said, I'm a square-head. I pulled the blankets over my ears. Pattie would laugh at me. Despite her saintliness, she had more of a sense of humor than I had. Maybe that was one reason she was such a survivor.

"Andy," she'd said to me once, "your life would be so much easier if you could just *believe* in the Ten Commandments and let it go at that. It must be a terrific strain to have to figure out every moral problem as though no one had ever thought about it before." She was, of course, right. Which didn't take the corners off this square-head.

The next morning Tad was badly hung over.

"Still, it was worth it," he said, as I handed him a cup of black coffee. "I have to get rid of tension some-how . . ."

For two nights he went to bed early and alone. The third night he had room service bring an elaborate dinner for two to his room, where he was entertaining a young man who wore tight white-duck pants stretched around his incredibly small ass and a black turtleneck sweater around his heavily muscled shoulders. At about nine Tad came to my room to tell me not to worry about him. His guest was going to spend the night, so I might as well turn in.

When I woke up the next morning, Tad and his friend were talking and cooking breakfast together in our kitchenette. They didn't ask me to join them and I went downstairs to the coffee shop. When I came back Tad was alone, cheerfully getting dressed.

"You disapprove of my friend," he said to me.

"I'm told it's an alternate way of life."

194

"He's not just fun and games. That was Carlos. He's big in the trade. I may have something for us there."

That morning Tad went out with his briefcase to interview the executives of big pharmaceutical companies and to do research in libraries, as he did every day, no matter how late the parties had lasted. As soon as he got back, he said, "Did Carlos call?"

"Nope."

"Maybe I shouldn't have mixed business with pleasure. Carlos could really help us . . ."

For the next week Tad kept asking about calls from Carlos, but none came.

"I don't know, Carlos is the only real lead I have. There've been plenty of offers, but most of these people are small-timers. They think they're going pretty big if they offer to sell me one whole kilo of coke."

"How's your legitimate research going?"

"Hell, I've found they make a lot of 'medical' coke here and distribute it through legitimate channels all over the damn world, but they look at me in a way that makes me scared to even ask questions about illegal sales. That's a *verboten* subject—a young college student just doesn't come in from America and ask questions like that . . . I doubt if we can buy coke by the ton—there's not enough of it. We'll have to go for a mixed cargo."

"You got any idea about how we would pay for the stuff or get delivery at sea, even if we could find someone who wanted to sell it in quantity?"

"Carlos has got the answers, he used to be big in the business himself, but now he acts like a kind of agent."

"How?"

"You tell him how much you want of what. He collects

195

it from a lot of different sources if necessary and puts it on your ship for you."

"What's his mark-up?"

"Big, I assume, but even if he doubled the price of the stuff, would we really care? Our profit would still be almost a thousand percent, the way I figure it. We could make damn near as much on grass as we could on coke if we got a big enough ship."

"How would this Carlos want to be paid?"

"Cash—American currency."

"Maybe twenty or more million dollars if we're really thinking about a big cargo, mixed or not. How could we possibly get it?"

"Dad could figure out a way in the States. That's his department."

"What makes you trust this guy Carlos? There'll be three or four of us on the trawler at most. He and his friends could jump us easy. He'd never even have to touch the cargo, just set up a time and place for us to deliver the money—"

"There's got to be that famous moment of trust, and I trust Carlos more than any of the others I've met."

"Why?"

"Just an instinct. And he's pretty big-time—he does business year after year down here. He'd want us to come back and do more business with him."

"If he could rob twenty million or so off us, he could retire fat and happy."

"Have you got a better way? We have to take a chance . . ."

Soon the telephone rang, but it was not Carlos. It was Seymour.

"What's going on, Andy?" he said. "How come I'm not getting more reports from you guys?"

"You better talk to Tad."

As soon as Tad got on the telephone with his father, his voice lost its usual confidence, sounded querulous, and there was that hint of the swish in his tone that I never heard when he was talking to anyone else.

". . . I don't think that's really necessary . . . All right, if you must, I just need a little more time. All *right*. Do you want us to meet you?"

Finally Tad slammed the receiver down. "He'll be here tomorrow. He wants you to meet him. He'll have his secretary call with the flight number and time."

Before I could reply, he went into his room and slammed the door.

I wondered how a man like Seymour, so staunchly respectable, would set about finding how to buy illegal narcotics when his street-wise kid had apparently failed.

A few minutes later Tad came into the living room wearing his trench coat.

"I'm going out, don't know when I'll be back."

"Where to?"

"To find Carlos."

"I better go with you."

"No. I have to do this alone."

"Damn it, I'm supposed to look after you. Can't you call him?"

"I tried that this morning. I couldn't even get through to him, but his office gave me his address. I think he wants me to come to him. If I can't trust him enough for that, how could we ever do business?"

"Where's his place?"

"Don't worry, it's very respectable. The International Hotel."

"How long before I should come looking for you?"

"There wouldn't be much point in that, would there? We're in his back yard. Maybe there has to be more than one moment of trust. Trust me now—I know what I'm doing."

He disappeared down the hall. My eyes strayed to a forest of liquor bottles which he had left on the living-room table. I wanted to get smashed, to blot all this insanity from my mind, but Seymour was coming soon, and he'd fire me quick if he found I'd taken a fall. Did I want a drink so much that I'd give up a chance at millions?

No. Not yet, at least. I ordered two hot-fudge sundaes from room service. After two hot-fudge sundaes, not even an alcoholic can stomach booze. At this rate I would soon be fatter than I was tall, but the tension in my guts subsided a little. I took a bath and tried to think of Pattie. In more ways than one, she seemed a long way away, part of a dim and distant past I'd been a fool to leave.

Lying in the hot tub, I tried to recapture my worries about paying my bills at home and the prospect of an impoverished old age. And then I began imagining what I would do when I'd made maybe ten million dollars. I'd tell Pattie that oil had been discovered on land to which I'd bought mineral rights long ago—I'd cook up some "miracle" like that. Pattie believed in miracles. She probably wouldn't ask too many questions. I'd tell her she could buy anything she wanted. She had long admired a house we often passed on our way to Coconut Grove, a stately old mansion of oddly modern architecture that seemed to grow out of the knoll of white coral on which it stood and that was surrounded by royal palms and tropical gardens. I'd tell her she could buy that house and I'd get her a Mercedes roadster like the one Tad had bought with some of his first profits in the trade and that she had often admired. I'd tell her she could send her kids, *our* kids, to any schools that wanted and we could spend our summers as a family traveling in Europe. And if traveling as a tourist bored me, I could buy a yacht, my own yacht for a change, a vessel which—unlike most rich men's toys—actually could go anywhere in the world safely and comfortably. After our big run, maybe I could buy the new trawler Seymour was looking for. I had studied three specification sheets he'd mailed to me, and they showed fine, powerful vessels, handsome in their strength if not their grace. Such a ship could be converted into a magnificent yacht. Almost all we'd have to do was to build cabins in her holds. Where would we go? The South Sea islands, Japan, even China was being opened up for yachtsmen. I'd always wanted to see China, the really unknown quantity—

I was interrupted in these pipe dreams by Tad, who returned much sooner than I had expected.

"Andy, are you in there?" he asked, knocking hard on the bathroom door.

"Yeah. Did you find your friend?"

"He's here and I want you to meet him." Tad sounded excited.

"Shouldn't I stay in the background?"

"He's here alone. We don't have to play any more games. I really trust this guy, Andy. I think we can get this whole thing wrapped up before dad comes."

"We can't make a final decision without telling him."

"I'm just setting up a deal for dad to take, like I said I would. Come on, Carlos is waiting."

"He's in a hurry?"

"Andy, he's not the kind of man you keep waiting."

When I came into the living room Carlos was sitting in the middle of the couch. I had seen him only briefly before and had noted only his odd proportions, very small below the belt, large and muscular above it. He was wearing tight black pants now and a white, V-neck cashmere sweater. A gold chain with an emerald about the size of a lima bean hung from his neck. His sleeves were tight enough to show big biceps. Obviously this man had pumped a lot of iron, but as I came close, I realized he was more than a body-building freak. He didn't have that dumb look I had seen in so many gymnasiums. From the neck up he might have been a poet or actor. His face was that of a highly intelligent man, sensitive too, if faces really told much, and he had the look of a man who had endured a lot of pain of one sort or another. His black hair was cut quite short and was not slicked down. His age was hard to guess; a very old twenty-five, a very young thirty-five, or anything in between.

"Ah, Andy," he said with a smile of great warmth, "Tad has been telling me a lot about you." His voice surprised me. It seemed to come from still another person, some sort of Englishman.

"He's told me a little about you," I said.

"Not too much, I hope . . . Now, shall we go directly to business?"

"Could we be overheard here?"

"Our local authorities are not very sophisticated about electronic devices, and they're more interested in politics at the moment than our kind of business. As for others who might be interested—I don't think they'd bother me or my friends."

"I see."

He must have sensed some of my skepticism about his immunity, because he went on almost immediately to say, "You must forgive our country. We are in an odd position. Our climate and our soil produce some of the finest quality material in the world in quantity. Millions of people all over the world crave our products. We need their money—Colombia still has millions who are desperately poor. But foreign governments, yours and others, frown on our commerce. They keep asking us to put a stop to it. Our government authorities of course would like to cooperate, but do they really want to stop a river of gold?" He held out his hands and shrugged, and I saw that his elegant cashmere sleeve was pushed up just enough to reveal a dagger tattooed on his left wrist. This was indeed a very strange man.

"Are you a native of Colombia?" I asked.

"Only the Indians are native Colombians. I have some Indian blood, but not enough to give me their feeling of righteousness. I am mostly of Spanish descent. My family has been here a good many years."

About three hundred, I guessed from his manner, or maybe that was just part of a pose. A Spanish aristocrat with a tattoo of a dagger?

"Where did you learn such good English?" I asked.

"A tutor, sort of a remittance man from England, I suppose, but a very good teacher. He got my whole family

201

to talking like Limeys. It confuses some people . . . Now about business. Tad tells me that you and your other partner plan to go into this thing in a big way."

"We're doing research," I allowed, wishing Tad had let me know how much he was going to reveal to Carlos.

"So I understand. That's a very wise way to begin. I must say it's rather naive, though, for you to expect to buy cocaine by the ton. The reason it's so expensive is that not much is produced."

"But they manufacture some hundred tons a year, I'm told."

"Most of it is spoken for long before it leaves the laboratories."

"May I ask what part you play in all this?"

"Didn't Tad tell you? I'm an agent."

"Yes, but I'm not sure what that involves."

"I know most of the sources of cocaine and most of the big sources of hash and the different grades of grass. I can put together a package for you. How much of it will be cocaine, I don't know yet. In part that will of course depend on the price you want to pay."

"Our other partner will have to work that out—"

"*I* can work it out," Tad broke in. "I know more about this than the old man."

"First I have to see how much I can get for you," Carlos went on, "but I can make up the rest of the package with a high grade of hash that will be worth more than three million a ton in the States. That is available in any quantity you want."

Tad was about to interrupt again but he read the warning in my eyes. I wanted to get a better feel for Carlos before we started talking business seriously and he seemed almost eager to oblige.

"There are of course plenty of agents around here, but I'm generally considered the most trustworthy and the most trusting. I actually am willing to deliver goods before I get paid. I take the risk."

"Aren't you ever disappointed?"

"If I were operating alone, perhaps people would cheat me, but I'm working with many friends, some of them Americans. They would perhaps not be familiar to you. Some call them 'the new breed.'"

"I've heard the term," I said.

"They are a little hard, shall we say, but actually there's nothing new about them. I consider them an extremely ancient breed. My ancestors, the Conquistadors, were not the most gentle of men, and the Indians of both North and South America were not always gentle to the white men. We face many distressing situations nowadays, but my ancestors did not have it easy. They needed gold to pay for their expeditions and to maintain their positions at home. Admirals and captains who did not return to Spain with gold did not remain admirals and captains very long."

"So I imagine." Whatever I had expected from Carlos, it had not been this curious conversation.

"My ancestors sometimes tortured the Indians to make them tell where gold could be found. And the Indians gave them gold, one way or another. When they captured a Spaniard, they sometimes poured molten gold up his rectum, or should I say anus?"

"Asshole," Tad corrected. "Hey, did they really do that?"

"Oh, it's all history—I didn't make it up. The

203

Spaniards and the Indians were not really gentle people and the pirates who came along afterward were also not so gentle."

"I've read a fair amount about them," I said.

"So have I," Carlos said with a brilliant smile. "Most people don't understand the pirates. They were not just simple . . . thugs."

"I didn't get that impression from what I read."

"History often presents the pirates as total bad and the governments of their time as total good. Actually, the governments of their time sent press gangs out to drag men into their navies. They lashed sailors to the bare bones for small offenses, keel-hauled them . . . I can't really blame the pirates for rebelling. The navies and the merchant marines were merely an extension of an iron-fisted class system. I like to think of the pirates as the first effective revolutionaries. And they were the first masters of psychological warfare. They invented the skull-and-crossbone flag and had many other ways to make their victims too scared to fight."

"I think a lot of them were just plain crazy," I said. "Greedy and crazy."

"More so than the governments of their time? Take Blackbeard . . . he's usually considered the worst of the pirates. I have made something of a study of him. Old Teach, they called him, a huge, very powerful man. Was he just a psychotic? Was he a genius at the uses of terror in warfare? Was he at heart a revolutionary who loved freeing the crews of merchantmen from their officers as much as he enjoyed his other profits? Or was he just a gigantic bon vivant, out for all the wine and women he could get? I tend to think he was a little of all of those things."

"Just how much of Blackbeard is history and how much myth?" Tad asked. "I mean, what did he *really* do?"

"Among other things, he liked to pretend he was the devil," Carlos said. "That scared whole crews into surrendering without a fight."

"I read somewhere that he wore glowing pieces of punk in his beard when he attacked. He arrived in a halo of fire and smoke." Tad, I noticed, was really caught up in Carlos' little history lesson, none of which was very new to me. What intrigued me was that the agent was going to such lengths to establish and perhaps even justify the brutality of the new and old breed of pirate. Was it sheer bluff? And why the need to justify it . . . ? Was he mostly doing a Blackbeard on us?

"Quite so," Carlos said, "I'm glad you know your history—do you remember the business about the hearts?"

"I don't think so."

"He liked to eat the hearts of his enemies. Once he slashed a man's chest open and grabbed his heart out so fast that he was able to take his first bite out of it before the victim lost consciousness. He said he'd always wanted to eat a man's heart in front of his eyes."

"Is *that* true?" Tad said.

"So the story goes," Carlos went on, smooth as silk. "Some of my American friends—the new breed or the ancient breed, whichever you wish to call them—debated for a long time whether it was possible to eat a man's heart before he lost consciousness. I didn't approve, of course, but when a man did not pay us for our goods and services, they eventually rounded him up and experimented. They used one of those Ghurka knives—have you ever heard of them?"

"Yes," I said, getting the point.

"Well, they got his heart out very fast, but it's a matter of opinion whether he was still conscious when they ate it. At least his eyes were open and he took a few more breaths."

"Good God," Tad said. "Did you see that?"

"Oh no, I left when I saw what was happening. But they did take Polaroid photographs in color which they insisted on showing me, and a few others. The word got around. Now no one ever tries to cheat us, and we can afford to be very trusting . . ."

"I get the point." I said it aloud this time.

"It's not such a nice story. You may wonder why anyone would want to deal with us at all."

"I might."

"Because we can deliver the goods aboard your ship anywhere you want. And because we can arrange sophisticated methods of payment. We don't go in for crates full of cash."

"How do you work it out?"

"It's not too difficult to buy gold legally in some places. Buy it and pay for it by check. Arrange for us to pick it up from your truck—we can even furnish the truck. The same can be done with emeralds, but that would be difficult when such large sums of money are involved."

"Yes. Our other partner is best equipped to work that out."

"There are many possibilities," Carlos said. "We are

not naive in this business. We can gather whatever cargo you want if it is available and deliver it anywhere at sea. After a few unfortunate experiences, we gave up running it into the States. We prefer to stay in our own back yard. And our services are relatively cheap in view of the fact that for newcomers like you we are indispensable. I advise you not to trust anyone else."

"In view of the fact that we are newcomers," I said, "we don't trust easy."

"Of course no transaction can take place in a total vacuum of trust, but the small-timers around here are notorious, especially when a fairly big deal is involved. Few are able to stand the temptation to take what they can and run . . . I represent a fairly big organization, with more men than can be made happy for long by any one deal, no matter how big." Carlos got to his feet. "Like the pirates, not all of us are out simply for money. Think of us as a free brotherhood with many battles to fight. Tyrannical governments did not disappear with Blackbeard."

"I'll tell my father all of this," Tad said. "You'll have my recommendation."

"Thank you," Carlos said. "I must be getting home—my wife worries about me. By the way, just as a rather bizarre curiosity, would you like to see that Polaroid photograph I was talking about?"

"No thanks," I said, as he took a thin wallet from his hip pocket. Tad said he'd have a look.

With elegantly manicured fingers Carlos picked a photograph from his wallet. Tad took it, held it up to the light for a moment, turned green and gave it back. Immediately he went to the bottles on the table and

207

poured himself a generous drink.

"It's a very upsetting photograph, isn't it?" Carlos said. "At least in Blackbeard's day, there were no cameras and people could almost forget."

"Will you have a Scotch?" Tad asked, his face going from green to chalk white.

"No thank you, I'm with your friend Andy on that. We're not punished for our sins but by them, they say. And liquor makes me fat, as well as stupid, and I can't afford to be either. Good evening. If your father wishes to see me, you know where my office is . . ."

When he'd left, I turned to Tad. "Do we really want to deal with such people?"

"Who else?" he said.

13

Seymour looked so completely his calm, respectable old self when I met him at the airport the next day
that I found myself expecting him to make even the
smuggling business rather humdrum. Although he was
not a physically impressive man, he could, when he
wanted, assume such a grand manner that many people
assumed that he must be important enough to deserve

courtesy. The customs officials called him "sir," not "*señor*," and I had the idea that people all over the world talked *American* to Seymour, even though they'd never even tried it before. He gave the impression of being tolerant of foreign languages as subjects for study in school, but sensible people who were capable of operating at Seymour's level all over the world would of course speak American English. And if they didn't, to hell with them.

"It's good to see you, Andy," he said. "It was a long flight." He gave me his baggage tickets. "Pick this stuff up for me, will you? I was exhausted before I started this trip. Things have been very active. I'll tell you about it. Meet me at that bar over there, okay?"

He did look tired and pale. I wondered if he'd taken to using some drug, cocaine, himself. The baggage clerk couldn't find Seymour's luggage. It had been lost, maybe left behind in Miami, he said. They would look for it and send it to our hotel as soon as possible.

I found Seymour hunched over a martini at the bar. I expected him to be angry about his lost luggage, but he only shrugged and said, "It was just clothes. I can buy more here."

Money—it must be wonderful to have enough money to make worry about details like lost luggage unnecessary. Well, soon maybe I'd have that luxury.

On the way back to the hotel Seymour slept in the back of the taxi, despite that fact that our driver, like so many of his compatriots, appeared to regard any journey as a race with all the other cars. He revived quickly, however, the moment we got there, and on the way up in the elevator, he said, "How's Tad been?"

"Pretty well."

He gave me a quizzical look but followed me silently to the door of our living room. Tad opened it the moment I touched it with my key.

"Hello, dad."

"Hello, son."

They were a strange pair, those two. They stood a few feet apart, tense as boxers waiting for the first bell.

"Mix me a martini, will you, Tad?" Seymour said. "Andy, I reserved a bedroom next to yours for myself. I'd be obliged if you'd see about registering me and getting the key."

I don't know what they said to each other while I was gone, but when I returned with Seymour's key, Tad was flustered and Seymour, sitting in an overstuffed chair with his martini, appeared even more pale and tired. The thought struck me that he looked almost dead.

"Sit down, Andy," he said. "You wanted to be a full partner in all this so you better hear me out."

I sank down on the couch, his key still in my hand.

"I'm under tremendous time pressure," he continued. "This deal we're trying to put together is part of my whole effort to consolidate and to liquify many of my family's enterprises. I believe I have succeeded in finding a purchaser, both for these enterprises and any goods we may purchase here. Do you understand that? It could be a very clean sale, conducted through perfectly legitimate channels, as far as the financial aspects go. But that deal of course can't go through until we deliver the goods. Meanwhile I have to stay liquid—I have to have more than twenty million dollars on hand for our expenses and for buying our cargo. Much of it I had to borrow. Do you have any idea of what kind of interest we have to pay for that kind of money these days?"

"A lot," I said, although I realized that this lecture—more to the point, Seymour's castigating tone—was for Tad's benefit. Tad said nothing. As I watched, he lit a joint, the first I had seen him smoke in months.

"Every day we delay costs me a fortune," Seymour said. "Every day diminishes our capital. Now I've been assuming, perhaps mistakenly, that with twenty million dollars of cash in hand, we'd have no trouble buying all the stuff we want."

"From what we've discovered, it just isn't that easy," I said, beginning to be irritated with him, but he didn't give me a chance to explain.

"Tad tells me that he has just one real contact after all the time you've spent here. If we have only one contact, we can't bargain about price. And Tad doesn't even seem to have any real background information on this fellow. Carlos, he calls him, and doesn't even know his last name."

"Dad, this isn't Wall Street."

"Business, boy, is business the world over—you have to know who you're dealing with. Andy, what's this Carlos like? Tad seems to get all tongue-tied when he tries to tell me."

"Carlos is a tough man to describe," I started, still not sure whether I'd trust him above any other agents.

"Supposing you try," Seymour said with exaggerated patience, "seeing we're thinking of giving him millions of my dollars."

"He's just an *agent*, dad," Tad said. "He'll buy the stuff for us and deliver it at sea. He's really selling local knowledge and connections—"

"Don't interrupt, I asked Andy a question. You saw the man, didn't you, Andy?"

"Yes."

"Well, what's he like? How do you size him up?"

"I'd say he's sort of a well-bred pirate, and maybe a political rebel . . . he's an odd mixture. He talks like an Englishman, says he's of Spanish descent and gives that general impression to me. His body looks as though he's pumped a lot of iron and his face looks very intelligent. He says or implies that he has a big, rough gang. He also seemed to me to imply connections with revolutionaries."

"Is he a fag?"

The question jolted me as much as it did Tad, but it was Tad who asked, "What the hell has *that* got to do with it?"

"I like to find out all I can about people I may do business with."

"I don't really know anything about his sex life," I said, for some reason feeling protective about Tad.

"Did you try to check up on him, ask around about him?"

"You just don't do that here with a man like Carlos," Tad said. "I am certain, though, that he's the top man in his field."

"Tad, I think you should tell your father about the Polaroid picture," I said.

"Hey, I don't know what to make of that. It might have been his idea of psychological warfare. He talked a lot about that."

"Tell Seymour about it."

"He showed me a picture of a man murdering another man. The point was to scare me, I guess. He says he can deliver drugs without immediate payment on the spot because he trusts people. He trusts that they'll be too scared not to pay him, because they'll be murdered if they hold out."

"Very reassuring," Seymour said.

"This is the kind of business we're in," I said. "You better tell him a little about the nature of that murder, Tad."

"He told us some stuff about the old pirate, Blackbeard, cutting a man's heart out and eating it before the guy even lost consciousness. One of his men evidently tried it. I don't know . . . I suppose a picture like that could be faked."

"And you want me to deal with *this* man?"

"Dad, I couldn't find anybody else. Nobody else is even willing to talk about cocaine by the ton. Except for Carlos, they're all a bunch of small-timers. I think he's driven everyone big out of the business."

"Tad, maybe you just ran into small-timers and thugs like this man Carlos because you took the wrong approach. You've got to get your thinking above street-level. Didn't I tell you that before?"

"You don't know what you're talking about down here."

"Or maybe you don't know what you're talking about anywhere."

Tad flushed. "Dad, if you can do better, go ahead—"

"I've already done better. Sitting in New York, I've done considerably better."

"You know how to buy the stuff?" Tad asked.

214

"Yes, I know how."

"You know how to pay for it and have it delivered at sea?" I said.

"I know that too."

"How?"

"By following sound business principles that I've tried to teach you since you were about eighteen years old, and which you didn't think were worth taking seriously."

"Dad, if you got a deal, tell us about it."

"If I have a deal which meets with your approval, my son, will you for once in your life admit that you have something to learn from me?"

My God, this was one of the damnedest family-therapy sessions I'd ever heard of.

"What's your deal?" Tad said.

They were staring at each other, hard.

"Wait," I said. "Carlos didn't seem to think it was too farfetched to imagine that this room might be bugged."

"Come into my room, then," Seymour said. "I just reserved it. They couldn't have known about that."

We went into his room, which was identical to mine. Seymour sat in the only stuffed chair, Tad sat at the desk and I sat on the edge of the bed.

"The old commodore used to say that there are three basic rules for success in business," Seymour began. "Investigate, investigate, investigate."

"In this case, how?" Tad asked.

"All human activities are pyramidal. The real leaders of everything meet at the top. That's why the lifestyle of your ancestors has some meaning, Tad. We tend to hang out in places where we meet men who know more and have more power than those fascinating people you seem to meet on the streets."

"Dad, if you have a deal, will you stop rubbing it in? What have you really got?"

"I started with rumors. Checking out rumors often pays. There are always rumors in New York that that big building or the other is really owned by the Mafia, or that such and such a corporation or bank is Mafia-controlled. I should add that I don't really know what the Mafia, Cosa Nostra, or whatever you want to call it, actually is or whether it even exists. It's fairly obvious, however, that there are large organizations which control such criminal activities as prostitution, loan-sharking, gambling and, of course, drugs." Seymour seemed less tired now, as if he were enjoying what seemed almost a performance. He paused, lit a cigarette and leaned back into his chair before continuing.

"I have always assumed that there is such a thing as an oak-tree corporation—that's my own name for it. An oak-tree corporation is big and it flourishes because its roots go deep underground, into the underworld, you might say. It stands to reason that any outfit which made millions of dollars illegally would invest much of it in perfectly legal, indeed obviously respectable enterprises which could launder the money and give the leaders a place in the community."

"Dad, do you have to make this into a lecture?"

"Just you keep quiet, Tad, and try to learn something from your old man for once. You don't seem to be doing too well on your own . . . Because these oak-tree corporations, as I call them, get large infusions of tax-free dollars, they can flourish more than most strictly legitimate enterprises, and they develop quite an

216

identifiable financial profile—identifiable to someone who understands a little about finances, that is. They almost never have to borrow money for expansion. That's one aspect of their financial structure."

"So far I'm almost with you," Tad said sarcastically.

"All right. Some of the oak-tree corporations have Ivy League front men, but when you find the people who have the real power of decision, they're a different sort—not necessarily your stock gangster character, but not Harvard Business School, either."

"Dad, could you get to the point?"

"I got to the point a lot quicker than you did and I'm telling you how I reasoned it out. It stands to reason that the men who wield the real power in those oak-tree corporations would eventually resent their front men and look for some kind of respectability and prestige for themselves. They'd buy big houses in the most fashionable suburbs—at least the second generation of them would, and all this has been going on a long time. Some of them would ache to join the best golf and yacht clubs."

"How did you meet one of those guys?" Tad asked.

"I investigated, investigated, investigated several companies whose financial structures had the oak-tree configuration. I found out who held the most power in them, and I called some of these men to discuss some perfectly legitimate business propositions I dreamed up. I got to know three of them and one of them seemed to want very much to become my friend. I asked him to dinner several times at the New York Yacht Club and gradually we edged our way into talking about business, real business, the business at hand. He's getting together a group which is going to buy me out at prices high enough to permit us to give him our cargo."

"That's great, but what has it got to do with getting the stuff down here?" Tad asked.

"Some of those oak trees have roots long enough to reach all over the world, including Colombia. There's a company here called Santana Chemicals, I believe, and it has a branch called Riva Pharmaceuticals."

"I checked with Riva," Tad said. "They're strictly legitimate and their whole output is sold far in advance of manufacture."

"Of course, but did you realize they're owned by Santana?"

"No."

"Then you didn't realize, of course, that Santana is in turn owned by a conglomerate which is in the process of being bought by a larger conglomerate which is based in New York."

"And controlled by your friend," I said.

"By my friend and his friends."

"What exactly does that mean for us?" Tad said. "Will the Riva company sell us the stuff?"

"Yes, but certain problems have to be worked out first. They don't have much more cocaine than we want and the disappearance of so much from regular channels will have to be explained. There may have to be a big fire up there. That won't be our business, of course. They'll take care of it."

"Both the buying and the selling will be done at very high levels," I said.

"Yes, but the deal is rather complex in spots. The conglomerate also deals in coffee here. One of my enterprises will be buying their coffee at somewhat inflated prices, even by current standards. But coffee is always a gamble, and there'll be no reason for the governments to get suspicious."

"Can they deliver the stuff to us at sea?" I asked.

"Santana Chemicals has several small freighters which are operated by long-time employees, trusted men. There'll be no problem about that."

"So you've got it all sewed up," Tad said, sounding more resentful than pleased.

"Except for the details. There are several men I want to meet here and much paperwork for me to do."

"Why did you send us down here?" Tad asked.

"Because I wasn't dead sure I had this end of it sewed up until a few days ago. Of course I had some idea I could manage it. Maybe I wanted to teach you something. You *are* my son. After all, your real name is Seymour Clayton III, not Tad, and maybe I wanted to remind you that you belong in a world where business can be done more efficiently than in the streets."

Tad just shrugged.

"I think we're going to make a great deal of money," Seymour said. Anticipating the question on my mind, he went on to say, "The final prices for both the purchase and the sale have not yet been established, of course. I'm still not sure how much cocaine will be available, but we'll fill up our holds with marijuana. I won't be able to talk in even ball-park figures until I know considerably more, but I expect we'll be dealing in very large sums."

"I can't believe you're for real," Tad said in disgust. "You didn't even want to go into it at first. You laughed

219

at me, and now you've taken over as if the whole thing was your idea."

"Smuggling *was* your idea, and I still think it's ridiculous at your level. It was my notion that it could be conducted on much higher levels."

I felt for Tad, more than I ever thought I would. But I was embarrassed and a little annoyed at being a party to this scene. "We still have the problem of transportation," I said. "There still could be hijackers. And I understand that the Coast Guard has some new appropriations for drug patrols. The whole thing may not be as easy as you think—"

"That's your department, Andy. I have every confidence that you can handle it."

"When do you want to buy the trawler?"

"As soon as possible. As I said, I'm running on borrowed money, in part, and I'm under great time pressure."

"You want me to fly to New Orleans right away to inspect those vessels you found out about?"

"Now let's make haste without too much hurry, Andy. There are a lot of loose ends we still have to talk about. I've accomplished a lot in the last few weeks . . . It's funny how things all come together sometimes. I even sold the *Patrician* to my new friend during one of those luncheons at the New York Yacht Club. I promised you an exclusive and I'll still give you your commission, of course. You'll need some money to buy some stock in our holding corporation. Otherwise it would be hard to make our payments to you appear proper."

"I'm grateful," I said, with something else than the abject gratitude that I knew was expected.

"You should be, Andy. This is a great chance for you. You should make more money than you ever imagined."

"Not without earning it, I suspect. For starts, how are they going to move all that cocaine to the coast?"

"It will be well guarded by trained troops. My friend has the connections here. Some of these corporations have enough guards to make a small private army."

"But it will be hard to keep an operation that big secret. If they're going to arrange a fire and all the rest of it, dozens of people will know about it."

"Do you believe hijackers will want to fight real soldiers?"

"With all that money at stake, they might try anything. With only the three of us—and maybe one more—on a trawler, we'd be pretty weak throughout the whole voyage."

"Once you get to sea, no one will be able to find you. You can steer an unpredictable course. I assume that you wouldn't take a direct route."

"For a day or more any light plane could spot us and send boats out to take us. It'll take us a couple of days to get clear of the Colombia coast."

"You may have more cooperation than you think. My friends have planes and boats. Some people may want to interfere, but plenty of others will want this deal to go through."

For some reason an image of Carlos flashed into my mind, perhaps a modern version of old Blackbeard himself. If Blackbeard had known of a cargo worth hundreds of millions of dollars, he would have gone to some effort to get it. Seymour might have friends here, but I guessed that Carlos had even more. There was at least a possibility that I was heading into a bloody war, the sort of war I liked least—the kind where my job would be defense, not attack. The attacker can always get the advantage of surprise. And all I'd have would be a slow ship, maybe a few sticks of dynamite, some light guns and no one I could really count on in a fight except Esky, if I could get him. The back of my neck started to prickle.

"Hell, the whole thing will probably turn out to be routine," Seymour said. "It's done every day."

"How about our unloading place? Did you check on Red Rock Cove?"

"I got it rented until the first of November. I even flew up and took a look at it. That was an inspired choice, Andy. How did you happen to have that in the back of your mind?"

"I guess every old sailor thinks about smuggling once in a while. Look, if you've got everything set up, why don't I go buy the trawler? It will take time to get her outfitted."

"That's just the point—it will take time to outfit her and bring her here. She should lay fifty or a hundred miles offshore until we know exactly when we can get the stuff to the coast and move it out to her."

"We'll have to get hold of a radio and establish some sort of a code—"

"Exactly. Andy, at this stage I'd rather you be the admiral of this operation than the captain of that ship. Didn't you tell me once that you know a good man who might help us?"

"I know one, if I can get him."

222

"Does he know his business as a sailor?"

"He's the best."

"Then have him fly here. Set up codes with him, radio communication and all the rest. Then have him go inspect the ships in New Orleans and choose one. We can send a couple of Colombians over to be his crew—he can say he's delivering the ship to a Colombian owner. My friend said he could get us a couple of seamen we can trust. Tell your friend to bring the ship over here and lie to off the coast until we give him the signal to come closer and load. The freight boat that brings the cargo can bring us out and the native crew ashore. You can take over command of the ship then."

"I'd rather command her right from the start."

"We need you here, Andy."

"Why? I can teach Tad to handle the radio communication."

"I could do that easy," Tad said.

"No . . . everybody here knows I'm a so-called big American businessman. I'll be entertaining their bigshots—that will be a necessary part of my deal. This is a very volatile place, both politically and because of the trade. It's even conceivable that I could be kidnapped, held as a hostage, either by revolutionaries or as part of a drug war. We need Andy here as a bodyguard."

"You could hire bodyguards easy enough," I said.

"Men I could really trust?"

"What do I do?" Tad asked.

"It would be a help if you just stayed the hell out of trouble. Have you been smoking your funny weed long?"

Tad flushed, jumped up and stamped out of the room,

and I couldn't blame him, even if he was behaving childishly.

"I don't know what to do with that kid," Seymour said.

"He'll be all right if you can stop cutting him down."

"I can't help it—I love him, but just looking at him makes me mad. Why does he have to be like that?"

"Take it easy on him, he'll come along."

"Which is another reason I'd like you here, Andy. You can handle Tad a hell of a lot better than I can. He's the weak link in our chain. If they were to kidnap anybody, it would probably be him. I don't want him wandering around this city, especially smoking that stuff."

"I'll keep track of him as well as I can—"

"All right. Now what's the name of this friend of yours who could bring our ship over here?"

"Esky—his nickname is 'the Eskimo.' His real name is some damn Danish thing no one can pronounce."

"Get him here as soon as you can. Put your calls through right away. Have you got a financial deal with him in mind?"

"I told you some time ago that he's worth a hundred grand for a job like this."

"See if you can get him for fifty."

"No. He's worth the hundred. As a matter of fact, he could probably bring a trawler over here alone, without getting Colombian seamen involved."

"A seventy-footer?"

"Two men often take ships like that shrimping and one stays busy with the nets. She'll have an automatic pilot and bridge engine controls. Beyond that, I think Esky could sail a square-rigger alone. He can do damn near anything."

"He sounds like our man. Get him here as soon as you can so we can work out the details. After a day or two with us, he can fly to New Orleans, inspect the ships I've lined up and pick one. I'll have a lawyer take care of the financial and legal details. How long will it take him to sail?"

"That'll depend on the condition of the ship. Esky could put a new trawler together fast. Maybe a week or two."

"How long will it take him to get her here?"

"Maybe ten days."

"All right. This is July Fourth, Independence Day—do you realize that?"

"It doesn't seem to mean much down here," I said, but Seymour chose to ignore the crack.

"If he takes a week to come here, talk to us and go to New Orleans, two weeks to get the ship ready and ten days to get here, that means we could make something like August the seventh our target date for loading, if I can get my paperwork done."

"All right, but schedules like that never work out."

"To be realistic, let's give ourselves two weeks' leeway and set August twenty-first as our target date. That's getting us into the hurricane season, isn't it?"

"With a new trawler, it *could* be an advantage."

"All right, that's your end of it, though I don't like the idea of going through a hurricane on a seventy-footer much myself, no matter how rugged she is."

"Hijackers won't like the idea of hurricanes much, either, and the Coast Guard will be busy." I hoped.

"It's your decision. Now try to call your friend, this

Eskimo, right away. By the way, why do they call him that?"

"He says he can smell icebergs in a fog and he looks sort of like an Eskimo—short but rugged, a sawed-off giant."

"Tough?"

"A lot of people have thought so."

"Reliable?"

"I trust him."

"Then call him and tell him to be here as soon as he can. We'll pay his travel expenses, of course. If you can't get him, can you think of anyone else?"

"Not like Esky."

"Tell me when you get results. Wake me up if you have to."

He took off his coat and tie, suddenly looking so pale that I asked if he felt all right.

"As well as can be expected," he said. "Of course I've been under a lot of strain, and smuggling isn't exactly what the doctor would recommend for a man with a tricky heart . . . The strain of failure would be worse, though. I was getting pretty close to the edge when I started to put this deal together." He lay down. "If we meet our target date, the last week in August," he added drowsily, "when would you get into Red Rock Cove?"

"Close to the middle of September if everything went right."

"That's when we'll get paid—that's when the final papers will be signed in New York, the minute you deliver the stuff."

"Have you thought of the possibility of hijackers at that end?"

"Of course, but these are reliable people, as this business goes. They're a huge organization."

I said nothing and there was a pause.

"We keep getting back to the fact that we have to trust someone," he said with a sigh. "Of course there's risk, a very great risk. Why else do you think the profits are so high?"

14

I went to my room and washed my face in cold water. For some reason I felt profoundly tired. I wanted to sleep and forget this business for a little while, but first I had to try to call Esky.

He'd be glad to get my call, I thought. He was bored with his work on the yachts and worried about his boat-bum future. He'd wanted to go into the smuggling business when I'd last seen him, but his friend had scared him off. Working with me and a man like Seymour would be different. I was pretty sure that Esky would jump at it.

Except was I really doing him a favor? One thing I was sure of: He'd want to make the decision himself, not have me make it for him. He'd be sore as hell if I knew of an opportunity like this and didn't tell him. Where else could he pick up a tax-free hundred grand?

I glanced at my watch. The time difference between Colombia and California confused me for a few moments, but I finally figured it to be about four-thirty in the afternoon there. The office of the yacht broker I knew in San Francisco who would be most likely to know Esky's whereabouts would be closed if I didn't make my call soon.

For some reason I suddenly felt as though I had to talk to Esky right away, that I needed a friend more than ever in my life, and Information in Frisco seemed to take an infuriatingly long while to get the number. Then the telephone buzzed so long in the yacht broker's office that I thought it might have closed early. Finally a girl answered and put me through to the broker, an old shipmate from the Honolulu races I hadn't seen in about four years.

"Andy, where in hell are you?"

"Colombia," I said, and realized that that one word meant drugs to any sailor. "I got a big delivery job," I added.

"Oh?"

"I'm looking for the old Eskimo."

"Esky's working for Strad Gilmore now. They're

230

getting ready to take his Twelve east."

"Can you get in touch with Esky? I have a good job for him."

"He has a good job now."

"No job on those Twelves can last long," I said, realizing that some explanation had to be made of the kind of job that might be available in South America, something that had nothing to do with drugs. "When the racing season's over, he'll be out on his ass. Tell him I have something permanent for him, an oil king's yacht, and that he won't have to be a butler. The owner has three stewards."

"Sounds good," the broker said. "I'll have him give you a call."

I gave him my number, hung up and then just sat there, suddenly wanting a drink more than ever. There was no one I could call for relief except Pattie. I hadn't called her yet, but she wouldn't really expect me to call from Colombia just to shoot the breeze and she would be sure to feel the tension in my voice. I'd also have to make up a lot of lies, and lying to Pattie would make me even more tense. I decided to go out for a walk.

Under the awning at the front of the hotel I saw a dark green sports car, one of those expensive Italian jobs. Two laughing men were in it. The car roared away as I approached, but I caught a glimpse of them. One was Carlos and the other was Tad. What the *hell* was Tad doing with him now?

I couldn't see any good possibilities and I wanted a drink more than ever. Instead I walked to a nearby park and jogged for five miles on a path where bicycles kept swerving around me.

In this place even running appeared to be dangerous.

When I got back to the hotel the little red light on my telephone was blinking. I hoped that Esky had got my message to call, but the hotel clerk had only a note which said "Call me, Clayton."

"Do you know where Tad is?" Seymour asked.

"I saw him drive off with his friend Carlos."

"Why didn't you stop him?"

"I can't run fifty miles an hour."

"Don't be a wiseguy, Andy. Did Tad look as though he was going willingly?"

"As a matter of fact, he was laughing."

"What does that mean?"

"Maybe Carlos is just his friend, among other things, and you made him feel like he needed a friend. If I were you, I'd let up on him."

"Somebody has to straighten him out."

"If you push him too hard, he could blow this whole deal."

"I don't think Tad would do that. He's still my son, he's still smart and he still knows I can show him how to make a great deal of money—"

"Granted . . ." It was ironic, I thought uncharitably, that Seymour had heart trouble, but then the Claytons had always expressed their affection in dollars and cents.

"Did you try to call your Eskimo?"

"I left a message for him to call me."

"Where have you been? I've been trying to get you for an hour."

"Oh, I just went out to have a few drinks."

"Do you *mean* that?"

"I sure felt like it, but I ran about five miles instead."

"Don't even make jokes like that. To be honest, I thought twice about picking you for this job—"

"I kind of thought that Tad and I had picked you for this job, or that Tad picked us both."

"Whatever. Remember that I'm counting on you, Andy. We're all going to have to be able to count on each other."

"Touching, isn't it?"

He did not laugh. "If you see Tad, tell him I want to talk to him, no matter how late it is. I'm worried about him—"

"Then take it easy on him. Good night, Seymour."

I hung up. I too was worried about Tad. Was he so angry, maybe so enraged at his father that he'd go over to Carlos' side? He'd spent a night with Carlos, after all, and obviously was a lot happier with him than with his father. If he and Carlos worked together, maybe they figured they could grab the whole cargo before we got clear of the Colombian coast.

A possibility—anything was a possibility in this crazy deal. But in the end I decided that crime, like other enterprises, depends on character. Tad might be temporarily enraged enough to do anything, but in the long run I didn't *think* he'd betray his own father. I also didn't think he'd betray me; there'd always, I thought, been some unspoken current of understanding between the two of us. I know I trusted Tad more than I did his father . . . None of which helped me get to sleep.

At a little before four in the morning, I heard Tad come into his room. That wasn't hard—he was stumbling around and knocked a lamp to the floor with a crash. His father came running and we both went in.

Tad obviously was stoned and I was a little glad that he smelled of booze. That, at least, was something I understood.

"Where have you been?" Seymour demanded.

"Up yours, old dad." He was standing with one hand on the head of his bed, swaying.

"Seymour, for God's sake leave us alone," I said. "Talk to him in the morning if you have to. You're only making things worse."

Seymour did. After he left I helped Tad lie down, loosened that clown-buckled belt of his and took off his shoes.

"I want to talk," he said.

"Tomorrow—"

"Now . . . My body's drunk but my mind is working just fine."

"I know how that feels."

"Carlos isn't such a bad guy. You know he had that terrible picture faked to scare people. Psychological warfare. That's what he said."

"Maybe . . ."

"I didn't tell him anything, Andy—honest, I didn't. He called up and said he wanted to meet me."

"Why?"

"He knows something big is up. It looks as though a lot of people know it. Dad thinks he's clever as hell, but you can't keep secrets down here. It's my fault really. It was my idea to make just one big haul and never any others. The greatest crime of the century . . . I was thinking about the police—they latch onto patterns of repeated crimes, that's true. But here the cops aren't the big problem. No one really wants to stop the trade down here. So the problem is other runners. They don't mind a *little* competition too much, but they don't want a guy like dad to walk all over them and make it big . . . hurts their pride, not to mention pocketbooks."

"So what did Carlos say?"

"These people don't want to stop us—they just want to be cut in. Like I said, it's partly a matter of face with them."

"We've been too greedy. Is that it?"

"Yes. But if we spread the wealth a little, these people will cooperate with us instead of trying to stop us."

"'These people' you keep referring to—is it Carlos' group?"

Tad nodded.

"How much do they want?"

"Fifty-fifty, Carlos said. I don't think even he has any idea just how big this thing is, although he claims to have 'eyes and ears everywhere.' That sounds pretty corny, but I get the idea he's not joking. He has political connections. I think he's interested in drugs mostly to get money for his cause."

"Maybe. Who the hell can tell?" I said, disgusted with this new complication in an already complicated business.

"If we gave him half, we'd still have plenty to divide among the three of us. I've an idea that dad's never going to give us any hard figures even when he gets them, but he sure is thinking big . . . Carlos wouldn't ask for cash or money. We could just give him half our cargo before it was loaded, then he'd guarantee us clearance of the coast—"

"We'll talk to your old man about it in the morning."

"I'm worried about that, it'll be a matter of face with him too. He can't stand anybody putting him down, or not being put down by him."

"He'll have to take on a dose of reality. How could three or four of us fight it out against practically the whole world down here?"

"I knew you'd see it—we've no choice, when you come right down to it. But I think they'll let us make our profit so we'll come back down here again with more money. We've got to be reasonable, though, spread the wealth . . . You talk to dad, Andy. I can't."

"Okay."

"And be careful, Andy. If we pull this thing off, take your money and run as far from him as you can. That's what I plan to do. He's an even bigger rat than I used to think . . ."

"I doubt that, Tad . . . Anyway, get some sleep. You've got to keep yourself together . . ."

"Thanks, Andy. You know, I trust you. That's why I wanted you in this thing in the first place. Sailors are easy to get, but you're the only man in the whole world I really trust . . . I like you too, Andy. Do you like me?" His voice was drowsy.

"Sure, Tad." I was beginning to feel uneasy.

"Sometimes I almost love you. Hey, I don't mean in a

queer way . . ."

"Sure."

"But queer love's better than no love. Wouldn't you say?"

"I guess."

"I don't think old dad loves anyone. I don't think he ever has. I don't think he even knows what the word means. Carlos knows. I'm going to see him to-morrow morning. You'd like him if you understood him . . . He's into politics. He used to be just a hot-shot operator, but now he has a cause. I wish I had a cause . . ."

He closed his eyes. I sat beside him for a few minutes and then covered him with a blanket before going back to my own bed.

Late as it was, I found it hard to get to sleep that night, and I woke up at eight still tired but too restless to stay in bed. To my surprise Tad was already drinking coffee in the kitchenette. Youth is a damned miracle; this time he hadn't even a trace of a hangover.

"Good morning," he said. "Carlos wants me at his place in about half an hour to meet some of his friends. Want to go? I don't mean for protection. I told him a lot about you and he said he'd like to get to know you."

More likely he wanted to lay on another dose of his psychological warfare, I thought. I hadn't entirely bought the story Carlos had fed Tad earlier about being so damn reasonable.

"What are you going to do?"

"He just wants to introduce me to some of the political

237

people he works with. No matter what dad says, I think they're people we're going to have to deal with, one way or another."

We took a taxi to the International Hotel, a place smaller than the Hilton but more fancy. I followed Tad into a big elevator with a thick red carpet. We got out on the twelfth floor and saw, directly across the hall, a glass door with a sign in discreet gold letters:

TOURIST SERVICES, INC.
OUR GUIDES SPEAK MANY LANGUAGES.
WE WILL HELP YOU ENJOY YOUR HOLIDAY
OR DO BUSINESS HERE.

There was an impressive little foyer, but no receptionist was at the desk. Tad pressed a button near a sign that said, "Ring for service." Carlos walked from an inner room almost immediately. In a conservative gray suit, he could have been a successful Los Angeles businessman, maybe a movie producer, yet.

"Good morning," he said. "I'm glad you brought your friend. There are people I want you both to meet. I hope you excuse the early hour. We've fallen into the habit of breakfast meetings."

While he was talking he led the way to a modest conference room that looked as though it had been arranged for sales meetings. Posters advertising beautiful Bogotá and Colombia lined the walls. At a long rectangular table four men sat drinking coffee. Three could have been middle-aged travel agents, maybe shoe salesmen, but the fourth was a tall, thin, young and intense man whom Carlos introduced as

Professor Rada.

"Good morning," Rada began in Spanish-accented English. "We don't have much time, so I'll begin right away. I understand that you people are planning to do some business here in Colombia."

"Maybe," Tad said.

"As our sign on the door says, our business is to help foreigners to do business here. I have a little lecture with which I usually begin. Will you permit me?"

"Sure," Tad said.

Rada motioned to a pretty girl in a green dress to bring coffee for Tad and me, then sat back and looked at us appraisingly.

"Our basic situation is this. Regardless of the morality and legality involved, our little country now gets more money from illicit drugs than from coffee, which once was our main crop. I'm sure statistics will bore you, but our income from marijuana alone this year will be close to two billion of your dollars. That is a very large amount of money for us."

"For anyone," I said.

"This marijuana is wholesaled in your country for anywhere from two hundred and twenty-five dollars a pound to three twenty-five, according to its quality, and of course the retail price can be twice that or more. You would think the farmers who grow it would be rich. Well, it may surprise you to know that the farmers get less than four of your dollars a pound for even the best grade of marijuana. The rest, the difference between four dollars a pound to the grower and as much as a thousand a pound to the consumer, all this goes to middlemen—ours and yours. That is quite an interesting fact, don't you think?"

"There are people here who don't like it," Carlos said mildly.

"Ah, yes," Rada put in with more irony, "there are people here who don't like that. And there are other facts which some of us here don't like. Colombia, unlike your great country, has virtually no middle class. We have a vast lower class and a small, self-styled aristocracy."

"Some of the people here don't like that either," Carlos said softly.

"Yes, some of the people here don't like that," Rada repeated, a little like a revivalist preacher picking up a chant. "It also happens to be true that sixty percent of our population must live on only nine percent of our national income."

"You can guess what the sixty percent thinks about that," Carlos said.

"Sixty percent of the people don't like it," Rada said. "So we have a great many unhappy people in our beautiful little country. The results are often unfortunate. We have just a few terrorists and revolutionaries, as our papers and yours often say. There have been unfortunate events, such as the recent occupation of the Dominican embassy by 'a few urban guerrillas,' as the papers said. That was most unfortunate, particularly the holding of your ambassador and the diplomats of so many other nations."

"I read about it," I said, though I had not followed the story in the papers much because I never quite understood it. What I *did* understand was that this little lecture was an orchestrated piece, and while I could guess where it was leading, I was as caught up in the performance as Tad obviously was.

"Our government was much congratulated on the way it handled that situation, and even the urban guerrillas received praise. A compromise was reached. You will find that we Colombians are sensible people compared to some you might find in, say, Iran? Opinions differ about how much political unrest there is here. Some say there are only these very few urban guerrillas. Others tend to believe that the sixty percent of the population who receive only nine percent of the national income are over-ripe for revolution, if not already supporting the formation of one."

"Some tend to believe that," Carlos said, with no smile.

"Some tend to believe that if billions of dollars are going to be made on drugs, the people who grow the crop should receive more than one sixtieth, one dollar in sixty, that the consumers pay for their product."

"A good many tend to believe that," Carlos said.

"Some say that the government of Colombia is the most stable democracy in South America. Others think it may be, shall we say, slightly to the right, the wrong side, of our ideal?"

"Slightly," Carlos said, still without a smile.

"There are bad rumors, rumors of the police holding people without trial, of torturing in prisons for political differences . . . And there are some who think that the rumors may be true," Rada said. "There are some who shout slogans which may grate on American ears."

"Such as 'Power to the people,'" Carlos said very softly.

241

"All power to the people," Rada repeated, with noticeable intensity. The words had the effect of an incantation on his friends, who no longer looked like ordinary salesmen. They were leaning forward in their chairs, their coffee cups forgotten, their faces taut.

"There are some who blame the capitalist hegemony for our problems," Rada said.

He had more or less got my sympathy up to this point, but he lost me with that word *hegemony*. I could never believe anyone who used language like that . . . Hell, people who mean what they say don't fancy it up that way. What the hell did "hegemony" mean, anyway? Here I was with my whole year of Harvard education and I wasn't sure . . . so what the hell did the factory workers and peasants mean when they kept shouting it at Commie demonstrations? "Down with the capitalist hegemony." I'd heard Castro quoted as saying, and crowds had cheered him . . . All right, I was wrong to put down a whole political argument on account of one silly word, but language like that and slogans of damn near any kind always did seem to me to mark the end of any real thought or honest feeling.

Rada had got himself all worked up with his own slogans and now was speaking with the self-conviction of a soap-box orator, which put me off further.

"There are those, here and abroad, who want to help our people," he was saying, and Carlos again echoed him.

That last stopped me even more than *hegemony* and the slogans. I could imagine Rada or Carlos trying to help "the people" or "our people," but I doubted they ever got it down to one suffering person, the way, for example, Pattie did when some poor old drunk woman called in the middle of the night. It's a hell of a lot easier to help the "masses," the "people" than getting down to one on one. I just didn't trust rhetoric like this. Besides, the atmosphere in this room had turned to hate, not any kind of love or compassion for "our people." The men who'd looked like salesmen sat with doubled-up fists as Rada repeated his slogans. I glanced at Tad and was relieved to see that he simply looked bored. I guess I'd been afraid that in his search for a cause he might have been sucked in by the rhetoric. But he was either too smart or too indifferent.

Rada soon felt that he wasn't reaching us, and Carlos looked uncomfortable.

"Not everyone sympathizes with us or understands us," Rada said, "but anyone who does business here would do well to understand that there are more than the uniformed authorities to deal with in Colombia. They have power, others may even have more . . . They do not deal in extortion, they deal in righting wrongs—"

"And they have many people to back them up," Carlos said, "and not all of them are unarmed."

"Okay, message received," I said sharply. I'd never liked threats.

"We prefer cooperation, not a fight," Carlos said. "We ask for your understanding, *and* your cooperation."

"Of course I do not make any plea myself," Rada said, with new briskness in his voice. "I have been giving you an orientation in contemporary Colombia. This is one of the services we do for foreigners who want to do business in our country."

"We sure appreciate it," I said. "Now if you don't mind, we have to be getting back to our hotel."

"I'd give you a ride but I have an important appointment," Carlos said.

"Sure," Tad said in a subdued tone. "Well, I'd say you gave us a lot to think about."

"My pleasure," Carlos said, his dazzling smile once more in place.

On the way down in the elevator, Tad looked depressed. "What do you think?" he asked, after we climbed into a taxi.

"I think we got told to pay up or ship out. What do you think of Carlos now?"

"I think even if he believes that crap he mostly wants power. He admitted that to me once. He doesn't use fancy words but he's mad as hell at the way he's been treated all his life, and he'll take any help he can get to get even with the bastards."

"Which bastards?"

"Anybody's a bastard who won't do what he wants." Tad paused and shook his head. "No, he's more than that. I think he really does feel sorry for the farmers. And the people who run this country probably are a bunch of bastards."

"Hell, *all* countries are run by a bunch of bastards. That's almost a law of nature. And all sailors feel sorry for all farmers. That's one generality you can believe. God, I got a headache. Political talk always gives me a headache . . . Well, old Carlos showed us his muscle, all

right—though I wish it had come without the bullshit.
I'll try to get Seymour to buy him off. I still don't know
how big Carlos and his friends really are, but they know
too much for us to ignore them. As far as we're
concerned, they're probably the most dangerous men in
this whole damn country . . ."

15

Seymour woke me up at nine the following morning, but for once I had had a good night's sleep.

"Sorry to bother you, Andy, but we've got to talk," he said briskly. "Come to my room for coffee."

I put on my bathrobe and went in without bothering to shave. Because he was nattily got up in a blue pinstripe suit, I felt disreputable, but I didn't really care. Somehow

I was still feeling a lot of Tad's anger at him, along with a fair amount of my own.

The sunlight was very bright and I sat at his desk blinking as he handed me a cup of coffee and offered up a sweet roll.

"Thank you for helping me with Tad the other night," he said. "I can't do a thing with him."

"Just take it easy. One step at a time . . ."

"I have an important meeting today," he said. "Usually I'll want you to go with me as a sort of bodyguard, but this is an important official and we're going to the best club in the country, so I guess I'll be all right. I'll give you the address and phone number. Check on me if I'm not back by three this afternoon."

"That could be hard—"

"Call the police if you have to. We're still perfectly legal."

"Seymour, if you're going to do business, there are some things you should know."

"Such as?"

"There are some people who will want to be cut in on this deal and it may be wise to spread the wealth a little. I don't want any more enemies than necessary. So far, there are only three of us—"

"Wrong. I have important friends here."

"That may be, but we still may have enemies, and with the profits we stand to make, it might well be wiser to buy them off instead of—"

"Are you talking about this guy Carlos?"

"Among others."

"From what you tell me, he's just a small-time hoodlum who makes a racket of scaring small-time

Americans who come down here trying to buy drugs. We're not small-timers."

"Maybe that's our weakest point. We're attracting a hell of a lot of attention. You can't keep secrets down here—"

"With what I've got behind me, it probably won't matter."

"Seymour, I suspect there's more than one power center down here. We may have to deal with several, and I'd rather grease a few palms than—"

"I thought you always fancied yourself some kind of natural fighting man."

"Maybe I'm that stupid, but if I am a fighting man, I'm the kind that doesn't like to fight until he can win. I got no troops."

"Maybe I do. I'll have some of my friends check up on this Carlos. If he really has power, we may have to deal with him. If he's just a small-time thug, as I suspect, maybe we can take care of him in other ways."

"Seymour, even a small-time thug can talk if you make him mad enough. Carlos obviously has good enough sources of information to know we're involved in something big. And I know he has revolutionary friends—"

"His main source of information is probably Tad, damn him. And anybody can have revolutionary friends. Even I have a few."

"I think Tad is being pretty smart about this."

"Good. Remember . . . I may have troops on our side—trained troops."

"You've got the government in our corner?"

"I'm not saying that. There are lots of trained troops in

South America, some for governments, some against them. And because of the political situation, there are a lot of armed guards, regular private armies, working for big corporations. Why do I have to keep explaining to you, Andy, that I deal at the top?"

"Okay, but where you've got a powerful top, you usually have a powerful bottom. Carlos could alert the whole waterfront to our deal. He could even alert the whole Caribbean. This trade has brought piracy up to date, and maybe it's making revolutions profitable. If the word gets out, our voyage home could be a run through a very long gauntlet."

"God, Andy, I didn't know you'd scare so easy. I'll make sure we find some way to get away from this coast. If you're as smart as I think you are, you'll head for Europe before you circle home. How in hell are a lot of small-time pirates going to find you?"

"I'd rather leave with as few people after me as possible. If it costs us a few million out of five hundred million or whatever, so what?"

"You don't have to put together this package. The profits may be high, but right now *I* have to handle the costs."

"We could pay in cargo."

"Andy, are you arguing *for* this guy Carlos?"

"I'm arguing to stay upright. A few extra corpses here and there mean even less in South America than with your oak-tree corporations, Seymour. It doesn't pay to get too greedy."

"Andy, no one is more pragmatic than I. I'll have this Carlos checked out. If he really is a threat, we'll do business with him . . . Andy, relax, your job is transportation and defense when we get to sea. The rest is up to me. And if I do say so, I've been doing pretty well. Trust me."

I said nothing.

"And keep Tad in line—I worry about him. I'll be back for dinner."

Taking an attaché case from his closet, he walked out of the room, looking like a good banker on the way to one of the usual meetings of his board of directors. I went back to bed, hoping I could sleep until Esky called.

I had barely closed my eyes, it seemed, before the telephone rang. I jumped for it. The operator said in Spanish that she had a collect call for Señor Anderson from Señor Eskimo. There was a lot of buzzing and crackling before the deep, exuberant voice of Esky said, "Andy, how the hell are you?"

"Damned if I know. Esky, how soon can you fly to Bogotá?"

"With or without an airplane? If you got an oil king's yacht waiting for me, I'll take off all by myself. Do you really have a good job lined up for me?"

"Fly down here and we'll talk about it."

"I ought to tell you that I got a pretty good deal here. Three grand a month for the racing season. Can you top it?"

"Yes. Get a leave of absence. After you talk to me, you can make up your own mind."

"You can't talk on the phone, eh?"

"Right."

"If you think I ought to drop everything here and come, I'll do it. I trust you, Andy . . . By God, it'll be great to see you anyway. Any chance we can ship out together?"

"A chance."

"Must be a bloody big yacht to need the two of us. I'll check on the plane schedules and call you back."

"I'll meet you at the airport," I said. "Esky, this is some deal—a man needs a friend."

"You got one—especially if there's money in it," he boomed.

Only about fifteen minutes later Esky called to say his plane would be due in Bogotá at one-thirty the next morning.

"The ticket's going to wipe me out," he said. "Can you pay me back as soon as I get there?"

"No problem. Don't worry about money."

"Man, I've worried about that all my life. How am I going to quit now? Have you quit worrying about money?"

"Not quite." My voice sounded tense, even to me.

"Well, I'll help you worry. Hang on. When you got the old Eskimo on your side, you got no more troubles."

Though it didn't make much sense in my situation, I somehow felt that was true. Glancing into Tad's room, I saw that he had gone somewhere. That worried me, but there was nothing I could do. I took a good hot shower and went down to the dining room for lunch. Once in a while, at least, I had to escape those rooms.

At the main desk I stopped and picked up my mail. There were three letters for me from Pattie. She had been writing regularly and I had found her expressions of love and descriptions of life at home even more painful to read than they were reassuring. Her pale pink stationery bore the faint scent of the lilac sachet she used—to keep the one desk on the old ketch clear for me, she had kept her writing paper with her clothes in a drawer. There was something especially innocent, poignant, about that fragrance, like Pattie's words themselves . . .

"I miss you so much and live for the day when you'll come back. The kids miss you too—you've already become more of a father to them than you know. Tommy was home for the weekend and loves his school. He wanted to know if I'd heard from you and I showed him your cards.

"I can't help wishing you had time to write more, but I know you must be very busy down there. I guess that 'nursemaiding' Tad would be enough to drive anyone crazy. I respect and love you so much for taking such a job for the sake of all of us and our future . . ."

Just the look of her small, neat handwriting was enough to conjure up the feeling of hard-earned sanity, unaffected, uncomplicated love, complete honesty. I was becoming more sure every day that hers was a world I should never have left, and the feeling was rising in me that, win or lose on this deal, I would never be fit to live in that world again. Since I couldn't tell her the truth about much of anything, it was very hard for me to answer her long letters. Lying on paper to her was no easier than lying in person. The words would not flow from my pen and I had to make do with flip comments on funny postcards, ending with "Terribly busy—will write soon."

After mailing cards to her and each of the kids, I felt very down. Too tired to run in the park, I took a long walk through the sunny Spanish city, hardly seeing anything beyond my own dark thoughts. I hadn't had a drink in seven years, but the results of a few of my old binges were easy enough to remember, even if alcoholic blackouts had mercifully obscured the details of most of the horrors themselves. Other people had lost weekends, but in the old days I'd lost a few weeks and even a few months. I'd been capable of walking around and looking sober enough to escape arrest even though I had no idea of what I was doing, or at least nothing I could remember when I finally sobered up. Apparently I had obeyed odd subconscious impulses, and I had liked to travel a lot when I was drunk. As a yacht deliveryman I had had an air-travel credit card, and when I sobered up I sometimes had to wait for the bill to see where I'd been. Once I woke up in a hotel in Mexico City without any idea of how I had got there—I'd started drinking in Miami. When I heard people talking Spanish, at first I thought I was still in Miami and asked a taxi to take me to my apartment. It took me about ten minutes to believe that the taxi driver wasn't crazy when he said that no such street as mine existed. I almost called the cops.

Why had I decided to go to Mexico City, where I had never been in my life? For years I'd tried to answer that one, and the only thing I could figure out was that my father and mother had gone there on their honeymoon and had often told me how beautiful it was. My mother had once jokingly told me that I had been conceived in Mexico City and must therefore be part Mexican. Maybe in my drunken daze I'd thought I was going home. At the time I didn't have any other explanation. Or even any other real home.

Some of my worst binges had led to acts that didn't

254

seem so innocent. Once I woke up naked in a hotel room in Chicago. I was alone, but someone had taken my clothes—all of them, including my wallet and identification papers. I was, as they say, naked and alone in a strange city, but that bothered me less than what I had done to make someone treat me like that. Who? Probably some woman I'd picked up, but would even the worst whore do that to a man without some provocation? My foggy brain had given me no answer. I had called AA and they sent a man to get me. I was wrapped in a sheet when I opened the door for him. He gave me his galoshes and his overcoat and walked through the snow shivering while he took me to a hospital. That was the first time I hallucinated and convulsed. Without hospital care I probably would have died . . . Once I woke up to find myself lying between a husband and wife in a big bed in a neat little house in Huntington, Long Island. We were all nude. I didn't know how I'd got into their bed or to Long Island—my last memory had been of a party in Manhattan. After one glance at my sleeping host and snoring hostess, I knew only that I wanted to get the hell out of there as fast as I could, and I had a big worry that my clothes would be missing again, as they had been in Chicago the previous year. To my relief, I saw my suit hanging on a nearby chair and my other clothes mixed in a tangle of theirs on the floor. Trying not to wake them, I crept out of bed.

"Where are you going?" the woman suddenly asked.

"I've got to get home."

"Why? Let's have some coffee and do it again."

Do what again? I was afraid to ask. Dressing in a rush and stammering out apologies, I ran for the door and up that suburban street, frantically waving my thumb at every passing car.

Obviously almost anything would be better than drinking my way into more nightmares like that. Maybe a movie would help. They'd been the narcotic of my youth.

The first one I came to was in a dingy theater in a very poor part of town. *Robin Hood* was the feature, a very old film indeed, and to my astonishment, I saw that it starred my childhood idol, Errol Flynn! Here at last was an old friend of sorts, the dashing celluloid hero of my youth, his handsome face and stalwart figure unscarred, as they say, by time. I bought some popcorn and sat near the front row, just as I'd done as a boy, getting as close to the action as possible. Errol was talking Spanish here and so were all the other characters, Little John and Friar Tuck—a whole family recaptured, almost. Errol was stealing from the rich to give to the poor, bless his heart, the way I'd dreamed of doing when I first saw this picture so many decades ago.

Maybe I still could give to the poor—a few paltry million or so. Maybe that would relieve the burden of my guilt and make Pattie love me, even after I'd confessed. And was smuggling really stealing? From whom? Everybody would get rich or happy in this deal and no one was robbed. The Indian peasants who grew the coca leaves and the people who processed them were all being given a market. A whole group of middlemen would get rich, and as for the people who sniffed the stuff, well they got their escape, and they were hardly innocent poor street kids, I reminded myself. Who was I to make a decision for rich people who chose to use cocaine?

So who *was* I really hurting? Maybe a few hijackers

would get killed, but they would be the thieves, not me. A man has a right to defend himself, hasn't he?

Except no matter how I tried to reason it all out, I still felt guilty as hell. It was a relief to turn my attention to the movie. To Errol up there on the screen in his green suit. No fear marred his happy smile. No guilts. After a while, I was Errol and all was well in Sherwood Forest.

I saw *Robin Hood* halfway through the second showing before I came to and remembered that I'd agreed to have dinner with Seymour.

Back in the hotel I found Seymour and Tad in the living room drinking martinis together. For the moment, at least, they looked surprisingly companionable, perhaps they had not been together more than about two minutes.

"Good timing, Andy," Seymour said. "I just got in and so did Tad. Can I get you a ginger ale?"

Seymour often said he admired me for giving up booze, but there was always something a little patronizing about his tone when he offered me ginger ale.

"Ginger ale will be fine," I said.

"What did you do with yourself today, Andy?"

"Went to a movie."

"How about you, Tad? You have a good day?"

"As a matter of fact, I did. I went to the American library to look some stuff up. I met an interesting girl."

"A girl, eh? Well . . . that's *good*."

Tad obviously felt the tone a slur. "She's an interesting person," he said. "I've asked her to have dinner with me tonight."

"What sort of girl is she?"

257

"A student. Nice. Idealistic. I'd forgotten that people like her even existed."

"Well, don't burden her with secrets, Tad. It would be neither wise nor kind to do that."

"Dad, do you *really* think I'm an idiot?"

"Sorry, but I got some information today that doesn't exactly make me think your judgment is infallible."

"*What?*"

"That pal of yours, Carlos—a friend of mine knows about him."

"So . . . ?"

"Carlos' father was sort of a poor relation of one of the old families here. He married an English tramp who came through here dancing in the nightclubs. They drank and drugged themselves to death before they could get into serious trouble, but Carlos is more enterprising. It seems he started as a tourist guide. A lot of damn fools asked him where they could buy drugs so he became an agent, as he says. That part's true on a very low level. He found he could scare the gringos with a lot of talk about pirates and soften them up for all kinds of deals. The authorities kept track of him but didn't bother about him much until he got into politics. He's sort of a half-ass revolutionary. I can arrange to have him picked up any time I want if he gives us any trouble."

"So you think that's all there is to Carlos?" Tad said.

"A cheap hood with delusions of grandeur—that's what my friend called him. He's going to have him warned to stay away from us."

"I think that's a mistake—"

"You know more about him than the authorities do?"

"I'd rather keep him our friend if we can."

"His *friendship* would cost a very great deal."

"I think he's trying to get money for his political cause, whatever it is. I think his tough hood bit is a cover for his politics. If he found he couldn't get a lot, he still might take a little. His people are pretty desperate."

"I bet. And if you gave him a little, you'd just be showing weakness and whetting his appetite for more. As a businessman, Tad, I've had to learn how to deal with people like that."

Tad shrugged. "I'm just giving you my opinion."

"Try to learn, Tad. Tell your friend Carlos to go straight to hell—tell him that comes from me. Then see if he does anything. If nothing happens, will you at least concede then that your old man sometimes knows how to deal with people—?"

"That's one thing I'll never concede," Tad said, got to his feet and went back to his room, slamming the door behind him.

"Well, I struck out again," Seymour said, rubbing his eyes wearily, then got up and mixed himself another martini.

I said nothing.

"What do you think, Andy?"

"I'm not going to get between you and Tad."

He almost looked disappointed, as if for once he had really wanted my advice, but he let the subject drop. "Did you hear from your friend, this Eskimo character?"

"I'm going to meet him at the airport at one-thirty."

"Good. I may not know how to handle my son with velvet gloves, but I think I do know how to get things done. Some spec sheets for more trawlers came in the

259

mail today. Look them over, make your recommendations, and send your friend to inspect one. I want to get moving. My business deals are shaping up fine. The longer we delay, the more talk there'll be, the greater the risk of something going wrong. Tell your Eskimo to get that ship here pronto."

16

Esky's plane was more than two hours late, and I must have paced ten miles in the airport, trying to keep away from the bars. That nervous tension was turning into a premonition of disaster that got worse every time I tried to reason it out. I should probably explain the entire situation to Esky before asking him into it, I decided. It wouldn't be fair to ask a man who trusted me to walk into a maze like this blind. Of course I'd have to take the risk of his talking, but I had to follow my own instinct sometimes, and what was one more gamble added to so many? What I needed most was somebody on my side.

I saw him coming through the gate, a low mountain of a man carrying a seabag on his shoulder. I was so glad to see him that I gave him a bear hug, and he reciprocated by lifting me about a foot off the floor, all two hundred and twenty pounds of me.

"Andy, you old bastard, you're light as a feather! You must not be eating right."

"There's been enough going on here to drive me off my feed, Esky, sure enough. I'll tell you when we get in the car." I had rented a new Ford. I still thought our hotel rooms might be bugged, and I wanted to talk to Esky in private.

"Okay, so now what's the deal?" he said, as soon as we got into the car. "Is it drugs?"

I felt foolishly relieved that he'd guessed, as if it lifted some moral responsibility for him from my conscience.

"I didn't see why else you'd be in this godforsaken place. How safe do you think your deal is?"

"I guess nothing like this is safe, but we're dealing with top people. Seymour Clayton himself, and his son."

"How much is in it for me?"

"A hundred grand for the voyage to Maine, half here and half when we make it."

"I accept. Man, I been so flat-ass broke I haven't been drinking nothing but beer for months. I been making good money lately, but I'd piled up some big debts."

262

"There could be a lot more money in this . . ."

"More than a hundred grand? There ain't more money than that in the world, is there?"

A cop patrolling the airport parking lot looked at us curiously and flashed his light at our license plate. I had no reason yet to fear cops, but I felt uneasy and drove away. Soon I was in the midst of the regular Bogotá grand-prix traffic race, with taxis swerving all around me.

"Wait till I find a quiet place," I said. "We got a lot to talk about."

The modern highways leading from the airport offered no quiet places. I saw a sign that said "Shrine," and thinking that that might be quiet, followed the arrow. We started up a road that wound up a steep mountain. After what seemed a long time we came to a parking place that provided a view of the city, which spread out like a sea of lights beneath us. This was something of a lovers' lane, I realized, because several cars were parked near the rail. I stopped my car at the end of their row.

"I won't go all the way," Esky joked, but I was too wound up by now to even pretend to laugh.

"Esky, we're talking about at least a five-hundred-million-dollar cargo."

"You ain't kidding, are you?"

"Nope."

"It must be gold."

"Nope. Cocaine, at least thirty tons of it. If we can't get that much we'll have a mixed cargo, but even good grass goes for a million a ton."

"How big a ship?"

"About a hundred-ton trawler—we want you to buy

one for us."

I told him the whole deal then, keeping nothing back. He said little and asked very few questions. When I was about halfway through, he reached back to his seabag and took out a pint of vodka. He took off the cap and held it toward me.

"Get that stuff the hell away from me," I said.

"Sorry, I forgot." He took a swig and put the bottle back in his bag.

It took me a good hour to tell him the whole story, including the friction between Seymour and Tad and the business with Carlos. "What do you think?"

"The first thing I think is that they got you all wound up. Man, it don't sound so complicated."

"How come?"

"For once in our lives we got a chance to make some big bucks. All I'm supposed to do is pick up a trawler in New Orleans and bring her to the Colombia coast. I can do that easy alone. You're going to meet me there on a ship with the cargo and the rest of the party. We'll use big life rafts to transfer the people and cargo if the weather's bad. Then we go to Red Rock Cove in Maine. If anybody tries to stop us, we'll try to stop them. What's so complicated about that?"

"Things can go wrong—"

"But what have we got to lose, old buddy? If we get caught, we'll probably get fined—"

"We could also get killed," I reminded him.

"So then what have we got to lose? The tail end of a boat bum's life. A few years of damn poverty. Would they be so hard to lose?"

"Things were starting to go good for me—"

"Think how much better they'll go when you got a few million bucks."

"I'll split with you, Esky. Right down the middle. God knows what my share will turn out to be. I'm supposed to be in for a third . . ."

"Hell, you shouldn't have to split with me—you planned the whole thing. I'll be pleased to take a lousy million off you, though."

"What will you do with it?"

"Hell, I've *always* known what I'd do if I had a million dollars."

"Build your own ocean racer."

"I used to dream about that when I was young. I got pretty tired these last few weeks, wrestling in all those bloody sails. But my ocean racer was going to come after the main part of my dream."

"What's the main part?"

Esky reached back and got his bottle again before answering. He took a sip and cradled it in his lap. "I'm going to get me a plantation somewhere, maybe Argentina, maybe Brazil, maybe the South Seas. I'm going to hang me a hammock between two coconut trees right on the edge of a beach. Then I'm going to stock my plantation with bananas, booze and bare-breasted women. And there, old buddy, I'm going to spend the rest of my life, which will be happy, if not necessarily long. I ain't joking, I aim to do it. And them bare-breasted women are going to be white, black, yellow and red. I ain't got no racial prejudice."

"How many?"

"Two of each, and no other men allowed on my plantation. I'll pay the women well—I hate unwilling

265

women. A special prize, maybe a thousand bucks, will go to the one who spends each night with me. I want them fighting over me and *wooing* me. Man, I been fighting for women and trying to woo *them* all my life. I aim to finish my years with them fighting over me and trying to please me."

"Some son of a bitch will try to break into your paradise."

"Andy, you're a very negative thinker. I'll buy me some big dogs, Eskimo dogs, naturally."

"Aren't you going to try to make any more practical plans than that?"

"Man, the thing to be practical about is not how to spend the fucking money but how to get it. You and I got business to do. We got to get duplicate charts with positions A, B, C and like that worked out on them, so you can tell me where to meet you. We got to work out a radio code. And what idea have you got about getting ourselves ready to handle hijackers?"

We talked half the night, and most of the next day we spent in the car, making detailed plans. Esky had so many good ideas about this smuggling thing that I suspected he'd been in it before, though on a much, much smaller scale.

"There's no problem about radio codes," he said. "We'll use the old international code for flag signals. Since everybody got radio telephones, most people have forgot that the old code for flag signals even exists."

"You want me to just look up the flag signal for any message and then radio you the letters and the numbers of the flags?"

"The Coast Guard might figure that out. Radio me the page number in the flag code book and the number of the first line of your message, counting from the top. Say you want to ask, 'What's your position?' Say that's on page one hundred, the third message from the top. So you radio me, 'Number one oh oh three.'"

"That's too obviously a code, and we're not supposed to use codes on RT," I said.

"So when you contact me, I'll say, 'What's Mary's telephone number?' And you'll say, 'Plaza nine-one oh oh three.'"

"Maybe this is too simple," I said.

"So double all numbers. By the time anybody figures it out, we'll be long gone. We're not dealing with hotshot code breakers."

"What if I want to say something that's not in the code book?"

"Practically every conceivable message is there. But just in case, we'll get two of those little basic English dictionaries. You can spell a message out word for word by giving me the page number and the number of the word from the top of the page. To tell me you're going to the dictionary, say you're going to give me some stock quotations. That way you can get away with transmitting a lot of numbers."

Esky seemed equally knowledgeable about arming a ship. "Hell," he said, "you can buy semi-automatic guns legally and I figured out long ago how to fix the firing pins to make them fully automatic."

"How did you happen to get involved with that?"

"I shouldn't have to tell you that. How many yachts

have disappeared in the Caribbean, Bahamas and even Florida waters lately? Thousands of vessels have disappeared over the past twenty years or so. Maybe half, maybe two-thirds are due to so-called natural causes, but the number started to shoot way up as soon as all this smuggling started."

"That's just about the time they started to mass-manufacture shitty little yachts and to advertise them as seagoing. I shouldn't have to tell you about seagoing houseboats."

He laughed. "That sure was a blast. But don't kid yourself, Andy. Most of the people who buy those shitty little yachts soon get too scared to take them to sea much. There's a lot of hijacking and plain old-fashioned piracy going on. Just because a lot of crap is written about it doesn't mean there's no truth to it."

"I know, even the Coast Guard admits that."

"So I figured a long time ago that the old Eskimo ain't going to be no two-bit thug's patsy. Whenever I go offshore I take a submachine gun with me. And if I'm on a big rich yacht that looks like it might be a prime target, I take along a few hand grenades."

"How do you get them?"

"Make 'em. It ain't hard."

"How?"

"I empty out a few boxes of shotgun shells, mix the powder with rusty nails or ball bearings and pack the stuff into beer cans. I stick a regular Fourth-of-July firecracker in the top hole of each can and seal it there with any kind of marine glue. I can lengthen the fuse as much as I want by taping together the fuses of more firecrackers, but the fuse that usually comes with one is about right for a good throw."

"I was going to get some sticks of dynamite—"

"That stuff's hard to buy—you need a license. I always try to stay *legal*."

"I don't think I have to explain much about getting ready for this voyage to you—"

"Just tell me where and when to meet you. I'll be there, cock at the ready."

"You don't sound exactly like a virgin in this business, Esky."

"Hell, I've never brought in more than a pound or so of grass. The problems of buying and selling the stuff always scared me. But you can't be flat-assed broke around the waterfront for long without thinking a lot about all that easy money. I've lain awake many a night trying to figure out all these details, just in case . . ."

"Me too, but the closer I get to all this easy money . . ."

He laughed. "Think how hard and how long you'd have to work to make a million dollars tax-free legit."

I did, and it was good therapy. For a while, anyway.

We went over the specifications of the various trawlers Seymour had found out about and decided that the best was a ship named the *Mary Anne*. She was not brand new; she'd made three voyages before her owners defaulted on their payments and the builder in New Orleans reclaimed her. She'd probably give less trouble than a vessel which needed a shakedown cruise and she had all the latest electronic equipment—radar, loran, radio telephone and sideband.

269

"You know sideband?" Esky asked me.

"Esky, I been in this business a long time."

"Some boat bums don't. I like this vessel. She's got two automatic pilots, so I won't be running around like a crazy man if one cuts out."

"You sure you can handle her alone?"

"The only trouble would be in mooring, and I won't even have to do that before you come aboard at sea."

Esky studied the price which was noted in pencil at the bottom of the sheet: $975,000.

"Your people going to stand that?"

"Seymour is only a piker about little things."

"If this ship is as good as she looks here, she's worth it, but do you want me to start with a low offer?"

"Seymour's going to have a lawyer in New Orleans handle the purchase as soon as you inspect her and say she's all right."

"How about the name, *Mary Anne?* You want to change that?"

"It's perfect—very forgettable."

Just before the stores closed we bought some small-scale charts and figured out courses. We saw no reason why Esky shouldn't steer straight from New Orleans through the Yucatan Channel to the coast of Colombia, roughly 2,000 miles, which shouldn't take more than about ten days for the *Mary Anne* with her huge Cat diesel. There was no reason for him to clear for a foreign port, we decided; he wouldn't actually be landing anywhere until we got to Maine, and big trawlers often wander all over the ocean in search of fish.

We penciled a choice of rendezvous points on

duplicate charts and gave them geographical names, instead of alphabetical letters, so we could radio in plain English, "Meet you at Charleston." Although we were going to delay making a final decision until after Seymour, Tad and I got aboard with the cargo, we debated the advantages and disadvantages of several routes back to Maine. We agreed that we should avoid both the Yucatan Channel and the Windward Passage, the usual ways to get around Cuba . . . Those were relatively narrow gaps in the chain of islands where we might be expected and could be easily observed. I wanted to head for Panama, then circle around to hug the coast of Haiti and the Dominican Republic before escaping the whole West Indian chain between Puerto Rico and the Virgins.

"I don't want to hug no land," Esky said.

"I figure we'd mix with coastwise traffic and a lot of other fishing boats. We'd be harder to spot from the air than if we were in the open sea. Some of these hijackers might have light planes."

"Even if they spot us it would take them a while to get a ship alongside us, and we'll change course every night . . . If we are hijacked, Andy, how do you think it will happen?"

"They'd have to use a boat a lot faster than a trawler to catch us. They must figure we'd be too smart to follow a straight course for long. Their boat would have to be big enough to carry a crew that could overpower us real quick—they wouldn't want a fair fight. I figure something like one of the old PT boats or rum runners."

"How about a whole bunch of fast small boats like

271

Boston whalers with three men in each? They could come at us like lightning from all directions at night—maybe in the middle of a rain squall, and there'll be plenty of those that time of the year. Our radar would be snowed by heavy rain and wouldn't pick up fiberglass boats much anyway."

"How would they get a fleet of small boats in position for that if they didn't know our route?"

"If we were spotted going up a coast line, plenty of small boats could be bought or stolen locally up ahead. Andy, you say we're playing for big stakes. A lot of people are going to do a lot of thinking."

"We better stick to the open sea."

"You're fucking A—the old pirates used to take a lot of their prizes from open boats near shore."

"We won't be lying becalmed like the galleons often were."

"No, but in calm water men could board a trawler under way from fast small boats easy enough."

"Unlikely, Esky. They'd have to have shore spotters along every route we could possibly take."

"They may be bigger and better organized than you think. I doubt that a bunch of unorganized pirates could account for all the hijacking that's been going on, all the thousands of missing vessels. Revolutionaries would be much better organized and equipped than simple pirates. They'd probably have radio communication from one country and one island to another. They might be part of the whole Commie thing."

"Hey, now you've got us sailing against Russia!"

"It's no joke, Andy. You say we're going to be carrying a cargo worth maybe hundreds of millions of dollars.

Drugs are an international currency. How many guns would even one million bucks buy? A hundred million is a hell of a lot more money than plenty of these little nations have in their whole treasury."

"That brings us back to Carlos," I said, frowning. "Seymour writes him off as a petty crook, but he is obviously caught up in some kind of revolutionary movement . . . He could set off the whole long fuse."

"Whether it's Carlos or somebody else, with a deal this big you're not going to be able to keep much of a secret anyway. The stuff will have to be carried somehow from where it's made to where it's loaded on the ship that's going to bring it to us."

"Seymour keeps saying he has that part of it taped. He talks about the stuff being guarded by trained troops."

"Do you think you can move thirty or more tons of junk without revolutionaries learning about it? In South America?"

"Probably not." There was a moment of silence before I added, "Carlos wanted to make a deal with us, a fifty-fifty split for his protection, more or less."

"Why should a bunch of revolutionaries settle for half if they can get it all? Andy, it's at least conceivable that Cuba could get into this with a whole navy and air force. I hear Castro's hurting for money. I imagine he could do with a few hundred million bucks' worth of drugs. From the way he shoots his own people, I don't imagine it would hurt his conscience much to gun down a few of us imperialist, capitalist drug runners for the sake of his great cause."

"He probably wouldn't lie awake nights much," I agreed.

"We won't have the protection of our flag, Andy— we got to remember that. No nice American Coast Guard or Navy is going to come on the double to save us."

Another moment of silence.

"Are you *sure* you want to get into this, Esky?"

"Hell, we got to understand the dangers, but I still figure we got way better than a fifty-fifty chance. If we weren't carrying such a damn big cargo, I'd figure our chaces of getting through, once the stuff is loaded, were nine out of ten."

"But we're not talking about being caught by the Coast Guard and being fined. We're not even talking about a fight with a few hijackers. We're talking about a whole damned war, with our one trawler against maybe whole fleets—"

"We've still got a damn good chance to slip through. You know how I really figure this right down in the bottom of my beat-up old heart?"

"How?"

"I've had a pretty good life. Us boat bums had a lot of fun. But I'm already too old to be much good on the foredeck of any ocean racer. I can't keep up with the twenty-year-olds. I'm going out of date, Andy, just like the wooden boats. I think old age can be fun for a rich man, but no damn fun at all for the poor. To tell you the truth, I've often thought about just jumping overboard some dark night with an anchor. I'd take that over sitting around parks on relief. This deal of yours gives me at least some kind of a chance for some good years. I'm *grateful* for it. What the hell have I got to lose?"

I found it hard to answer. I at least would not be alone in my old age.

"You don't feel that way, do you?" he said. "You got a family now and all that."

"Yes . . . you know, Esky, plenty of times I ask myself why I got into all this. Things weren't so bad for us in Lauderdale. I worried about money a lot, but we always managed to get along. I was happy a lot of the time—"

"To tell the truth, Andy, I was a little surprised to find you in a thing like this. I never figured you for the type. Everybody knows I've always been a wild man, but you were always just about the most straight-arrow boat bum there ever was. Old reliable Andy, take no chances. That's why you made out so much better in the delivery business than I did."

"Just a square-head sailor," I said. "My grandfather described himself that way. Just a square-head sailor who wanted to give everybody a square deal. Hell, I never really was that . . . Just seemed to be, I guess. But I had some crazy juices running. Still do . . . But it's been a nightmare for a long time. I can't talk to anybody except you. I can't even talk to my wife."

"If we make it, you can go back to your wife—"

"I get a feeling that nothing is ever going to be the same, even if we make it. If . . . God, Esky, revolutionaries, Commies maybe—we're volunteering to fight a whole war with nothing but one trawler and four men."

"I painted too black a picture. It's a big ocean."

"I'm sorry I brought you into it. You were doing okay

275

on your own out in Frisco. It's not too late for you to go back and forget all about this—"

"It's not too late for *you* to quit."

"I'm in too deep."

"Why? You haven't done anything illegal yet. You haven't crossed the line. You won't have crossed the line until you load the stuff on that trawler and take command."

"I couldn't let the others down."

"Are you going to get into drug running for a Boy-Scout reason like that? You've done your part of setting this thing up. I can take that ship anywhere in the world without your help."

"Unless you have to fight—"

"Hey, Andy, I know you're one hell of a fighting man and all that crap, but if we're caught by the kind of opposition I think we may get, what good is one more man going to do? You'd go under just as quick as any of the rest of us if we got really jumped. Do what you want to do. If you want to go home and forget all this, do it."

"Okay," I said, "I'll shut up." I realized my irritation was at myself, not Esky, for my damn backing and filling. I knew all the reasons I wanted to go, and to stay . . . why lay it on Esky? And, crazily, I remembered a great old Jimmy Durante song . . . "Did you ever have the feeling that you wanted to stay, wanted to go? . . ." Except I wasn't lovable Jimmy Durante, and what I was doing went a ways beyond his famous act of breaking up a piano . . .

When I took Esky to the airport for his flight to New Orleans, he gave me his bear hug and lifted me a foot off the ground again in farewell. As I watched his powerful squat figure with the big seabag balanced jauntily on one enormous shoulder go into the throng at the departure gate, he turned, grinned at me and made a funny little open-palmed gesture with his left hand which seemed to me to say, *"What the hell?"*

17

Now we had to wait. We guessed that it would take Esky about two weeks to take delivery of the *Mary Anne*, or some other ship if that one didn't pass his inspection, and about ten days to get to the Colombian coast if the weather was reasonable, but of course any number of things could disrupt that schedule. I had to buy a radio telephone and a sideband outfit. For a few days I kept myself busy doing that, studying the equipment and trying to figure out where to install it. The simplest legal way was to buy a small boat of some kind at Barranquilla, the port where the stuff was to be taken out to meet the trawler. Any kind of craft with a cabin on it that could float inside the harbor could house the transmitters and receivers, but it would be cheaper to put them in a panel truck, and I figured that I'd get much better range from the top of one of the nearby hills than in the harbor. The use of marine transmitters in a car was illegal, but since our aerials looked little different from C.B. stuff, there was small chance of detection.

Seymour quibbled about the cost of a secondhand panel truck, though he approved the purchase of a big trawler without comment. Finally he agreed that buying a truck would be better than renting, because the people who rented cars demanded a lot more identification than some sellers did, and we would have to abandon the car with its equipment in Barranquilla when we sailed. The fewer easily traceable loose ends we left behind us, the better.

It wasn't hard to buy a beat-up Dodge panel truck for cash from a little secondhand car lot, and I was able to register it under a false name without any questions. Small steps toward a vast illegal operation . . . Had I already crossed the line . . . ?

Once I got the radio equipment working, there was not much for me to do. As Seymour wound up the details of our deal, he had a lot of conferences with big-shots in imposing office buildings and seldom felt he needed me as a bodyguard. My main job was keeping track of Tad, which did not turn out to be hard to do because he spent most of his time with his new girl in our hotel living room, and for some reason they appeared to welcome my company.

His girl's name was Faith Parker and I made it my business to find out all I could about her, because Tad obviously was telling her too much about our plans. He assured me she was "utterly trustworthy," but this character judgment did not seem to me to be immediately apparent. My first impression was that she was a big, jolly fat girl in her mid-twenties—rather a sexy one, with enormous breasts which she usually covered only with a partially buttoned shirt or thin sweater. She had an infectious laugh that hardly sounded consistent with her speaking voice, which was much like the Claytons', very upper-class New York, until she got enthusiastic or angry, which was often. Then she got strident and occasionally obscene in a way that was funny because she chose such odd occasions for her earthy spells.

I could see why Tad was so taken by her; among other things, she was the only person I had ever met who could cut Seymour down to size. I was there on the memorable occasion when Tad introduced them.

"Hello, poopsie," she said to him.

He looked startled.

"Any man who can't laugh when he's called 'poopsie' is a real poopsie," she said.

"I see," Seymour said with a determined smile. He sat down on the end of the couch, as far away from her as possible. "Tad has been telling me quite a lot about you," he added.

"He's been telling me quite a lot about you too, poopsie. You should be ashamed of yourself."

"My dear young lady—"

"Now don't get uptight. I'm not really mad at you. If you could just get your eyes off of my tits and onto my face, you'd see that. I feel sorry for you. I want to help."

"That's very kind of you," Seymour said. "If you don't mind, I have some work to do . . ."

Without actually running, he walked as fast as he could to his room. Faith's exuberant laugh rang out.

"He's a perfect example," she said.

"Of what?"

And I soon wished I'd never asked. Faith Parker was a far more serious woman than I'd realized. Indeed she was a fanatic of a kind I'd never met.

"Seymour's an example of a man who's rich but miserable to himself and everybody else, just like my old man," she began. "Of course with a name like Seymour you might think his personality was predestined," she added with a laugh, "but it's largely his own fault."

"I see," I said gamely.

"My whole family is miserable, everybody but me," she went on.

"I'm sorry to hear that."

"Don't be sorry for me. Is your family miserable?"

"I don't think so, especially not my wife, most of the time."

"You may not know her very well. How about your parents?"

"You got me . . . they were pretty miserable."

"And you?"

"Can I ask what your point is?"

"My first point is that almost everybody in the world is

282

miserable. Do you concede that?"

"Faith, that's sort of sweeping," Tad said.

"Shut up, little poopsie. You were dying when I met you. Do you grant me my first premise, Andy?"

"I don't mean to quibble, but I suppose that depends on your definition of 'miserable.'"

"Now don't give me a lot of shit. The poor are miserable because they're poor, the middle class because it's uptight and wants to be rich, the rich because they're afraid they won't stay rich long, and they all feel guilty, bored and worried as hell most of the time without knowing why."

"What are you going to do about it?"

"She *knows,*" Tad said.

"I can hardly wait to hear."

"First of all, we can discard the usual remedies for obvious reason," Faith said. "Most people think they'd be happy if they could only get rich and stay rich, right?"

"That applies to a lot of people, yes."

"Of course that's a ridiculous concept. There aren't enough goods in the world to make more than a tiny percentage rich, and wealth is relative anyway— everyone wants to be richer than everyone else. But the competition for wealth leads to wars, revolutions and crime. Do you buy that?"

"Why not."

"Revolutions never work for long because they just redistribute wealth, and any way they cut it, there's never enough to go around. Right? So we have a world full of miserable people, almost all of whom are hoping and working for something they're never going to get.

They work on assembly lines or walk around trying to sell crap to each other or juggle figures in offices. The men go home to dull, complaining wives and the wives wait for dull, complaining husbands. They raise dull, complaining children and watch *television* together. So millions of people drink a lot. They also buy a lot of grass, pills, all kinds of shit. And governments try to stop them. Why?"

By now I realized this one asked only rhetorical questions.

"Governments are always worried about drug addiction. That's no fun for poor people in a country where drugs are illegal, and it's rotten for anyone who uses crude drugs without medical knowledge. But it's medically possible to keep people happy for years without hurting them. Pure heroin doesn't hurt you until you come off it. Some rich people stay on it for years. With research it may prove possible to keep a person in ecstasy for a lifetime. Maybe we wouldn't even need drugs. Rats prefer a small electrical current delivered to a certain pleasure center in their brain to eating, even when they're hungry. They prefer it to mating. Experiments have proved that—they fix it so the rat can connect himself to the current and make a choice. They choose the current every time."

"Should we all just hook ourselves up and forget our troubles?"

"That concept really bugs you, doesn't it?"

"You have all the answers."

"Look, if it were chemically or electrically possible to keep people in a positive state of happiness, even in orgasm for seventy years, would you object?"

"If someone invented a seventy-year orgasm," I said, "somebody else would write a book saying that one is not enough."

"So go for the joke," Faith said. "If someone offered you seventy years of continuous orgasm, wave after wave of it for seventy years, would you prefer it to life as you've known it?"

"I confess."

"And there would be much less work to do—no luxury goods, just one vast place where people could be kept in the proper state of bliss. Obviously everyone would have to donate a certain portion of his life, maybe five years, serving in a work force that would run the place, grow food and take care of the bare necessities of life for everyone. Others would have to volunteer to raise children—"

"Who'd defend the country if another country attacked?"

"The whole world would have to volunteer to go on this plan at the same time. It could happen if one small state proved it could keep most of its people in constant bliss. Then what would all the struggles be for? That shocks you, you laugh, but dreams prove you can experience anything outside of reality. Neurosurgeons know that the brain can be stimulated in ways to produce any kind of sensation. We can short-cut this damned thing we call reality. We can give people any kind of happiness they want without physical goods."

"No more science, no more art . . ."

"My plan would be voluntary. Anyone capable of making himself happy without artificial stimulation would be free to do it. Maybe just the people in slums, the guys on assembly lines, all the poor suffering souls would opt out of this Goddamned reality into the new world. An end to mass misery . . . Have you got a better idea?"

"Not at the moment."

"Tad talks about his drug run as the greatest crime of the century or something, but the greatest crime of this century really is abandoning hope."

"I think she's right," Tad said. No big surprise there.

"I want to set up a research center to create mass bliss. It's ridiculous to spend so much money on trying to cure diseases which just continue miserable lives. Most of these diseases are probably a symptom of misery anyway. The way things are, a hell of a lot of people want to die, consciously or subconsciously."

"And you think I can help you do something about that?"

"Tad says he's going to give me his share of your operation to get it started. Thirty million dollars or so will go a long way. Twice as much would be twice as good."

"That's Tad's business—"

"I'd like part of your share too. What would you *do* with so much money? Do you have a way to buy hope?"

"I don't think I'll really start worrying about that until I get the money."

"I know—you've got some big odds against you, especially because other people know about this—"

"I hope you haven't been telling a lot of people."

"Hey, it's around . . ."

"Great."

"And I want to get in on it. What better way to start my venture than by bringing cocaine to the people? In the present crude state of science, cocaine is probably the most effective, harmless drug there is. I regard this as a crusade."

"Well, that's certainly a new way to look at it," I said.

"Who's going to do your cooking for you on that trawler your friend the Eskimo went to get?"

"Are there any details you've missed?"

"Tad and I are like one person, our brains work as one now. What he knows, I know."

"You can trust her more than you can trust me," Tad said. "She's strong, Andy. I think she's the strongest person I've ever met."

Well, I thought, Tad had finally found his cause, harebrained though it was.

"You want to go as cook?"

"Damn straight," she said. "Anything. If I know that this trip will build me my research center, I'll fight for it like a wildcat. I'm stronger than most men, fat as I am."

"Have you talked to Seymour about this?" I asked Tad.

"I want you on our side when I do that."

I could imagine how much Seymour would want this lady as a shipmate, all other considerations aside.

"You can tell him that the safest way to shut me up is to let me join you," Faith said. "I am strong, like Tad said, but I have a weakness. I can talk a lot . . ."

"Suppose you joined us."

"I wouldn't endanger our cause for anything. I haven't breathed a word about it outside this room since I realized how *positive* this whole thing could be."

At least she'd keep Tad happy and out of other kinds of trouble, and we could use a cook, and probably the best way to keep her quiet was to take her along. With her

287

sense of righteousness, she could probably throw hand grenades at hijackers as well as any man, and one more on our side wasn't to be looked down on. Even her.

"I'll talk to Seymour about it when he gets over being introduced to you," I said. "Try to get on with him. He put this thing together."

"I honor him for that," Faith said.

All her talk about mass bliss had ended by giving me a headache. Maybe her mass bliss would be better than wars and slums, but it was nothing but a crazy dream and I had my own dream, or nightmare, to deal with.

Right now I wanted to go home and pick up the pieces of my old life. And as more letters came from Pattie, I wanted it more and more . . .

Dearest Andy,

I've had some bad nights just lying there and missing you. I know I'll never drink again, but the temptation kept growing—I kept thinking that you wouldn't know, and I'd get on the wagon again before you got back. So I called Jane, my old sponsor back in Miami, and God bless her, she drove right up in the middle of the night and we talked it out. The AA people have been wonderful, both the old group in Miami and the new one here in Lauderdale. They've been dropping in to see me and asking me out to dinner a lot ever since they realized you were gone. It's wonderful to think we have such *friends* all over the world. I realize you must be terribly busy, but I worry about you. I love your funny cards, but Andy, your heart's my heart, and I feel that something's wrong. Write me a long

288

letter and tell me I'm silly or call me up and tell me not to worry . . .

I called her but my throat constricted when I tried to make up stories. I couldn't get much out and she didn't sound much reassured, no matter how often I said I loved her, which was the only truth I had to offer.

I made a different decision every hour, and really no decision. The waiting was hard and I stayed near the telephone, waiting for calls from Esky. Two days after he left me, he called to say that he had inspected the *Mary Anne* and she was a fine ship. She just needed a few superficial repairs which wouldn't take more than a few days. The lawyer was putting the sale through. Esky was going to fill her fuel tanks, eight thousand gallons, enough to go halfway around the world, because fuel was cheaper in New Orleans than farther north, and he needed it for ballast. The lawyer had approved.

"All the other preparations we discussed are under way and I'll leave on schedule," he said. "I'll get new life rafts. I expect we'll have good fishing."

Faith's steady conversation about doing research to provide mass bliss instead of mass misery for the world got on my nerves and I was glad when Seymour was asked to visit some big-shot who lived in a villa about twenty miles outside of Bogotá. The papers were full of stories about recently discovered revolutionary plots, drug-related murders, kidnappings and thievery.

"I think I better take you as a bodyguard, Andy," he said. "It's not just because of our project. I think that any

289

apparently rich American might need a little protection almost anywhere in South America these days."

He wanted me to drive for him the next afternoon, but the more I thought about it, the more I realized that as a driver I couldn't offer much protection. If we were jumped, I'd either die or put my hands up like anybody else. There must be a way to get some better edge than that. After thinking about it, I suggested that he get two native drivers, one for the Cadillac he had hired for this state visit and one for our panel truck, which could follow him. I could sit in the back of the panel truck, out of sight, with whatever weapons I could devise, and if we were stopped by a small group, maybe I could be effective. At least I'd have a chance for some element of surprise.

Seymour seemed pleased by these arrangements. Evidently he had been more frightened by all the violence reported in the papers than I had realized.

"Andy, you really seem to know what you're doing," he said.

"Don't expect miracles from me, Seymour. The best man alive against more than one is on very shaky ground—"

"Do you want a bigger crew on the trawler on the way home? I've got friends who could send a dozen armed guards with machine guns—"

"And they could take over the ship, couldn't they?"

"They'd be company guards, picked men, long-time employees—"

"Forget the men. Just get me the machine guns. Fifty-caliber if they have them, with plenty of ammo."

"How are you and me, Esky and Tad going to handle

so much?"

"We at least won't have to worry about a bunch of guards we know nothing about hijacking us. By the way, has Tad asked you about taking Faith along?"

"That terrible girl?" He seemed almost to shudder.

"She'll cook and it's one way to keep her quiet. Tad can't keep quiet with her."

"It figured. What do you think?"

"Take her."

"All right, if it will keep Tad happy, and her shut up."

I knew that the girl would be pleased, but when I started to tell her about it that evening, I had an attack of old Andy conscience. Why was I arranging to have this odd dreamer go on a voyage that might well get her killed?

"Seymour has agreed to take you as cook if you want to go," I said, "but do you have any idea how dangerous this operation is?"

"Most smugglers get through. They do it every day."

"Not with cargos this big. We may have more than hijackers after us. A haul this big could be of interest to all kinds of people, whole governments—"

"Maybe I know more about that than you do. Before I got into drugs I was into politics. Well, I have a cause of my own this time. And where Tad goes, I go . . . Say, I still know some of the comrades," she said. "Maybe it would help if I leaked them some wrong information about the course we're going to take."

"It might help; say we're going straight through the Yucatan Channel."

"Where are we really going?"

"I don't know yet."

"You know, after all this talk, I bet this trip is going to

turn out to be easy. In about a month I'll bet that Tad, you and I will be celebrating in New York."

"Knock on a lot of wood," I said.

"I'm not superstitious."

"I'll knock on it for you," I said, and tapped the table. But I'd heard another part of that superstition: knocking on wood for other people doesn't work.

18

I should stop worrying about the distant future and start thinking about my trip with Seymour the next afternoon, I decided, as I tried to get to sleep that night. If I was going to be a bodyguard I should have more to fight with than a pistol. In the movies pistols were marvelously accurate, but in real life I'll take a semi-automatic 12-gauge shotgun every time. I'd seen that some were available in sporting stores. Tomorrow I'd buy one. From now on, it would be a good thing to have in the panel truck.

In the morning the clerk at the store asked to see my passport. No reason why a rich American like me shouldn't prepare to do a little hunting in the hills, was what I hoped he'd think as I showed it to him. Without question he sold me two boxes of buckshot and a Remington semi-automatic which had good balance. The smell of gun oil took me back to the old *Angry Angel*.

After I'd bought the panel truck I found that a tattered set of quilted pads for moving furniture had been left in the back. Since I probably would have to sit there all afternoon and part of the evening, I added a pillow and some blankets from my room, and then threw in a clutter of large cardboard boxes so I could stay hidden if we stopped at a gas station. I also took two almost empty Scotch bottles from the bar Seymour and Tad had set up on the coffee table, emptied them into other bottles and rinsed them out. One I filled with drinking water, and the other I took along for urine. Now, even if we got stuck in traffic for long periods, I figured I could handle most emergencies.

Shortly after I'd lunched alone on a tray in our living room, Seymour came from his morning meetings. He was even more spiffily dressed than usual in a new blue suit he had just bought and he was carrying an attaché case in each hand.

"I hope we're going to reach some final agreements today, Andy," he said, leading the way to the hotel garage where drivers were waiting in our vehicles. Mine seemed disappointed by my shabby panel truck and somehow suspicious, though I hadn't yet mounted the aerial and our radio equipment inside which had been covered with cardboard boxes. The shotgun I had wrapped with its ammunition in the furniture-moving quilts, and there was no reason for him to be alarmed—except that I, this big old American, insisted on lying down in the back of the truck instead of sitting properly beside the driver. The man seemed to be insulted, and kept saying, "Why there?" in broken English. "Why not up front with me?"

Suddenly I had an inspiration. I opened the whiskey bottle I had filled with water, took a swig, and settled comfortably down on my pile of quilts, a big, dumb smile on my face. That he understood and with a laugh started the engine.

"Follow the Cadillac," I said, indicating Seymour's car as we emerged from the garage onto the crowded streets.

"Follow that Cadillac"—the phrase kept repeating itself in my head as we careened around corners in the usual traffic free-for-all. More than ever I felt as though I'd become an actor in some television melodrama. Maybe I *had* turned into Errol Flynn after all, though he had usually been given better dialogue than that. The water in my bottle tasted faintly of Scotch, in my imagination at least, and the cork was still fragrant. After one sniff I decided not to let it near my nose again. Whiskey was not a sophisticated drug, as Faith Parker saw such things, but it could whisk away reality almost as well as the gimmicks and chemicals of her utopia, and suddenly it seemed to me that any dream was better than this business of hiding in the back of a truck with a gun. Sure, part of me wanted to opt out, but no matter what I finally decided on, I had to finish this job I had *today*, which was guarding the life of a man I didn't even much like, whom I had indeed hated, I now realized, during large parts of my life.

"Stay clear of the Claytons," my father had often warned me. "They'll use you and throw you away."

I had no clear idea where we were going, except to a villa of some big-shot friends of Seymour's somewhere beyond the concentric rings of suburbs which surrounded the city. For a while we drove on a superhighway no different from those at home, but the only way I could see out the windshield was by kneeling on the quilted moving pads, and that was uncomfortable. Otherwise, except for a small glass pane in the rear door and the side windows in front, there was no way I could see out of the panel truck. I lay down and napped until I felt the driver slow and turn off the main road. We began to cross a slum area. At first it was not much worse than the poor districts of most American cities: drab, decrepit buildings and littered streets crowded with ragged dark-skinned people, various shades of copper here, but few blacks. Some of them stared with obvious resentment at the big black Cadillac ahead of us and I wondered why Seymour felt that he had to travel in such style. At home he often drove a rather shabby station wagon. People with a yacht and a house like his could afford reverse snobbery when it came to cars on the North Shore of Long Island, but in Colombia Seymour evidently thought he had to play the stereotyped role of a top American businessman, even when that might be dangerous.

The slums got worse as we crossed this strange plain surrounded by jagged mountains. When I had stayed near our hotel, Bogotá had seemed to be a rich city, with slums no worse than most, but here people were living in what appeared to be a giant dump, trying to make homes out of piles of tin roofing and old crates. Even though the temperature there rarely climbed above sixty degrees and a strong wind was sending beer cans rolling down the streets, many of the big-eyed children wore nothing but a few rags around their loins and some were pathetically thin.

The real crime of this century was the abandonment of hope, Faith had said, and I guess I believed that, without knowing a cure. I saw no hope in drugs, none in politics and none in formal religion. Hope for me was just my wife and a bunch of old ex-drunks of all faiths gathered in church basements, trying to take twelve simple steps to sanity.

But hate surrounded me here. On the weathered walls of a tenement house someone had used red spray cans to paint a huge, crude, upraised fist, and that symbol appeared in many places. Ragged people turned to look at the big Cadillac and shouted angrily at it. Faith in the power of hatred—apparently a lot of people had that.

We passed many churches, the only buildings in these slums which were not threatening to fall in on themselves in a heap of rubble. On the crests of the distant mountains we could see the giant crosses which had been erected near the shrines. What kind of faith had moved the men who cleared those mountain peaks for such a purpose? Probably they were just working for wages. The shrines were treated mostly as a tourist attraction now, but still, some of the people who knelt before the crosses must have some sort of hope.

As far as I could see, most people still worshipped money, and lived in hope of that, not heaven. Even, or especially, the rich worshipped money, never mind that it seemed to visit special torments on them. Seymour's whole family probably felt crazy because they had no poverty to blame their misery on. Seymour needed more than any of us ... if his money didn't buy him happiness, more might. In his fashion he was drugged on illusion.

And what about me? I was going to be sitting on a compact cargo worth several hundred million dollars, the illusory answer to almost everybody's most desperate problems, so of course a great many people would try to get it and almost inevitably there would be a fight. It would be Esky, Seymour, Tad, me and a fat girl against the world.

And of course the reason why the essence of coca leaves grown in those blue mountains, the dust of the Andes, was worth so many hundreds of millions of dollars was that so many people in almost every country craved a ticket to a trip out of "this damned reality," as Faith called it, even more than money, it seemed.

My mind went back to those church basements in which we old drunks of all faiths had stood in a circle holding hands and repeating the Lord's Prayer together after confessing sins to each other and asking the help of a higher power to do better. Many of us had been dead broke, but to my initial astonishment, those AA meetings had not been depressing. The people in those church basements had smiled more than the people at bars and nightclubs did, though they also laughed less. The old alcoholics, some of whom hadn't had a drink in twenty years or more, had a curious habit of looking each other in the eye.

For an hour or so, some of us at least got a kind of vision in those church basements of what the human spirit could achieve without drugs and without dreams of wealth. Maybe that vision was what the people who had started all the great religions had had in mind and which their descendants, down through the centuries, tried to recapture in churches, temples and shrines. I had no idea why that vision appeared to illuminate the faces of old drunks in church basements more than I had seen it help communicants in more fashionable congregations, but it had been only at those meetings of our "fellowship" that it had seemed real to me, stronger than booze or any other drugs—a new kind of hope?

Except, I'd abandoned that for dreams of easy money—the greatest crime of the century, indeed—and those dreams were still too much with me to get loose from them. They had me, just as booze had had me once, and I was afraid to go through the convulsions of withdrawal.

And right now a harsher reality of a different kind was surrounding me. We were passing through a public square in which some kind of a meeting was being held and an angry crowd turned from their speaker toward the Cadillac, which was trying to go around them. There were shouts and upraised fists, and a teenage boy threw an empty wine bottle that bounced off the big car's shiny black front fender.

Our drivers speeded up. We skidded around a turn and escaped into deserted alleys. The dilapidated buildings around us thinned and soon we were speeding through a verdant countryside, green fields with tall grass waving in the wind like the sea itself.

My driver turned to me with a grin.

"Marijuana!" he said, with an expansive gesture.

So there we were, driving through an ocean of drugs which didn't look much different from wheat fields. Every once in a while we came to small villages, where people seemed to be living in even worse poverty than in the slums—small, windowless huts made of mud and stone, hard-packed paths instead of side roads, in which a few scrawny chickens scratched among the empty bottles and tin cans. Naked children stood in the chill sunlight and stared at the big Cadillac, which had to slow down and swerve to avoid hitting a dazed-looking goat which limped away on three legs when our drivers blasted their horns. This imperious honking brought a group of ragged men from the biggest of the hovels, which was evidently a bar. For a few moments they danced around the Cadillac as though it were a bull and they were matadors and picadors. They slapped its black flanks with the flats of their hands and yelled at it. One tall cadaverous-looking man tried the driver's door and hung onto it until he was dragged as the car speeded up. After the Cadillac escaped, the crowd turned its anger on my panel truck. Small stones pock-marked the windshield. As the crowd thickened around us, I even considered firing a shot in the air and loaded the shotgun, but the driver worked his way free and speeded up so fast that I was thrown backward onto the quilts, cradling the gun on my chest.

"La hende brava," he said to me, which I took to mean, "the angry crowd" or "the brave crowd" or some mixture of the two. He shrugged, grinned and took a limp

cigarette from a tin that had contained pipe tobacco. He lit it, offered it to me, and after I shook my head, inhaled it deeply. I'd read that marijuana can affect driving ability as badly as alcohol, and he soon started speeding up almost enough to hit the rear of the Cadillac before braking so sharply that I had to brace myself against the back of the front seat with both hands. As the miles of marijuana fields reeled by, he began to talk rapidly between puffs in a mixture of Spanish and broken English. To my surprise I gathered that he was only nineteen years old; his small, tense face looked ageless. He was training to be a jockey, he said, and if he won a few more races, he might not have to be a chauffeur anymore. Some jockeys make big money. A few get to be millionaires . . .

After an hour we started climbing into the mountains. There was no traffic here. We seemed to be the only cars in this world. Steep cliffs, some of which had been blasted into fields of jagged boulders, surrounded us as we negotiated one S-curve after another. It was impossible to do more than crawl on this road. It wound along the edge of cliffs in many places, with no rail between us and a sheer drop into a gorge I could barely glimpse below. The view was breathtaking, no less so than the perils of this torturous road.

We had just dipped into a small valley with great piles of gray gravel on both sides of the road when suddenly all four tires of the Cadillac blew. We almost hit it as it swerved to a stop at the side of the road, and at the same time our tires blew. When I looked through the rear window, I had just one glimpse of a plank with upturned spikes. It was being jerked off the road by a rope which led between two piles of gravel. Looking ahead as we came to a stop just a few feet behind the Cadillac, I saw three men in wide-brimmed hats step from behind another pile of gravel. One was carrying a heavy revolver, one brandished a rifle and the third held a machete. As they approached the front of the Cadillac, its driver suddenly jumped out with upraised hands and my driver quickly followed suit. The man with the rifle walked toward my driver and suddenly struck him on the head with the butt. At the same time Seymour's driver was hit hard with the handle of the revolver, and both men went down. No words were exchanged and except for the sharp *chunk* of the blows, the whole thing was oddly like a silent movie. The man with the revolver opened the back door of the Cadillac and Seymour stepped out, looking remarkably calm. He even forced a smile.

"I'll be glad to do business with you people," he said. Then the man with the revolver gave him a hard shove. Seymour staggered and the men laughed. The man with the rifle headed toward the back of my panel truck and I quickly covered myself and the shotgun with the padded quilts and cardboard boxes.

I heard him open the rear door of the truck and held my breath for what seemed a very long time. Finally I heard him slam the door shut. After waiting what seemed another eternity, I climbed to my knees and looked over the back of the front seat through the windshield. Five in all now, they were gathered around Seymour and the man with the revolver, who had stuck his weapon into his belt, was examining Seymour's wallet. I saw they had just hit Seymour—his nose was bleeding heavily—but he looked more angry than scared. The guy had guts. At

302

least he hadn't called for me and I noticed that he didn't even let himself look at my truck.

Moving as quickly, as silently, as I could, I opened the back door of the panel truck. Carrying the shotgun in one hand and a spare box of shells in the other, I ran behind the nearest pile of gravel, which was only about ten feet to my left. This gravel dump, as it turned out to be, was safer for me than a panel truck with a tank that was still about half full of gasoline. After crawling to the other side of my pile of gravel, I peeked out and saw that the five men were still busy with Seymour. They were shouting at him now, very rapid, guttural Spanish I couldn't understand, and the leader, if that's what he was, hit him across the mouth with the barrel of his revolver. Seymour opened his bloody lips, but no sound came and he still did not look toward the panel truck. His eyes looked very frightened now. The man with the machete produced a coil of rope and they started to tie Seymour's hands behind his back.

They still did not know I existed. My new shotgun held five shells. It made only the smallest click when I cocked it. The men were still shouting and cursing too much to hear. I heard my driver moan from where he lay sprawled on the ground, but if he had recovered consciousness, he was too scared or too smart to show it, and was soon still. The men were standing closely around Seymour and there was no way I could open fire on them without hitting him.

While they hog-tied him and went through his pockets, I tried to decide whether they were just going to rob him and leave him there or whether they were planning to kidnap him. Before I could decide that one, there was more shouting and the leader hit Seymour on the head with the butt of his revolver. Seymour fell heavily and lay at the feet of the men. Which gave me my chance.

All five were in a tight little group around Seymour's writhing body and I aimed at their chests, pouring out all five shots as fast as that semi-automatic would fire. I wasn't even conscious of the barks of the gun. I wanted to make sure I got the men with the rifle and the revolver first, and I killed them fast enough so that they couldn't fire back. There were splashes of blood on their faces before they crumpled. My first shots went a few inches higher than I had planned, but still did the job.

I kept on firing and the other three men fell into a squirming tangle. Before moving from behind my pile of gravel, I reloaded my gun, noting with an odd sense of detachment that my hands were trembling a little. By the time I got the gun cocked again, Seymour was crawling out from beneath the bloody pile. Some of the ones I'd hit were twisting around, and I couldn't tell whether one might have a concealed pistol. No point in taking chances. As soon as Seymour crawled clear, I again emptied the shotgun into that pile. Not all the motion stopped, but now it looked convulsive. After again reloading the gun as quickly as I could, I ran fast, zigzagging through the gravel dump. No one was hiding behind the other piles, but I found a rusty Ford truck parked with its engine still running. By the time I got to Seymour he was still dazed. We said nothing as I helped him to the Ford. We'd have to abandon the Cadillac and the panel truck, I'd decided, in case there were any more of these people in the hills.

"Can you sit up?" I said, as I put him in the seat beside the steering wheel.

"Yes," he gasped.

"Take the gun. I'll go get the drivers."

My driver was surprisingly light. He'd been playing possum, as I had suspected, and came to as soon as I lifted him, but he couldn't walk fast and I ran with him in my arms to the Ford. Seymour's driver was limp and fat enough to give me trouble. I dumped him in the back of the truck, where my driver held his head in his lap. I started to get behind the wheel, but I was still worried that one of the attackers might be conscious enough to take a shot at us as we drove away. Running back to the pile of bodies, I pulled the top ones away and sorted arms and legs out until I found the revolver and rifle. My ears were starting to work again—there were a lot of groans. Twelve-gauge shotguns at close range do messy work. This was not like the movies. There was a lot of blood, tissue, the real horrors of gunfire. The man who had held the revolver lay on his back with his shirt around his shoulders, still trying to hold his intestines in his belly, or had been when he died. I'd never killed anybody ashore before; somehow it seemed cleaner at sea.

Carrying the pistol and the revolver, I got into the driver's seat of the old Ford truck and got out of that gravel dump fast. All I could think of was that those five men probably had friends, and I wasn't sure what the local police would do when they found what I'd done.

"You want to go on or back to Bogotá?" I asked Seymour.

"Bogotá—hospital," he said.

So I started back the way we had come. I wished I'd

305

taken the quilts from my old panel truck to cover the unconscious man in the back of this old Ford when we went through the villages and slums, and suddenly I remembered that I had abandoned our marine radio equipment. That could easily be replaced, but there might be questions when it was found. Making a sharp U-turn, I went back. I hated seeing that gravel dump again, but it didn't take long to rip out the receivers and the transmitters, wrap them in one of the quilts and toss them in the back of the Ford with another quilt for the unconscious man. The bodies were not utterly still; buzzards were wheeling low overhead.

I got started back toward Bogotá as soon as I could. We had gone about ten miles before anything passed us going either way. The first vehicle we saw was an army truck full of soldiers, crawling up in dead low gear, and I wondered what they'd do when they found the bodies.

"Do you want to stop and report to the police?" I asked Seymour.

"Better just let it go."

"Our drivers might report it."

"They didn't see much; we can take care of them."

"Did you use your real name when you rented that Caddy?"

"Yes, but I can take care of those people . . . Everything can be taken care of down here . . ."

He spoke in a monotone and his eyes were dull, his face covered by blood, his own and that of the others. Shock—Seymour had probably never seen blood. I was starting to get the shakes myself. Darkness came before we approached the impoverished villages and no crowds bothered us. Soon after we got onto the superhighway

Seymour's driver came to and sat holding his head as though he had a bad hangover; blood stained his forehead.

"Maybe nobody needs a hospital," Seymour said. "Are you all right, Andy?"

"I wasn't hit."

"You saved my life." He sounded surprised.

"They might just have robbed you and left you by the side of the road."

"They were going to hold me for ransom—that's what they said. I probably would have been killed. My money's so tied up now that no one could get much together for me." He paused. "If they'd taken me, our operation would have collapsed. I haven't got the whole deal signed, sealed and delivered yet."

I found myself guiltily wishing that they *had* taken him, that I'd been knocked out and come to too late . . . then this whole nightmare would have been over . . .

"I'll have to call the friend I was going to see," he said.

I said nothing.

"Do you think those people had anything to do with our operation?" he asked suddenly.

"I doubt it. You said yourself that your money's still too tied up to be available for ransom, and the people you're dealing with must know that."

"Do you think those bastards were some kind of revolutionaries or just simple thieves?"

I wondered if it had occurred to him that Carlos might have been behind the attack, if he was regretting having written the agent off so quickly. But I couldn't decide about Carlos myself and so I didn't bring him up. "I have an idea that the organized revolutionaries, if there are any here, just can't wait for us to take our cargo to sea. Probably those guys were just hungry. Killing-hungry."

"They didn't look too organized," Seymour said, gingerly touching his bruised nose and cut mouth. "They weren't very smart, either. They didn't check out the back of your truck."

"We were lucky." I was imagining dozens of other men swarming aboard our trawler in the middle of a rain squall some dark night. Surprise would be on their side then.

"You saved my life," Seymour said again after a few moments, as though he were trying to make himself believe it. "In the end of this thing you'll be paid more than any reward I could give . . . Meanwhile, you have my thanks, Andy. I don't know what we'd do without you. My part in putting this whole deal together is about done. The rest of it's going to be up to you."

"And Esky."

"I count mostly on you . . . Look, we've all been under a lot of tension. In a few weeks it'll all be over and you'll be able to buy anything in the world that you want. Think about that."

I tried to visualize that house in the tropical garden that Pattie had always admired, but the reality of the fly-covered pile of corpses kept spoiling the view.

"I'll have the drivers take the radio equipment up to our rooms and I'll take care of them," Seymour said. "You better take this old truck away from the hotel and just leave it somewhere."

When we got to the hotel Seymour had the drivers carry the radio equipment to our rooms and I drove the old truck a dozen blocks away from the hotel before leaving it in a vacant lot. The shotgun I disassembled and wrapped in a quilt before walking back to the Hilton. The fact that my fingerprints were all over that old truck occurred to me and I walked back to wipe off as much as I could. I guessed the police wouldn't check too carefully. If Seymour took care of the drivers, who would report the thing? Even if they decided to talk, they'd been knocked out before they saw much.

Of course the Cadillac could be traced to Seymour if he was unsuccessful in taking care of the rental company, but he *seemed* to have friends in such high places . . .

I left the motor of the Ford truck running, as it had been when I found it. Maybe someone would steal it, removing me from any association with those dead bodies up in the hills. . . .

When I walked past the lot the next day, the truck was gone. The five men I had killed—unreported, unlamented as far as I knew, though perhaps some widows and children were weeping somewhere—began to seem no more than one of my many bad dreams. The nightmares of the past worried me less than the ones I was sure would come next.

19

Three days later Seymour told me that his partners had arranged to have a helicopter fly him to a new meeting place, a villa by the sea some two hundred miles away.

"You come with me, Andy. I'd like you to see what kind of people we've got on our side."

"Who are they?"

"That's a bad question. Businessmen. Some from the States, some local aristocracy. A few of the local political leaders may be there. They're . . . learning to trust my discretion."

The chopper picked us up at eleven the next morning. The pilot was a twenty-five-year-old American, a boyish-looking young man who told me he'd flown three years "in 'Nam." He looked as though he took hikes with Boy Scouts on his days off. But then I had thought Carlos looked like an actor or a poet, I reminded myself.

Less than an hour after taking off, the chopper whisked us over a high ridge of the blue Andes and followed a stretch of mountainous coastline, very picturesque, not unlike New Guinea. It descended over a horseshoe bay with narrow cream-colored beaches laced by surf, more like Bermuda or Hawaii. We landed in the middle of a private golf course, and a fancy golf cart with a fringed red and white canopy met us. It was driven by a handsome young black man in a white house jacket and black pants. A West Indian, maybe a Bahamian. He had an English accent.

"Mr. Seglia apologizes for being unable to meet you himself," he said with careful formality. "He is busy entertaining other guests, but he asked me to welcome you and to take you directly to him."

"Thank you," Seymour said, but he looked annoyed. Maybe he judged his status here by the rank of the people who met him, the way I used to when I got off the train to visit him on Long Island. The idea of such an insecure Seymour was new to me, and damned pleasing.

I'd not expected the villa of the people who engineered

312

a billion-dollar illegal operation to look like a retired dentist's Florida beach cottage, but the golf cart took us into surroundings more opulent than anything I'd been able to imagine. A tropical Versailles—formal gardens with fountains, pastel-colored buildings, both old Spanish and modern, with red-tiled roofs, artificial lagoons made to look natural, and a swimming pool almost big enough for a dinghy regatta. The pool was surrounded by a terrace, part of which was shaded by royal palms, a vine-covered dome of metal latticework and the soft green awnings of cabanas which formed wings to what would have been called a fancy bar and restaurant if it had been a public building. The golf cart wound through narrow roads of hard-packed white coral which ran between gardens of scarlet poinsettias and other brilliant tropical blossoms. It bounced right onto the terrace and stopped at the edge of the shade cast by the vine-covered dome.

My eyes had grown so used to the bright sunlight that at first I couldn't clearly see the man who came from the shadows to greet us. Tall, white suit—I had a vision of a handsome and easy-mannered South American aristocrat, and in a place like this, I felt that's the way he should have looked. But as my vision sharpened, I saw that he was much less genial than I had imagined him, older, maybe seventy, and maybe not too well. He had a long, narrow face that was very pale, an oddity in a country where only deep suntans seemed natural, and his eyes and mouth were surrounded by puffy crepe-paper skin. He looked a little like photographs I had seen of old Somerset Maugham, but without Maugham's weary resignation. This man's eyes were not resigned to anything he did not like, and his voice, upper-class

American English with only a slight Spanish accent, was like a commanding general's greeting a general of only slightly inferior rank.

"Ah, my dear friend, Seymour," he said, extending a long, narrow hand. "I apologize for not coming to greet you in person. We have invited so many people here to meet you that my talents as a host have been severely over-extended."

"I appreciate your inviting me to this meeting," Seymour said.

He did not introduce me, and except for giving me a brief, penetrating glance, Mr. Seglia paid me no attention.

I followed Seymour as Seglia took him into the shade and introduced him to a circle of nine men who were sitting in luxurious beach chairs around a low oval coffee table of polished teak. They were not the stereotypes of gangsters or movie-Mafia types. Just such a group of men might be seen sipping cocktails at the Bath Club in Miami Beach or at any good country club. Quiet, thoughtful men, conservatively dressed for the tropics, mostly in tan or light blue Palm Beach suits. Some wore white shirts with subdued neckties, some had expensive-looking open-collar sports shirts. Most were of average height, between the ages of forty and sixty, and their only common denominator was over-weight.

Their names sounded like Miami—that is to say, like all the countries of the world, but mostly Spanish, Italian and Jewish, with a few old English or American clans represented. No good Scandinavian names were included. I was the only square-head smart or stupid enough to be even on the fringes of this group.

They of course didn't talk about business right away, not with a whole troop of black and Indian servants bringing drinks and canapés of lobster and shrimp. They discussed the weather, the stock market, inflation and international politics—all were devoted anti-Communists, and self-righteous about it. How come I hated both the political right and the left, but each side made me sympathize with the other?

Their comments were oddly predictable, and therefore boring, when they weren't discussing their business. I found the striped lizards with quick-flicking black tongues which darted out of the vines overhead more interesting.

I ate a lot of lobster and shrimp and drank cold ginger ale. At least the ginger ale was top quality, dry and with a lot of real ginger in it, probably British. The helicopter took off, circled away and soon came back, settling onto the golf course. This time Seglia got up and walked alone to the waiting golf cart to meet it. Seymour and the others exchanged what I supposed were knowing glances. There were no explanations, but apparently the new arrival was a VIP politically, maybe a high official of the government. I never saw him. A whole train of golf carts arrived to take Seymour and his friends to some more private place for their luncheon meeting.

"I hope you don't mind waiting for me here," Seymour said to me. "They'll bring you anything you want. Take a turn around the grounds. It's quite a showplace."

The canapés and ginger ale had left me with no appetite for more lunch. A half dozen girls with their startling proportions accentuated by bikinis sunned around the other end of the gigantic swimming pool. No older women or children were visible. Either they didn't exist in this place or were kept out of sight.

After Seymour had gone off with his "partners," I walked around this never-never land, detouring around the girls because I didn't like the picture of myself standing there and ogling, and couldn't imagine what kind of conversation I might have with them anyway. Fat men, beautiful young women, an incredible number of black and Indian servants tending lawns, clipping hedges, growing flowers, marking tennis courts—I'd forgotten that this kind of luxury ever existed. It made Seymour's estate on the North Shore of Long Island, even in the thirties when armies of servants had worked there, look like camping out.

This Versailles-in-the-sun of course represented real power over people, both fairly unreined political power and the clout of great wealth in a country where most people were close to starvation. As I strolled around those gardens and palm-fringed lagoons with arched bridges, it seemed as if the breath of power and fear could almost be heard, like the hiss of the irrigation system which bathed much of the grass and flowers in a soft rainbow mist. The gardeners and even the pretty girls I saw bicycling or playing tennis glanced at me with obvious unease, not certain of my status, and seemed to quicken their pace as they passed me. There were a few who approached to ask if they could help me in some way, but it was painful to see how much effort and even fear lay behind their careful smiles. These were not servants who could quit and get a job as good any time they wanted or go on relief, I guessed. Their livelihoods, maybe even their lives, probably depended on their ability to please Mr. Seglia and his friends, a job that might not always be easy to bring off. The atmosphere of fear put a chill on the luxury of this vast estate even in the early-afternoon heat. I tried to exchange comments about it.

"There is air conditioning in all the buildings and a nice breeze by the beach," was the only reply I could get, and even those words sounded uneasy, as though the speaker were afraid he might fail to be hospitable enough to satisfy a possibly important guest. I could almost understand how Seymour had been able to dismiss Carlos and his new-breed friends as petty hoods. There was an undercurrent here that was far more insidious than any of the threats Carlos had voiced.

I returned to the coffee table where Seymour and his friends had sat. An elaborate bar was visible through a glass wall nearby. It was air conditioned enough to make me shiver at first, and no one was there but a black bartender in a white jacket. Feeling as though I'd wandered into some nightclub after closing time, I sat drinking more ginger ale on cracked ice. Lizards pursued flies buzzing against the glass wall, and licked them up with cold-eyed relish. The tiny suction cups in the soles of their feet were pressed flat against the glass, their shiny bellies a pale, delicate yellow . . .

I was bored, and glad when Seymour finally showed up about two hours later and the golf cart took us to the helicopter on the golf course. Seymour looked pleased.

"Everything's going fine," he said to me, as we waited for the boyish pilot to pour cans of gasoline into the chopper, a job he insisted on doing himself, much to the chagrin of an encircling army of servants. "We're going to have top-level support in this whole operation, and when I say top-level, you better believe it."

"That's good," I said.

"You don't sound very impressed. Did you get a good look at this place?"

"I walked around a little."

"My father used to live almost like this, before all the servants disappeared. No one can live like this at home anymore."

"No," I said, wondering why anyone would want to. I'd come a long way since the days when I had envied the Clayton lifestyle, I realized, and in some respects that hadn't been so very long ago.

The helicopter carried us back to the international airport, and we soon returned to the Bogotá Hilton, which was beginning to seem more like reality than anywhere else I'd been lately. When I was hanging my gabardine suit in the closet I saw the shotgun I had wrapped in shirts and left on the top shelf. Those five ragged men I'd shot had probably hated the people I had briefly met today far more than I did. Maybe I'd shot the wrong people. Waylaying a Cadillac and holding a rich American for ransom seemed almost innocent compared to the crimes that had created and maintained that vast estate with its cringing servants and its rainbow mists of irrigation in the tropical sun. But at heart I loved the banditos and the strident revolutionaries no more than I did my new "partners." I wished *I* had a cause I could believe in and fight for. At the same time, the self-pity in thinking of myself as a righteous rebel without a cause, a devout man without a religion, disgusted me. Pattie had told me once that she had felt like a lost person crying in the wilderness until it occurred to her late one night that only damn fools allow themselves to get lost.

"I think I know why you love navigation so much," she'd said to me another time. "You're a man who always wants to know exactly where he is."

At sea that was easy. I still labored under the old sailor's delusion that all the trouble of the world could be left ashore.

20

The shock of our bloody encounter in the gravel dump passed but the vision of those twitching, gory bodies kept recurring for days and appeared to acquire new meanings. It proved that violence could flash from fantasy to reality without warning. Didn't the fact that I'd saved Seymour's life mean that I could quit now if I wanted to? After all, I'd already made a real contribution.

Or did the fact that I'd already killed five men in this operation, whether in self-defense or not, mean that I'd "crossed the line"?

I was lying in bed thinking on all this early one morning, when the telephone rang and brought me out of it. It was Esky.

"I'm running a few days ahead of schedule," he said. "Everything's set for sailing. The weather report is good. I'll meet you at Charleston in about ten days if our luck holds."

Charleston was a rendezvous point we had established fifty miles north of Barranquilla.

"Great," I said, trying to sound enthusiastic.

"Don't forget to keep radio watch at twelve and six every day, both a.m. and p.m.—the agreed-on channels. My nets are in good shape and I figure that the *Mary Anne* is going to make a great haul. Everything's A-okay, all systems go . . . You still worried, Andy?"

"Me worry? What for?"

Esky laughed. "Hang on, old buddy. We're going clear to the end of the rainbow."

"So now we can really get things rolling," Seymour said, when I reported Esky's departure from New Orleans.

"Have you got all the paperwork finished?"

"Signed and sealed. The delivery, so to speak, is up to us. Before we get to that, though, my friends are going to have quite a lot of work to do. Things will move fast now."

"What's the next step?"

"There's going to be one hell of a fire in the Riva plant

322

and warehouses. A lot of cocaine is going to go up in flames."

"Then what?"

"A lot of bales marked 'Morning Mist Colombia Coffee' will be trucked down to Barranquilla and stored under guard in warehouses there."

"Not our responsibility yet?"

"Their responsibility. When Esky reports that he's about a day's sail away, all those coffee bales will be loaded into the holds of the *Señorita*, a little coastwise freighter, and we'll be able to move any time the Eskimo gets here."

"I better pick up another panel truck, install the radio equipment and get on down to Barranquilla. With any luck I can keep in touch with Esky on sideband right along. I should be able to contact him soon."

"Reserve rooms for all of us. As soon as our cargo leaves here, we might as well all wait there. Keep in touch with me by phone. I'll be right here in my room now most of the time."

The shootout at the gravel dump had scared him enough so that he rarely left the hotel alone.

I bought an almost new Chevrolet panel truck this time; Seymour agreed that our operation was too big to complicate with a penny-wise radio car that might break down on the highways and invite police inspection. It didn't take me long to install the equipment with a bank of four new twelve-volt batteries I figured I could charge at night if I could figure a way to park near an electrical outlet. A motel would be good for that. I'd find some out-of-the-way place on the fringes of Barranquilla.

Before I left the Hilton I checked at the front desk to

get my mail. There was a letter from Pattie.

Dearest Andy,

I can't sleep at night because I feel in my bones that you're in trouble. It's no mental telepathy, I've known and loved you for a long time, Andy. I know your voice and I know the kind of letters you used to write when you were on delivery trips and don't write anymore. I love your postcards, but when you just start making jokes, Andy, and refuse really to talk about anything, I know you're badly troubled about something.

I keep trying to imagine what it is so I can try to help you with it. Have you gone back to the booze? I'm not going to yell at you for that, but for God's sake if it's true come home so your old friends and I can help.

Okay . . . this is hard to ask . . . Do you have another woman down there? Is that making you feel too guilty to write? Andy, I'm a grown-up and know it's tough for any man to stay alone for long, never mind an old sailor like you in a foreign port. Give the señorita or señoritas my best as long as she or they treat you decent. But please don't tell me about her, or them—I am jealous and *not* a saint. Lie to me about that, but don't feel guilty about it. I'd rather you go to bed with a woman than with a bottle. And even if you need both, I won't care if you'll just come home and let us help each other again.

Or maybe it's something else. I read strange things about the part of the world where you are now and you've talked to me about Tad a lot. I'm not entirely stupid and I can imagine that things down there could get pretty complicated for you. I know that you've been terribly worried about money and I know I've contributed to that strain with all the burdens the kids and I have put on you. Here, at least, I can give you some help. I've got a job! Mark needed a new secretary and I'm it! The typing-at-home bit was okay when the kids were younger, but now there's no reason why I can't hold a real job. I should have done it long before now, but somehow I was scared of it and I'm a creature of habit. Anyway, I have a regular job now and I think I can do it well. The pay isn't great, but it's enough to pay for Tommy's tuition. Life could be so great if you'd only come home!

I shouldn't beg. I'm sure you know what you're doing—you always do. Maybe I'm just being selfish. I'm lonely, damn it! And I'm not old enough yet to like sleeping alone. The hell with whatever you're doing there. The hell with Seymour and Tad. You're needed here. Please come *home*.

All my love,
Pattie

That letter did it for me. It tipped the balance and caused me to finally make up my mind to walk out of the whole smuggling deal as soon as I could, as soon as I could honorably get out of it . . . God. I was still so confused that I wanted to be "honorable" about all this. I'd killed five men, a fact which still did not seem quite real, but which I couldn't forget. Errol Flynn never seemed to worry about all those men he killed in the movies, but the real Errol Flynn, the poor old alcoholic actor I had known, had had enough sense to stay the hell away from real wars. He had suffered such agonies of conscience every time he got drunk enough to try to sock someone in a bar that he had to get even more drunk, and I doubted whether the poor guy ever actually hurt anyone in his life.

I'd not been that smart, but I was beginning to be. I'd done the whole transportation-and-defense part of their crazy operation together, and in Esky had found them the right man to run it.

There was no need to question my decision, but I began to sweat as I rode the elevator up to Seymour's room. He was sitting in the living room of his suite with Tad and Faith.

"Hey, Andy," he said, "I thought you'd already started for Barranquilla."

"I've got some questions."

"From the look of you, they sound serious."

"They are."

"All right, Andy. What's on your mind?"

"I'm afraid I want out."

There was an instant of silence.

"Andy, we all go through times like this—"

"Let him go," Faith said. "He never really got the vision anyway."

"I'd go along with that," I said. When he asked why, I tried not to say anything phony about an attack of conscience . . . I put it in terms of the odds having gotten too long, lousy security. Seymour said that could be handled by last-minute change of plans, and then he got down to it . . . "I'm not sure that my partners, here or in the States, would let you just quit right now, Andy."

"What the hell can they do about it?" Knowing damn well the answer to that.

"Do you have any idea who I'm dealing with at home?"

"Is the Mafia going to send a hit man after me?"

"Let's just say I don't believe our partners would like the idea of a man who knew *all* about this operation just up and quitting and going home. They could be very dangerous for you. I don't know how they'd work it out."

"That's their problem." Bravado was cheap, or rather *could* be very expensive.

"It would be better for you to quit with the good will of everyone concerned, wouldn't it, Andy? Let me talk to our partners. Maybe we can work something out."

"How long will it take?"

"Say a week—a lot of people will have to be contacted. I'll have an answer before our ship arrives."

"All right." All wrong, but what was the good alternative?

"Meanwhile, please keep up the work you've been doing, go down to Barranquilla and establish radio contact with your Eskimo. Take Tad with you and teach him all about it."

I got up to go.

"Wait a minute," Seymour said. "Tad'll have to pack his things."

"Me too," Faith said. "Where Tad goes, I go."

"Very touching . . . Andy, seeing you've got a few minutes, would you mind coming into my room with me? There's something I'd like to show you."

327

I followed him into his room. He sat at the desk and motioned me toward an armchair.

"There's something I want to show you," he said again, and took a flat case of black leather from the desk drawer. "Colombia produces more than drugs and coffee. Such as emeralds."

He flipped open the lid of the box. An old Spanish necklace was spread over black velvet, shining green stones and gold. It was beautiful, but I said nothing. I could only feel that Seymour was running true to form, had in fact become almost a caricature of himself.

"I bought it for Virginia," he said when I kept silent, "but in her present state I don't think she'd get much pleasure out of it. Why don't you send it to your wife?"

I could visualize Pattie opening that box and putting the necklace on. She'd love it, and it would also worry her. Pattie was no fool, she'd wonder where the money for it came from.

"No," I said, and told Seymour why.

"Your wife has no idea of what you're doing?"

"That's right."

"That's admirable, but what are you going to tell her when you hit it big?"

"I'm not going to, Seymour."

"Shouldn't you give her a chance to have a say-so about that?"

"She'd want me to get out."

"Well, you of course know her better than I do. She has children, doesn't she?"

"Yes."

"How many?"

"Three."

"Education costs so much these days—"

"We'll *manage.*"

"Would you mind if *I* sent this necklace to her, as a gift from me? I can't very well tell her about your saving my life, but I can say you've taken very, very good care of my son."

"I guess."

"And if some emergency comes up, she could always sell it. These matched emeralds should bring enough to send at least one child through college—"

"I *still* aim to quit, Seymour."

"I understand that. Just let me see if I can make the proper arrangements. In business it's always a good idea to keep your partners' good will—especially our partners . . ."

21

As Tad, Faith and I started driving in the panel truck to
Barranquilla, I realized I'd at least promised to keep on
playing along until Seymour could maybe win some sort
of pardon for me. In about ten days, Esky was going to
have that trawler waiting off the coast, and I would either
have to cross the line by taking command of her, or else
have to run like hell to try to get home. Meanwhile I was

supposed to find motel rooms where I could run a wire to charge our batteries and teach Tad how to operate the radios. That all seemed fairly clear . . . if I didn't look at it too closely . . .

Barranquilla turned out to be a fairly typical Caribbean port of the sort I had expected Bogotá to be. It was hot, humid, dusty, dirty and surprising only in that it seemed to be so busy. The wharves were crowded with ships of all kinds and construction was booming ashore. Drugs apparently brought prosperity to some . . .

We rented rooms in a shabby motel on the outskirts of the city and I did my first job, which was to teach Tad to operate the radio equipment. During the days when he had gone as deckhand with me on delivery jobs, he had already learned a lot about it and so didn't need much instruction.

We drove the truck to the top of the highest hill we could find and found a place to park off the road, behind a copse of bamboo. Soon enough we raised Esky on the sideband.

"I'm rolling along with a fair wind, making a good thirteen knots," Esky's exuberant voice boomed. "I'll see you in Charleston about a day ahead of schedule if this weather holds."

I was so edgy that the news that he was coming at thirteen knots seemed a bad omen. Everything about this voyage seemed jinxed.

Now there was nothing for me to do except wait a week to hear from Seymour or make the decision to quit anyway as soon as Esky arrived. I had a mental image of that big black trawler charging through the seas, coming closer . . . Nothing had always been the hardest damn thing in the world for me to do—it had usually been in periods of idleness that my drinking had got me down. I walked around the waterfront a lot, looking at the ships and wishing I were headed home on one of them.

While I was touring the wharves I got an uneasy feeling that I was being followed. A small dark man in blue jeans and a patched blue shirt appeared to go everywhere I went. Of course many of the sailors dressed like that and many of the *mestizo* people looked much alike to my American eyes, but this fellow had distinctive black stains like ink blots on the knees of his dungarees.

Well, if I was being followed I shouldn't be too surprised, I told myself. Seymour had probably told his partners by now that I was a defector. I'd no doubt that organized crime controlled much of the drug traffic in the States, and it would have representatives here, where so much of the stuff came from. Those people would hardly want loose ends lying around in a deal as big as ours. If I quit, a loose end was what I'd be.

Question: Would I be in more danger as captain of that ship or as a defector ashore? Who the hell knew?

I had a week to think that over and try to survive. I decided it wasn't too smart walking around the town, and decided to stick to the motel, loaded my shotgun and kept it near my bed.

But alone in a motel room for a week wasn't easy. There was no air conditioning and little breeze from the window. Tad and Faith kept pretty much to themselves, lost in the dialectics of private and mass bliss. They occupied the room to my right and the partitions were thin. They were a noisy pair, but they at least seemed happy most of the time.

The room on the other side of me was occupied by a thin American girl who worked as a waitress in the motel's bar, and I gathered that she did considerable business on the side with the construction workers and sailors of all nationalities who frequented it. There was a great deal of boisterous swearing and laughing in her room, with assorted thumps and grunts. When the walls of the room started to close in on me I went to the bar and sat sipping ginger ale. At least there were people there, but before long that particular crowd seemed worse than being alone.

In a kind of panic I looked around the room, as though I were locked in a place with no doors. A pretty girl in a black dress gave me a tight-lipped smile, got up from her table and came toward me.

"You sailor?"

"Me sailor."

"Want good time?"

Suddenly she looked very beautiful to me, not more than about twenty years old, a mixture of races, big breasts, narrow-waisted and with a curiously innocent face. Esky had once said that whores in very poor countries are usually much nicer than the ones at home, where girls really have to be crazy to get into the business.

Pattie had told me that she would rather have me take a girl than a bottle . . . Anyway, there was a pretty good chance I'd never see Pattie again. When I'd felt this way during the war, women, any I could find, had helped a lot, and mostly they'd been remarkably kind to me. Hard-bitten army nurses I had met in Hollandia, New Guinea, little Australian shopgirls, even Honolulu whores— mostly they'd seemed to sense the fear and had done their best to help me burn it out. Maybe this girl saw my panic too. I badly wanted to believe that.

I nodded to her. She put her hand on my wrist and I saw that she had bitten her fingernails to the quick, though she'd tried to pretty up the result with red polish, which made her hands look more wounded than ever. I decided to give her a hundred pesos, two hundred, a thousand, who cared? She looked like she deserved a lucky night.

She guided me away from the bar through curtains at the back of that ill-lit room and down a dark hall. The thought struck me that this might be a trap, either one set by a relatively innocent thief or by Seymour's partners. Somehow that didn't seem to matter. I followed her into a dark room where only a little daylight filtered through a small dirty window facing an alley full of trash. She struck a match and lit a candle on a bedside table. The brown blanket which covered the bed looked dirty and empty beer cans littered the floor, but the girl herself, as I saw her in the candlelight . . . wanted to see her . . . had nothing sordid about her. Her tight-lipped smile was a little shaky, as though she were even more scared than I was. She had a right to be; when I looked at her closely I saw she'd tried to cover a bad bruise on her left cheek with powder. Her business was no damn picnic.

"Hundred pesos?" she said.

By local standards that was probably outrageous but I gave her three hundred. She grinned and I wished she hadn't done that. She revealed brown and broken teeth,

335

which for an instant seemed to turn her young face into a death's-head. Apparently her grin had cost her customers, because she quickly pressed her lips together and her eyes seemed to ask me not to turn and run. Quickly she unbuttoned her dress, revealing full, beautiful breasts. When she turned to hang her dress on a nail on the back of the door, I saw that her buttocks were black and blue and covered by bite marks. Feeling weak, I sat on the edge of the bed.

"No like?" she said, standing before me and cupping her breasts in her wounded hands.

"I like."

She knelt before me and started to fumble with my fly. The thought of her shattered teeth . . . gently as I could I pushed her away and stood up.

"No like?" she repeated, and her eyes seemed to be more pleading than ever. She unbuttoned my shirt and unbuckled my belt. I'd lost so much weight that my trousers started to slide down around my ankles. Feeling absurd, I stripped and tossed my clothes to the bed. Seeing that I was not erect, she attempted a little erotic dance, shaking her shoulders and rotating her pelvis. Clumsy and awkward though she was, the very intensity of her effort to arouse me was kind of stimulating and she did have fine breasts. The airless room was hot and her efforts made her sweat. She lay on the bed, held her arms out to me and continued to work her pelvis. When I didn't respond immediately, she parted the lips of her vulva with both hands and grinned at me again, her shadowed face more like a death's-head than ever. A kind of horror wiped out desire. I grabbed my trousers, struggled into them, took my wallet from my hip pocket and extracted a handful of bills that I tossed on the bed. While she counted them I quickly put on the rest of the clothes.

"*Gracias,*" she said. "Want me do more?"

God . . . I started to touch her face, to try to reassure her, but she shrank back and this time her lips parted in a grimace of fear, which was worse than her grin. I ran.

My mouth was dry when I finally climbed onto a barstool, I wanted ice water, or so I told myself.

The thin girl who occupied the room next to mine was tending bar. "Rum?" she asked.

Yes . . . Goddamn it . . . The horrors that surrounded me had gotten to be too much. My nerves were shot, I felt I couldn't get back to my room without a drink.

I nodded abruptly, the girl poured me a shot of golden rum. My hand showed only a slight tremor as I took it and tossed it down. Down . . . down . . . That was my direction . . . I put the shot glass on the bar, motioned for a refill.

"Beer too?" the girl asked.

"Beer too."

The ice-cold beer seemed exactly what I needed, and with the help of a little more rum it refreshed and calmed me. My head stopped feeling as though it were going to explode.

No reason to make a big deal about going off the wagon . . . I'd not been the type to fall into the gutter the moment I touched booze. Sometimes I could drink a month or even two before the need to finish the bottle right away took hold . . . A few days of grace, even a few hours' release from this killing strain, that's what I needed . . . a few drinks would calm my nerves, make it easier to make decisions, afloat or ashore . . . My choice was between two kinds of insanity—the insanity of bursting nerves or of booze. Booze was preferable. I bought a quart of vodka from the thin waitress. The smooth glass felt good in my hands as I carried it back to my room. As I uncapped it I caught a glimpse of myself in the mirror over my bureau . . . an old drunk unable to stay away from a bottle, even after seven years of sobriety. I recapped the bottle, but of course it was already very late . . . My encounter with the prostitute had left me with unsatisfied desire, on top of the pity and the horror, and the booze intensified that. Well, did I want to go to my death chastely, was I trying to be perhaps the first and the last of the chaste drug runners? . . . "I regret I have been so chaste," old Somerset Maugham was supposed to have said . . . "Chaste is waste"—God, I wanted Pattie so much I could almost feel her beside me when I sank down on the bed, but Pattie was a lousy long way away and the conviction kept growing in me that I'd never see her again . . . What was I going to be, the faithful husband, sentimental pirate, true to the marital ideals even in a Barranquilla brothel?

I needed a substitute. Substitute, prostitute . . . Colombia must offer thousands of girls, not like the poor girl I'd just been with. I wanted a girl, damn it, a genuinely pretty girl, maybe two at the same time. What was really wrong with that fantasy that I'd occasionally brought to reality when I was young and too drunk to do much about it? Compared to killing five men in a few minutes a sexual orgy seemed pretty damn innocent. And compared to getting killed . . .

338

Long-buried memories of times in Australia came back to me. In those days there had been deep fear, much like that I felt now. And in the days when the Aussies had been certain that the Japanese were about to invade their country, the girls had shared the fear of the soldiers, and shared fear had often turned into shared love for a few nights at least . . . A girl's room in a garage apartment in Brisbane, or had it been Sydney? My girl and I had the bedroom while her sister and some lieutenant-commander, who'd seemed very old to me at the time, had been in the living room. The lieutenant-commander had drunk so much that he passed out. We had, of course, all been drinking, but the rest of us had been young enough to last longer, and it had seemed very logical, as well as funny, for the three of us survivors to wind up in the same bed. In the morning we all had hangovers, but they hadn't been bad enough to keep us from trying all the various combinations again. I'd ended by spending two days with those sisters, and when I left them to go back to my *Angry Angel* in New Guinea, we'd vowed to be friends forever, a new kind of liberated friendship before the sexual revolution even began.

Of course I never saw my sisters again, but now, in my new fear, I wanted them here, *now*, and the thought that they were in their fifties or sixties if they were alive at all seemed a very cruel joke.

Time had been wasted, my sisters had been turned into old women, but I, more the fool, still had the illusion of eternal youth, and substitutes, prostitutes must be available in this place. Not the girl with wounded fingers and the death's-head grin. Not the thin waitress who lived next door and tended bar, but she would know

339

where I could find what I badly needed . . .

I decided to ask her, but my legs wouldn't work right. Suddenly I heard heavy footsteps in the corridor outside my door and fear drove away desire. The footsteps echoed down the corridor; they would return, I was sure. It was too late for the relief of a woman—my time was running out. I saw scar-faced Italians in New York packing automatic pistols in briefcases to go out on a routine assignment: tying up a loose end. Me. Oriental-faced *mestizos* were prowling the waterfront here with knives hidden in their shirts. The thin-faced waitress probably worked for them—she always knew where I was, they'd planted her in the next room . . . I deserved it, I'd gunned down five men without giving them a chance to surrender . . . the squirming pile of bodies seemed for a moment to exist in my room. Flies were crawling on open, staring eyes.

I buried my face in my pillow, found my mouth full of feathers—I'd chewed right through the slip. Spitting out feathers, I sat up, and laughed. A mouthful of chicken feathers, for God's sake. I saw a streak of blood my cut finger had left on the bed. It seemed to spread, the whole bed appeared drenched in it and I was dripping with it.

I had to wash off the blood, I ran for the shower. I got cold water first, which shocked me back into a little sanity. I thought I heard Pattie crying. It was me . . . I got into bed, sweating and shivering. Time seemed to stand still—like in death. Was I dying? I hoped so. . . .

I have no idea how long I lay there, my muscles rigid. Gradually I began to calm down a little, but I still had a decision to make. I'd better make some plans for running.

As soon as Seymour's friends found that I had actually gone, they'd be sure to send people after me. Or already had.

The trouble was that I could not calm down enough to think. On the way back to my bed I saw the bottle of vodka on my bureau. It seemed like an old friend, and I grabbed for it. Alcohol would give me a few calm days at least, which was priority for me now. My hand shook a little in anticipation as I poured just one little shot of vodka into a glass. It tasted oddly antiseptic, but then there was that warm glow and at long last my nerves started to relax. I allowed myself one more drink, a slightly bigger one, before I put the cap back on the bottle. This time I would ration myself. Five shots a day at most.

Now, of course, I was able to think clearly. Lying on the bed, I planned to dye my hair black, dress like one of the visiting merchant sailors and carry a seabag when I went to the airport. Before doing that I'd tell Seymour I'd decided to make the trip with him. Maybe then he'd have his partners call off their dogs and I'd be on a plane back to Miami before they found out my defection. The best time to cut out would be just before I was supposed to board the trawler. Seymour would make sure to enforce radio silence once we all got aboard. If I disappeared at the last moment, he might find it difficult to report that fact and his partners might think for a long while that I'd sailed.

All this seemed very clever to me, and I had one more shot of vodka before I slept. That was only five for the day, after all. No one could say I had had to finish the bottle the first time I had a drink. Good boy, Andy . . .

22

I bought hair dye, some merchant seaman's clothes and a seabag for my disguise. I also laid in a stock of some excellent vodka and Scotch. Seeing this would almost undoubtedly be the last drinking I'd do in this life, one way or another, I might as well have the best. . . .

Five days later, when Esky reported that he was only a two-day run from our rendezvous point, Seymour flew in from Bogotá. The first thing he did when I met him at the gate of the Barranquilla airport was to hand me a copy of an English-language weekly published in Bogotá. On an inside page it carried a story of a big fire at the Riva pharmaceutical plant.

"Two large warehouses went up in flames and a considerable quantity of pharmaceuticals were lost," the reporter had written, "but the laboratories were little damaged. The cause of the fire is being investigated."

"All according to plan, eh, Seymour?"

He nodded and went to collect his baggage. We were followed by two large men who looked like Spanish cops, in spite of their businessman's clothes. At first I thought that they were just looking for their baggage, but they also followed us when we went to the car.

"Don't worry," Seymour said when he saw me glancing over my shoulder. "They're with me . . . I hope you've thought better of your idea about leaving us. I talked to my partners about it, here and in the States, and they were quite upset. After all, you're a key man—"

"I'm sorry I even mentioned that, Seymour. I admit I get down sometimes, but sure, I want to go. I've had enough time down here to think it through . . ."

"I'm very much relieved to hear that. Our partners were so upset about even the possibility of your changing your mind that they asked me to leave these two gentlemen behind us with you."

"That won't be necessary now. I'm *definitely* going."

"They want to make sure of that. And of course these gentlemen can also protect you. This is a dangerous place. Think of our friends here as bodyguards."

"You don't really have to keep me a prisoner, Seymour."

"Not as long as you behave," he said with his bland smile. "Take our friends back to the motel with you. Arrange for cots for them in your room."

"Not much I can do about this, is there?"

"Not much. Oh, I should introduce you."

Stopping just before we got to the car, he motioned to the two men. "Andy, I want you to meet Paul and André. They're very reliable men. We'll have more armed men on the ship to help us. All of them will report directly to me."

"You're the skipper."

"Oh, no. My old title of owner will do. You'll still be the captain. Now if you don't mind, I'll ask you to go back to your motel with these new friends of ours. I'll take a taxi. I'll be staying with a friend who has a villa on the beach, but I'll be in touch every day on the phone."

Paul and André were not exactly great conversationalists. They said absolutely nothing during the drive back to the motel. They inspected my room thoroughly, confiscated my shotgun without a word, and declined the drinks I offered them with a shake of the head. I didn't know they could talk at all until Paul, the bigger of the two, picked up the telephone and asked for two cots. The manager apparently demurred, until Paul barked something in fast Spanish and the cots quickly appeared. André immediately lay down on his and went to sleep. Paul sat in the room's one armchair and stared vacantly ahead.

So that was that. I was going to be put aboard the trawler with the cargo whether I liked it or not. And once

I was there, of course, I'd better do what I could to help the ship survive.

I reached for a bottle of Scotch and poured myself a stiff drink.

It was curious logic, but I figured I'd probably be safer drunk than sober. At least a far-gone alcoholic would present less of a threat to Seymour's partners. And if they loaded me aboard the ship against my will, and if the Coast Guard stopped us, I'd have a cause. I'd been shanghaied. I put on my bathrobe and swiftly tucked a bottle of Scotch under it, holding it tight against my stomach. Since I had kept my back to Paul during that sleight of hand, I doubted he'd seen me. He made no effort to stop me when I went into the bathroom. After turning on the hot water and taking off my clothes, I climbed into the tub, lay down and opened the bottle.

Of course I finished the bottle of Scotch there in the bathtub, and inevitably there must be some blanks in the part of this account which immediately follows. Apparently my guards called Seymour as soon as they found I was dead drunk. I remember lying on the bed while Seymour yelled at me.

"Goddamn you, Andy, you drunken son of a bitch," was the way he started, and then I tuned out.

Once when I came to a little, Seymour, Tad, the two guards and a thin little man I'd never seen before were gathered in a sort of circle around my bed.

"I say throw the bastard in the harbor," the thin stranger said. He had a deep voice, an American accent.

"For God's sake, he can't do us any harm in this condition," Tad said.

"He'll come to eventually, get rid of him now."

"If we can bring him around, he can still be useful to us," Seymour said.

"I can get him sobered up," Tad said.

"Do you trust this boy?" the deep voice said.

"Hell, he's my son," Seymour told him. "We'll be in the restaurant, Tad. Call us if he gives you a hard time."

They went out and there was a moment of silence.

"Can you hear me?" Tad finally said.

"Yes."

"Can you understand me?"

"Nothing—I understand nothing."

"You've got to sober up, they'll kill you if you don't."

"Probably kill me if I do, too."

"No—we have a chance. You've got to sober up."

Suddenly he ripped my blanket off, felt all around the edge of the mattress and found a bottle I'd stashed. "You've *got* to sober up. I need you, Andy."

I lay wondering whose side Tad was on. He probably hated his father more than I did, but that didn't mean that he could bring himself to work against him. And if he did find the courage to do that, he'd be trying to work out some plan for his own survival and his girl's. He'd care about me only as long as he thought I could be useful . . .

I wanted to sleep and sleep wouldn't come. The room seemed to hum. I don't know how much time went by before I felt a cold washcloth on my face and Tad saying, "Try some coffee."

I sat up and took the cup he was holding toward me.

"Do you know why dad flipped when you wanted to quit? He was going to let you make the run yourself, you and Esky. He was going to pull out at the last minute himself. He thought he could trust you to make the run."

"That figures. He'd risk his money but not his neck."

"He wanted to pull me out too. He was going to fake a heart attack after the stuff was loaded and I was going to have to stay behind to look after him. We Claytons do the planning, he said, but we don't get involved in the rough stuff. You've thought I was a patsy in this all along, haven't you? Well, I'm smarter than you think, Andy, and stronger. I'm the one you've got to work with."

"I don't want to work with anybody—"

"Listen to me, you won't have a chance alone."

"And with you?"

"The thing was my idea in the first place, wasn't it?"

"Congratulations."

"I had to take dad in to get started, but you don't think I trusted him, do you? I know him better than you do."

"So?"

"I never thought he'd pay us our share, Andy, even if it all worked out. Did you?"

"I didn't think about that much."

"He's going to control all the money in the process of laundering it, isn't he? You're counting on him to pay you your share. But what are you going to do if he doesn't, sue him?"

"That's the least of my worries."

"Maybe, but think about it. With good old dad, you lose if we lose and you lose if we win. That should put you on my side. You and I are both in the same boat. He was never going to pay me either. Oh, he'd give us both a little something. He'd say he was taking care of our stock for us, but it would always be the wrong time to sell it. He'd always be in control of us. We'd never be able to get rid of him.''

"You're sure of that?"

"Dad's thing is to stay in control. I knew it for sure when I told him I wanted to go on this damn trip even if he stayed ashore. He said he'd never pay me a cent unless I did what he told me to do. And when I asked him about you, he just smiled and said that you'd settle for very little, that you could hardly take your beef to court."

"So we both lose if we lose, and lose if we win. Perfect."

"We can still beat him, Andy. We can take over the ship, we don't have to follow his damn plan."

"He's going to take guards—"

"We could take care of them—"

"That depends on how many they have and how good they are. Anyway, we'd never be able to sell the stuff. I think he's made some deal to deliver it to the whole bloody Mafia. They'd come after us."

"All right, he's got big people on his side, so we have to get some on ours. Who has he got on his side? Organized crime at home and maybe here. Maybe he's got some of the politicians on his side here—the guys way over on the far right. So we go to their natural enemies, the guys on the far left. We make our own deal and we get their help."

"Carlos?"

"Sure . . . he's in touch with revolutionaries, and not just here."

"They'll cut our throats quicker than anybody. They'll just take the stuff and run—"

"They're practical people. If we cooperate with them, tell them where they can jump us, give them our route, we can keep in touch by radio."

"You been working with Carlos all along?"

"I've been listening to *any* offers I can get. Carlos can send men, ships."

"If Seymour takes on troops there'll be a fight. People will be killed, maybe us."

"The other troops will be outnumbered. And ours will be men with families here."

"So Carlos is the man you want to trust."

"Carlos won't try to control us when this thing is done. I told you . . . basically he's a revolutionary. As for me, I just want to take my money and run. Faith and I'll take it from there . . ."

"Where?"

"Carlos will help me if I help him—"

"So we come back to trusting Blackbeard?"

"Andy, are you going to be better off trusting him or trying to get out of this alone?"

Actually I felt that my only hope was to try to figure a way out alone. Or with Esky.

"I got to know if you're on my side," Tad said. "We've got a lot of planning to do—"

"Okay, I'm on your side." It would be better for me, I decided, if *everybody* thought I was on his side.

As soon as I started to sober up the guards André and Paul replaced Tad, and the day Esky was due to arrive at our rendezvous point offshore Seymour took over for an hour by himself.

"How you feeling, Andy?"

"Great."

He took a small automatic pistol from his pocket.

"My friends insist that I carry this. It seems kind of

ridiculous with you and me."

"Want me to carry it for you?"

"It wouldn't do you any good," he said, and slipped the gun back in his pocket.

I waited.

"I've been thinking about you, Andy. I mean, you saved my life and I saved yours. They wanted to—"

"I heard."

"I still think you can be useful. Has Tad talked to you?"

"Not really."

"He got sore at me, wanted me to promise him his share as soon as we got in, and of course I couldn't. You understand the complexities of a deal like this—"

"Not sure I do. Enlighten me, Seymour."

"My partners are buying into my whole operation on top of the table in return for favors we're doing them under the table. My stock will go up and I've been able to put a good block of it in your name and some in Tad's. But you wouldn't want to sell out too much right away. You wouldn't get a good price for it that way. A little at a time . . ."

"I understand," I said, and I did understand that if I followed his plan he would be in control forever, just as Tad had warned me.

"I'm getting the feeling, Andy, that like Tad you don't have much faith in me."

"Seymour, I have as much faith in you as you have in me, and you're the one with the gun in his pocket."

"Circumstances . . . but it wouldn't make much sense for me to cheat you if we carry this thing off. There'll be plenty for everyone—"

"Everyone alive . . . I hear your partners get rid of captains when they've done their job."

"You're not dealing with these people. You're dealing with me."

Hardly a good argument, but I decided the best ploy for me would be to continue to make each man believe I was on his side.

"All right, Seymour," I said, "we've known each other a long time, I guess we can trust each other if we can trust anyone."

"And we have to trust someone, even in a deal like this. By the way, just as a token, I've brought you something."

He took his polished pigskin wallet from his pocket, opened it and gave me a green piece of paper. When I unfolded it, I saw that it was a certified check for $50,000, payable by an outfit called the Valley Publishing Company.

"Who are they?" I asked.

"Friends of mine. Here's a legitimate contract. You're sort of a writer, I've seen your articles in the boating magazines, and I remember that you always wanted to write. So here's a legal contract to write a book with an advance of fifty thousand."

He took an envelope from his pocket, opened it and gave me a mimeographed contract.

"Sign here," he said.

"I've gone big-time pretty fast, haven't I?"

"I'll level with you, Andy, I want you to remember that I'm still in a position to do you favors. Remember that if I need some."

I took the pen, signed the contract and handed it back

to him.

"Win or lose on our deal, that check will be good," he said. "Don't try to write up our little expedition, though, your critics might use more than a typewriter."

I told him he'd made his point, and wondered how much rubber was in the check.

That night Tad told me that our cargo had been loaded into the coastal freighter *Señorita* and that Esky was only a hundred miles from our rendezvous point. We'd go to sea in the morning.

"How's the weather?"

"Good. We may be able to go right alongside the trawler to unload."

I didn't know whether I was glad or sorry about that. A hundred ideas for escape were running through my mind, but the one inescapable fact was that even if Esky and I could make it away from the Colombian coast, a lot of very nasty big-shots would be looking for us, at sea or ashore . . . That last night I spent under guard in the motel was a long one.

Shortly before dawn Tad came in and told the guards that he would take over while they got breakfast.

"This will be my last chance to contact Carlos by telephone," he told me. "Dad may not let anyone use the radio when we get to sea. Just give me some idea of the route we're going to take."

"Yucatan Channel," I said, figuring that that would sound plausible and put at least one set of enemies as far off the scent as possible.

"How many days?"

"We'll be making twelve knots by the most direct route. Let your friend Carlos figure it out, according to the weather."

"Andy, you wouldn't be getting cute, would you?"

"I can't guarantee anything, Seymour may set a route."

"Carlos' people may be checking us with light planes along the way. If we lie to them, they might be sore when they catch up with us."

"Then tell them that your father is going to set the route at the last minute. He probably will anyway. Seymour's no fool."

"Neither is Carlos—you better start to believe that."

As soon as my two guards returned, Tad left, apparently to place his last call to Blackbeard, as I kept thinking of him. My guards told me to get dressed and pack up. For the time being, at least, there were no decisions for me to make.

Seymour, Tad, the two guards and I rode to the waterfront in a shabby van that had been chosen because it would attract little attention. It stopped near the end of a wharf alongside which a beat-up 500-ton coastwise freighter was moored. The freighter was identical to many others in the Caribbean, surplus U.S. Army supply vessels, FS boats, World War II vintage. The *Angry Angel* had taken food and ammo from her type many times, and seeing this familiar hull so down at the heels was a little like seeing an old friend on skid row. About 180 feet long, this vessel had her name, *Señorita*, in new white paint on her rusty bow. Her gray superstructure had been patched with red lead and her decks had not been painted in years, but I noticed that she had a new radar antenna and new cables on her freight booms and winches. The red copper paint at her waterline looked fresh and I could hear the low rumble of a powerful generator running.

An offshore wind was keeping the ship about four feet off the wharf and the gap was bridged by a single heavy plank about twelve inches wide. It occurred to me that this gangplank would also lead me across another kind of line . . .

In the wake of the passing tug the *Señorita* rolled a little . . . I was at sea again and before long I would be in command of my own ship, at least in name. Colombia soon would be left far behind. I had no idea of what waited for me, but at sea this game would at least go according to rules I understood. The sea was where I lived.

23

My guards took me to a compartment which used to be the officers' wardroom; now it looked like a flophouse, with uncovered mattresses on the old benches and a coffee-stained table. Seymour was sitting there in a spotless tan suit, looking out of place, and Tad lounged beside him with a green beer bottle in his hand.

"We won't be sailing for quite a while," Seymour said.

"It's good to see you, Andy. Welcome aboard."

"Nobody exactly piped me aboard, but it's better than the motel," I said. I made myself smile because I figured that I could handle Seymour better if he didn't know how angry I felt. I'd never been a very good actor, though, and Tad was sensitive enough to feel what I felt.

"Relax, Andy, our cargo's been loaded. I'm about to start testing samples to make sure it's as advertised."

"I'll have some men go with you to help move the bales," Seymour said. "I don't think we have to worry much about the quality of the goods. My partners are reliable about those things."

"Dad, I have all the testing equipment—"

"Fine. At any rate, I haven't signed the final papers yet. I'm waiting for your okay."

"This is going to take me a couple of hours," Tad said.

"You have all afternoon. Andy, you won't have anything to do until I tell you that you're in command. Take it easy and don't leave the ship. I've got a few last-minute items to take care of ashore."

Seymour left, putting on a spotless new Panama. The man in the white hat. My guards played pinochle and drank coffee at the table. An old navy Chelsea clock on the bulkhead ticked loudly. It was seven minutes before eleven a.m. I assumed we would leave soon after dusk and transfer the cargo to the trawler in the dark. Although the portholes were open, the little compartment was hot and a buzzing electric fan barely moved the humid air. Humming flies clustered on the table where spilled sugar had coagulated. Suddenly I felt mortally tired.

For nights I'd hardly been able to close my eyes. Well, for the time being, at least, things were beyond my control . . .

Four hours later I was awakened by Seymour. He had three men with him. One was a thin, coffee-colored man in a khaki uniform and a gold-encrusted cap bearing the insignia of the Colombian merchant marine. He introduced himself as "José Rodrigues, the regular skipper of the *Señorita*." Rodrigues gave an overly ingratiating smile, but as the captain of a ship owned by Seymour's new partners, I guessed he probably had to smile a lot.

The second man was small, nervous and ferretlike, and kept glancing around the wardroom as though looking for a way out. He wore an expensive-looking suit of pale blue silk, and a big diamond ring flashed on his right little finger. Seymour introduced him as "Mr. Jones, an experienced merchant-marine officer."

Seymour and his two friends were dwarfed by a tall, fat but strong-looking man who wore navy blue pants and a clean white sports shirt, its open neck showing heavy black chest hair. I'd long had a habit of sizing a man up to see if I thought I could take him in a fight. This one could take me if I wasn't very careful and very lucky, I figured. He was overweight, but his shoulders and biceps were huge, and he was twenty years younger than I. When he looked at me, his big, heavy, deeply tanned face appeared to be very self-confident; also sullen, hostile, maybe contemptuous.

"This is Captain Apo," Seymour said. "He's an experienced captain of the big new tankers."

359

"I hear you're a yacht skipper," Apo said in a deep voice, correct English but heavily accented. Greek?

"A deliveryman," I said with a rather forced smile. The captains of the big tankers always think that a man's worth is measured by the tonnage of his command, but old sailors like me tend to think of them as factory superintendents, not seafarers. Mutual contempt by two kinds of men who could not do each other's job. A trawler was a small enough ship to fall more in my area of competence than in a tanker man's, I figured, but it would be wise to let this mountain of flesh go on thinking I was just an idiot. Thinking . . . ?

"With so many captains aboard, we have to get our lines of command straight. I want no confusion."

"I am not confused," Apo rumbled. "My orders are clear."

"You understand that I am in command of this operation," Seymour said.

"As long as you are delivering the goods where and when ordered," Apo said.

Seymour fitted a cigarette into his long holder. "If anything should happen to me, you take over. Until such a contingency, you're on standby but will stand radar watches."

Apo grunted and asked for a cold beer.

"Look in the refrigerator in the galley. We have a girl who's going to cook, but she's not aboard yet."

The ferretlike man got up and fetched a beer for Apo.

"Mr. Jones, you are basically Mr. Apo's assistant or mate," Seymour said, when the little man sat down. "You're accountable to him, but to me too while I am

360

in charge."

"Yes, sir," Jones said nervously. He looked as though he felt accountable to everyone.

"Where does all this leave me?" I asked.

"Andy, you better think of me as an admiral. You'll be my captain during the final run to the States. You won't be in command until I give you the word. If you want to give orders to Mr. Jones or Mr. Apo, do it through me, but remember that they're mostly on standby and will keep only radar watches. You and your friend Esky will be in day-to-day charge of running the ship on the final run. Captain Rodrigues will be in charge until we meet the trawler. We'll also have an armed guard, about twelve men. Some of them will be qualified to act as deckhands. When they're deckhands they'll take orders from you. As armed guards they'll take orders from Mr. Apo."

"Who's going to be in command if we have to fight this ship?"

"Me," Apo said. "The soldiers will be under my command."

"You've had experience in naval combat, Mr. Apo?" I asked.

"We ain't going to fight no naval war."

"If we're attacked by hijackers, I'd like to have Andy in command because of his combat experience," Seymour said. "But if the soldiers are needed to settle problems aboard our own ship, Mr. Apo will be in charge—our partners have insisted on that. All clear to everyone?"

Apo shrugged his massive shoulders. I figured that he would do whatever he wanted to do, no matter what was said. He would always consider himself in charge.

"We'll be getting under way at eighteen hundred. Andy, I'm sorry, but my partners want the guards to stay with you until we sail. I know it's not necessary but . . ."

They all left, except for my guards, who had silently continued to play cards throughout the exchange. I lay down, thinking it would be good to get aboard the trawler with Esky. With the old Eskimo aboard, I might be able to make things happen . . .

I didn't wake up until they started the engines. Most of those old army supply ships had been driven by relatively light converted truck diesels, two on each screw, but these engines had the deep rumble of a pair of heavy new Cats. Nothing but the best for hauling stuff, even on short runs to transfer it to another ship at sea.

It was twelve minutes before six p.m., and through the porthole I could see that the sunlight was still bright. It seemed silly to leave on such a mission before dark, but soon I heard orders being given in Spanish. André and Paul, my guards, got up and abruptly left—their job was done. I followed them on deck and watched them jump ashore, where they stood on the wharf to make sure that I stayed aboard.

A lot of men in khaki uniforms without insignia had come aboard while I slept. Rodrigues stood on the bridge and shouted orders. Three men who wore nothing but dungarees obeyed his commands to take in the mooring lines. The heavy manila hausers were hauled in quickly, despite a lot of shouting and apparent confusion, but the board which had served as a gangplank was forgotten. It splashed into the water as the screws started to rumble in reverse. The vessel backed away from the wharf, and as the strip of brown, dirty water which separated us from the land widened, I found myself wondering whether I would ever touch shore again, whether I would ever see Pattie again. The thought of her strengthened my determination to get out of this mess somehow, and soon I'd have Esky to help me. We'd be two against I didn't know how many, but a pretty good two, come to think of it . . .

The sky was clear and lights were just blinking on in the city as we turned and started out the main channel. Barranquilla was a river port, I knew, but I wasn't sure how many miles we would have to go to reach the sea. Not many, judging from the charts I'd glanced at. Suddenly I realized that it was six o'clock, a little after, which was the time that Esky would be standing by for radio messages. The last I'd heard from him he was only thirty miles from rendezvous point.

"Seymour," I said, going to the bridge where he was standing, "can I use the sideband to talk to Esky?"

"I'm going to have to be in charge of all radio transmission. Just code your message and give it to me. I'll send it and bring you the reply."

"I didn't know you knew how to use sideband."

"There's nothing to this voice stuff—I've been studying it."

Using the international flag-signal book I'd purchased, I coded a message to request Esky's position and to ask him to stand by according to plan. Seymour went into the radio shack near the bridge and soon came back with Esky's answer: "Am in position. All A-okay."

"He seems a good man, all right," Seymour said.

"Have you got a weather report?"

"Southeasterly winds, fifteen to twenty knots, clear skies."

"We won't be able to put the ships alongside. We'll have to use the big life rafts to transfer the cargo."

"Just take it one step at a time, Andy. Let events unfold."

"What does *that* mean?"

"Come into my cabin, Andy. I guess there's no reason to keep my plans a secret anymore."

He'd taken over the captain's cabin. The old army "C.O." sign was still over the door. I had been in many such cabins—a bunk, a desk, a chair, no luxury other than the privacy a captain enjoyed. Seymour motioned me toward the chair and sat on the bunk, leaning against a rolled-up blanket and pillow. "What's up?" I said.

"There've been major changes in the plan . . . unexpected circumstances . . ." He sounded bitter.

"What's happened?"

"I got some very disturbing news last night, personally disturbing and more."

"What?"

"Tad—my own boy's been working against me, Andy, against all of us."

I played dumb.

"The police have been keeping tabs on that Carlos. They picked him up yesterday morning and asked him a few questions. The cops in this part of the world can be very persuasive."

Carlos might not have been one of my favorite people, but I felt sorry for him.

"The bastard's got wider connections than they'd thought—political, Castro, the lot. Tad has been working with him. *They've* been planning to hijack us. I didn't want to believe that my own son—"

"A lot of rich kids have joined all kinds of revolutionary nuts," I said, trying to sound sympathetic.

Seymour sighed. "I can't let myself think about it now," he said. "My first job of course was to figure a way to evade whatever hijacking operation has been set up. Tad has given them the details of all our plans—about transferring the cargo to the trawler, going to Red Rock Cove, all of it."

"So what are we going to do?"

"Fortunately, my partners are very resourceful. Of course we can't do anything according to the old plan. In the first place, we won't transfer the cargo to the trawler. We'll continue to the States aboard this vessel. She doesn't have all the latest electronic gadgets that Apo would like, but she can make it. You'll get her through—"

"How about Esky and the trawler?"

"They'll be a decoy ship. We'll tell Esky to head through the Windward Passage. He should draw off our potential attackers while we go another way."

"What will happen to Esky?"

"He can just give up the moment he's stopped and hand them an empty ship. She's insured."

"They'll kill him."

"Andy, no one said this operation was risk free . . ."

The thought of setting Esky up infuriated me. "I need Esky here. I can't run a ship this big myself—"

"You've got plenty of people to help you."

"I need a man I can trust, and so do you. Have Apo run the decoy ship."

"My partners want Apo to stay here. He's their representative—"

"Then have Jones do it."

"I doubt if he's able. He's just Apo's toady."

"Then put Rodrigues on the trawler. He'll do the job if you pay and scare him enough."

"I'm not sure that my partners would approve—"

"Look, Esky didn't agree to run any decoy ship. He signed on to sail with me."

"He'll do what he's told. My people are rough—"

"Esky won't give a damn. When he gets angry, he's a wild man. Your own partners told you that when they checked him out. If he feels he's been double-crossed, he might ram us with that trawler right here and now. Or he's liable to run her ashore at Barranquilla and go to the authorities, radio the Coast Guard about the whole operation."

"If he did any of that he wouldn't live too long."

"He wouldn't give a damn about that either."

There was a moment of silence. Seymour ran a hand through his hair, which looked whiter than ever. "Well," he said slowly, "that's a consideration. I'll radio my partners."

"Tell them if you don't take Esky aboard I'll quit too, even if I have to dive overboard. They won't care, but you might, Seymour. When the chips are down you can trust me a hell of a lot more than you can your damned Mafia navy."

"You wanted to quit."

"True, but I'd never kill you in cold blood. Those guys would, and just might. Why do they need you now?"

"Because their bosses still stand to get money out of me. I haven't paid in full yet—"

"Well, you still need Esky and me. They could hold you hostage or beat the money out of you. And if we hit a hurricane with this old bucket, you may need more than Mafia tanker men to get you through."

"I know that . . . I'll have Rodrigues run the decoy ship . . . it will take some doing, though . . . Now, there's something else in the new plan you should understand . . . a third ship will be involved. If the *Señorita* doesn't return to Barranquilla soon, as she's supposed to do according to the original plan, some people might figure she's gone on to the States. Fortunately my partners have three of these old army ships, all the same model . . . FS boats. It wasn't hard to name another *Señorita* and to make the paint jobs similar. This ship was going to rendezvous with us and take Rodrigues back to Barranquilla. Now she can go back without him. I guess they can say that we had trouble with Rodrigues. Disappearances don't seem to cause much talk on the Barranquilla waterfront."

"If a different *Señorita* goes back, won't her different crew cause talk, even if the ships look alike?"

"We just need to fool enough people long enough to give us a chance to get well to sea. It's worth trying. We also won't be going to Maine, of course. We'll lay to off the South Shore of Long Island and small boats will take our cargo in, rum-runner style. It worked in the old days."

"That's where the Coast Guard may get us."

"We're part of a big organization now, Andy, an independent part but we have people on our side. Some of them will arrange to have distress calls keep the Coast Guard busy far away from us while we're unloading. You know, this ship is about twice as big as a trawler, and her holds are full."

"Double the profits?"

"Something like that, although we couldn't get as much cocaine as we wanted—the rest is marijuana. I figure it can all go for almost a billion. Fantastic, isn't it?"

"Unreal to me." And it still was.

"You'll be a real millionaire if you stick with me. Now I have one more immediate problem . . ." He lit a cigarette and took a long drag before continuing. "I figured we'd have to do something like this when I realized that that crazy girl was blabbing around town. She's aboard now, God bless her . . . but maybe it's just as well they told Carlos' people about the trawler and Red Rock Cove. There may be a lot of surprised people . . . Now I have something tough to ask you to do, Andy. I'd like you to stay here with me while I tell Tad that I know about the plans he and Carlos were making. It's a terrible thing to admit, but I don't want to be alone with him when he learns that I knew about the whole thing. I'm a little afraid of my own son."

"I don't think he'd hurt you." Actually I wasn't so sure.

"What do you think he had in mind for me when Carlos and his friends took us over?"

"I don't know. Mostly I think he wants to beat you, show you up, not kill you—"

"If he's willing to turn me over to revolutionaries, he's sure as hell willing to take some chances with my life."

He picked up a telephone on the bulkhead and called the bridge. "Send my son down here, to the captain's cabin, right away."

Seymour sat down on his bunk, got up again. Opening a drawer, he took out a bottle of gin.

"I don't usually drink it straight," he said, and took a swig from the bottle. Before he capped it, he took two more, and I wondered whether it was fear or anger he was trying to blunt. He put another cigarette in his long holder with a slightly trembling hand, had just lit it when there was a knock on the door.

"Come in." His voice unusually edgy.

Tad had recently put on clean dungarees and a white T-shirt. His look of self-confidence faded as he saw his father.

"There's no point in drawing this out," Seymour said. "The police picked up Carlos yesterday. He talked."

Tad sank down on the edge of the bunk next to his father—there was no other place to sit. His face suddenly looked like tallow.

"My partners were understandably quite disgusted with you. It took all my arguments to get them to turn you over to me," Seymour said. "We've changed all our plans, of course."

Without a word Tad left the stateroom.

"God, I don't know what he'll do now," Seymour said.

"I doubt if he'll kill himself, if that's what you're worried about," I said sarcastically, but Seymour missed my tone and went on with his act as the concerned father.

"Keep track of him for me, will you, Andy?"

"I have a question first. What happens to this ship after small boats have unloaded us?"

"She'll go back to Barranquilla. Apo and I are to go ashore on Long Island with the cargo. You and Jones were supposed to take the ship back, but now maybe Esky can do it."

"I'll stay with the ship," I said. Maybe Esky and I should insist on going ashore with the cargo too, but I doubted Seymour's partners would give us long to live in either event. Somehow Esky and I would have to figure a way of escape . . .

Tad, I soon found, had retreated to the stateroom he shared with Faith. She opened the door when I knocked. Tad was on his bunk.

"What did his father say to him?" Faith asked.

I didn't know how much she knew about Carlos and Tad.

"Old dad taps out," Tad said drowsily. "He always does."

"They had a fight and Tad got a shock," I said. "Do you know what he's taken?"

"Seconal—"

She gestured toward an open briefcase on a chair. The inside had been made into a traveling drugstore—rows and rows of bottles of pills and capsules.

"I've got anything he needs," she said. "How about you? You don't look so good."

"Have you got an aspirin?"

"Everything but that. How about Valium?"

"No thanks. Watch Tad. Stay with him."

"But what *happened?*"

"Ask Tad," I said, and went off to the bridge.

24

The ship was just emerging from the river and heading for the open sea. Daylight had faded, but a three-quarter moon and bright stars made the breakwater gleam. As we cleared it, the ship began to roll a little. Rodrigues was in charge on the bridge, but Apo sat on a stool near him, a massive, silent, brooding presence.

Seeing that I was soon to command this ship,

nominally at least, I inspected the bridge closely. This shabby vessel had a gyro compass, loran and radar. Also an automatic pilot and a deep-sea depth finder, as well as bridge control of the engines and an elaborate panel of warning lights. She apparently lacked only a satellite navigational system and the sophisticated radio equipment which Apo and Jones probably had learned to depend on aboard the giant tankers.

Glancing down on the welldeck I saw that tarpaulins had been stretched across the freight booms. About a dozen young men who looked like soldiers despite the lack of insignia on their khaki uniforms were lying on sleeping bags or sitting with their backs against piles of duffle.

I went up to the flying bridge. Seagulls were wheeling in the moonlight around the ship and there was that clean smell, or absence of rank odors, that one gets when putting to sea. Jones and two other men were bolting a heavy machine gun in brackets which had been prepared for it, and others had already been placed on the bow and fantail. They were now being covered with tarpaulins wrapped loosely enough to disguise them.

As we cleared the coast with its sheltering headlands, the roll of the ship increased and a few of the soldiers on the welldeck rushed to the rail laughing. Soldiers at sea always act about the same. When it got a little rougher none of these boys would be laughing and I wondered how much protection they could give us. The motion of the ship had already turned most of them languid. They were slow to secure their rifles and gear, which were beginning to slide around the deck.

While I was standing on the flying bridge, Seymour

joined me.

"Is Tad all right?"

"He's in his bunk. Faith is with him . . . The boy'll probably be all right, in time," I said. "I wonder, Seymour, if the same could be said for us?"

"A good point." He didn't seem much happier than his son did. I almost felt sorry for the boy and the father. I'd had a taste of it with Tommy. . . .

Figuring that it would take us about three more hours to reach our rendezvous point with Esky, I decided to continue the inspection of my future command, if that's what she could be called. I went down to the engine room. It was the best I'd ever seen, as spic-and-span as the exterior of the ship was shabby. Two yellow Cat diesels, the size of whole automobiles, crouched side by side. Ahead of them two new yellow generators, almost half as big, shone in the fluorescent lights. The engines stood on solid new beddings over reinforced bottom plates. They had elaborate fuel filtering systems and mechanisms for cleaning the oil. Pegboards on the surrounding bulkheads held spare parts and tools, all of which had been outlined in black against white and labeled to show where they should be put back or replaced.

An old man with the strong, craggy face of an Indian chief and wearing only dungarees was sitting on a stool near a built-in desk with the engine logs when I came in. Seeing my admiration, he proudly showed me around. It occurred to me that one way Esky and I might escape was to find some way to sink this ship near enough to land so that we could get ashore some way. In such a grand engine room such conjectures seemed almost sinful, even if they did involve saving my life and Esky's. Still, I noted with satisfaction that the new bottom plates ended at the bulkhead which formed the forward end of the engine room, and an inspection of the bilges showed me that they were rusty, the old plates worn thin. This would be a fairly easy ship to sink. One hand grenade properly placed . . . And knowing Esky, he had armed himself for this voyage with those makeshift grenades he'd told me about.

Deciding to have a closer look at the soldiers, I walked to the welldeck. I counted fifteen men—more than I'd figured. Most of them were *mestizos*, more Indians than Spanish, small, copper-colored men, wiry and strong. None were older than maybe forty, and some appeared to be in their late teens. They were well turned out, well armed and appeared to have had military training. Their army uniforms were clean but showed bits of thread where insignia had been ripped off. Their heavy brown shoes shone and a few carried well-oiled U.S. .45 automatics on U.S. Army belts. Twelve glistening M-16s were laid out in a row on a tarpaulin on the after hatch. A boy who did not look more than about eighteen was whistling while he fitted clips of ammunition to each. Apparently he'd never heard that there's an old sailor's superstition against whistling aboard a ship.

Four soldiers were shooting craps in the bright moonlight, and they cursed as the rolling of the ship made the dice jump off the hatch, where some of the M-16 guns were threatening to slide. One thin boy who sat cross-legged a little apart from the others was softly playing the harmonica.

The oldest, a bald man who would have looked like a

sergeant even outside of uniform, looked at me with hostility but he thawed some when I smiled and said, *"Buenos noches."*

"Buenos noches," he replied. *"Captain?"*

"Sí."

They started to ask me where we were going, how long it would take to get there and what kind of weather I expected. They did not, of course, know that the ship was slated to return to Colombia without ever coming into port in the United States. Return to Colombia if she was lucky. Which seemed more and more unlikely as I thought about it.

"New York?" one boy asked with a grin. And another, who seemed to know about the Colombian drug-trade center of that city, grinned and said, "Jackson Heights?"

Others spoke fast Spanish, too fast for me, but I recognized the familiar questions: What ports will we visit, how long will we stay there, how much of the time could they spend ashore? I evaded by saying I spoke little Spanish. These men would probably be angry when they learned that they were not to be given any liberty before returning to Barranquilla—if we were even allowed to complete the round trip, I reminded myself—and their anger might be useful at the right time.

The young soldiers hardly looked like drug smugglers to me. They looked like the kind of kids who are always drafted into the front lines in any war for any cause, and who usually die first . . . as these men *might* if I had to sink this ship . . .

I couldn't bring myself to think about it now. I inspected the holds. Most of the after hold was full of carefully crated "coffee" bales, wood over heavy

377

waterproof plastic. When I examined a few which Tad had opened in the process of testing the contents, I saw that the cocaine had been packed in regular one-pound coffee cans. That hold was capable of carrying 150 tons, but there was some pig-iron ballast on the bottom of it and about a third of the space had been devoted to dry and canned stores for a long cruise.

The forward hold was jammed to the hatches with bigger bales, burlap over waterproof plastic, and when I took a look at the ones Tad had opened, I saw that they contained bricks of marijuana, compressed by a trash compactor. Those FS boats were rated as 500-tonners. Seymour had said the whole cargo was worth more than a billion dollars and maybe that was correct, though I'd learned that Seymour tended to talk in big sums when he wanted me to do something for him, small sums when it was time to pay. I believed Tad had been right when he said that Seymour intended to give very little, no matter how much money this voyage made. The profits in his final report would be reduced by high expenses, low sales figures and so forth. Seymour had started greedy with his plans for a trawler, doubled his potential take with a ship twice as large.

Next I went to the forecastle, which offered three tiers of pipe berths in a V-shaped compartment. The soldiers had covered the bunks with U.S. Army blankets, despite the fact that it was a hot and airless compartment even at night—which was why the men were sleeping on deck.

Going aft, I found Faith in the galley, which adjoined the old wardroom. She had a two-gallon pot of coffee steaming on the oil range and was making ham sandwiches. Her T-shirt was smudged, and she looked already exhausted.

"How's Tad?"

"Asleep. Can you show me how to run this damn oil stove? I can't get a low flame."

I explained the range to her.

"God, I had no idea there was going to be so *many* men aboard here," she said. "I'm not sure I'm going to cook for anybody. Tad told me a little. This isn't much of a crusade for me anymore."

"No . . ."

"I don't blame Tad for trying to go in with Carlos. His father has been trying to kill him ever since he was born. And Carlos would have paid better than Seymour, who's planning to keep it all for himself . . . You don't look so good, Andy. I thought you were a man of the sea, our intrepid captain and so forth . . ."

"I'm not exactly here on my own terms, you know—just look around. We're playing a dangerous game, and that's all you need to know right now . . ."

As the time for meeting Esky and the *Mary Anne* neared, I began studying the horizon ahead through the binoculars. Moonlight was dancing on the water and a few white clouds looked almost luminous, but for tonight, at least, the Caribbean reminded me of the wartime South Pacific in its deceptive softness. Esky had radioed that he was waiting for us at the rendezvous point, but even with the prospect of having Esky at my side I was all too aware that we were nearing the dangerous part of our voyage. From now on we were prey to hijackers. The only consolation was that Carlos' people would have trouble finding us because I'd had sense enough to keep the exact location of our rendezvous a secret between me and Esky. There was no way that hijackers could jump us there, unless they were following us now.

Apo, I found, had already thought of this possibility. He was standing in front of the radar set, studying its screen, on which the dim outline of a small chart of the land astern of us still glowed green against gray.

"Anybody following?"

"Nobody that shows up here."

Well, I thought, it won't take more than a half-hour to send Rodrigues over and bring Esky back. If Rodrigues went willingly . . . I noted that Rodrigues was no longer on the bridge and that Apo was clearly in charge. Seymour had no doubt finished his radio conversations with his shadow partners and was now giving Rodrigues his orders. Faced with a choice of running a decoy ship which almost certainly would be attacked, or returning to the murderous anger of his employers in Barranquilla, Rodrigues would probably do what he was told.

Returning to the flying bridge, I stood sweeping the luminous horizon ahead with the binoculars. On the boat deck astern of me, Jones appeared with five men and began to prepare one of our two lifeboats for launching. It was a small, much dented metal boat without an engine and I doubted if Apo's men could handle oars or a small boat of any kind in the considerable seaway which was now running. Transferring men from one ship to another in a lifeboat in such conditions called for a kind of seamanship that almost no one had these days. The fact that Apo was planning to attempt it encouraged me. Either he was smarter than I'd thought or more stupid

380

about old-fashioned seamanship, and I had more confidence in his ignorance than in his intelligence.

Going to the bridge, I found Apo still studying the radar.

"You'll have trouble transferring the men in the lifeboat in this seaway," I said.

He glared at me, King Kong annoyed. "It's too rough to take the trawler alongside," he said.

"Use a rubber life raft."

"Nobody can row those things."

"Put Rodrigues and whatever men he's going to take with him in a raft. Back away and give them plenty of sea room. The trawler can then come alongside the raft as it drifts."

"Is that the way the yachties do it?"

"That's the way a sailor does it."

Apo grunted. "All *right*, we'll do it that yachty way." Turning to a man near him, he said, "Tell Jones to secure the lifeboat and to break out an inflatable."

Round one for me, I thought. Or was it . . . ? It might have been smarter to let him go on thinking I was an idiot until the last round of our inevitable set-to, wherever and however that would come, but I couldn't very well risk not having Esky with me when it did.

In such bright moonlight I should be able to see the *Mary Anne* at a distance of about five miles, I had figured, and I began to worry when I couldn't catch even a glimpse of her. She was, I reminded myself, a very small ship, with a low black hull and white superstructure, not bad camouflage for a moonlit night. I kept studying the horizon ahead more intently with the binoculars and

381

finally I saw a glint of moonlight on metal, the radar antenna on her masthead. At a distance of about four miles, the *Mary Anne* looked even smaller than I'd expected; like a toy ship, a tiny model, drifting on the vast face of the ocean under thickening but still luminous clouds.

Apo picked her up on the radar at almost the same moment I saw her, which either meant that the *Mary Anne* didn't present much of a radar target, or that our set wasn't working very well.

"Hey, Yachty, if you can send blnker light and have your friend on the trawler read it, then tell him to stand by to pick up men on a life raft and for further instructions from them."

He handed me a new hand-held blinker light.

"Wait until we're right close."

Neither the *Mary Anne* nor the *Señorita* was showing lights and the trawler looked deserted as she lay rolling, drifting with the seas on her quarter. The thought that hijackers might already have taken her, that maybe they'd killed Esky and now were waiting just for us, grew in my mind as I sent my first blinker message to her: "Who's in command?"

Immediately a light blinked back from the trawler's bridge: "Esky here. Who dat?"

"Andy here," I blinked back. "All plans changed. Stand by to pick up life raft with men and further instructions."

"Wilco."

Apo's soldiers and Jones almost managed to screw up even the simple task of inflating a life raft and lowering it over the side. It was a big one, the kind we'd planned to use for transferring the cargo, and as the carbon-dioxide cylinder ballooned it up, the wind almost took it off the welldeck. Finally the big yellow doughnut was secured alongside as we headed into the seas at dead low speed. Apo was not good at handling a small ship. He could have kept her bow into the seas without building up any headway, using the twin screws, and he should have turned away from the wind a little to put the raft in a lee. I didn't want to antagonize him though, and the situation was manageable enough as Seymour, Rodrigues and three of the soldiers climbed into the raft. There's nothing very complicated about casting off a big, soft inflatable, but there was a great deal of shouting and confusion on the welldeck, and finally Apo went down to oversee the operation. Soon he returned to the bridge, backed the ship down, and let the raft with her passengers bob ahead. We kept on backing to give the *Mary Anne* plenty of room for maneuvering. Esky was quick and expert as he circled to leeward of the raft, headed the trawler into the wind and turned enough to shelter the inflatable in his lee. Then he ran from the bridge to the welldeck and took the line Rodrigues tossed him. Esky was about the only man I knew who could make running a 70-foot trawler alone look easy. . . .

It took about two minutes for Seymour to make whatever explanations were necessary for Esky. Through the binoculars I saw Esky run to the bridge, and soon afterward he returned to the raft with his seabag on his shoulder. I hoped that he'd bring some of his hand grenades with him and, knowing him, was almost sure he would. He climbed into the raft with Seymour after carefully lowering his seabag. Rodrigues and his men had

383

already gone aboard the trawler. Seymour cast the raft off and the trawler backed away.

"On schedule," Apo grunted.

He was looking to the southeast with his binoculars. Training mine in that direction, I saw another FS boat approaching, a mirror image of ours. The name *Señorita* had been painted in big white letters on her bow, and splotches of red lead had been added to match ours on her gray superstructure. The captain of this new *Señorita* was not too smart. He could not read blinker light and wanted to come close enough to talk with a loud hailer. Not seeing that we wanted to maneuver to pick up the life raft, he got his ship between us and it. Apo got on our loud hailer.

"Stand clear while we pick up raft," he bellowed. "We'll talk later."

"What say?" someone asked with a Spanish accent.

"Keep the fuck *clear*," Apo yelled.

That the new *Señorita* seemed to understand, and she circled away from us. Apo maneuvered us alongside the life raft without trouble, and Esky bounded to the welldeck after lifting his seabag aboard and helped Seymour to make the climb. For a few moments Esky was lost in the shadows of the winches. With his seabag on his shoulder, he finally followed Seymour to the bridge.

"Greetings, bud," he said mildly. "Nice night, ain't it?"

"Lovely."

He took a match from his pocket and sat on his seabag in a corner of the pilothouse, picking his teeth. Apo ordered the men to cast the life raft adrift and we backed away from it. What did a five-thousand-dollar rubber raft

384

matter in an operation like this?

"Thank you, Mr. Apo," Seymour said. "Now I think that Andy can take command for the rest of this voyage . . . under my direction."

(Seymour . . . a captain's captain. Great . . .)

"She's all yours, Yachty," Apo said, and went into the radio shack.

"Head for Grenada," Seymour said to me. "We'll try to get through the islands that way."

"Take over, Esky, and steer east slow while I figure a course."

"Aye," Esky said, and approached the wheel, where one of the young men in khaki was acting as helmsman. "Come left slowly," he said.

I went to the chartroom and figured a course toward Grenada. After giving it to Esky, I told him to ring up full speed ahead, and the engines quickened their beat.

"I think we'll have a safe period of several hours at least while our friends chase the trawler," Seymour said. From his tone, he might have been talking about investment strategy rather than armed hijackers.

"When they catch it, they'll start looking for us," I said. "Did you set up radio communication with Rodrigues?"

"Of course. Apo's men will be standing twenty-four-hour radio watch and Rodrigues will tell us the moment he's approached by any ship."

I nodded. Not so dumb, my captain's captain.

"My partners and I are not exactly inefficient," Seymour said.

"I see that."

He seemed pleased, almost unreasonably so, as if *my*

approval were important to him. I was briefly reminded of that long-ago time when his father had given command of the *Patrician* to me, of when Seymour had come to me for help when he was flunking out of school, and more recently for help with his son and with this damned smuggling scheme. I was realizing what I'd been blind to all my life, that I had in many ways seemed threatening to Seymour, penniless and powerless though I'd always been, by comparison. Insecurity and envy in a man like Seymour, especially with the power of his new partners behind him, weren't exactly a harmless combination, though, and I became even more anxious to get a chance to talk to Esky in private. I set the automatic pilot on the new course.

"Seymour, will you take over for about half an hour?" I said. "If we're going to run this ship, Esky and I should look her over pretty carefully. I want to start by going over the charts with him."

"Okay, Jones will take the radar and I'll take the watch."

"Let's go to the chartroom," I said to Esky.

We closed the door but talked in whispers anyway.

"You bring hand grenades?"

"Three."

"You got questions?"

"Seymour told me most of it. Where do you stand with them?"

"I tried to quit, they wouldn't go along. They brought me aboard under guard."

Esky gave a low whistle. "Well, at least that'll be good for you if we're ever brought into court."

"I doubt they want us to live all that long. I've an idea

Seymour's partners don't intend for us to live much beyond the end of this voyage, no matter what happens."

"I figure you're right . . . they won't forget you tried to quit."

"Sorry I've fouled you up—"

He grinned. "I got fifty grand in advance. Now we just have to figure how to get me and you out of this thing alive so I can spend it."

"Any ideas?"

"We got to figure a way to get off without giving them a chance to shoot us."

"We could jump overboard with a life raft at night—"

"They'd circle back and fix us as soon as they'd found we had gone."

"Not if we left a hand grenade in their bilges."

"That would fix 'em, all right . . ."

"Jones is a fool, Seymour's smart but not very tough, and Apo is smart *and* tough—at least that' the way I figure it."

"We can take Apo out at the right time. Hell, Andy, I'm betting on us, the boat bums against the Mafia navy at sea . . ." He clapped me on the back.

"We better look the ship over," I said.

We started at the stern and made a close inspection, more detailed than I had by myself. We ended in the double stateroom Esky and I were to share. Someone had put his seabag on his bunk. The top had been untied and the top layer of T-shirts was spilling out.

"I guess Apo inspected my bag for arms," Esky said with a grin. "I figured someone would do that."

"God, what did you do with the grenades?"

"I had them on top in a ditty bag, and the first thing I

did when I climbed aboard was hide them."

"Where?"

"They're just stuck in the middle of a coil of fire hose. I'll go get the little beauties . . ."

He went on deck and came back a few moments later with a small canvas bag, and proudly showed me three king-sized beer cans with fuses protruding from glue at an opening in the top. Taking a big jackknife from his pocket, he pulled the mattress from his bunk and slit open the inner edge. After pulling out some stuffing and wadding it in his pockets, he crammed the beer cans in.

"Good to sleep on," he said, as he remade the bunk. "They'll make me rest real good."

25

After Esky had taken a swig of vodka from a bottle in his seabag, we returned to the bridge. We saw that despite the rolling of the ship, men were lying on the forecastle head, doing some work on the bow.

"They've painted out the lettering and are attaching new name boards," Seymour said. "Now we're the *Denise* of Martinique and we're flying the French flag. No government wants to stop French ships just on suspicion. The Frogs are kind of touchy about that."

"Good idea," I said, and it was. But not for Esky and me.

"We've got Martinique papers for the *Denise*. As I said, my partners are very efficient."

He seemed almost childishly proud of all this back-up clout.

"Well, Esky, what do you think of our ship?" he asked.

"There's a lot the matter with her," Esky said, "but nothing Andy and I can't handle."

"My partners assured me that she'd be ready for sea in every way."

"Seymour, I don't think much of your partners as sailors. You better be glad you got Andy and me aboard."

"What did you find wrong?"

"The compasses haven't been compensated since they put the new engines in."

"We've got gyro—"

"Never can rely on that—never can rely on anything electrical. She also hasn't had speed trials since she got the new engines. There's no RPM curve. Andy and I can make one."

"Don't we have a patent log?"

"Not that we can find. And the transducer of the depth finder wasn't left bare when they painted her bottom. The damn thing don't work right."

"Anything else?" Seymour looked worried.

"The port engine's oil pressure is low—happens with new engines. We'll watch it. Except for the section under the engine beds, the bottom is old and flaky. I

390

wouldn't want to take her through a hurricane, but we can probably dodge any bad storms if you get the right weather reports."

"Mr. Apo will make sure we do that."

"You better let Andy and me interpret those reports."

"I will."

Esky was even smarter than I'd thought; he was setting Seymour up to trust us more, and the representatives of his partners less.

"If I'm in charge now, I'd like to have lookouts stationed on the bow, flying bridge and fantail," I told Seymour. "Will you have Apo do that?"

"I'll see to it," Seymour said. "I'm glad to have you and Esky aboard."

I nodded, and hoped he'd be damn sorry before this trip was over.

For half an hour Esky and I stood on the starboard wing of the bridge. It was a nice night, and except for the fact that we were running without lights, this voyage was beginning to seem as routine as any other. The guy on watch on the flying bridge was softly playing a harmonica.

"One of us better get some sleep, Esky," I said. "It's going to be watch on watch with us for a long time."

"How beat are you?"

"I slept half the day."

"Then I'll turn in. We both better get as much sack time as we can while the hijackers are chasing the *Mary Anne.* How long you think before they catch up to her?"

"They probably won't let her get far from the coast."

"That's what I figure. Damn, I don't want to be taken

over by no hijackers until we get a chance to figure something out for ourselves."

"We got a lot of stuff to fight with aboard here," I said.

"Against Cuban gunboats, maybe. Well, hell . . . it's a big ocean."

Standing my watch on the wing of the bridge, the first question I had to answer once and for all was whether I was finally dead sure I wanted to somehow abort this voyage and try to escape at whatever cost, even if the only way was to sink the ship, maybe with everyone but Esky and me aboard.

The faces of the young soldiers kept flashing into my mind. Deep-sixing them would be a kind of black-hat thing to do, and I still cared about hats, no matter how ridiculous that was for a one-time almost smuggler. I still wanted to be Errol Flynn, wanted to play a hero's role if only in my own imagination. I wasn't supposed to be a bad guy in a black hat, at least I didn't want to be. Well, Errol, only a black hat would cold-bloodedly plan the destruction of about fifteen young soldiers and several others for his own survival. What about other choices?

Like what? Maybe Esky and I could manage to run the ship aground or engineer a collision with another vessel, but I was sure Apo would have us killed before we could be rescued and get to a court. Maybe Esky and I could contrive to attract the attention of the Coast Guard as we approached the coast, but I was also sure that we wouldn't be alive by the time the officers boarded us.

Or maybe with Tad's help we could deliberately play into the hands of the hijackers, revolutionaries, pirates, whoever the hell they might be. I didn't think, though, that hijackers would be likely to treat Esky and me too kindly, whether they were rebels or just greedy thieves. With Apo and his soldiers aboard, there'd be a firefight if hijackers tried to board us, which would provide plenty of opportunity for Esky and me to get ourselves killed, no matter what side we wanted to be on.

No, I'd have to work with Seymour and Apo to avoid hijackers. And if we could manage that, we *might* be able to work some kind of an accident so sudden, or in such a crowded place, that Esky and I could escape without sinking the ship.

I remembered that Seymour had said we were going to lay to off the South Shore of Long Island while small boats unloaded our cargo. During the hurricane of '38, I had lived in fear of beaching the old *Patrician* on the South Shore near Montauk in a hurricane surf. Even in calm weather, when the fog was thick, fishing vessels and small freighters occasionally beached themselves on the South Shore through simple errors in navigation. The currents were strong there and unpredictable. On one dark rainy night during Prohibition, my grandfather had told me, a rum runner had run full tilt onto the beach at Southampton while trying to enter Shinnecock Inlet. There was a Coast Guard station there, and the Coasties had been able to wade out in knee-deep water to capture the rum runners. Much to the delight of beachcombers, the ship broke up in the surf and scattered the sands with cases of Scotch.

Why couldn't Esky and I fix up an "error in navigation" like that? Well, one reason was that Apo would keep careful track of the ship's position with radar and Loran, but those machines could be made to fail in a way that might seem normal, and Apo himself could be taken out at the right time, as Esky had said.

Even with Apo and the machines out of the picture, it wouldn't be easy to beach a ship in clear daylight or bright moonlight without giving early warning to Seymour, Jones and everyone else aboard . . . but it was August, a month of fogs and heavy thunderstorms off the South Shore of Long Island. If we were lucky and the weather was right . . .

So beaching the ship was a possibility. Suddenly I had a clear vision of Southampton Beach as I remembered it from the days of my youth—crowds of young people making love and drinking beer on blankets so close that they almost touched each other. If we beached the ship in such a crowded place, Esky and I could run ashore and be surrounded by people before anyone could catch us. At least that was one way we could escape without killing everyone else aboard, and though it seemed a slim chance dependent on all kinds of conditions beyond my control, it still seemed the best hope.

Esky and I could arrange to keep the ship's company busy aft as we approached the beach. Maybe we could start a fire in the lazaret. Maybe we could get Tad to help us—a third hand might be needed when it came time to deal with Seymour and Apo. It was always difficult for me to tell where Tad stood, but he had been so angered by his father that I guessed he'd welcome a chance for his own revolution. And the girl would probably stick with him. That would make four of us against more than twenty, counting the men in the engine room and all the soldiers. Well, four might fool twenty, and Esky alone was better than any dozen men.

At least this shaky plan was better than none, and maybe some other would come up as the voyage progressed. But first of all we had to evade the hijackers. I wondered how long it would be before they caught the *Mary Anne* . . .

The answer to that turned out to be only a little more than nine hours. I was asleep in my bunk when Esky came from the bridge to tell me about it.

"Seymour got the word from the trawler," Esky said. "Rodrigues said that two shrimp boats loaded with men were closing in on him, one on each side. Then the sound of shooting came over the radio and that was the end of it."

"Exit Rodrigues," I said.

"Maybe they didn't kill him. Anyway, they'll be looking for us now. If Rodrigues lived long enough, you can bet they made him tell what kind of a ship we've got and anything else he knows."

I got out of my bunk to ask Seymour to tell Apo to get the ship ready for a fight. Apo was ahead of me. The men had already taken the tarpaulins off the machine guns and were loading them. The bald sergeant on the welldeck was giving hand grenades to the soldiers.

"I don't think anything's going to happen for several hours," Esky said. "They got to find us first. Let's change course about fifteen degrees every hour."

"Right. Start now and plot it."

"Wilco. Like old times, ain't it?"

All that day nothing happened and the troops gave their hand grenades back to the sergeant, who stored them in hammocks which he rigged on the bulwarks of the welldeck. The young soldiers laughed, stripped in the bright sunlight and threw buckets of sea water at each other. Jones volunteered for long radio watches, and when others replaced him he pestered them for news about the outcome of horse races and athletic events all over the world. When off watch he sat huddled over racing forms.

Apo sat on a stool in the bridge, looking more like King Kong all the time, his scowl heavy, his vigilant eyes malignant. In his huge right hand there was always either a bottle of beer or a cup of coffee. Apparently he drank beer until he got sleepy, then switched to coffee, but he clearly had a need for constant liquid intake. This observation, combined with my memory of Faith's briefcase full of drugs, gave me another idea: At the right time, it might be possible to take care of Apo by doping his beer and coffee. Jones or one of the soldiers usually served as his waiter, but Apo had an eye for the full-blown charms of Faith. He solemnly winked at her whenever she appeared and laughed when she sort of flounced away. If Faith really came over to our side, she could put anything she wanted in Apo's drinks, or anywhere else . . .

I'd passed a certain line, I noted. Doping people's drinks, arming ourselves with machine guns, beaching ships no longer seemed at all unrealistic or melodramatic to me; they were simply a part of my surrounding reality. To deny it would have been the true unreality—and stupidity.

At about dusk of our first day of that voyage, only about five hours after we heard from the trawler *Mary Anne*, a light plane passed overhead, returned and circled low over us. It finally roared only about a hundred feet over our mast before heading back toward the Colombian coast.

"Well, I guess there's no doubt that we've been spotted," Seymour said unhappily. "It'll take time for them to get ships alongside us, though. You're going to change course, aren't you, Andy?"

"We're zigzagging every half-hour."

"Good, I doubt they have anything both fast enough to catch us and big enough to fight us."

Any little country's gunboat might do it, or a whole fleet of fast small craft, but I said nothing.

The next day was the summer Caribbean at its best, hot but windswept. Thundersqualls built on the horizon, but obligingly passed us in the distance. Flying fish skipped from the tops of the waves and one landed on the welldeck, where the soldiers pounded on it and ate it raw, arguing over slivers of the meat. I felt a strong kinship for that flying fish. They might seem to be playing as they dart from the wave tops, but they're leaping to escape one set of jaws and often land in another, if the beaks of the gulls don't grab them in flight.

I envied the porpoises, which really are playful. Great schools of them circled our ship and crossed back and forth under our bow. Porpoises live in fear of nothing except steel nets and killer whales. Only two things to worry about. Not so bad.

That night and the next morning nothing happened, and I began to hope. The wind faded, but did not die completely, and there was no glassy calm of the sort that often precedes a big blow in the Caribbean. The ship stopped rolling and the soldiers held wrestling matches on the hatches. I was surprised when Apo came out on the starboard wing of the bridge and said almost casually, "I've got a radar contact. Range, twenty-two miles, bearing one seven two. I've had him on the screen for about five minutes and he's heading toward us. We better call the men to battle stations."

"Okay," I said. "You want me to sound the general alarm?"

"I'll just pass the word," Apo said, sounding almost bored, and walked to the welldeck. The wrestling stopped abruptly and the men scattered to the machine guns and to the hammocks of grenades.

I telephoned our cabin and woke Esky up.

"We got a radar contact," I said. "Can't see anything yet. Apo is having the guns manned."

"I'll be right up."

Seymour had been alerted by Apo, and after telling Jones to report our position and the radar contact to his partners, he stood by me on the wing of the bridge and studied the horizon with the binoculars. At first we could see nothing. Then there was a flash of white bow spray and a big, fast sport fisherman materialized, approaching at about twenty-five knots on a course to intercept us.

"He's too small to fight us," Seymour said. "I doubt if he's more than forty-five or fifty feet."

"Not too small to dog us and call in bigger ships," Apo said.

"Maybe he's just out looking for fish," Seymour said.

"Maybe," Apo said, but didn't sound convinced.

As the sport fisherman neared I saw that it was a big

Bertram, a boat that cost about a half-million dollars, but it badly needed paint and the dacron dodger over the helmsman on the flying bridge was gray and torn. The owners of half-million-dollar Bertrams don't ordinarily let them fall into such disrepair. Her engines hummed smoothly, however, as she circled us, keeping just far enough away to avoid gunfire. Three men on her flying bridge were studying us through binoculars. Her streamlined little mast carried a lot of radio aerials as well as two for radar, I noted. This was no doubt one of the thousands of yachts that had disappeared in the Caribbean in the last few years, but it was certainly operating in the service of no yachtsmen.

"They're reporting us, sure as hell," Seymour said.

After circling us twice while they studied us, the Bertram slowed and let us go a mile ahead before she fell into our wake and followed.

"Well, I guess there's no point in zigzagging," Seymour remarked dryly.

"I have a little shadow . . ." Esky said.

Apo remained stoldily silent. He sat on his stool, writing with a pencil on a yellow pad.

Occasionally the Bertram fell almost far enough back to be invisible but she was obviously keeping us on her radar screen and every few hours caught up enough to check us visually. Her strategy was easy enough to figure out. We were headed for Grenada, where the government was reported to be in sympathy with Castro and assorted other revolutionaries. It wouldn't be hard for them to arrange for a fleet of any required size to meet us, now that they would always know where we were. Everyone aboard realized this and everyone looked damn depressed. Everyone except Apo, that is. He kept giving pieces of yellow paper to Jones, who went with them to the radio shack.

"Don't worry so much," he said to Seymour. "They got friends, we got friends. We'll see how this works out."

It seemed obvious to me that the fishing cruiser following us was a constant danger no matter how many friends Apo had. I wondered if we could suddenly double back on our course and take her with our machine guns. It might work if we did it at night or in the middle of a rain squall that might fog her radar. She was staying only about a mile astern at the moment. Approaching each other at twelve knots, we would close that gap in less than three minutes, and their radar man might not see us unless he was especially alert. If we moved the machine guns on our stern and flying bridge to add to the firepower of our bow gun, we could give the guy a real burst.

Seymour liked this plan, and Apo rather condescendingly agreed to have the guns moved. That night the moon was too bright to allow such a maneuver. We needed a dark night or a rain squall, but the next three days brought us only clear Caribbean skies.

Before the weather obliged us we got company.

"I got another radar contact," Apo reported casually on the morning of the third day.

The vessel that came over the horizon from the south was a trim gray modern subchaser, about 120 feet long, of the kind that many small nations in South America and the Caribbean use as gunboats. Her decks were bristling with a variety of small cannon and machine guns.

"One of ours," Apo said. "My partners have friends in high places in the governments around here."

As the subchaser drew near, the sport fishing cruiser suddenly took off at full speed and soon disappeared over the horizon astern of us.

"That little son of a bitch at least knows when he's had it," Apo said.

The subchaser paralleled our course at a distance of about 2,000 yards. The men on her deck wore white naval uniforms, but she flew no flags of any kind. I wondered what little governments were working closely enough with organized-crime syndicates to support them with naval power, and what payoff they would get. Apo seemed to be enjoying my look, but he wasn't about to enlighten me.

26

The arrival of the subchaser, with a three-inch gun on her bow and two 40-millimeters on her stern, was a mixed blessing to Esky and me. Now that Big Daddy was here, we might have little to worry about from hijackers, and if smuggling was really like the old rum running, the same might apply even to our own authorities when we entered the United States waters. The big money of organized crime talked, even in the corridors of government power. Sometimes especially . . .

Trouble was that the crime syndicate "protecting" us made our plans for escape damn near hopeless. Southampton Beach was a nice idea, but Apo and his crew had been put aboard to prevent such escapes and Seymour was certainly no fool. And even if Esky and I were able to escape in a crowd on the beach, how long would the over-bosses let us live? After we'd aborted their billion-dollar operation, we wouldn't exactly be their pin-up boys. Just their targets.

But I'd heard that the Mafia preferred not to stir up trouble unless there was some immediate practical reason for it . . . and once this ship had been beached and the operation ended, what could Esky and I do to them? . . . We had no idea of their actual identity . . . Maybe we *could* still get home free. Maybe . . .

I wished that my old *Angry Angel* could come roaring out of the surrounding mists and blow this damned ship to hell. Well, my old PT boat was long gone, but I was still here, maybe I could be an angry angel for it—one last time . . .

Esky in his own way was a kind of angry angel too, though admittedly an unlikely one. He just didn't like Seymour or Apo, and his feeling came from his guts—not too angelic a place, I guess.

"They're a couple of sure enough bastards," he said to me. "It'll be a real pleasure to screw them proper."

"Do you really think we can do it?"

We were in our stateroom, whispering in the dark, while Seymour took the watch for a couple of hours.

"Your idea of beaching her is going to be hard to pull

off, but I can't think of anything else," Esky said. "When the time comes, we're just going to have to try it and take our chances. The way I figure it, we don't have a whole hell of a lot to lose."

So now, for the first time we began to make a serious, step-by-step plan. We talked about the risks of asking Tad and Faith to join us, and decided to do it.

"Maybe they won't be much help now, but if we ever get in court we might find it hard to convince a judge that a couple of boat bums like us managed to beach the ship alone," Esky said. "The jury might think we were just trying to take advantage of a damn accident . . ."

While Faith was cooking dinner that night, I went to Tad's cabin. He was lying fully dressed on his bunk, pale and listless, when I entered.

"Andy . . ." He raised himself up on one elbow and gave me a sickish smile.

"How you doing, boy?"

"Not good."

"What are you going to do when this trip is over?"

"Get some wheels and get out if I can."

"If I found a way to screw up this operation, would you help me?"

"You're damn *right*." Color began to come back to his face.

"It might mean really wiping your old man out, even landing him in jail."

"It's what the son of a bitch has deserved for twenty years. I could prove that."

I asked about Faith and he said she felt as he did.

"I'll do anything you tell me to do," Tad said. "Andy,

you've always been a sort of conscience for me—"

"You got a bad conscience, then."

"No, seriously . . . when a man is rotten, his son *should* fight him. Has a right. I said rotten. How about evil? I mean it, and you know a lot of the reasons."

"I guess . . . Yes, I knew, but it still made me uneasy to hear a son—any son—talk like that about his father, even a father like Seymour . . . Now, you get Faith lined up with us. And tell her we should be as nice to everyone aboard this ship as we can while we're putting this thing together. At least pretend to make peace with your father—"

"*That* will be hard, but I'll try . . . You won't tell me what the hell you're going to do, will you?"

"Not yet."

"I can't say I blame you for not trusting me."

"Tell Faith to butter up Apo—"

"She'll hate that."

"It's important, Tad."

"Then she'll do it."

The next thing Esky and I planned to do was to put the radar and loran sets out of commission: They would give Apo, Seymour and Jones too much advance warning if we tried to beach the ship. I had noted that both pieces of equipment were almost new, the radar a Decca, the loran from Texas Instrument Company, both good. On closer inspection Esky noticed something else: They were both 12-volt models of the kind manufactured for small yachts, not ships this size, which generated both 120 and 220 volts. They had been taken from some of the yachts that had disappeared in the Caribbean, I guessed, and had been installed aboard this vessel with transformers to give them their 12 volts.

"You know what that means," Esky said to me.

"Stolen equipment."

"More than that. We could blow that equipment by sending a hundred and twenty or even two hundred and twenty volts through it. That wouldn't be too hard, and if we did it in the middle of a thunderstorm it would look like it was hit by lightning."

"Apo and Seymour would still be suspicious as hell—"

"Any radio equipment can be blown in a storm and this ship hasn't been set up with much lightning protection. They might suspect, but they couldn't be sure. Besides, Seymour will need us until we get in."

"When do you figure to do it?"

"The first big lightning storm we get."

"How? With that equipment right on the bridge, there's no way we can do it without being seen."

"A hundred and ten volts will be enough. I can get that from the chartroom. I won't have to go near the bridge. The transformers are in the radio shack. The wire from them to the loran and radar goes right through the chartroom, along the overhead. All I'm going to need is about three feet of wire for a jumper and I can get that from the desk lamp in our stateroom."

"You're a genius, Eskimo."

He gave me what can only be called an arch look.

"After killing polar bears with bone knives, it's a piece of cake."

I was impatient for even the first action—putting the

electronic gear out of commission, but we ran into few of the thunderstorms we might have expected for August in the Caribbean. Plenty flashed on the horizon all around us, but our ship seemed to be living an oddly charmed life. With our escort steaming two thousand yards ahead of us, we escaped the island chain of the West Indies near Grenada and passed into the South Atlantic.

It had always been difficult for me to believe that God, or whatever higher power there be, really cared much of a damn about me, but Pattie had got me into the habit of prayer and it had often made me feel calmer, if nothing else. So I prayed a lot for a good lightning storm. What I got were waterspouts. They weren't an unusual pheno-menon in this part of the world at this time of the year, but I'd never seen a more awesome display. Heavy dark clouds like thunderheads funneled down to touch the sea and then rose, sucking up a great column of whirling water hundreds of feet high. Waterspouts are really small marine tornadoes. Some old sailors say they're harmless, and I never heard of a ship being hit by one, but maybe that was because no one ever lived to tell the tale. Waterspouts could account for some of the disappear-ances in the Caribbean and South Atlantic. Often I'd seen two or three at the same time, but now I counted six all around us. The ship seemed to be steaming through a giant plaza surrounded by columns to an angry heaven.

All the men on the ship except Esky looked scared as hell. Seymour took to his martinis in his cabin, and even Apo nervously paced the bridge, draining his beer bottles quicker than usual and flinging them into the offending sky and sea. The waterspouts majestically twisted in a circle around us, like an enormous merry-go-round. Most dissipated into mist in a few minutes without coming close to us, but one monster kept growing and started to head toward our bow. Even the last breath of wind around us died, and we could hear the rush of the spout, a roar that my imagination built into something like Niagara Falls.

"Anyway, if it kills us, it will take us *up*," Esky said. "We sure as hell will find out what heaven's like."

When the waterspout was perhaps a thousand yards ahead, our escort turned at right angles to it and opened fire on it with its three-inch bow gun and 40-millimeters. Attempting to kill such a monster with those popguns seemed pretty foolish, but old sailors had long taken comfort from the superstition that waterspouts could be stopped by guns, and I'd even seen yachtsmen shoot .22 rifles at them. In obedience to the superstition, or its own mysterious nature, I'm damned if the waterspout didn't dissipate just before reaching us and gave us no more than a fierce but brief gust of wind that ripped the tarpaulins off our machine guns, plus a deluge of tropical rain that left a few small fish flopping on our decks. When it was over, the men cheered wildly, but there was more relief than exuberance on their faces. Somehow they looked as though they had just been pardoned by a priest.

I went right on praying for thunderstorms as we followed a semi-circular course designed to take us out to sea and back to the south coast of Long Island. We got a stroke of luck I hadn't expected: the radar went on the fritz all by itself. Such things often happen, which is why naval vessels carry radar technicians, I pointed out to

Seymour, and maybe I only imagined that he was looking at me with suspicion.

Apo had his men haul him to the truck of our mast in the boatswain's chair to inspect the bar antenna, which had stopped revolving. He discovered that the fierce wind from the waterspout had broken a flag halyard and tangled it in the antenna. When it had tried to turn, a bearing had gone.

"Goddamn yachty equipment," he thundered, when he came down.

"It wasn't made to operate in a tangle of line," I said.

"The sets we have on the tankers wouldn't be bothered by a damn flag halyard," he said. "And on the tankers we have stand-by sets."

"Maybe you should have stayed on the tankers—"

"Everything about a yacht is Mickey Mouse," he said. "Mickey-Mouse boats, Mickey-Mouse equipment and Mickey-Mouse *people*. They got no right to make a radar out of stuff light as that."

"Everything for a yacht has to be light. Weight slows them down."

"So you get Mickey-Mouse equipment manufactured by and for Mickey-Mouse people. Hell, nothing is made honest anymore. I got a brand new Caddy at home that had to be taken to the repair shop twice the first month I owned it."

For five minutes Apo continued his tirade about crooked manufacturers, which he expanded to include crooked businessmen of all kinds. Which was funny, in a way, considering who he was.

Apo's fury at "yachty gear" and "crooked manufacturers" pleased me. Now I figured that he wouldn't be surprised when the loran set went out. Esky was carrying his pocketknife and a coil of wire he had taken from our desk lamp, and he said it would not take him more than a minute to knock that receiver out. Now all we had to do was wait for lightning.

We had been at sea a week before my prayers for a thunderstorm were finally answered, and they were answered with a vengeance. It came on a hot, airless dusk; bolts of lightning stabbed down from roiling black clouds that surrounded us. The thunder followed the flashes too quickly to be timed, and Seymour was worried about being hit.

In the midst of the excitement over the storm, Esky slipped into the chartroom "to check our position." I kept my eyes on the loran receiver, and soon it sent up a small puff of smoke. No one else on the bridge noticed it and Apo didn't realize that the loran was *kaput* until he tried to get a position on it about two hours later.

"Mickey Mouse," he roared. "Now the goddamn loran is out—"

"Might be lightning," I said. "It was all around us . . ."

Muttering, Apo unscrewed the panels on the set.

"Burned out," he said with disgust. "Why didn't the bastards who installed it ground it right?"

"Not many electronic experts in Barranquilla, I guess . . ."

"And we don't even have a stand-by set. We'll be navigating like Columbus."

He did not, apparently, even suspect Esky and me, and his rage at the equipment and people who had installed it helped divert Seymour's naturally suspicious mind. Apo ordered Jones to take sun sights to check on my navigation every morning, noon and afternoon. Jones used air navigation methods, which are quicker, easier and less accurate than nautical procedures. When his results differed a few miles from mine, Apo himself broke out a sextant and took his own sights, which were accurate. He and Jones did not bother with dusk and dawn star sights, though. He got into the habit of taking his last sunsight at four p.m. and his first sunsight at ten-thirty in the morning. That would give me eighteen and a half hours every day during which they would not be checking my navigation. At twelve knots I could get far enough inshore of our supposed position in that time without making any obvious course changes. With luck, the beaching operation should at least be possible.

Even with all the zigzagging we had done and our semi-circular course, we got almost halfway home during our first week at sea. Figuring that the danger from hijackers was over, our escort left us the next day. She made no signal, wished us no luck. She just abruptly changed course and disappeared over the horizon to the south. I still had fantasies of being jumped by revolutionaries, pirates, name it, but we saw nothing except big tankers, a few container ships and an occasional trawler during the next few days. None came close.

In late August the Atlantic was as hot as the Caribbean had been. Not unexpectedly, Jones soon picked up radio reports of a hurricane building a few hundred miles astern of us. I figured that the chances of it hitting us were slight, and Apo just grunted when he read the reports, but Seymour's tired face looked more worried than ever. He asked for reports on the hurricane every hour and stayed in his cabin most of the time, calling for frequent supplies of ice.

Faith brought it to him. She also answered Apo's constant calls for beer and coffee, and even managed to grin when he patted her ass. . . .

"Being nice to that bastard is the hardest thing I ever did," she said to me one night, when she found me alone on the starboard wing of the bridge.

"I'm afraid it's necessary, until—"

"Hell, I'll lay the bastard if you want. I'll do anything to get back at these people."

"You won't get any money for your project—"

"I wouldn't anyway. These people are all out for themselves, and look what they've done to Tad."

Tad, like the rest of us, had contributed to his own troubles, but now wasn't the time to say so.

"How much do you really know about drugs?" I asked.

"A lot."

"Could you knock Apo out for me if I wanted?"

"I guess."

"You could put stuff in his beer or coffee?"

"Just about any downer would do it . . . Seconal, Nembutal, any barbiturate."

"Would he taste the stuff?"

"He takes so much sugar in his coffee he probably wouldn't taste anything else, and he likes his beer so cold it wouldn't let him taste much."

"How closely can you time it? If I say I want him knocked out at, say, eight at night and wanted him kept out of it for at least two hours, could you manage that?"

"I think so. You want him just knocked out cold or put gradually to sleep?"

"I don't want to make him or anyone else suspicious. Can you just make him so sleepy he'll decide to sack out on his own?"

"Just tell me when . . . Do you mind telling me your plan?"

"I'm sorry . . ."

"I know, I'm lousy at keeping secrets. Are people going to get killed?"

"I hope not."

"Will there be fighting?"

"It's possible."

"Would it help to get the soldiers doped up? God knows we've got plenty of stuff aboard."

"Not a bad idea. I'd like everybody aboard except for Esky, me, Tad and you doped up as much as possible from here on out."

"Can you get me some of the stuff from the holds?" The boys all want to be friendly with me. I'll pass out presents."

"I'll inspect the holds tomorrow and get what you need."

I stayed on the wing of the bridge for a while after she left, thinking that it was beginning to look as if we really might make it. Esky, Tad, Faith and me—a more unlikely combination of people was hardly imaginable, but maybe we had the brains to pull it off. God knows, we had the motive. Staying alive.

It was not hard for me to keep Faith supplied with stuff from the holds and she reported that the soldiers accepted it from her eagerly as she stood chatting with them every evening on the welldeck.

The idea of drugs helping me to run a drug ship ashore sort of appealed. My worry, though, was that Apo and Seymour would smell the marijuana smoke in the forecastle and take some sort of action to sober their men up. Nothing to do but hope they'd get on to it late.

We turned west to complete the last 500 miles. The men, in their shipboard boredom, became more and more grateful for the "presents" Faith gave them each night. Under the influence of the grass, there was a lot of sloppy guitar playing, both Spanish and Colombian versions of rock and roll. Our vessel began to sound like a cruise ship full of drunks. As they used the drugs, some of the men just lay nodding out on the hatches and a few on cocaine argued belligerently.

Apo, of course, soon noticed this, but didn't seem too surprised—I guess that people who run drug ships aren't unaccustomed to the crew getting into the cargo. Hell, the old pirate ships had often gone under because their captains couldn't keep their men away from drugs and booze. Old Blackbeard himself had become addicted to the morphine he found in ships' medical chests and had finally been killed because he hadn't bothered to get in his anchor when warned that the Navy knew where he was and was sending a boat after him.

Apo was a good pirate captain, though, and did his damnedest to restore order. His methods were brutal, if not particularly effective. Periodically he'd charge down on the welldeck and into the forecastle, using his huge hands to club the men who obviously had been taking drugs, and he had Jones roust out the whole compartment, making a close inspection of all bedding and clothing. Finally he'd line the men up buck naked on the welldeck while Jones was going through their khakis and told them he'd shoot any man he found breeching the cargo. He also locked one man who was far gone on cocaine in a paint locker, where the temperature was about 120 degrees and there was no ventilation. This poor guy was almost dead when Esky sneaked down and let him out.

Perhaps because of the intolerable tension that Apo created, the men seemed more eager than ever to accept Faith's presents. She had taken to leaving the small packages hidden in ventilators because she was afraid that Apo would suspect her nocturnal visits to the crew.

"It don't make much difference," Apo said privately to Seymour. "We got those boys here to fight and there ain't going to be no fighting now. I just got to keep them in line so they don't make too much trouble for us."

27

The hurricane which built up astern of us passed close enough to give us rain and mountainous seas for two days. Befuddled on drugs, the men were now also seasick.

As we neared the end of the voyage, I began to think of the future—assuming I had any future at all . . . The fifty-thousand-dollar certified check that Seymour had given me might or might not prove out to be good, but that no longer seemed very important. Pattie and I would get by, one way or another, and my old worries about money now seemed crazy beyond belief. I just wanted to *see* her and *be* with her. Aside from the love and need I felt for her, I'd begun to think of her as the only sane person in the whole crazy jungle we called the civilized world. Corny bromides like "staying on the right side of the Lord" and "It doesn't matter if you lose everything as long as you can keep your self-respect" didn't *sound* phony when Pattie said them, mostly because her actions fitted her words. Pattie was no hypocrite. She could even say "I can make myself happiest by helping other people" without sounding sanctimonious. She just made these words seem a statement of fact, which she honored by doing all in her power to make her family happy, as well as going out in the middle of the night to answer calls from women who called AA for help.

Pattie knew how to live. She had learned the hard way after a terrible youth, and her face showed her happiness over her discoveries. She was a middle-aged woman, but people still turned to look at her on the street, not because of her physical beauty, which was still real enough for me, but because of that look on her face, a kind of genuine happiness, the rarest look of all. She had the secret.

I would go back to Pattie, and although I'd almost run drugs and had killed five men, I still had some self-respect and would have more if I managed to beach this drug ship and brought this whole billion-dollar operation to a crash end . . .

One morning after I had taken my dawn star sights, I

looked out at the pastel pinks and blues of the horizon and felt a curious lift. Maybe I'd fail in the attempt to abort this operation. Maybe I'd be shot or maybe it would all end in a fiasco when Seymour or the others saw the shore looming close and took charge. But at least I was trying to do something that was right for a change, and Pattie was right—there was a kind of peace to be found in that, maybe courage too.

Such thoughts were too deep, and too naive, for an old sailor like me, but right now I believed them, and they gave me a curious measure of serenity as I planned to beach a drug ship with a billion-dollar cargo.

We approached the 200-mile limit off the South Shore of Long Island. The weather remained sunny, with a gentle southeasterly breeze and very little seaway, both good and bad news. The weather reports gave small hope of fog, which would have made the beaching easier. On the other hand, rough weather would have made us delay the approach to shore for unloading in small boats, and I was feeling a growing sense of urgency, wanting to get on with this thing, to end it as soon as possible.

Just before we reached the 200-mile limit, Seymour received final instructions from his partners on the radio. We were to lay to twenty-three miles east of Moriches Inlet on the South Shore of Long Island at ten o'clock the following evening and wait for fast "Cigarette"-type speedboats and sports fishing cruisers to unload our cargo. That suited me. Any of the area surrounding that inlet would be good for beaching, and it was only about fifteen miles from Shinnecock Inlet and Southampton Beach. I wanted to run the ship ashore at

Southampton because I was pretty sure that the beach would be crowded there on just about any August evening, and of course I liked the idea of ramming the ship right into the front yard of the Shinnecock Coast Guard station. I did not want the authorities to think that I had beached the ship by accident and was just trying to escape responsibility by pretending I'd done it on purpose. If I delivered the ship right into the front yard of the Coasties, my intention to surrender her should be pretty clear.

Dusk came soon after we passed the 200-mile limit, and I took my star sights, getting a small triangle which put us three miles ahead and to the east of our dead-reckoning position. Both Apo and Seymour watched me plot this on the chart.

"We got plenty of time to get there," Apo said, obviously pleased with himself. "We might as well get a hundred miles nearer before we slow her down."

"I guess that the Coasties could pick us up at any time now," I said, and I did worry about that possibility. If the Coast Guard caught us in spite of the false SOS's Seymour's partners used to decoy them from our position, I suspected that Apo would never let Esky and me live long enough to testify ashore, and he might even fire on a small Coast Guard patrol boat. A lot of people, including Esky and me, could be killed. Beyond that, my plan to run the ship up on a crowded moonlit beach had begun to take on a special quality for me, a bloodless cleanliness, and I didn't want anything to mess it up.

"Our partners have rather elaborate plans to take care of the Coast Guard," Seymour said with a smile.

"Such as?" I tried to sound casual.

"Right now a charter schooner is sending Maydays about a hundred miles to the east of us," Seymour said. "They've had an explosion and they're sinking. They have fourteen people aboard—that's what they're reporting. The Coast Guard will have to investigate. They'll find nothing and will have to go into search patterns. That will keep them busy for a while."

"Except the Coasties are getting fed up with false Maydays," Apo said, "so just before we start to unload, we're going to toss them some real meat."

"Oh?"

"The boys are going to see that one of those big Montauk headboats goes down, the kind that carries passengers. We're going to give them the real thing."

"Nobody will drown," Seymour said quickly. "Those headboats carry rafts and life preservers—"

"Good thinking."

"With a billion-dollar operation we can't take chances," Seymour said defensively.

"No, we can't . . ."

In my mind's eye I could see one of those crowded boats that take people out fishing for the day go down, probably with a small time bomb in the bilge. The Coast Guard would need time to get there. Women, old men and children screaming in the ground swell, which was usually big off Montauk even in calm weather. Damn right there would be loss of life, but our partners couldn't "take chances . . ."

My desire to ram this vessel ashore grew into a lust. Seymour, Apo and their partners had everything figured out, except for one Eskimo and one square-head. They were self-confident, even complacent as we started our

421

final run toward the Long Island beaches. Esky and I had been bought and paid for, after all, and beyond that, we'd been given ample reason to be scared into submission.

Still, maybe Seymour and Apo weren't as calm, as complacent as they seemed. Seymour stayed in his cabin and sent out for more and more ice. Apo took to hassling Jones, who was finding escape of a sort by following the results of horse races on which he'd placed bets during the last radio transmission Apo had allowed him.

"You're sitting by that damn radio too much," Apo said. "Go down and start getting the ship ready for unloading. Roust out the gear."

"Plenty of time for that," Jones said. "My results will be coming in. I got a bundle riding on three different races."

"Write the dope down for me and I'll get the results for you. I got to be standing by on radio anyway."

An hour later Apo told Jones that all his horses had won. The little man was ecstatic.

"Jesus, now I'm really in the clear," he said. "I can even get a new car when I get ashore . . ."

After Jones had wallowed in his euphoria for an hour, Apo told him he'd been kidding, that all his horses had lost.

"Do you *mean* that?"

"That's the way it happened. I didn't want to tell you." Baloney.

"Tell me the *truth*."

"That's it, they all lost."

"Is that the honest-to-God truth?"

Apo laughed and cut him off. The pleasure Apo took in

422

inflicting pain, even in such a small way, sickened me almost as much as the thought of that fishing boat full of passengers. Somehow it was all part of the same thing. I wanted to ram this ship ashore so hard they'd never find the pieces. . . .

Dawn found us about a hundred miles off the beach, due east of a point almost midway between Moriches Inlet and Shinnecock Inlet, according to my star sights. I slowed the engines.

"I figure we got about eight hours to kill," I said to Apo and Seymour. "I'd rather kill them out here than farther in."

Apo grunted and Seymour nodded. Which pleased me. Now Apo would find me going according to plan when he took his sun sights. After he charted his four p.m. line of position, I'd have six hours at twelve knots to go where I liked, as long as my course remained northerly. That would give me time to be fifteen miles to the east and twenty miles to the north of our rendezvous point with the small boats at ten p.m. Plenty of navigators had made errors bigger than that after a long voyage without even trying. Seymour had never learned enough navigation to keep track of the ship's position, and Apo shouldn't notice too much once Faith started doctoring his beer and coffee. . . .

Proceeding slowly on course about a hundred miles offshore on a fine summer day, we saw numerous sports fishermen and sailing yachts. A Coast Guard airplane roared overhead, going southeast, probably looking for the charter schooner which had sent out a Mayday.

Aboard our ship the soldiers sat in the hatches playing cards, shooting dice and smoking grass, tossing the roaches overboard when Apo approached.

With Apo drugged out of the picture and Tad keeping Seymour busy with arguments in his cabin, I hoped no one would notice our approach to the beach that evening. At the final moments a fire in the lazaret would draw everyone aft, and I'd ram the ship ashore at her flank speed of thirteen knots, a good unlucky number for her.

But my momentary self-confidence scared me. Obviously anything could happen. It was time to pray, not to be cocky.

28

Esky and I had a conference for making final plans in our stateroom at four-thirty that afternoon, soon after Apo had plotted his final sun sight. After creeping along at four knots all day, we were about fifty miles from his rendezvous point and right on his course. If we continued at slow speed, we would meet his fleet of small boats at just about the right place and time, ten p.m. I needed just a few more revolutions of the propeller and a slightly different course to get me to my destination, Southampton Beach, at the same time.

"I think we better have Faith start making Apo sleepy," I said to Esky. "I can edge the RPM's up real gradually, but the bastard is pretty alert."

"If she can't make him sleepy, I can," Esky said, showing me a sock he'd loaded with rock salt from the ship's ice-cream freezer.

"We don't want to stir up a fuss."

"But if there's a fuss, we got to win it. You better carry one of the grenades. Stick it in your pocket upside down and it'll look just like a can of beer."

"I will, but I still think we may be able to do this quiet and easy. Tad said he thinks he can keep his father busy yakking in his cabin, and Faith is giving him something to put in the old man's martinis."

"Just in case that doesn't work, give the boy this salt sock. I can make another."

"Okay. You ready to start a fire in the lazaret when I give the word?"

"I won't need more than about thirty seconds. I got some oil from the galley range and soaked some blankets in it. I even got some kerosene from the stand-by running lights, so I can touch it off quick."

"How long can you make it last?"

"Long as you want. I got four big plastic bags full of oil-soaked blankets, and they're storing a bunch of old tires for fenders in there."

"You better let the whole pile go up—we don't want them to put it out right away."

"Then don't ask me to start too soon. That fire could

426

easily get out of control, and we'd never make it to the beach."

"I'll wait till the last few minutes if I can. I hope there won't be a bunch of soldiers sitting up on the foredeck when we approach land. I'm going to have Faith give them some booze in the forecastle. She'll tell them they got a right to celebrate the end of the voyage."

"Those guys are plenty sore at Apo," Esky said. "He's been shoving them around too much, and they've just figured out that they're going to be shipped back to Colombia without being given a chance to get ashore."

"Maybe a few would come over to us, but I don't know which ones to approach," I said. "Anyway, Faith will try to keep them happy in the forecastle."

"How about Jones?"

"He's so wrapped up in his racing forms that he doesn't know what the hell is going on. Once we get Apo off his neck, he'll stay glued in the radio shack. If he doesn't, he should be easy enough to take care of."

"Looks like we got it made," Esky said with a grin.

"Keep your fingers and heads crossed," I said.

Next I went to see Tad and Faith, whose cabin was near ours. Tad was lying on his bunk and Faith was massaging his back. They quickly agreed to the plans Esky and I had made.

"Do you think you can bring yourself to knock your father out if you have to?" I said to Tad, as I handed him the salt sock.

"Hell, I've been wanting to do that all my life, but I probably won't have to. He's sopping up the martinis pretty good, and he'll just love what I'm going to say to him."

"What's that?"

"That I'm sorry for everything I've done and I'll promise to do anything he says in the future. He just loves to make plans for me. He'll sit for hours telling me everything I'm going to do for the rest of my life."

"Well, your job is to keep him in his cabin, no matter what. Faith, yours is to put Apo to sleep, starting now."

"Don't worry about that ape. He's been trying to get me down to his cabin for days, and I've got a dose for him big enough to knock out an elephant. We're going to have a few drinks together."

She got up, brushed her hair, unbuttoned the top of her blouse and started for the bridge. I followed her a few minutes later, and found her and Apo head-to-head.

"Take over here for a while, Yachty," Apo said. "I got business below."

He slapped Faith's bottom and they left the bridge. I waited a half-hour before gradually starting to speed up the engines and making the slight course change which would bring us into Southampton rather than Apo's rendezvous point. It was just about five o'clock in the afternoon. The next five hours would be the most crucial ones. Surprisingly, I felt calm. Well, I'd done everything I could do, and for once in my life I was sure that what I was trying to do was right.

Dead sure.

It was a nice afternoon, hot, the sky slightly hazy, but the seas were almost as calm as a lake, fine for the unloading operation which had been planned. Preparations for it were probably now under way in many small ports where the fast drug-running boats were kept, looking like yachts. The headboat Seymour's partners planned to sink to draw off the Coast Guard was, I worried, maybe at sea now, with a time bomb or some radio-controlled explosive in her bilges. I badly wished I could warn the Coast Guard about that before the thing had any chance to go off, but Jones would raise an alarm, or more likely shoot me on the spot, if I tried to get into the radio shack. At least the seas were calm. The Coast Guard should be able to haul those people out of the water without too much loss of life . . . I had to hope for that. There wasn't a way in hell to warn them.

At dusk I took my final star sights, and couldn't repress the morbid thought that I might never again stand on the flying bridge of a ship, trying to reflect those tiny pinpoints of light in my sextant's mirror. Antares, Regulus, Arcturus—the names of the navigator's stars were like those of old friends. Somewhere I'd read that the stars might be dead, burned out, but that they were so far away that their light might keep coming to us for centuries. I had the sudden thought that I might be a dead man, or one soon dead, trying to find his position by consulting dead stars. No calm now, no confidence . . . I was plain scared. So much could go wrong in the final hours or minutes. What if someone saw the shore that would be looming ahead in the moonlight before long? What if someone, anyone, saw Shinnecock Light or other navigational lights blinking ahead and raised an alarm?

The first thing I should do if that happened was to toss a hand grenade into the forecastle, before all those soldiers came out. Esky and I would then stand a chance of taking over the ship with the help of Tad and his girl, especially if Apo was heavily drugged.

What if Apo tasted the drugs in his drink and refused to swallow them?

Stop it. Get on with it.

My star sights showed me to be right on course, my own course, not the one ordered by Apo and Seymour. If we kept on at ten knots, we would hit the beach at ten o'clock; there seemed some odd comfort in the double appearance of the figure ten in this calculation. A good sign? At any rate, Apo didn't seem to have noticed the gradually quickening tempo of the engines. Faith must have done her job.

After plotting my star sights I went back up to the flying bridge, the beer-can hand grenade in my jacket pocket. The last glow of the sunset was bright red with green bands and purple clouds, all reflected in the still waters. Regardless of the rhyme, "Sailor, take warning . . ." when the glow finally faded, it grew very dark. The nautical almanac had told me that a half-moon would rise at eight-thirty-three. That would put it on our starboard beam, better than having it setting over the land ahead, spotlighting the beach for anyone aboard our ship who happened to glance in that direction. Other tables told me that the tide would be three quarters high at ten o'clock, and that was good. The higher the tide, the better, because I didn't want to hit some outlying bar; I wanted to ram her bow right up on the beach, where Esky, I, and all the others could jump ashore without having to swim through dangerous surf. At any rate, there would not be much surf on a still night like this. So far, God or nature seemed to be cooperating pretty well, even though there seemed little hope of the thick fog that would have made the operation much easier and safer.

At a little after seven that evening Faith came up on the flying bridge.

"Apo's deep under," she said. "It took longer than I expected, but he'll be out of it now for at least six hours. I gave him an injection to make sure, after he passed out with the Seconal."

I nodded. And just then a gentle wind sprang up from the northwest and brought us the fragrance of land. After weeks at sea, I had always found the smell of land sweet, but this whiff of August gardens, new-cut lawns, even the acrid hint of smoke, seemed to be the breath of life itself . . . "The real tragedy is that so few people seem to enjoy life," Pattie had said to me once. "They hope for immortality but don't know what to do with the afternoon ahead . . ." If I ever got home free I'd damn well know how to enjoy life, even when it hurt. Somewhere I'd read a poem that called a bird "a stone burst into song." The ghostlike forms of white seagulls circling us in the starlight reminded me of that poem. They were admittedly stones burst into squawks, but the grace of their flight seemed to carry some small hint of a serenity beyond what most mortals know. This mortal, anyway.

At about eight o'clock Faith carried a big soup caldron in which she had mixed a punch of vodka and grape juice to the forecastle. The men who had been sitting on the welldeck followed her there. The sounds of their voices and laughter soon grew. With that punch and the marijuana she was handing out, the soldiers ought not to give us too much trouble. Unless one or two happened to wander up on the bow at the wrong time and saw land close ahead . . . I telephoned our stateroom and asked Esky to take bow watch until he lit the fire in the lazaret.

At eight-thirty Tad startled me by appearing beside me on the flying bridge.

"Don't worry, I got dad under control. He's happy to take it easy in his cabin."

"You better stay with him."

"He wants me to give you a message. I think he's afraid to give it to you himself."

"What?"

"He talked to his partners and they want you and Esky to take this ship back to Barranquilla after she's unloaded. He can't talk them out of it."

"I bet."

"It makes no difference now, but I thought you'd like to know."

"It makes me damn glad we're doing what we're doing. I'm sure they have about the same plans for this ship that they've got for that headboat off Montauk."

"Probably. Anyway, I've got dad treating me like the prodigal son, although he doesn't seem sure he's happy about it. He's going to train me to take over his business. Of course the training would last maybe twenty years, as long as he lived, and I'd end up like my brother, Cy. Thank God, you're giving me an out."

"Maybe you better get back and keep him busy."

"He's arranged for his own boat to meet him when they start unloading. He wants me to beat it ashore with

432

him right away. The excuse will be that he has to finish up the paperwork for the sale.''

"You're sure he's not getting you to change your mind?"

"Forget it," and he hurried below.

Tension kept building. A quarter to nine. If things went right, we'd hit the beach in just a little over an hour. Right before the moment of impact, Esky, Tad, Faith and I would lie down on the deck, to offset the shock. We'd jump up while everyone else aboard was being knocked off his feet. I remembered Southampton Beach well. Near the dunes there was a row of bathhouses and some telephone booths. The first thing I'd do would be to call Pattie. In a very real way, this was her operation. I'd be reporting to the real captain.

After telephoning Pattie I'd call the Coast Guard to bring in the men from the local station if they hadn't already seen the beaching, or maybe I ought to do that first. I checked to make sure I had two dimes for the telephone.

Living in this daydream of the future was dangerous. Pay attention to the business at hand until you feel the sand under your feet. You're not home free yet.

29

The half-moon was now rising above a thin strip of
clouds on the horizon to the east, on our starboard beam.
Through the binoculars I stared into the darkness ahead.
Land must be just about ten miles out there and
Shinnecock Light in theory should have been visible
before now, but an evening haze often reduced visibility
on the South Shore, especially in August. Nothing was

visible ahead. Perhaps at the last moment there was a bank of fog near the shore. No, it was only a haze, but that was still a help.

Shinnecock Light was very faint when it finally appeared. Behind it the glow of other shore lights could easily be confused with moonlight on the clouds, but I was still glad to see that Esky was alone on the bow. And to hear the sound of singing and guitar playing from the forecastle's open door.

Nine o'clock. One hour to go. Jones appeared on the flying bridge.

"Where's Apo?"

"Sacking out."

"Time to break open the hatches and get ready for taking the boats alongside."

"I guess he trusts you to do it. He told me to have you take care of it."

Jones looked surprised, and pleased. He went to the forecastle door and yelled at the men. The soldiers weren't exactly pleased to break up their party, but a few did what he ordered. The hatches were opened, and light balloon fenders were rigged over both sides. When Jones yelled for more fenders, I was afraid the men would go to get the tires in the lazaret, but they found more of the softer kind, more suitable for the light speedboats they expected to take alongside.

Forty-five minutes. An outboard runabout circled us and a girl yelled that our running lights were out. I waved thanks and put them on. Jones went to the radio shack and a few minutes later telephoned me on the flying bridge to say that the radio was full of reports of the Coast Guard rescue operation for the headboat that had sunk off Montauk. I was glad that he hadn't come to tell me in person. Shinnecock Light now blinked brightly and a variety of shore lights blazed in the haze only seven and a half miles ahead. Anyone who glanced over the bow would get quite a surprise.

The sergeant was yelling for the last of the men to come from the forecastle and was gathering them on the welldeck to rig the cargo nets.

It was time to start the fire in the lazaret to draw everyone aft. I telephoned Esky on the bow and he trotted toward the stern. I went to the bridge, where the soldier helmsman stood concentrating on his compass course, oblivious of the lights glowing in the haze ahead. Putting the ship on automatic pilot, I told him that he could go help the men with the cargo nets. He had just stepped away from the wheel when Esky shouted, *"Fire aft, fire in the lazaret!"*

I hit the old general-alarm button and there was that hysterical klaxon bleating which I remembered so well. Everyone except me raced aft. Black oil smoke billowed into the moonlight from the fantail, swept aft by the motion of the ship and the slight headwind. There was a great deal of shouting and a tangle of hoses as the half-stoned soldiers rushed about. Seymour and Jones tried to outshout the men.

Apo appeared, staggering. He was drugged, but still had forced himself to respond to a general alarm and fire. He stood clinging to the rail, too befuddled to do much more than emit a sort of bull-like roar.

Esky joined me on the bridge.

"Is the fire well started? I don't want them to put it out fast."

"No chance."

The confusion on the fantail mounted, with men sliding and slipping on the decks which the firehoses were soaking. Tad and Faith came to the bridge, looking scared.

"Now what?" Tad said.

"When we get real close, lie down. After we hit, jump up and run like hell for the shore."

Thirty minutes. More confusion, more billowing black smoke aft. Through the binoculars I could see the beach clearly ahead—the half-moon was now high enough to help. A ground swell was making more surf than I'd expected, enough to be dangerous for swimmers, but I hoped I'd be able to ram the bow well past it. I rang up flank speed, the engines quickened their beat. With the fire, I hoped no one would notice.

Now I could see people on the sand—blanket parties. Bless this hot August night. Bless all the beer-drinking young lovers of Southampton.

Fifteen minutes. I changed course ten degrees to the left to make for a gap in the surf. Locked in the automatic pilot again. We were in shoal water now and the waves started to hump up at our quarter.

Ten minutes. Esky arrived on the run, his face black with oil smoke. He took one glance ahead and yelled, "Ram her, jam her . . ."

Now it would be too late for anyone to turn the ship. The waves at our quarter started to break.

Five minutes. Somebody on the beach saw us and shouted. For them we must be clearly silhouetted in

438

moonlight. People started running from every direction toward our point of impact. Good. Our whole ship's company was still busy with the fire aft. Some black smoke eddied back to the bridge. I started to cough and gag.

Three minutes. We touched bottom, just a shudder. I was afraid we'd stick too far from the beach, but all five hundred tons of her went charging on.

Seymour was too panicky about the fire to notice we had touched bottom. He came running up to the bridge to say I should slow the ship to reduce apparent wind. Good advice. I smiled at him.

And then he glanced over the bow, saw that we were almost on the beach—"*Andy.*"

I didn't answer. After making sure we were going to hit full on, not at an angle, Esky and I lay down on the deck with our feet against the forward bulkhead, bracing ourselves for the shock. Bewildered, Seymour grabbed the wheel and tried to turn it.

Tad appeared and tried to pull his father away from the wheel.

Esky and I had lain down on the deck a little too soon, and there was an agonizing wait that seemed endless.

Seymour managed to pull the clutch levers into reverse. Too late. Those big Cats screamed.

There was a heavy bump, a crunching bounce and then we hit the beach hard. Seymour, Tad and no doubt everyone else aboard were knocked off their feet. There was the roar of surf breaking over our stern, but we had rammed through the worst of it and the bow was almost high and dry.

"Let's *go*," Esky shouted to me. I followed him as he

ran down the welldeck, where men were just starting to pick themselves up. We jumped over the side. The water was only waist deep, but it felt surprisingly cold.

Half swimming, half running, we scrambled up on the beach. The crowd was pressing all around us, gathering in a circle around the ship. Hands reached out to help me as I stumbled and fell in soft sand, but I got up and kept running toward the bathhouses, which I could see dimly on the crest of a dune ahead. Glancing over my shoulder, I could see that Esky had been delayed by the crowd, but he was charging after me like a broken-field runner. Everyone around us was laughing and shouting.

While I stopped to wait for Esky and extract my precious dimes for the telephone from my wet pocket, I looked back. The soldiers on the ship were jumping over the side to run ashore. A few enterprising young swimmers were already climbing to the welldeck, passing the soldiers at the rail, and many more were following them. The bow of the ship was not more than twenty feet from dry land, and children were wading toward it. I wondered what Seymour and Tad were doing now, but put them out of mind when I turned and saw two telephone booths near the bathhouses. Clutching my two dimes like lucky pieces in my right hand, I ran across the beach. The soft sand caught at my feet, everything seemed in slow motion. Finally I reached the two booths, but someone had plugged up the coin slots of one with chewing gum, and a fat woman was shrieking into the other—whether to report the excitement around her or in some private trouble, I couldn't tell. Esky, who had caught up with me, slapped her on the back. When she turned indignantly toward him, he pointed to the beached ship.

"Emergency, lady," he shouted.

"Anybody killed?" she said, but she hung up and stood aside to let me into the booth. Through its glass side I saw three Coast Guardsmen from the nearby base already running toward the ship. With a shaky finger I dialed my almost forgotten home number.

Pattie answered at the first ring.

"It's me," I shouted. "I'm *home*."

"Thank the Lord," she said.

"Look," Esky said, hitting my shoulder.

I stared at the ship. Tad and Seymour were grappling on the wing of the bridge, in a way that looked almost like an embrace. The swimmers now crowding the welldeck were falling all over each other, pushing and grabbing in the open hatches. Apo was clinging to the rail, roaring at them, but barely able to stand.

The Coast Guardsmen were yelling at everyone to get off the ship, but the swimmers continued to throw bales from the hatches and to smash them open.

I closed my eyes and turned back to the telephone. At more times than I can remember in the past, telephone wires had been my only connection with sanity. Love.

"Pattie," I said, "are you still there?"

And, of course, she was. Just as she'd always been.

Epilogue

Immediately after that telephone call to Pattie, Esky and I went to the Coast Guard station near Shinnecock Inlet to make a report. I think the hung-over chief boatswain's mate who was in charge that night believed us, but after telephoning his superiors he said that he was sorry, we'd have to be locked up until a full investigation was made. And so my reunion with Pattie took place with a glass wall between us.

She looked more tired and worn than I remembered, and also more beautiful. I told her everything that had happened, trying to stuff it all into the half-hour they gave us. She had not one word of censure for me, but she was scared.

"What do you think will happen now?"

I hadn't given much thought to that during the past week. My nightmare was over, that was the fact—fancy—that gripped me. Of course it wasn't so simple.

Esky, Tad, Faith and myself were locked in separate cells and questioned for days; so were Seymour, Apo and everyone else aboard the ship, except most of the Colombian soldiers, who escaped in the crowd and probably found their way to compatriots in New York. Gradually the authorities came to believe that Esky, Tad, Faith and myself at least were telling the truth. In exchange for our evidence we were pardoned for helping organize the greatest single drug run that had ever been *stopped*, but that wasn't the end of it.

The authorities kept us in protective custody until the trials took place. Seymour, Apo and Jones were given jail sentences, though their lawyers appealed, and the prisoners were allowed to go free on bail. I hadn't expected much else, and wasn't particularly surprised when most of the drugs later disappeared from the vaults where they had been stored. There were charges of police corruption, some dropped, some going before grand juries that are still in session.

To protect us from the crime syndicate whose plan we'd deep-sixed, the U.S. Government offered to help Esky, Tad, Faith and myself to establish new identities in some part of the world where we couldn't be found. But how could people like us become someone else? Esky could change his name and might even be persuaded to dye his hair and stay ashore the rest of his life, but there was no one else in the world like him. The first time he had a few drinks in a bar he was sure to tell his story to most any pretty available girl who would listen, and the first bartender who told him he had had one too many would find himself airborne. Anybody who wanted to find Esky would simply have to check the police files for reports of flying bartenders.

Faith was even worse at keeping secrets. And since Faith showed every sign of sticking close by Tad's side for the immediate future, he wouldn't find it easy to slip into anonymity either.

As for me, I would have the job of trying to hide not only myself, but my wife and our three children. I didn't have a high opinion of the Mafia navy or Seymour's damned "oak-tree corporation," but I assumed that the leaders of an extensive crime syndicate would be smart enough to locate a whole family.

"It may be necessary for you to split up, at least for a while," a government man said. "After all, it may be a matter of life and death, not only for you, but for them . . ."

I tried to face the fact that for the sake of everyone I loved I should try to live alone, maybe for the rest of my life. But without Pattie, I had a fairly good idea of what would happen to me. My old enemy within would kill me even if I escaped all the others. Besides, if my enemies wanted me badly enough, all they'd have to do was kidnap my family and demand my surrender. Pattie and the children would be in more danger without me than with me.

Pattie agreed that there was no safety in hiding. We still had hope in the hard-boiled practicality of the criminal syndicate, if not in its mercy. They'd kill us to shut us up, but we'd already told all we knew, and *maybe* they wouldn't want to advertise themselves for the satisfaction of punishing us. So I did nothing but talk into tape recorders during the first few days of my imprisonment, and I urged the others to do the same.

It also occurred to me that the syndicate would be less likely to kill a public figure than a nonentity whose murder or disappearance might go almost unnoticed. The very opposite of hiding might bring safety . . . I hoped. I decided to do everything I could to stay in the public eye as long as possible.

In the immediate aftermath of wrecking the drug ship it wasn't too difficult for me to get publicity. Photographs of the beached vessel and of Esky, Tad, Faith and me appeared on the front pages of newspapers all over the world. While we were forbidden by the authorities to meet with the press, Pattie told my story to the reporters, and the interviewers found her to be an appealing subject for articles. When our testimony was released during the trials, Esky, Tad, Faith and I became as briefly famous as Seymour and Apo became notorious. To his credit, Esky didn't much enjoy being a public figure; what he really wanted to do was to hole up at a beachfront motel with some girls for however long his money lasted. He did, however, have his own answer to our fears of being punished by criminals. On the one television show he agreed to go on, he said he'd formed an association of more than fifty old boat bums who had sworn to attack the homes of several known Mafia leaders with explosives if anything happened to him or me.

Tad, like the rest of us, was besieged by reporters, but he was so tortured by the role of the son who testifies against his father that he kept himself under with drugs and refused to talk to anyone. And while Faith appeared to love all the attention at first, she became surprisingly subdued after a while, even toning down her advocacy of mass bliss, and finally disappeared to points unknown with Tad.

So I became the one who was asked to appear on all the television shows. I was asked to stress that it was naive to think that there's really easy money in drugs, or that drugs can be harmless. Some people seemed to want me to lead an anti-drug crusade, but crusades aren't exactly my thing, and I suspected that preaching against things doesn't help much.

What I especially wanted to do was to understand the moral storm I had passed through and maybe help other people to understand this kind of passage, which I guess comes to most of us in one form or another, though for most in less melodramatic ways. As I got into this, I remembered that I actually had a contract to write a book, an arrangement I was able to dissolve when I found the company was associated with some of Seymour's more disreputable partners, but the publicity given to our self-aborted "greatest crime of the century" attracted other publishers. I began trying to put the tapes I had recorded into some kind of a coherent account of everything which had happened to me. Out of this came several magazine articles, as well as a book, and now there is even talk of making a movie.

I am grateful for the fact that I am beginning to be able to pay my family's bills, but the feeling that I am capitalizing on a crime I helped to start still bothers me, and I know that it troubles Pattie, even though she reminds me that my reward is for rebelling against a crime, stopping it and reporting it.

As my tales turned into something of a business, some people, including my son, Tommy, began to regard me as some sort of hero. I enjoyed Tommy's admiration, and my whole family is grateful for the modest house we bought with my deserved, or ill-gotten, gains, but I had this growing feeling that something was wrong.

"When you come right down to it, what *is* the moral of my story?" I said to Pat one night.

"Maybe real stories don't have morals," she said. "Only people do . . . I think most people at least *try* hard to do right. And some of them, when they fail, manage to pick themselves up and try again. That's where the hope for us all is."

"The hope for us all . . ." Pattie's clear voice made that phrase ring. Some people might not buy her uncomplicated faith. Not me. I had lived in a world without hope long enough.

With it, I was really alive for the first time in my life.